Forgive The Monster

The Isolated

{1}

Forgive The Monster

The Isolated

Diana Regolizio

Trigger Warnings

Abuse (emotional, physical, sexual, abusive relationship); alcohol; anxiety (panic attack); blood; death (murder, death threats, dead body); depression; drugs [cannabis, lysergic acid diethylamide (LSD), benzodiazepine (benzo), drugging, needle, pills]; forced marriage mention; guilt; hallucinations; kidnapping; loss of a loved one (fiance, parent, child); manipulation (gaslighting, toxic relationship); memory loss; mind control; paranoia; racism ("respect your kind," paranormal parallel to nationalism); rape (off screen, implied, mentioned); self harm (mention of cutting, fall-from-great-height attempt); suicidal thoughts, mention of suicide attempts; trauma; violence; vomiting.

Table of Contents

Defining Choices, 2011

The Day of the Dance, 2011

All or Nothing, 2011

The Aftermath, 2011

A Letter

Dear Ruth Van Sloan,

While I am a friend, please do not try to find me. You have a more important task, which will become clear by the end of this letter.

Please forgive this rough translation. It's much more poetic in its original Italian.

A pact was forged between the feuding parties of Otherkind:
The callous Domsuco,
who gained life energy from the blood they drank,
And the amiable Wishers,
whose magic stemmed from their very thoughts, desires and fears.

The pact forbade Domsuco from feasting on Wisher blood,
Nor could Domsuco seize control of a Wisher's mind,
Nor enter their home uninvited.

But Human life was free game.

In exchange for safety,
And for the Humans' peace of mind,
The Wishers put into place an illusion unlike any other.

A Global Veil;
The perfect mask to hide

The scars of a Domsuco's bite.

To power such an illusion necessitated a sacrifice,
To which the First Born Son of the Sences-sanim Wisher line
volunteered himself, as well as every first born son in his lineage thereafter.

The later Sencessanim Wishers tried to re-work the illusion
To disallow a practice so barbaric,
And in their ventures created the Domglory.

"Oh Domglory,
"may you have might,
"corporeal invincibility
"and means to an army of lesser ability.
"May you stand with us unless banished by congregation,
whether willingly or for the wellness of the people.
"So mote it be."

You are aware of your heritage, Ruth. You know who the next Wisher's Son is. When the sacrifice is ignored and the world seems to conspire against him, you'll know what to do. The stone for the Summoning Spell is in a separate package.

Sincerely,
An old friend

Jack at Seventeen, 2009

1. The First Death

Jack

Jack typically didn't wake up to his phone going off at four in the morning, but that day he did, and he couldn't sleep since. It was Grandma Ruth. "Oh, I was just checking in," she'd insisted, clearly more concerned than she'd meant to let on. "Just…you still wear that bracelet, right?"

He knew what bracelet she was talking about. "Uh. Yeah," he'd answered. It was his very first birthday gift—literally, the day he was born, she gave it to him, for protection. He didn't always wear it, but for her sake he tried.

Thankfully the last day of summer heat had passed, so now he could hide it beneath his jacket sleeve. With it's knotted rope band and runic wooden beads, it didn't work with his look. He wasn't a witch—he didn't believe in that stuff like she did.

As touching as her concern was, he wrote it off as trivial superstition. What had kept him awake was what day it was, and what he had planned.

Backpack hanging off one shoulder as he trudged down the school's tiled hall, Jack pulled off his black beanie and ran his fingers through his dark overgrown hair. He twisted in his locker combination and, just as he pulled the latch, his eyes were covered. Two hands, girlfriend-sized, cold.

A knowing smile tugged his lips. "Smells like fish," he said. "You had a good morning?"

"Ohhh, wow, masturbation joke, clever." She went nasal and overboard with the impressed sarcasm, and he liked it. She let her hands drop to his waist.

He finished opening his locker, then turned around to hug her fully. Sarah stood at about his height whenever neither wore shoes, but when they were in public as they were now, her Doc Martens put her about an inch taller than him. Her nerdy graphic tees and black denim pants were just a size bigger than his, and while she did have a stocky build, this said more about his stature than it did about hers. Jack was a lanky shit, and he accepted it.

Her darker, honey blonde hair was short with a pixie cut. Paired with her youthful blue gaze and mischievous grin, she looked like the sort of woman who would play Peter Pan on Broadway.

"Hey, woman." He kissed her soft, freckled cheek.

"Hey, boy." She kissed his lips. He reciprocated.

A soft *beep*, followed by a satisfying *shutter* and a flash of light. A taller, slouching boy with peach fuzz and blotchy cheeks lowered the camera from his face. "Sorry, that was perfect; had to get it." This was a typical interaction with him.

"Sup, George?" Jack greeted.

The boy emitted a low breath. "This year's kicking my ass, and it's hardly even started."

"Tell me about it," Sarah groaned.

"And with my sister here, and now she's joining the cheerleaders—she's gonna befriend dudes *your* grade, and it's gonna be weird because I'm probably gonna hear them doing it in the basement—"

Sarah put a firm, reassuring grip over George's shoulder. "One thing at a time, man."

George sighed, "Yeah. Yeah."

"And Monica can handle herself."

Jack withdrew his math and science books, then aggressively pushed his locker shut to ensure it closed all the way.

They strode down the hall, past all the other students and to their homeroom class. Sarah stepped inside first, crossing to her seat. Jack took his seat beside her, and George followed to his seat behind him.

A substitute teacher nobody recognized stood at the front of the room. Maybe in his late twenties; receding hairline and average build. His name was written in neat, large letters across the wall-to-wall dry erase board, *Mr. Giannopoulos*. When the bell rang to signal the start of homeroom, he began roll call, unenthused; bored. "Sarah Becker?"

She raised her hand.

He checked off his paper. "Luke Donovan?"

The only kid in school whose build screamed *steroids* raised his hand. George scratched the back of his neck, looking anywhere else.

Jack's mind wandered as the sub continued down the list. He wondered if Sarah remembered what day it was. Neither ever forgot; they always had something planned, but it was still early so it was possible her head was still stuck on everyday routines.

"Theodore Van Sloan?" called Mr. G-opoulos.

Jack raised his hand with a correction, "Jack. Just Jack."

The sub wrote it in his notes. "Jack," he echoed.

With a folded piece of paper already in her hand, Sarah reached to the floor as if to pick it up. "I think you dropped this," she muttered as she let it fall on Jack's desk.

Unfolding the note, he found it read, *Happy Anniversary, betch.* He grinned. She did remember.

He wrote back, *Woman.*

...

The rest of the day crawled. It made him anxious. The classes he had without Sarah were good in the sense that he didn't need to worry about cracking and letting her open her gift early. Lunch and gym and the times between classes, however, he got dangerously close. He would tell her, "You'll never guess what I got you," but then she'd start guessing and he'd have to try his best to neither confirm nor deny anything. She said, "So it's some kinda jewelry, then."

He closed his mouth and said nothing else until they parted ways. Nothing, save for, "You'll find out when you open it, and you'll open it when the moment's right."

Unfortunately, any moment which left him alone with his head distressed him. There was a chance she wouldn't receive his present well.

Finally the school day ended. They'd already decided to start the evening at her place, so they began their walk through the school courtyard to where she was parked.

He stepped along the short brick wall which got higher as the sidewalk downwardly sloped.

"Is it one of those corny locket necklaces, where you keep half the pendant and I keep the other half?" she asked, walking the sidewalk below him. "Is it heart-shaped?"

He laughed with a whining moan. "Ow. No. God, you're making this painful."

"Look, I don't know when you intend to do this, but I already know it's jewelry; I'm gonna figure it out before we get there."

She could've been right. *Ring* wasn't a huge leap from *necklace*.

He paused at the wall's edge, just before the corner down from which he'd usually jump. Bringing his hands to his hips, he surveyed the setting. The sky was partly cloudy with the sun in plain sight. The world's shadows began their evening stretch and everything appeared slightly more yellow, glowing. The courtyard was clean, and prettily landscaped with colorful flowers—purple, white, pink and yellow. They were alone.

"Alright," he decided. Not a second later, his heart raced and he smiled. He tried to reel back his enthusiasm and maintain some level of cool, but it took all he had to just keep from laughing.

She raised an eyebrow like she didn't trust it. "Alright?"

"Yeah." He dropped down from the wall, landing gracefully beside her. He paced a couple feet to work off some of the nervous energy, then back, taking a full breath. His false sense of confidence depended on how playful he made it. "Well, as you know, this is our anniversary—"

"Wait, we're *dating?*" She gasped.

He laughed, "Shut up," kissed her temple, then went back to it. "We've been dating for six years, since before we even knew what sex was—"

Her gasp was doubly exaggerated. "You mean it's *not* just naked cuddling?!"

"Goddammit woman, I'm trying to make a moment."

"Dude, you're blowing my mind right now."

"You don't even know," he mutedly whined.

Eyes softly squinting, she quieted. She might've finally figured this was gonna be big, and while she might not have guessed what it was yet, he knew she wasn't gonna interrupt anymore.

He vaguely gestured to their situation. "This is good, right? You're happy, I'm happy? Anything comes up, we'll work through it?"

She nodded, face unchanged.

He pressed his lips together, hoping to remember anything he might've missed. "Yeah. I wanna keep this going." He pulled the jewelry box from his pocket.

"Me too." She didn't understand yet.

As he slowly sank to one knee, her jaw dropped and her eyes widened. Her voice cracked a lower register, "Duuuude."

"No pressure. The ring's a gift no matter how you answer, I just... I wanna show you I'm serious. And I think you're the real deal."

"I think you're the real deal too, but before college?!"

"Long engagement, no marriage until we both graduate."

Verging on hyperventilating, she forced a couple calming breaths and nodded. "Okay."

"Okay?"

"No! I mean—keep going, let's do this right."

His smile widened. Now he knew her answer. "Alright, Sarah Becker." He opened the box. Her eyebrows rose in the middle, and he reveled in it. "Will you marry me?"

The white gold band took the shape of delicate, interwoven leaves. A brilliant cubic zirconia sat raised in the center, because fuck blood diamonds.

"Oh my God," she gasped, "how did you pay for this?"

It took all his birthday money, and five months of only contributing half the bill money his dad demanded of him.

"I mean, yes!" she blurted, "Yes!"

"Shit yeah." He took the ring from the box and stood, sliding the band to her finger. "Do you recognize it yet?"

Her eyes excitedly widened, and now she stared intently. A few seconds in, and he knew she was stumped.

"Was it used in a movie?" she asked.

"The only movie-versions I could find looked like they all came out a twenty-five cent vending machine, but yeah."

That was all she needed. She laughed, free hand over her mouth. "Fucking nerd, it's Nenya, isn't it?"

Galadriel's ring of power from Lord of the Rings. He nodded and laughed, "Takes one to know one. Nerd."

She laughed too, or wailed, "All I got you was a pizza with the pepperoni on top in the shape of a heart and the living room to ourselves and a list of animes on Netflix we haven't seen yet and popcornnn!"

"That's it? Damn, woman, never mind. Engagement off."

She gave him a mean look, and although she still grinned he knew this didn't mean she wasn't plotting some sort of cute vengeance.

But in all seriousness, "That sounds dope, you kidding?" he said.

"Yeah?"

"Yeah!" He kissed her. She kissed back. Both knew neither intended to stop anytime soon. He held her closer. She let her backpack drop.

"Hey! No PDA!" called a distant voice he didn't care to recognize.

At first glance it looked like Sarah flipped him off, but it was her newly bedazzled ring finger. Still, they didn't stop kissing.

"Never mind," replied the passerby, who continued on his way.

Jack couldn't say how much longer they remained like this, or if anyone else saw. He didn't want to let her go. If he let her go, it meant the moment ended. It would've been too soon.

. . .

There weren't any cars in the driveway when he and Sarah pulled up to the garage at her place, which was strange. Her parents were usually home by now, to pick up the younger siblings from the bus stop.

All was explained once they got inside and found a note on the fridge. It read:

> *Lovebirds,*
>
> *You get the living room until Chuck E. Cheeses' closes. Nothing can be promised after that (you know the little ones).*
>
> *Behave, be safe, and happy anniversary!*
>
> *With love,*
>
> *Ma Becker-Hall **and Mr. Dad***

It was clear who wrote what.

Jack set up the Netflix while Sarah called in the pizza and fetched the blankets. "What are we watching first?" he asked when he figured she was off the phone.

Her voice, however muffled, projected clearly through the wall, "Howl's Moving Castle! I've read it but haven't seen it yet!"

He trusted Miyazaki, so he contentedly brought it up in the search bar. He hit play, and paused at the exact moment the movie began. Rather than sit on the couch, he took the recliner, extending the legs and leaning as far back as the seat would allow. When Sarah came back, he motioned for her to sit with him. This was their usual spot. It allowed them both to lay back and see the TV, and it lent itself the position for optimal cuddles.

She grinned, the blanket like a cape over her shoulders. Rather than sit with her back to his chest, she straddled his lap and tugged his collar. Taking the hint, he sat up, and so she pulled him into a kiss. "Fiancé," she growled.

He wrapped his arms fully around her middle, wishing it was possible to hold her closer. "Woman fiancé," he teased back. They kissed again. And again.

It was all mostly innocent, though thirty minutes passed and they still hadn't started the movie.

There came a knock at the door.

"*Yes,*" Sarah moaned. Jack wasn't touching her at this moment, which meant this was solely a response to the pizza.

"I'll get it," she said, "And no peeking."

"Okay."

She delivered a quick kiss to his cheek before she stood, adjusted her shirt, and strode around the wall and to the room behind him. The front door opened, and "Hey," she greeted. He couldn't hear much after that. He assumed there was still a surprise she didn't tell him about—maybe a note she had wanted to add inside the box. If she and the pizza guy were still talking, they were whispering.

In any case, he couldn't focus. He was engaged, and it dawned on him again and again. If life was a rollercoaster, he found his screaming buddy. They would scream through college, backpack through Europe, start a small business, run an orphanage—who the hell knew; the possibilities were endless. He couldn't think of a better person to explore them with.

He didn't realize he had fallen asleep until he woke up. He couldn't have been out for more than fifteen minutes; the paused frame was still on screen, and Sarah hadn't returned with the pizza yet.

Still groggy, he waited. He couldn't hear anyone talking, or moving. The pizza guy had to have been gone by now, which meant Sarah was up to something else.

"Woman?" he called.

No answer.

She said no peeking, so he checked the bathroom first. The door was open, lights off. No one inside. He looked into her room from where he stood in the hallway, and she wasn't there either.

Louder this time, he called, "Sarah?"

No answer.

He grimaced. "I'm gonna peek!" he warned, striding back toward the front of the house.

He hoped for a frantic *You wouldn't dare, you heathen!* but still, there was nothing.

He found the pizza on the counter and felt the bottom of the box. Still hot. He couldn't have been asleep for more than a minute.

Maybe she went to grab something from her car. The front door was still unlocked.

He stepped out into the brisk cold night, and a wave of dread hit him. He couldn't place why. "Sarah?" he called again. There was still no answer, but if she was in the middle of doing something, she could've just been distracted.

He strode around to the side of the house. There sat her car in the driveway. No one there.

He muttered, "Where the hell…" She could've been in her parents room, for whatever reason. Maybe looking for candles.

Perturbedly gnawing his bottom lip, he turned and headed back down the stone path which led to the door, approaching the lone oak tree which obscured most of the front yard.

He froze. Something was different.

A weight, gently swinging, several feet off the ground. A long narrow shape, dark through the dying leaves. Wind whistled through the branches, followed by the higher, wheezing groan of wood.

Snap

Jack jumped and the shape fell, taking several dead limbs with it. He didn't know what possessed him to run closer, but he did, fumbling to pull out his phone and turn on the flashlight. Its weak ray illuminated rope wound tightly around denim-clad ankles.

Sarah's ankles.

Her chest was raised, back draped over a tree root, neck awkwardly bent.

Shirt, chin, neck, blotched with blood.

Wide eyes. Mouth agape.

"Wh…What?" he croaked, dropping to his knees. "Sarah…what…"

He couldn't breathe whole breaths. His eyes danced and he couldn't focus or fully register what he saw.

He needed to do something.

He pulled her up from the tree root, resting her head on his lap so he could shine the light on her face. Her eyes were open. Bloody cheeks.

He needed to do something.

Fingers numb and hands shaking, he dialed 911.
Dispatch answered.
His face was wet. Cold.

"Yeah," he managed after a silence, "She… She was hanging by the ankles."
"Your *location,* sir," the lady on the phone repeated.
Location. "I… Eleven Maple Lane." His voice shook.

"Okay, what happened?"

"She… answered the door for pizza, and… I don't…"
How could he have slept through this?

"Sir?"

"*I don't know!*" he cried, louder than intended. His throat found relief in not holding back, but he had to keep it together. "She's not—responding." He took her hand.

It was drenched. Dark. Her finger was gone. The ring finger.

Her throat was open, slit.

Everything went slow and far away.

The dispatcher spoke.

What if Sarah could still hear him?

He still had the phone to his ear, but no one was saying anything. His other hand covered her open throat.

"Hey. Hey, uh." He had to reassure her. He couldn't sound scared. He put the phone on the wet grass and held her. "You'll be alright, okay? You'll be alright."

Sirens. Flashing lights. Blue and red.

Maybe he fooled himself into thinking she wasn't long gone before he ever made it outside. Maybe this was easier to bear than her having passed alone and scared while he peacefully slept.

2. At The Station

Jack

Six months passed since the homicide. There were no leads. There was no evidence. Because no one could be indicted on an assumption, no one faced legal consequences. However, Jack worried about the whispers throughout the community, and the fact he was still under investigation. Mostly he'd overhear pieces of conversations from people he didn't even know.

"I saw him propose to her."

"So he killed her when she said no."

"It looked like she said yes, but I guess not."

"Must've said yes to save face, then dumped him once they left."

Idiots, Jack thought. *The fuck do they know?*

One night, at about two AM, Jack gave up trying to sleep. It was a school night, but then, what did school even matter anymore? There were only three months left.

He did what he always did on nights like these. He stuffed his backpack with everything he knew he would need for the next day, grabbed a sleeping bag and walked to the cemetery. It wasn't a long trek down the backroad and across the street. He was there within thirty minutes.

He unrolled his sleeping bag beside Sarah's tombstone, propping up his backpack as a pillow. He felt more at rest already, laying down and staring up at the stars beside her.

He let out a breath. "Your family moved away this morning. I'm not sure if they told you."

Silence. He expected nothing else.

There was more he wanted to say. Rather, he *wanted* more to say. Talking helped clear his head. "I'll miss them. They said they were sorry to leave me, but I get it. They couldn't bear it here anymore, and the rest of your family's all out west anyway, so now they're headed to LA." He bit his lip. "I'll be okay, though. I'll be out of here soon enough, too, right? NYU already sent my acceptance letter. I could drop out now, get my GED. Speed up the process. People here suck."

Silence again.

He laughed, "You'll get a kick out of this; remember that girl Kim I told you about? Moved into town recently, goes to The Velvet a lot, got me and my sister fake IDs? She asked me out today."

He knew this was the part Sarah would've burst out laughing, eyebrows up and hand masking her open mouth, *Are you serious?*

"Yeah," he answered. "Don't know what made her think I'd say yes, but... And I should've just said 'no,' but she caught me off guard so I pretended like I couldn't hear her and changed the topic."

Flashing lights, blue and red. A police car pulled up to the cemetery entrance. Jack frowned and, like an idiot, stood for a better view.

The car door slammed shut, and an officer strode past the gates. "Jack?" she called.

He didn't answer. He froze.

"Come on, kid. I know you're there."

He couldn't think. But he knew he had to do something. It was either cooperate, or act suspicious.

"Yeah?" he answered.

He shielded his eyes when the beam of her flashlight reached his face. When it turned to the gravestone and sleeping bag, he knew what she was looking at. "I couldn't sleep," he explained.

She was a silhouette with the police lights behind her, the red and blue like a flashing halo catching the outer strands of her short, tight curls. She wrapped a hand about her forehead so she could squeeze her temples. "God, this is some bullshit," she muttered. He recognized this was one of the cheerleaders' moms, Officer Robinson. The pair pretty much had the same voice, except Officer Robinson's held a slightly more rounded resonance.

"What?" he asked.

"You're just a kid who misses his girlfriend."

He didn't know where she was going with this.

She sighed and dropped her hand. "It's past hours. You're trespassing."

"Oh. Uhh…" He knew this. He didn't think it'd be a big deal, though.

"That's all I was called here about, but now I gotta ask: does the name Kimberly Michaels mean anything to you?"

He wracked his brain. Then it hit him, "New girl?"

"Damn," she muttered. "Now I gotta take you in for questioning."

His gut twisted. "Why? What happened?"

"Same thing that happened to Miss Becker over there." She gestured toward Sarah's grave. He followed her pointed hand. He couldn't form a response yet.

Officer Robinson nodded back toward her car. He remained where he was. It felt surreal. Suddenly he would never see Kim again.

And the killer was still killing.

"Don't worry," Officer Robinson said when he still made no move closer, "*I* know it wasn't you. And who knows, maybe whatever you tell us will aid in catching the *actual* guy this time."

As nice as it was to have someone believe him, he didn't feel at all reassured. Kim was dead. He had the odd impulse to text her about it later. He didn't have anyone else to help him through this, but...

Now he had no one.

Feeling like a ghost, he collected his backpack and sleeping bag. Officer Robinson waited patiently as he said goodbye to Sarah, and together they walked back past the cemetery gates.

...

Jack blinked slowly under the fluorescent lights from his seat at the interrogation table. The room was bare save for the table before him and three chairs — his, the interrogator's, and an empty one on the interrogator's side.

Jack remembered he was supposed to answer something. "What?" he asked, voice gravelly with exhaustion, going on thirty-four hours without sleep. He didn't feel tired, though; he felt dumb. He couldn't focus.

To further skew his focus, he knew Sarah's dad was a detective, and was probably watching everything on the other side of the one-way window. Not the dad who moved with her mom to LA, but her bio-dad, who was probably not gonna sleep until the killer was caught. It would have been nice if the guy hadn't listed Jack as the number one suspect.

The man who sat before him had introduced himself as Detective Schultz. He seemed younger than the others, clean-shaven with ruddy cheeks, a squared jaw and copper colored hair.

"I said it must be rough," Detective Schultz said, patient and gentle, though it felt like a practiced veil over an abrasively comedic personality. "Having to be back here again," he finished.

"Oh shit," Jack yawned as he leaned back in his seat, impatient with how early-on they were in this chat. "We're still in the rapport stage."

Detective Schultz chuckled, knowing better than to try and deny it. This was the part in the interrogation where they would try to lull Jack into a false sense of security and have him open to being honest, while getting a read for his tells. It worked on him last time because he didn't know any better, but this time he knew any kindness they showed him was just part of the routine. While they hadn't been able to use anything against him last time, he wouldn't rely on being so lucky again this time.

Anyways, if Detective Schultz had tried to deny his tactic, he would have lost Jack's trust completely. "You read up on interrogation methods," Copper-head praised. "Smart man." He smiled warmly, as if to a kid, but Jack didn't care for the attempted pretense. He wasn't offended, but indifferent. The guy was just doing his job. Jack had other things to bother himself with, like mind-numbing guilt; and the notion that he'd already met his soulmate, and living without her was like trying to read a story that had already finished, but for whatever reason it still had a daunting five hundred pages left before he was allowed to put the book down.

"I'll play along," Jack muttered, "but I'm losing my usefulness…so…fast." He didn't know how he was supposed to finish this sentence, but was content to know this phrasing would suffice.

Detective Schultz nodded. "That's alright." He shifted his weight to lean slightly closer, still with that soothing conversational vibe, but it was clear he was getting more serious. "Have you ever been to the Velvet Club?"

"Nah, man," Jack lied, not caring if the detective believed him. Of course Jack wanted to help the investigation where he could, but he wouldn't so easily admit to doing something illegal. "Are they doing the eighteen-plus thing?" he asked.

The detective didn't grin or chuckle this time, but seemed slightly disappointed. "Hm. No need to act clueless. It looks like just about every kid your age has a fake ID. It's not why you're here."

"Kids with friends get fake IDs," Jack quipped back. "I don't have friends."

"No, you have friends," the detective insisted, pitch rising as if he actually believed himself, and cared.

Jack stared back at him, deadpan. Waiting. Would the man try to continue to convince him, or would he move on?

"There's George Hernandez." Copper-head put up a finger to count, *one friend.*

"George is a fucking…" Jack stopped himself, then sighed. He didn't want to get heated here. But George hadn't hung out with him since the rumors started that Jack had killed Sarah. Of course George didn't believe them, but he knew being associated with a rumored girl-killer would have him just as shut out of every social circle as Jack was. George didn't have the pull to flip it.

But George also didn't have the balls to stick around and help a buddy out.

"So you guys aren't getting along right now," the detective guessed. "That's fine; that happens. What about your sister?"

"Pass." His sister Gabby had stuck with him on paper, and she'd hang out with him when she could, but it wasn't the same natural bond he'd have with an *actual* friend.

"Well," Detective Schultz continued, unfazed, "at least you and Kimberly Michaels are bonding nicely. Helps that she's new to town, doesn't it." He smiled, like this was something to smile about.

Jack stared back, waiting again.

"She's posted selfies with you all over her social media," Copper-head added.

Jack kept the stare. He was too tired to find what he wanted to say, but he knew playing this game wasn't getting them anywhere.

"What is it?" asked the detective.

"I already know why I'm here."

"Oh? Why's that?"

Jack kept silent for a beat, thinking, but practiced at keeping it out of his expression. Officer Robinson probably wasn't supposed to have told him anything. So he offered a different angle. "Why would you have seen Kimberly Michaels' social media posts? Either you're investigating her or she's dead."

"Hm. That's a truly astute observation for a kid with little experience here."

Maybe Jack had taken too long to come up with this angle. Still, he asked, "Is it a crime to be astute?"

"I think you already knew why you were here before I mentioned her name."

"You got any proof?"

Detective Schultz opened his mouth as if to respond, then paused, a hand to his earpiece as he tilted his head and listened. His eyes closed and Jack watched the outline as his eyes rolled back. One hand fell flat on the table while the other slid along the side of his head in a contained show of frustration. "She told you."

Welp, so much for keeping that a secret. "Yeah," Jack said. "Probably because she knows it's pointless to treat me like a criminal. So can we get on to the part where I'm actually useful?"

The single door flew open and into the adjacent wall with a *SLAM*. Jack hastily registered dark yellow stubble, angry blue eyes and disheveled blonde hair before his back met the wall and there was no floor beneath his feet. He couldn't place at what point he'd hit his elbow, but it throbbed.

The face too close for comfort belonged to Detective Gerald Lloyd. Sarah's bio-dad. "Really, punk? Playing it *'cool?!'*" he sneered, then bellowed, *"Do you feel cool now?!"*

Still surprised he was against the wall, Jack felt his eyebrows raise higher at the sudden loudness.

Schultz stood with some urgency, though was still cautious as he approached with a hand out. "Now, Lloyd," he warned. "You know you can't do that."

Sarah's dad didn't seem to hear, or care, but continued to scream, "You're a liar and we have proof, you little shit! There's footage of you leaving the Velvet, today, *with Kimberly Michaels!*"

"That doesn't prove anything!" Jack yelled back.

Detective Lloyd lifted his upper lip in a snarl, teeth showing beneath a rough mustache when he growled, "It proves you move on pretty quickly, don't you think?"

Everything in Jack quieted. He felt decently put together before, even with his exhaustion. Now he felt awake. Alert. Hungry for some kind of reckless release. Nothing mattered anymore, right?

Jack looked Sarah's dad dead in the eye, and kept his tone at a practiced calm when he replied, "You made a new family for yourself pretty quickly, don't you think?"

It was almost funny when Jack recognized that same odd calm come over Gerald Lloyd before the man pulled a fist back in preparation to launch.

Detective Schultz finally sprang into action and caught the punch by the wrist, stopping him. "I'm trying to cover your ass here, Lloyd! Let us handle it!"

Lloyd didn't fight it, but didn't immediately ease off. He laughed and offered Jack a manic, sarcastic grin before dropping the grip on his jacket. Jack stumbled in place against the wall as he found his footing. Schultz released Lloyd's wrist.

"Alright," Lloyd said, still at that odd, manic calm. He took his seat at the second chair. "Explain where you and Kimberly Michaels went after you left the Velvet."

"Check the parking lot footage," Jack replied. "We left separately."

"Where did you meet up?"

"We didn't."

"Why's that?"

"We didn't plan to. It's a school night."

Lloyd scrunched his nose with a laugh and shook his head. "Think you're smart, don't you?"

"Don't gotta be smart to know the days of the week."

"Prove you didn't meet her again that night."

"My family saw me come in."

"What time?"

"However long it takes to get home from the Velvet, plus whatever time I left."

"Were you with them the whole night?"

"I was in my room."

"Prove it."

"Well shit, if I knew I'd need to film myself in my room I would've."

"So you can't prove you were home the whole night."

"My car hadn't left the driveway."

"But you didn't drive to the cemetery, did you?" Lloyd wore a grin that said, *got you now.* "So the whereabouts of your car hardly mean anything."

"I'll give you that. Now can I hear your attempt at proof that I *did* meet up with her later?" When there wasn't an immediate clap-back, Jack inclined his head and feigned surprise at their incompetence. But Lloyd's smirk renewed. He peered back at Detective Schultz, who opened the case file and placed a photo over the table. Jack stepped closer to see it, angling himself so the glare of the overhead light wouldn't completely obscure the image of a men's flannel shirt draped over a chair. It looked like Jack's size, and he *did* wear a lot of flannels. A few had gone missing, which gave this "evidence" a bit of a creepy-chills factor.

While he knew what they were hinting at, he didn't want to seem too smart for his own good—he didn't want to look guilty by denying something too quickly. "Why am I looking at this?" he asked.

"You mean it doesn't look familiar?" Lloyd asked.

Jack couldn't help his voice rising, "It's a flannel shirt; anyone can have a flannel shirt."

"A flannel shirt with your hair on it?"

Had *Kim* taken one of his shirts? It didn't matter; this wasn't looking good, and nothing he told them would be helpful if they were just going to try and force a guilty confession out of him. He remembered reading that detectives were allowed to lie about evidence during an investigation; there might not have been a flannel at Kim's house at all.

While asking for a lawyer was useless because no one would defend him fairly, and denying everything was growing complicated, he had one last resort. "I plead the fifth. I don't have to answer any of this. I thought I was here to help."

Detective Schultz rolled his eyes with the helpless rise and fall of his hands to his thighs. This meant the end of the interrogation; Jack was under no legal obligation to stay there.

While equally displeased, Sarah's dad kept his unworried, sarcastic front. "That's fine. You can do that. But you're still under investigation." He darkly grinned, voice sickly sweet when he added, "I'll see you again. Jack."

. . .

It was a little after four AM. Jack sat at the station's lobby, waiting for it to be a decent time to call Gabby for a ride to school. He didn't have money for a taxi. He was sure if Officer Robinson was there that she would've helped, but she wasn't, and none of the other officers were on his side, or even neutral. Not even Detective Schultz was truly neutral; he was just okay at pretending he was.

With an alarm set on his phone to six AM, Jack sank in his chair, stared at the wall across from him and tried to think sleepy thoughts. It would be hard to quiet his mind now. Fluorescent lights, nowhere to lay down, no Kim to talk to, no Sarah to talk to... The fact one of his flannels ended up in a murder scene...

"Did they bring you in, too?" asked a small, feminine voice beside him.

He turned his head and found a petite girl with curly red hair. Freckles, like Sarah. About his age, if not the slightest bit older. Her lips were thin, and her jaw was squared. Her skin clung to her face, leaving little fat in her cheeks and below her chin. With hair so red and pigment so pale, she could've passed for a ceramic doll.

While he wasn't trying to make conversation, he also wasn't trying to be rude. Her eyes were so wide and she sat so stiffly, it was like any insensitive move would break her.

He nodded in answer. "You?"

She nodded back. "For the dead girls."

The plural caught his attention and he sat up. "Girls?" Yes, he knew there was more than one, but why was this girl in for *both?*

"Kimberly Michaels and Sarah Becker," she answered.

He doubted it could've been her, but he couldn't help an accusatory tone when he asked, "How are you connected?"

She turned her gaze past him, voice shaking, "The first one, I… Where I worked, they wouldn't let girls make deliveries, for safety reasons, but that night we didn't have any male drivers, and I was the only one with a car, and…" Silence as she struggled for words.

Finally he pieced it together. "You brought the pizza."

She nodded. "The door was open, so I called to see if anyone was home. No one answered. I didn't know what to do, but the pizza was already paid for, so I put it on the counter and left."

"Your story sounds like horse shit. How did you not see her on the way in?"

Wide-eyed, her gaze snapped back to his.

He saw his mistake. "Mine sounds like horse shit, too. How did I sleep through it?"

"So you believe me?"

"I don't see a motive. And I doubt you could've... strung her up as high as she was." *A dark shape, dangling, falling through the dry branches —*

She seemed to relax with a few silent nods, but she remained stiff. "Well. It doesn't help that I know Kim, too. Or, 'knew.' It's 'knew' now because...past tense..."

"It's okay, it uh. Takes getting used to."

"I never even saw the first one alive. Sarah, I mean."

A pang in his gut. His guard wasn't up anymore, so he felt all this like he usually would. Any reminder, any mention, just... He'd have some sort of physical reaction, every time.

His discomfort must've been obvious; the frail girl immediately spouted, "I'm sorry —"

"It's fine," he murmured, even though Sarah was only ever supposed to have been alive, and to have met her alive shouldn't have been a rare commodity.

"This is all new territory for me," the girl said, "and I don't think it's hit yet."

"It's okay," he promised.

"I met Kim at The Velvet a few times," she continued. "I called her out for being under age, and it confused her at first, but then she saw I was just playing, and we laughed, and... I was just at her house earlier. I was the last to see her, just like I would've been the last to see Sarah Becker, and I'm so—so—I'm freaking out."

"Don't. Of the two of us, they'll blame me."

She quieted as she again took him in. "I'll worry for you, then."

He managed a small, reassuring grin. "Thanks, but don't. I didn't do it, so there isn't any definitive proof, and without definitive proof I can't be convicted. I'll be alright." This was what his dad had told him, and Jack had no reason not to trust him on this. Yeah, the dude was socially destroyed with PTSD after serving in the army, but after becoming an independent PI, he learned a thing or two about law.

The way the girl's gaze remained locked on his had him think that maybe she thought he was being too optimistic. Maybe his dad was just trying to keep him from freaking out.

She dropped her gaze to her fingers which sat intertwined over her lap. He noted several indentations over her hands, as if she had been nervously digging her nails in for hours. "I think instead of 'good cop, bad cop,' they're just...all bad," she speculated. "Trying to intimidate us. Because if they were as rough with you as they were with me—"

"They were rough with you?"

"I don't mean physically, but they seemed so certain I did it."

This was reassuring. "So it's not just me, then."

She shook her head. "I'm beginning to think they're like this with everyone."

"Is there anyone else they took in that you know of? That they're questioning?"

Again she shook her head, this time with a shrug. "I only happened to see you because you were still here."

He bit his lip. He needed to know who the other suspects were.

"So your name is… Theodore Van Sloan?" she asked.

"Just Jack." When he realized this was an introduction, he put out his hand.

The girl weakly smiled and extended her own, arm trembling. "Just Wyn."

"Good to meet you, Wyn." They shook.

Her smile widened. "And you as well."

...

He ran into Wyn a few times after that, which made life a little better. She was much less nervous than their first encounter implied. Usually they'd spot one another at The Velvet and she'd buy him a drink. He wouldn't ever ask, and whenever she offered he'd always say 'no,' but it was as if she knew he couldn't afford his own—not since he lost his kitchen job. Every employer after that was hesitant to hire him, or to keep him after the fact.

At first his dad lectured him for not trying hard enough, but after they went together to *literally every business in town*, and *none* accepted him, the man begrudgingly acknowledged Jack's plight. Everyone low-key suspected he was a serial killer, especially since Kim was found dead upside down with her throat slit the same as Sarah, and no one wanted to risk extended contact. This was unfortunate, considering how Grandma Ruth was moving back in with them as a dependent. Without Jack's usual contributions toward bills, money was about to be *tight*.

The weeks which followed Kim's death revealed there still weren't any leads on the actual guy, but as far as the community was concerned, Jack was still the convenient scapegoat. The newspaper went so far as to allude to the killer as

Sabertown's own "Jack the Ripper." His mom drove to the press the first time it happened, tore them a new asshole and threatened to sue them for libel, but in actuality she couldn't. While the implication was heavy, the article — and every article about the murders after that — was carefully worded so that it never outright said Jack was behind anything. It was like a connect-the-dots puzzle with most of the dots already connected—you didn't need it all there to see what they wanted you to see.

His attention drifted from his studies, and so he neither graduated nor went to NYU. Because he was still under investigation, he was indefinitely trapped in county jurisdiction. Sabertown had him by the balls, and this suited Detective Gerald Lloyd just fine.

One Year Later

3. The Summoning Spell
Lydia

Still in her work uniform — an unflattering, black and red Rainy Day Grill T-shirt and jeans — Lydia sat at her dining room table, feet throbbing, and long, dark hair pulled back in a sloppy bun-turned-ponytail. She was too young for the strands of gray locks and wrinkled brow which grew evermore apparent over the past year, yet there they were. She shifted her pudge and withdrew reading glasses from her apron pocket. She had worked a double shift that day. Longer than what most fourteen hour shifts felt like. And now there was *this* to deal with.

The newspaper sat in an unfolded heap before her, beneath the quaint four-light chandelier—the only light on in the house. Although she already heard the news, she kept reading the article's opening paragraph.

**Sabertown's 'Jack the Ripper'
Strikes Again!**

Ashley Baker (17), last seen
conversing with Theodore
"Jack" VanSloan, was found
dead this morning outside
her car, throat slit, hanging
upside down by the ankles.
Sound familiar?

She could hardly read past the headline, though she knew
she didn't need to. After the third incident, they all began to
read the same. Teen girl, found with her throat slit, hanging
by her ankles so all the blood drained, recently seen with
Jack. Her son.

Lydia knew he was innocent. Of course, no mother would
believe their child could do something like this, but Lydia
knew Jack couldn't. It was never a thought which crossed
her mind; she was shocked to hear what other people were
saying.

She thought she would eventually become numb to each
new murder, but she never did. As with last time and the
time before that, her heart dropped and she had to force

deep, steady breaths. "This can't continue," she managed through a strained throat, a hand over her mouth.

Ruth, a healthy 78 years old, significantly lean and only taller than most children, responded with a stern nod as she set a mug of tea before her. Her long white hair sat atop her head in a thinning, fluffy bun.

She held a mug for herself in one hand, absently rubbing her daughter's shoulder in the other. "Tonight would be the night to do it," she said, and for a moment Lydia was confused. Ruth explained, "It's a new moon. Almost midnight, and therefore almost Monday, the start of a new week."

"You mean, this is the night for another spell?" Lydia verified, monotone and unenthused.

Ruth nodded. "We have everything we need."

"Ma, please? This is a human psycho, not a vampire."

"*Domsuco,*" the old woman corrected, a hint of fire touching her otherwise frail voice, but she was too sweet of a person to ever truly sound intimidating.

Lydia rested her face in her palm. All she wanted to do was sleep, or cry. While the situation was dark, she couldn't stop herself from laughing. If there wasn't anything she could do, why resist a laugh at the absurd lengths their desperation had pushed them?

Ruth, of course, turned more stern at the sound. "Lydia. I *know* what I saw those years ago. I *know* the Curse of the Wisher's Son is real — "

"Please, Ma, I'm trying so hard — "

Ruth plowed on, her agitation lending her more volume, "And Jack is the Wisher's Son of this generation! Unless you want what happened to my brother to happen to your son..." She licked her lips and opened her mouth, eyes flitting as she searched for the rest of her words.

Lydia looked away. She didn't have the energy to argue. With her husband missing, it was up to her to provide for her household. With the little time she had to spend with her family between working and sleeping, she didn't want to sour any moment. Especially not when arguing wouldn't get them anywhere.

Ruth set her mug down on the table and stepped into Lydia's line of view. The old woman's eyes softened at what she found. "There it is. I thought so."

Tears blurred Lydia's vision. She wiped them away with her thumb before they could fall.

Ruth crooned, "Dear, I know it's hard to believe sometimes."

Lydia huffed a quick breath through her nose.

49

"No, I know," the old woman insisted. "When faith is all you have left, it's scary. But what is the first thing we learn about magic?"

Lydia turned to the window and found their dog, Lestat — a moseying dark blur in the yard, ears up as he sniffed the ground. He jerked away and playfully ran the opposite direction.

"…Magic always works," Lydia finally answered.

Ruth nodded and smiled. "That's right."

"Just not always right away, or how you would expect it,"

"Mh-hm."

While she felt she was doing well before, Lydia heard her voice raise and the snark seep in when she added, "So it's all completely up to chance, and when it *does* happen we're just deciding to interpret it as 'magic at work.'" She stood and noisily snatched the newspaper from the table, shoving it three times into the garbage before it successfully wedged through the too-small opening.

Ruth patiently waited for the quiet that followed. However frustrated, she was just as painfully patient when she asked, "Whether you believe it or not, what harm would a spell do?"

Lydia stood by the trash can for a moment longer, wondering why she was dizzy before she figured it was because she stood up with her reading glasses. She took them off and let them dangle from her fingers.

No, she didn't believe in any of this, but... these spells were their last resort. She couldn't turn her back on that; she had to find the energy and try. For Jack.

She crossed back to the table and took her tea, placing her glasses back in her apron pocket. "What's different about this one?"

After a short silence, her Ma nodded, accepting this courtesy for what it was. "The other spells we did, we did with the aim to banish whatever evil attached itself to Jack. However, evil has free will, and there's only so much we can do about that." Ruth crossed to the antique hutch, which had survived the move from her old place in New Orleans without a scratch on it. "This is the time to call for help," she murmured as she opened one of its cabinets. She withdrew four white candles and laid them on the table. When she returned to the hutch, her eyes locked on an item and she paused. Then frowned.

Lydia noticed. "What?"

Still uncertain, Ruth touched an open letter sitting on its surface, then removed a weighty, black onyx stone about the size of her fist. "This may be a wildcard," she warned, "but…we can summon an entity powerful enough to fix this."

While her regular talk of magic already seemed pretty ridiculous, this came across as especially contrived. Lydia tried not to sound too skeptical. "Entity, like a demon?"

"I don't think so." Ruth commenced setting a candle per each cardinal point on the table. "It isn't typically as literal as that, to my understanding; we're dealing with energies. Think of it as…" She paused and gave it some thought. "Good luck and bad luck," she finished, setting down the last candle. "Rather than ask the universe to get rid of the bad, we ask for good." Again she paused, though last time it was because she didn't have the words. This time she was hesitant to say them. "Unless… Well, I suppose we'll find out."

It's a rock. "I trust it if you trust it," Lydia said instead.

Ruth frowned at the stone for a moment longer before placing it at the center of the table. "I'll need to make a few adjustments to the incantation. If you finish setting up, I should have it ready by then."

Lydia's feet screamed louder at the thought of moving again, but the slightest possibility of saving Jack took priority. Allowing a moment to brace herself, she nodded and sought out the matches.

It was decent timing. Ruth finished her adjustments as Lydia finished setting up. They called the corners and made the circle as they always did, then proceeded. From their seats across from one another, they held hands and read from Ruth's page on the table.

"Oh Domglory,
"Return to us now.
"May your power surpass any Domsuco,
"And may your kindness keep you grounded,

"So you may recognize who to trust,
So you may pursue justice with neither vengeance nor guilt,
So you may cleanse evil and herald true peace,

"We summon you to protect the sacrificial Wisher's Son,
"And find a new solution to this centuries-old feud
"Between those who create with their thoughts
"And those who destroy.

"May you stand with us unless banished by congregation.
"So mote it be."

They didn't notice the immediate change in the air. Their dog, Lestat, pawed at the back gate, and when it opened, he darted out into the blanket of night.

4. Reminiscence And Rebirth

Alice

Alice's heart was always an enigma, and there was nothing figurative about the way it beat for Theo. She remembered the day they first met. It was 1939; she was eleven and he was twelve. Before that chance encounter, her heart would beat at a regular rate regardless of the situation; calm or excited, it wouldn't slow or hasten.

It was a summer afternoon. She frequently wandered the woods, but that day she dared go further. Part of her wanted to get lost, just for the sake of adventure.

Thmp, thmp, thmp -

It was a subtle sensation at first, when her heart gradually quickened. She didn't feel it in her chest, but in her soul. She was happy, but couldn't put a finger on why. The leaves never before had appeared so green, nor the sky so blue.

She wandered further, and her heart responded accordingly. She laughed, learning a level of excitement she'd only ever read of before.

Thmp-thmp-thmp-thmp —

It was at this point she knew it was, in fact, her heart. Now that she knew how it felt, she couldn't let it stop. She picked up her pace and it was as she predicted: it beat faster. For lack of a better word, it tickled. The giggles that followed erupted from a place beyond her control.

She emerged into someone else's backyard and froze when she saw a boy reading by the pool. His hair was wet and sun-bleached, and his skin was tanned with summer. Even from across the way she could tell she liked his face. There was something about it to be associated with innocence, or sincerity. Kindness, put simply.

There was only one person in town who had a pool. This was the mayor's house. She was spying on the mayor's son.

Typically there would be a fence to keep wanderers such as herself out, but after taking in more of her surroundings, she saw she stood in the exact spot the fence had been broken down. The tools to fix it were nearby, arranged in such a way that Alice assumed they had been flung in a fit of frustration.

She turned her attention back to the boy, who must've been looking at her for a while now. She felt the warmth of embarrassment, but still the exhilarating sensation of her heart racing.

"Are you lost?" he asked.

After looking back into the woods, she answered, "I don't think so." She couldn't see her home, but all she had to do was venture straight. "Has your house always been here?"

"For as long as I can remember," he replied with a strange grin.

She peered back at the collection of tools. "Do you need help fixing this fence?"

In his smile and tilted head, she could see he was caught off guard and that she had somehow endeared herself to him. "What's your name?" he finally asked.

She wasn't sure how anything she said could've been construed as cute, but her heart was racing and her smile didn't falter; nothing else mattered. "Etsu Aisuru."

"What?"

"Call me Alice."

"Oh, Alice. Where are you from?"

She pointed back toward her house.

He offered a mock-suspicious stare. "You're not a Japanese spy, are you?"

"If I were, would I tell you?"

"Ah."

"And your name?"

"Theodore Jackson Van Sloan." He dogeared the page he was reading, closed the book and placed it on the nearby end table. "They call me Theo."

Alice wasn't sure what to do next. "Is this the part where we shake hands?"

He shrugged, then stood. From across the way she could tell they were about the same height. "I guess that depends." He began his leisurely cross to her, and her to him. "We can bow like the Japanese. Kiss like the Argentinians. Shape our hands into lotus buds like in Thailand."

"What about *here*?" she interjected.

"Here?" The manner in which he proceeded was as if she asked the exact question he wanted to answer. "You know why they call us the melting pot?"

She shrugged, and couldn't help but laugh when he exaggeratedly dropped his jaw.

"We are a blend of thousands of cultures," he answered. "I guess that means we do what we want."

"Or, it means we do all of them."

"All of them?"

"At the same time."

He paused, undoubtedly trying to visualize it. He snickered when he succeeded. "At the same time. Okay."

After some discussion and goofy laughs, they decided one hand would serve as a lotus bud. The other would reach out for a handshake, and as they were bowed they would deliver two quick kisses to the face.

Unfortunately, they would not complete this task. Once Alice's hand touched his, her heart leapt and she gasped, tripping backwards over a sun lounger and landing into the pool to avoid the cement. Theo, who tried to pull her back, only fell in as well. She was upset to have possibly ruined one of her favorite dresses, but still her heart beat so quickly, she could hardly focus on such things. She playfully splashed Theo for letting her fall, and he in the same manner splashed her back for taking him down with her.

Many moments passed before the pool proved too cold and they got out. Theo laid down some towels so they might snack on baby carrots and potato chips and dry in the sun.

This was the same day she met Goldilocks. If Alice was eleven and Theo was twelve, the younger girl had to have been eight when she and her parents pulled up the driveway in their '30 Stutz Monte Carlo Sports Sedan. It was nothing compared to the mayor's convertible, straight from the factory '39 Horch A Cabriolet, though when compared to what everyone else in town had, it was certainly worth talking about—and Alice *did* talk about it. The luxury vehicle had the same class; the same long nose and sleek, rounded accents. Alice marveled at how much she could see reflected in its tan painted sides as it slowed to a stop, and while she was content riding in her father's rusted pre-war pick-up truck, for a moment she envied whatever little girl got to ride in the back of this.

One of the back doors flew open and the petite blonde was out in an instant, already in her bathing suit and ready for the pool. Her breath stuttered as if to flip-flop between which way to greet him before she called, "Theo!"

He hadn't glanced over his shoulder yet, but Alice knew by the look on his face he didn't need to; he was expecting them. He grinned and peered back. "Well, if it isn't little Goldilocks!"

The girl hurriedly approached the gate, her parents only now stepping out of the vehicle behind her. "Hello, Theo!"

called her delicate mother, and her round father waved as well.

"Hello, Mr. and Mrs. Dodds!" he waved back.

Mrs. Dodds used her hands for a visor as she peered their way. "Oh!" she exclaimed, "And who's your new friend?!"

He turned back to Alice, nodding toward the gate before standing. Alice followed his cue and stood as well. Goldilocks opened the door and let them in as Theo led the way over. "This is Alice," he answered, and to Alice he introduced, "Mr. and Mrs. Dodds, and Winifred." Goldilocks was Winifred.

Mr. Dodds murmured something into his wife's ear, and while the children clearly weren't meant to hear, Alice couldn't help but catch her father's name, Hisao. Mrs. Dodds frowned in response, either disinterested or displeased. "Oh," she said.

Alice had begun to notice this sort of thing amongst the adults. They were never mean to her, but they were never entirely kind either. And for whatever reason they gave her father some trouble, again, not overly mean, but also not kind. She knew Theo was kidding when he asked if she was a Japanese spy, but she wondered if this was a true fear her neighbors had in regards to her father. Regardless of the fact he had moved here far before the war started—and from France, an allied nation, at that. An American's fear was deaf and blind, and he was an easy scapegoat.

Mrs. Dodds wouldn't glance Alice's way now, but only addressed Theo. "Does your father know she's here?"

Theo squinted, and Alice knew he picked up on it, their awkward attempt of a balance between keeping their distance and being polite. "It's no secret," he replied. "All he's had to do was look out the window."

"Well, someone ought to tell him," she sighed, mostly to herself.

Mr. Dodds nodded, then smiled for the children. "You all play nice, now; we'll be inside if you need anything." He even smiled at Alice, and for a moment she was relieved. But then she had to wonder, was this to be polite, or kind?

The adults went inside and now it was only the three of them. Alice sensed Winifred's unease, though after glancing between her and Theo, Alice gleaned her own background had nothing to do with it.

Theo must've sensed it, too. He laughed, "It's okay, Winifred, she's bonkers like us — maybe worse."

Winifred peered her way, but didn't say anything. Alice knew this wasn't completely the issue, either; the real issue was something more territorial. Alice was an interference. After a moment, the younger girl dropped her gaze with a sigh. "I — g-g-guess — I, I mean…" She took a breath as if to start over. "O-okay."

"I reckon you want to swim?" he guessed, and she nodded.

As much as she enjoyed swimming, Alice had just dried off, and her dress could only endure so much. Not only that, but she knew when she wasn't welcome. "I should be heading home," she murmured, and surprised even herself with how disappointed this made her. Going home meant returning to a mundane existence in which her heart worked a monotonous rate, with nothing new to excite it. The sense of exhilaration she had just being near him — it would fade with every step that lead her through the woods and back to her property.

Theo seemed put off as well. "Home?" Then he smiled, as if relieved. "You mean, to fetch a swimsuit?"

She clamped her lips between her teeth.

Now when Winifred looked between the two, she seemed more empathetic. She took Alice's hand, as if to say something, then dropped it the second a new idea came to mind.

She darted to the picnic blanket, carefully dragging it to the pool side.

Theo caught on and laughed, "So you can stay dry and be involved at the same time. Clever girl, Winifred!"

She blushed, turning her face away as she completed her task, fixing the snacks neatly back into place once the blanket was as close to the pool as possible. Theo began the cross over, and Alice followed. In a lower voice he explained to her, "She probably won't say a word to you all day, but don't take it personally — I think it was weeks before she said anything to me. Lucky for us, I can talk enough to entertain a party, two hours, no stopping — I know, I've done it before."

"Impressive," Alice commented, though she wondered what sort of party would let a child speak for so long without interruption. Shortly she remembered children often had birthday parties — children with friends, anyway. This wasn't to say Alice didn't have friends. There were some classmates who played with her, but this seemed to only happen within the window of a school day.

He raised his voice for the little blonde to hear, "You understand we can only jump in on the far side now, right?"

She nodded, beaming with excitement. Finally, it was time. When he told her, "You go on and get started without me," she didn't need to be told twice. With a running start and an excited scream, she threw herself in. The splash was most satisfying.

Theo went back to addressing Alice. "Fetch your swimsuit if you must. Otherwise, sit back, take in the sun, enjoy the show. She only ever lasts maybe an hour in there before she gets bored."

Now that the environment had become more welcoming, Alice felt no need to leave just yet. She sat with her feet in the water while the other two swam and occasionally hung on the wall beside her, keeping her company. Winifred stepped out of the pool often, never quite done with it, but not so infatuated with it that she couldn't continuously grab a baby carrot, or play with Alice's hair. Alice always had long, straight black hair — very inviting to any girl who knew how to braid. Theo, never being the sort to isolate himself, had Winifred teach him how to do it so he may join in the fun.

It felt right. With Winifred on her left, Theo on her right, and her heart pounding at a rate she didn't know how to adequately describe, she knew that while she was content before, she was happy now.

Bless memories. What a beautiful source for entertainment and inspiration, they were. No one would see, but her eyes watered as she lay in the suffocating darkness of her earthy underground residence. She wasn't in the best of circumstances, but she had been there long enough to grow accustomed to it. Yes, her eyes watered, but there was a smile to accompany it.

Bless memories.

She sometimes imagined Theo there with her, just as she remembered him: twenty years old, confident and charming. They would exchange their playful banter, or political thoughts, or musings on life.

He said something odd on this particular day. Dark brown hair combed back and neatly parted to the side, he softly smiled, kissed her face and whispered, "You're being summoned, darling. Good luck."

Purples and blues, and a fourth primary color she couldn't describe, but assumed was ultraviolet. Golden-lavender?

Her eyes continued to adjust.

Patches of earth and soot speckled the cracked cement walls. Antique lanterns caked in old candle wax hung from their wall-mounts, rusted and black. She remembered now. These once had lit her underground domain. Still, she couldn't remember how she got there.

A brown spider scurried up her arm. She couldn't swat it; she couldn't move.

Thmw—a quick pulse throughout her body, stunning her every fiber and thought. The spider paused on her shoulder, as if having heard.

Silence.

Thmp, louder, clearer. She wheezed a groan, writhing, falling off the cot. Her face landed flat with the ground.

But Theo wasn't really there. Or was he?

"Theo?" Another surprise. She could speak aloud, although it hurt and produced a sound like air sadly grating through a dirty pipe.

Thmp! Her body spasmed and she yelled, throat catching. When her arm flew upward of its own accord, she seized the opportunity and grasped the cot's metal frame. The material dented under her iron grasp as she pulled herself up.

Thmp! and another *thmp!* a second later, coursing through her with a fiery agony. She screamed as she flung herself to a lantern. It fell under her weight, but with a speed too quick to see she grabbed the hollowed-out hole which remained in its wake.

The room sickeningly tilted, reminiscent of a slowly rocking ship. Her fingers and toes twitched and curled inward as they cramped. It hurt to let them be, but it also hurt to move.

Gritting her teeth, she flung herself to the next lantern, then to the next, faster and faster until she was out of her place of rest and into the adjoining tunnel. Her every additional heartbeat ached worse, but she grew stronger for it.

She staggered, then jogged, then sprinted. It had been so long since she had such energy. Considering how deep she was underground, she reckoned Theo had to have been directly above her.

But then her heart slowed. Her legs nearly gave out.

"No," she growled, but continued to stagger. "No, no—" Her knees buckled and she fell with a harsh grunt. She scrambled back to her feet, only to fall again.

Though the thumps grew faint as the beats lost their punch, she crawled. Her limbs tingled with weakness and she panicked, but there was nothing she could do.

Her heart stopped again, entirely.

She clawed at the earth, dragging herself forward until she was, again, completely immobile.

The longer she lay there, the more she doubted the memory of her heart beating, and of herself sprinting down the hallway. However, here she was, still strewn across the ground with her arm outstretched, mid-crawl.

The sound of rain, growing louder, yet it wasn't raining. Her ears imagined it so vividly.

A light entered the tunnel, its rays reaching the wall. The sound couldn't have been rainfall, so it had to have been applause or, more likely, the footfalls of an incredibly quick man.

The light was brighter now. She detected his scent more clearly: metal, leather and electricity, if that was possible. The steps slowed to a more recognizable rate. Finally, she was faced with the full, blinding force of the flashlight. However pained, she barely mustered a petty groan.

"My God, Etsu," the man muttered. He turned her on her back, and though she was blinded, she could still make out enough of his features. Hair, thick with tight black curls, neatly trimmed. Subtle age lines about his brow and eyes. Dark, ebony skin. A look of determination by default. An amputee from the left elbow down. This was Bishop, who hadn't aged since the last time she saw him, which meant she hadn't been gone for long. But then, if he was a domsuco, he wouldn't have aged.

His clothes were different. He wore brown leather boots, sturdy enough for manual labor, but slim and lustrous enough to imply this was not their intended purpose. His pants were denim, but darker. His open, boxlike tweed jacket reached past his hips and could've been dark green or brown, and the turtleneck sweater beneath might've been burnt orange.

He sighed and knelt beside her, setting down his bag. Holding the flashlight with his teeth, he withdrew a plastic sack of donor blood. It seemingly glowed, with that new color she couldn't describe. Upon tearing off the corner, he sat Alice against the wall and poured its contents down her throat.

She nearly coughed, but instead swallowed the thick, lukewarm substance. Her stomach growled, demanding more. She noted her hands, and how her once-sunken digits filled out to regular finger-plumpness. It was a funny observation. She remembered a time when her fingers were so narrow, she couldn't imagine them any thinner.

Her muscles reawakened as her energy returned. Instincts took over and she shoved Bishop aside, feeding herself with the fervor of an animal.

He took no offense. "I brought what I could," he said, voice deep, rich and honey-like, though she barely listened. He spoke more, but something was off. She knew she had felt real blood just a moment ago. She still felt the bag against her lips, yet as she drank she felt less of the effects.

It clicked. She was doing as most children did with juice boxes; she drank nothing, but forced out little droplets, making loud sucky-noises in the process.

"Where's Theo?" she rasped, letting the donor bag drop with her hand. Bishop narrowed his eyes; she had cut him off mid sentence. Usually she would have apologized for interrupting, but she had to save her energy for the words that mattered. "Have you seen him? Recently?"

"No. Why do you ask?"

She pondered her best, most terse response. "He's here," she decided.

"Here?" It wasn't clear if he believed her. She watched the gears turn as he considered that, perhaps, her senses were to be trusted. "If your heart beat again, it could explain how you were able to move so far."

"You... knew?"

He gestured back toward the room from whence she came. "I installed a security system. Motion detectors. For the instance if anything changed, I would know."

"You...*knew?*" Bishop knew she was here. He left her like this.

He only frowned to himself for a moment before handing her another blood bag. Every thought she had vanished as she tore in, a savage once more.

"That's my last," he said.

She paused. She wanted to cry. This wasn't enough.

She drank slowly.

"If you are coming back, I suggest a change in wardrobe."

She considered his implication as she finished a sip. It might not have been solely his choice, then. That she stayed here. "My dresses?" she asked.

"Outdated."

This didn't make sense. Her dresses weren't trendy — they shouldn't have been outdated already. However, considering the change in men's fashion, as worn by Bishop... She was certainly here for more than five years.

He realized her issue. "What year do you think it is?"

" '66?" she guessed. "'67?"

Bishop wouldn't give away much, but something in his expression made her think she was wrong. She had been in here longer.

"What's the last thing you remember?" he asked.

"I..." Now she had to sort through what was a real memory and what was her isolation-induced imagination. "We kissed. Theo and I."

"When?"

"Mine and Gene's anniversary." Suddenly it became clear how awful this was, and here she'd stated it like a cold matter of fact. Gene. It didn't matter that she couldn't stand him; he deserved better.

Bishop's eyebrows rose and it was a minute before she realized her cruelty had nothing to do with it. "So you don't remember how... All in due time, I suppose. Can you stand?"

She grabbed the wall and stood on wobbly legs. Whether she could walk was a different question.

Bishop slung the messenger bag over his shoulder and rose to his feet. "Come," he said, draping her arm over his shoulder, "Let's go." In this manner he escorted her down the tunnel. She had to wonder if this was all real or merely convincing. This wouldn't be the first time she thought she was leaving the underground.

Rusted hinges *creaked* in the distance. Alice exchanged a glance with Bishop and his frown confirmed he heard it as well. They were still underground. If no one had been here in years, what would inspire them to come here now?

The longer she listened, the more she could make of women — or teen girls — laughing, conversing through excited whispers. Their voices faded when another sound overwhelmed her every sense.

Heartbeats. At least four pairs.

"Bishop," she managed, though she barely had the mind to continue.

He paused and waited nonetheless.

"I'm...starving." She dropped her gaze, avoiding whatever look he could give her. She was willing to drink human blood, and she didn't care whose.

"So feast," he suggested. His tone indicated a different look than she imagined. It still carried his smug 'I told you so' attitude, but there was something else. He felt sorry for her.

But he was supposed to tell her to pull herself together. He was her tether to sanity—she would have listened.

She remembered she still could have been dreaming. Her dream-self deserved something fresh, and the best part was there wouldn't be any consequences. The teens weren't real.

Her gums tingled and she felt her canines elongate. While she couldn't recall a time she had done this before, it all felt familiar —

Her footsteps echoed, and whenever she forgot what she was doing, they reminded her she was running.

Rays of a flashlight ahead.

Terrified faces, stretched with screams.

Alice grabbed the arm to a boyish-looking —
No, this was Theo, twenty years old, terrified in the woods —
No, this was a girl, in her teens. The girl was scared, and Alice had her by the arm.
Alice closed her eyes. Reality needed to fix itself.

There were three or ten of them. One had to have been a twin, or so many of them looked the same. All the same clothes - jackets and pleated skirts.
Alice relished in what smelled like pennies and sweat, warm down her throat and satisfying a thirst which she initially thought was an ache she would be forced to bear for the rest of time.
The screams cut short and gave way to gurgles, one by one. The ache loosened, and any other pain in her body dulled until it was no more. Finally, she felt...*alive*.

5. To The Hospital

Alice

Alice sat perched atop a closed, centered tomb, sucking fresh blood from her sleeve. The color intrigued her. It was that fourth primary color, electric lavender-gold, and *glowing*.

She lowered her arm from her mouth and peered over what damage she wrought. Splats of blood decorated the cobwebs and stone walls, each drop a glaring pinprick in the dark. Separate pools of light spilled from each teen's punctured neck, the four of them splayed across the floor, wide-eyed, but still breathing. Each wore varsity jackets with their names sewn in, and Alice knew the embroidered pompoms over the left chest meant they were cheerleaders.

She felt like an animal. Or worse. This was real. She was sated, and now she had the sense to know this was really happening. She brutalized four innocent—

"They *were* searching for domsuco." Bishop leaned against the entrance threshold in a show of nonchalance. When Alice gave him an incredulous look, he corrected himself. "Fine, they said vampires, but of all that is in this world, what's the closest you can get?"

"That's irrelevant." With her guilt and worry growing exponentially stronger, Alice turned her gaze back to the girls. She felt Bishop's observing stare on her back.

"Sometimes I forget who you are," he muttered.

She wasn't sure what this had to do with anything. She didn't have the mind or the energy to ask.

He added, "The Domglory was called to this earth to protect mankind. At her heart, she is a savior."

This didn't change the fact that she'd brought four teen girls to the brink of death. "Why didn't you stop me?" she whispered.

"It was not my place to stop you. This is basic code of conduct; you marked them, therefore they were yours."

"Code of conduct?"

"It's wired into every domsuco, Etsu; keep our existence secret, and respect our kind."

She didn't have anything to say to this. It was too... too... She couldn't think of the word. "Are you a monster now?" she asked, more curious than accusing, though concerned nonetheless.

He was quiet with thought, though his expression didn't give away much.

He turned his attention to the girls. "They'll live," he promised. "Come, we'll take them to the hospital." He crossed to the one whose jacket read, *Monica Hernandez.* "I work there again now, you know," he continued, "It keeps me current." He turned Monica's face for perfect eye contact and stared, no blinking. At first her muscles were tensed with fear, but then she went completely limp. He spoke in a slow, clear manner. "You and your friends had too much to drink before you blacked out. This is all you remember since entering the crypt." He stared into the girl's eyes for a moment longer, then looked away. The girl's head lulled forward.

He turned his gaze back to Alice. "Are you waiting for an invitation?"

"I... How do I do that?"

"You've done it before."

"I don't remember."

He huffed. "I'll walk you through it again, I suppose. It isn't difficult." He motioned her closer. However uncertain, she approached and knelt beside him, following his gaze to the next cheerleader. Her skin was dark, but lighter than Bishop's — more golden brown. Regal features, with high cheekbones and narrow eyes. Her hair was big with tight black curls. Her jacket read, *Crystal Robinson* and was otherwise the same as the others', meaning…she was from their same school. *Meaning they aren't… segregated anymore?* How much had Alice missed?

"The first step is to calm them," Bishop coached. "Their involuntary response will be to trust you, and that's your way in."

"How do I — "

"Read her. Figure it out."

Alice despised vague instruction, but she started with the eyes, same as Bishop.

Crystal's eyelids fought to stay open, and it seemed by fear and sheer willpower that they remained that way. Her breaths staggered, and now a rasping sob came attached to every exhale.

"You'll be alright," Alice muttered, voice low with no room for false pretense. "You and your friends will be at the hospital within minutes. I'm sorry this happened."

The girl didn't respond, but her breaths calmed. She wasn't fighting anymore, possibly because she couldn't. Possibly because she lost too much blood.

Alice hesitated before taking the next step. It didn't feel right, forcibly altering someone's perception, or memory. But if Bishop was certain it was what had to be done, she had to trust him; he was her only connection to the domsuco world, and still her only tether to reality.

"There's something I need you to do first, Crystal," Alice continued, and she gave her the same order Bishop gave Monica. After that, she wasn't sure if there was a proper way to end it, so she turned back to him.

"Yeah, that's it," he confirmed.

She wasn't so sure. It didn't feel like anything magical.

Once she and Bishop did the same with the last two girls, he and Alice each carried two, one over each shoulder. Alice followed Bishop's lead out of the crypt.

A gust of cold, fresh air hit her chest the second he opened the door, and inhaling felt like a sinful pleasure. She didn't realize it had been difficult until it proved almost too easy now. For a second she wanted to stand and do only that.

This pause allowed the rest of the world to present itself slowly, and so she wasn't overwhelmed.

Something about nightfall excited her. It wasn't always this way, but the feeling was familiar. She felt more alive— more awake. The moon was bright and lavender; the stars were a cliche of shining diamonds; the sky resembled the darkest blue depths of the ocean with gleaming, swirling, wispy clouds of that indescribable color, like nebulae in the distance.

A tangent of a thought occurred to her. She couldn't remember testing the sunlight with Bishop since she had transitioned into her stronger, immortal state. She knew she had to have, but she couldn't remember the outcome. Did she burn in the sun like other domsuco, or was she really special?

A field of tombstones stood before her—some cracked, others completely eroded. She didn't recognize the area, though the air still felt and smelled like October in Pennsylvania. "Where are we?" she asked, stepping down from the exit's ledge.

"Erie Cemetery," Bishop answered. "Guess where you've been all this time?"

She thought he'd just said, so now she waited for the answer.

He smirked and nodded to the area behind them. "Vampire Crypt."

She looked back. The weather-stained cement walls were unsettling enough. The two white pillars aside the door gave the impression of Post Revolutionary times. She supposed the two chiseled leaves of the insignia above the doorway curved and met in the shape of a *V*, but beyond this she couldn't see any other vampiric indicator.

"How did I get here?" she asked.

He subtly shook his head and commenced walking down the steep hill, testing his footing with the extra weight on his shoulders. "You, um." He bit his lip, struggling with a decision. She knew it was because he still would rather she remembered on her own time. "You were hidden," he decided, "buried. I later dug you out, but you wouldn't return with me."

Her eyes narrowed. This didn't sound like her, but she still didn't know the surrounding circumstance.

"Follow me to the hospital," he instructed. "Run when I run, and slow when I slow."

She nodded.

Teens secured over his shoulders, he took off, imitating a car in regards to how he gained speed, gradually. Alice kept pace beside him.

"Do I still have blood on my face?" she called over the wind. Her ears rang as a result.

He recoiled but continued on. "Please, don't shout. And a little. I wouldn't worry; you look more distressed than suspicious."

Again she nodded.

"We're about to hop the fence," he warned. "In three, two, one — "

Together they jumped, and together they landed, effortlessly continuing their stride.

"Good!" he called. It wasn't a fence much taller than the hurdles from high school gym class, so she wasn't as impressed with herself.

"Now," he continued, "it isn't terribly late, so the streets may still be busy. I'm taking us down a path we won't be seen."

He led them through a series of backyards, hopping more fences as they appeared. The foliage became a blur of dark purple autumn as they passed. The rubber heels and soles of her stompers shredded with every step. The cars she glimpsed all appeared more masculine than what she was used to; more boxed, less rounded. Dark, neutral colors. Not designed to impress, but to get from point A to point B. This was disappointing.

Thmp.

It caught her off guard; incorporating it into the way she already breathed produced a sensation best described as a reverse burp. She doubled over and resisted the urge to clutch her chest; she still had to keep the cheerleaders over her shoulders.

"That was definitely Theo," she said, catching back up to Bishop.

While he had to have heard, he showed no indication.

They were outside the hospital within minutes. It was huge—box shaped buildings surrounded by box shaped buildings. Bishop led the way to glass sliding doors. No one was there to let them in, and Bishop didn't slow in the least. Before she could gather the air to warn him, the doors opened by themselves. She slowed as she neared them.

There were buttons near the entrance, but no one there to press them. When she glanced about for clues, looked up and saw what she assumed to be security cameras, she supposed someone had let them in from afar.

"Etsu!" Bishop called, and she resumed her run through the doors. "We need help!" he called back into the sterile lobby, white walls and pale blue furniture.

Doctors rushed in, or nurses, or candy stripers. The uniforms were different from what Alice remembered, so she wasn't sure who was who anymore. Most were women, rolling empty stretchers from the nearby hall. They all had semi-circle scars on their necks. Some old, some fairly recent.

"What happened?" Alice muttered.

Bishop followed her gaze with a quick glance then shook his head, the motion short and subtle. "Don't draw attention to their own bites. They don't know they're there, and it's better this way."

Better this way? But the personnel were upon them before Alice could attain a more detailed elaboration. She laid her teens down gently on the stretchers, and one of the medics put an arm to Alice's shoulder as if to lead her along before Bishop blocked them.

"She's fine," he explained. The woman nodded and hurriedly followed as the others rolled the teens away, Bishop keeping pace beside the nurse as he relayed his version of the situation.

Thmp. Alice clutched her chest with a gasp, and the woman spun around. "That doesn't look like 'fine'," the medic grumbled, heading back her way.

Bishop was right, though, Alice didn't need help. She couldn't pull attention away from the teens, and she needed to find Theo. She didn't need to be here anymore.

She turned and reached for the doors, which resisted her attempt to slide open. She waited for them to open on their own, then sped into the night as soon as she could fit past.

6. Anxious To Reunite

Alice

Cold wind in her long black hair. A glowing nighttime of purples and blues. Fireflies like fluorescent green stars zipped past her as she sped.

Still Alice battled with the wonder of reality—whether this was all in her head, and whether that made this any less real. She felt more certain before, when she was with Bishop and modern technology, but being alone in the woods allowed for the memory to feel like a dream again. One thing she learned was, in either scenario, she didn't like that she attacked the cheerleaders. In whatever situation that followed, she had to do what was morally right, even if it wasn't real. For her own sake.

Did this make her selfish? Or, if the girls were in her head, could selfishness have applied?

Thmp.

She gasped and stumbled, gripping a tree before she could collide face first. The bark crumbled in her gasp and the wood beneath splintered her palm.

Every time her heart pulsed, it was too strong to have been imaginary. She fought to remember it, though when her chest was silent for the several following minutes it proved too easy to forget. Always, she would wonder again if her heart really beat.

"This is real," she muttered, knowing she would feel the movement of her voice in her throat, praying this would keep her grounded. "I am sated, therefore I have eaten, therefore this is real." This became her mantra as she decided on a new direction and took off sprinting again. "I am sated, therefore I have eaten, therefore this is real."

If it wasn't the '60s, it had to have been the '70s; she couldn't have been gone for much longer than that. Theo would've been a middle-aged man. She giggled at the thought of him with a full mustache and a portly, older man's gut. There wasn't anything wrong with extra weight—it was to be expected if his career didn't require much manual labor. He was by now a lawyer, no doubt. Or a politician like his father.

She slowed as more possibilities flooded her mind. He was a family man. He would have married. She couldn't blame him, with her being gone for so long. It was possible he found Winifred, now that he didn't need to stay in town for the sake of Alice's dependent heart. It was possible they got back together.

Alice forced fuller breaths and regained her speed. Winifred would have been good to him. If he was happy, and if her old friend was happy, Alice was happy. Now that Alice's life didn't depend on Theo's proximity, she could travel and find a new romance—

She couldn't finish the thought without her throat tightening.

"Etsu!" echoed Bishop's voice from a distance.

She slowed to a stop. "Yes?"

Snap, crack, whoosh!

Bishop skidded to a stop, a pile of dead leaves forming at his feet and climbing his legs. "Etsu, what are you thinking!" The pile blew away.

She answered, "I need to—"

"Think!" he finished, striding closer as if he wanted to shake her by the shoulders, though he never made contact. "You need to think! Do you have any idea how many people saw you disappear from the hospital—how many people I had to charm so they wouldn't remember?"

"I—"

"And Marius! Theo's not the only one who makes your heart beat, remember?"

Factoring him into her plans still felt like an alien thing. Marius. The monster who killed her father when she was twelve. The creature who terrorized her town with dozens of deaths, targeting anyone with strong Anti-Japanese sentiments or anyone else who had a problem with Alice. She and Bishop guessed it was all for the purpose of framing her and therefore isolating her—to what end, they still couldn't fathom.

No one was entirely sure what Marius was, or how to kill him. Alice remembered his collection of weaponized narcotics and wondered if this was a hint—if, perhaps, he was once a human whose sole power was in whatever he could create. In any case, his obsession with her must have been due to her being the Domglory.

Perturbed, she gnawed her lip. "Is… Is Marius still…?"

"He's been looking for you," Bishop affirmed.

"Where is he?"

"I don't know, but he's never too far for too long."

She lowered her gaze, thinking. "Where's Theo? Is he not in town?"

"I wouldn't know. I spent the last twenty years avoiding the people we knew so they wouldn't see how I haven't aged."

There was something he wasn't telling her. His ability with cosmetics would've allowed him to interact with the neighbors longer if it was only twenty years that had passed since she was buried. All he would have to do was color his hair grey.

She was gone longer.

"What year is it?" she demanded.

He caught her gaze, clearly gauging her probable responses. When apparently none were too damaging, he muttered, "Two thousand ten. Theo… may not have made it."

A pang in her chest. "May not, or didn't?"

"I can't say."

"Can't or won't?"

"Can't." The word still felt open to interpretation.

Alice stared him down. He stared back, waiting. She couldn't read anything else while he was still so anxious.

She turned away, pushing her hair back with both hands, weighing the new possibilities. If her heart was responding to Marius… While she was more powerful now than she was when they had last met, she couldn't guess if this was enough to properly combat him.

If Marius intended to hurt her, he'd have to catch her first. She'd feel him coming, so she'd always know when to run.

"Can Marius feel me the way I feel him?" she asked.

"I wouldn't know," Bishop answered. "I don't think so."

"Then all I need to do is not be seen."

He scoffed. "He'll hear your heart and know you're there."

Again she pushed her hair back, fingers catching in her matted knots. "I can't do nothing," she muttered, pacing away, "I can't do nothing, it has to be Theo; he's still alive; perhaps he's transformed like me —"

"He's more likely dead."

"*No!*" she screamed with an intensity she didn't know she had. "If he died, I would know!" She paced away again, muttering again, "I feel him; he's here."

Bishop let her mutter for some time before gently grasping her arm. "We've been over this, dear. It could be Marius."

What if Marius had her and this was all a drug-induced coma dream in her head? Her heartbeat might not have felt any different, if this was the case.

Thmp.

She screamed, doubling over and clutching her chest.

Bishop lowered his face to hers so she'd see his eyes. "I'll allow that Theo may be alive," he rushed, "but please consider the alternative, for both our sakes—"

Decision made, Alice darted off, retraced her steps to Erie, and worked her way south to Sabertown, where she used to live. If Theo, or Marius, wasn't still there, *then* she'd try running any which direction and see where her heart led her.

She traveled far more quickly than she and Bishop had with the cheerleaders—far faster than any car. It was pure instinct which saved her from colliding into trees and the occasional deer. There wasn't any room for doubt, for she knew the moment she doubted her footing would be the moment she tumbled out of control.

Thmp! Louder, stronger.

She growled through the pain, more prepared this time. She was right to run home; her heart was certainly quickening.

The blood-flow through her limbs started as a soreness in her biceps and thighs, which she ignored. There was a sensation in her forearms and legs as if her veins were expanding—as if they would pop from beneath her skin. Still, she persisted.

Thmp…Thmp…

Her legs began to crumble beneath her every stride, though she refused her posture to betray it. A part of her wondered if she was crazy to so eagerly torture herself, though one could argue this was the mentality of anyone who knew true love.

Thmp. Thmp   Thmp. Thmp

Her hands and feet cramped, wanting to curl inward. She stumbled and staggered, losing her balance, but she gritted her teeth and pushed faster still.

Thmp, thmp. Thmp, thmp.

Theo was near enough that if she ran much longer, she would pass him.

She slowed. It was time to utilize a different skill. Relying still on instinct to steer her, she focused on sound.

Crickets chirped. Twigs snapped and dry leaves rustled. Creatures of the night gnashed their teeth and cried their calls. Cars accelerated over the asphalt, with the sound of engines more powerful than she ever knew. People chatted, some argued, and the songs to at least three different radio stations played. She would hear Theo's voice any second now; he dominated any conversation he had, and he was near enough to hear.

Something smelled like burnt rubber.

Cliff ahead.

She stumbled to a stop as the woods began to clear, and the balls of her feet smarted. This was where the smell came from, her shoes. Allowing some time to catch her breath and examine her soles, she noted the clearly visible stockings on the underside. She needed new stompers.

Peering over the cliff's edge, she found a busy strip mall. Too many cars were in the lot, and too many people crowded the sidewalk outside the restaurants and bars. Taking in the sheer multitude of objects and bodies, she paid closer attention to the details, as if this would help. It only proved more overwhelming.

People used to dress to impress. If this was the case now, people must have been impressed by another's lack of motivation. No one seemed to care about basic steps of self-grooming. Women abandoned skirts and dresses and anything feminine. Men wore trousers two sizes too big, shirts untucked. She hated it.

The vast majority of people here, too, had scars on their necks, like the hospital staff. Were there honestly so many domsuco in town? Or did it only require a few to affect so many necks? Had it always been this way?

The pangs in her chest subsided to dull throbs, though her heart rate remained the same. This same distance would have had her writhing just hours ago. Perhaps if she stayed here until the pain became a non-factor, she wouldn't appear as a screaming fool when she reunited face-to-face.

She had to be patient.

His car — or, what she assumed to be his car — pulled into the lot. Marius wouldn't have needed a car, so this provided some reassurance. When a couple stepped out from the vehicle, both in dark knit hats and peacoats, she couldn't see either of their faces. She couldn't tell their age, but their scents became more clear. The minerality of rain, warmth of amber, softness of roses, and volume of smokey cream. The scent wasn't as harsh as what she remembered of Marius', but it wasn't as honey-like as what she remembered of Theo's. With the woman's scent mixed in, it was difficult to discern what was hers and what was his.

To be prepared in the instance he did turn out to be the monster, Alice lifted a fallen branch from the ground and tore off a sizable stake. From her vantage point atop a boulder she sat, pained and panting, but taking it all in. She waited.

...

The moon sat significantly higher in the sky. While her heart still kept a steady beat, her chest didn't hurt so much anymore. It was time to find him.

She cut a quick path through the woods and appeared before the strip mall within seconds. Her heart reacted with an immediate lurch and she nearly crumpled to her knees. This was the fastest it had beat since she was underground. She needed to approach him more gradually.

The first store in line was a quaint little boutique with displays of warm-hued dresses and jewelry in the windows. She wanted to dismiss it, but in the end decided it was best to make a quick stop.

There sounded a mechanical *ding* as she opened the door.

The lady at the counter spoke without looking up, "We close in literally one minute." The scars on her neck poked from beneath her collared shirt.

"That's all it will take," Alice replied without factoring in the absurdity. Or, was it possible to find new shoes so quickly at human speeds? Time was a foreign concept now.

Once the lady looked up, her mouth slowly fell open. "Are you…okay?"

Alice had no idea what she was talking about. Considering she only had a minute to find shoes, however, she wouldn't squint at the woman for long and hope to figure it out.

She scanned the walls until she found footwear. There were some flat-soled, bulkier styles with far more rubber involved than what she was used to, but she was relieved to find simple, daintier shoes were still readily available. With the makeshift stake still in her grasp, she tried on a pair of heels.

Too big. This might now take more than a minute. "Sorry," she said. "I was always a seven and a half."

No response. She stepped further down the aisle and found the same shoe at the next size down. It fit. Still on her feet, she crossed with them to the exit, her old shoes dangling from her fingertips.

"You're not paying for that?" called the woman.

Alice turned around just as she reached the push bar. She forgot this step. She still didn't have money.

It was a last resort, rush decision when she stared into the woman's eyes. The woman stared back.

"I'll pay you back," Alice said.

The woman didn't respond.

Alice wasn't sure if this was hypnosis at work, but in any case, she left without further incident, tossing her old shoes into the trash bin outside.

Thmp thmp, thmp thmp...

She passed a pet shop. Then a bar. Her heart quickened as she approached a diner, then slowed as the diner drifted further behind her.

She recognized this diner. Of course. It was the same place she and Theo would go with Winifred after school. It was still here.

This was the place, then. This was the moment. If it turned out to be Marius, she still had her stake. If it was Theo...

With a deep, cleansing breath, she turned back to the diner and pulled open the door.

Noise, chatter, slurping, chewing, gulping. Silverware scraped and clacked against ceramic dishes. A radio played from the speakers, which were installed in several places along the ceiling. The singers within all but screamed, and the instruments were distorted like nothing Alice had ever heard. All she could recognize was a drum set.

Even while the scents of fried food and body odor overwhelmed her... the nostalgia was stronger. Even with all its differences, and with Alice's own changes, there was the same family friendly atmosphere. The booths were still reflective and red like painted sports cars. Every table appeared made of shiny red or white plastic. Black and white tiles checkered the floor. Nothing was wood, and now she wondered who made up the majority of nighttime visitors.

The sense of nostalgia faded. Every neck in sight was marred with the memory of domsuco fangs. No one seemed concerned.

Alice stepped past the threshold, allowing the door to slowly close itself behind her.

The rattling in her chest intensified, *Thmp-thmp, thmp-thmp.* Suppressing a pained whimper, she closed her eyes and thanked herself for waiting on the cliff for as long as she had.

She scanned the area. He was somewhere in this room, within earshot and within sight. If only she knew where to look. Every table and barstool was taken; he was hidden in the crowd.

A nearby sign read "Please Wait to be Seated." She didn't plan to dine, so she stepped past it.

Her heart slightly slowed. She had passed him, somehow.

A tap at her shoulder.

She spun around to find a peeved waitress —maybe eighteen, nineteen years old, with pretty features arranged in such a way that did not flatter. "We don't have any seats available right now," she began, "but if you'd *wait* to be seat-ed, we'll have one ready in about fifteen minutes." She didn't need to be so rude about it.

Alice was about to object, but then considered her suggestion. If she waited by the door, Theo would eventually come to her. It stood to reason, because he would eventually leave.

Finally the waitress looked her up and down. "The costume party's next week."

Costume party? While Alice wasn't sure what she was talking about, she acknowledged with a polite grin then stepped past her, back toward the waiting area by the front. As she neared the window and saw her reflection more clearly, she slowed to a stop. Finally she saw what everyone else was seeing. She looked like death. Dirt and faintly glowing blood were smeared on her face. Her hair was matted, some leaves and twigs sticking out. Dried, lusterless blood made a large stain down the front of her shirt, a hole in the chest as if she was shot. Her skirt had torn in several places, from the top of the thighs down. She couldn't see Theo like this. She couldn't be in *public* like this.

She turned back to the waitress, who was still standing there, watching. "Where's your restroom?" Alice asked.

The waitress pointed toward the back. Alice strode along faster than what felt natural. She found the darker, secluded hallway, and was grateful the signs for "Male" and "Female" hadn't changed. She pushed into her appropriate door and hurried to the sinks, resting her wooden stake on the counter. With soap and water, the grime washed from her hands, arms and face with surprising ease. She removed the outdoors from her hair, and finger-combed the knots to the best of her ability. While she couldn't get it perfect, her style now at least resembled something more tame. There just wasn't anything she could do about her clothes.

She retrieved her stake and leaned against the back wall, thinking. She should have listened to Bishop; she shouldn't have tried to rush this meeting. She wasn't ready—for Theo *or* for Marius. Now she had to leave here without him noticing, whoever he was.

Her heart gradually quickened, signaling his approach. She could place his muffled footsteps through the wall—the dull *tap* of rubber to tile.

His scent of sweet smoke grew stronger. This was Marius, then—Theo wouldn't smell like this. Marius had seen her, and now…

Her chest ached as she considered Theo's state and whether he was alive, but she couldn't think of this now. She had to prepare.

Her grip tightened around the stake the closer Marius approached, and she crossed to the door. It was about time she got the jump on him. It was about time she claimed the upper hand.

She gripped the door handle as her heartbeat sped.

Thmpthmpthmpthmp—

She raised the stake in preparation and pulled the door open just as his steps sounded on the other side. His air escaped in a quick breath as her forearm landed across his chest and she pinned him to the wall —

ThmpThmpThmpThmp— She gasped, stake snapping in her grip. It felt like hot prongs in her chest, or as if her heart burst, yet still it kept racing and bursting again and again.

Her eyes danced for what felt like a full minute before she found his face. No reaper-like hood. Pale and young. His fierce brown gaze locked with hers, gripping her. Reminiscent of a Tiger's Eye stone, golden yellow radiated from his coal black pupils. Within she found a default rage she had never seen before. She would have expected this of Marius, but…

This was Theo. Somehow younger than she remembered. And *angry*.

Hair, darker than earth and completely without luster, reached past his ears, over his eyes, from beneath a black knit hat. His face was paper white with the minimum pink pigment which meant he was alive. Narrow chin, sharp jaw.

"Get the fuck off me," he growled.

She could hear his heart racing, and feel it. He didn't try to push her off, and the give of his sternum let her think she could break it, easily.

"I... Theo?" she whispered.

He squinted, and the hostility in his eyes gradually gave way to a more concerned confusion. He asked her a question, but she couldn't hear. Her peripherals went dark, as if someone turned off the lights behind her —

She heard a knock at her bedroom door, well past midnight. Of course it was Theo, and of course he knew she couldn't possibly have been asleep. Something happened previously. Possibly two things, one that day and the other earlier that week. She still couldn't remember what, but it led to Theo having stayed in the guest room down the hall for the past several days.

She answered the door and there he stood. It was intense, the way his gaze pierced hers. He could have been crying before he came, but it was too dark to tell. In any case, it concerned her.

"What's wrong?" she asked.

"Oh, Dollface," he rumbled, and she barely made out the words. "You, asking me if **I'm** alright..." He offered a playful smile, though still there was a sadness to it.

She was too worried to smile back.

He sighed and dropped his head, deflated. His voice was low and gentle. "I... have something for you. Meant to present it this morning, but with all that happened..."

She watched in silence as he scrambled to finish his thought. Finally she replied, "I understand."

"Well. I told you exactly when I would do it, and I can't have you running around calling me a liar."

She knew he was still being playful, but if he was talking about what she thought he was talking about... She didn't know how to respond. He had a hand behind his back. She never imagined it would happen this way.

"I'd be damned if you up and leave tomorrow and I didn't get the chance to ask," he continued.

"What is it?" she whispered.

He hesitated, then from behind his back withdrew a brilliant red rose. Tied to its stem was the most delicate, gorgeous diamond ring she had ever seen. It might have only been a small fraction of his wealth, but she knew full well it cost more than her worth.

The bridge of her nose tingled and her eyes moistened. He was doing it.

He waited for her gaze to return to his before he proceeded. "I want you by my side for the rest of my days. It might be selfish of me. It might prove difficult, but I don't care."

"Theo—"

"You have nothing to prove to these people," he insisted. In a perfect world, this would have been the case. He read her doubts and so promised, "If they try you, they'll have to answer to me." After waiting a moment for her to object, he knelt.

She didn't know what to feel. She didn't know what to say.

The memory was interrupted, plopping her back into the diner. The scent of metal and leather meant Bishop was near. The young Theo held her upright by the shoulders now, wide-eyed. They were still in the hallway.

"Theo? What…?" She didn't know what she was asking. She didn't know where to start.

"I, uh, don't think I am who you think I am," he said, "But listen, is there someplace you should be? Mental facility, or…?"

Trees flashed passed in a blur as she darted through the woods. A white horse ran in the distance, spooked, bleeding. But she couldn't recall this ever having happened.

Diner again. At some point she had gripped the wall for support.

"Etsu," muttered Bishop's voice. The young Theo stood some paces away, staring past them as if half asleep. Under trance.

Her mouth and chin were sticky with blood.

"Etsu!" Bishop yelled in the distance.

She tore herself from this vision before she could let it come together. It made her sick.

Strangely, she didn't find herself back at the diner. She was in the woods—a different woods, her hair blown back and her face more chilled. She ran here. How much time had passed?

Bishop was with her, steering her.

"Bishop, something's happening." She was scared enough to yell, but aware enough to know not to—not after his reaction last time.

"You should have listened to me," he replied, leading her down a remote driveway. There at the end stood an isolated, single-story cabin. Together they took to the porch steps. He unlocked the front door and led her in. "You were alone in the dark for eighty years; you're not mentally stable."

That was it, then; she had lost her mind. Growing more disturbed by the second, she turned to switch on the lights. When her hand met the wall—

The wall was a tree.

Slowly she turned about and found she stood dead-center to a clearing. The woods were stagnant with eerie, silver moonlight casting harsh shadows over the old world.

Now she felt no shame. "Bishop!" she cried, "I don't know what's happening!"

"I'm right here."

She knew she was alone, but she had to check. Cautiously scanning each direction, she verified the wood was empty. A double-take confirmed that, beneath a canopy of trees, a ceiling light illuminated the end of the hallway in Bishop's cabin. She staggered after it. As she neared, she noted his arm around her.

Helping her down the hallway, Bishop ranted, "Your heartbeat triggered you. We could have prepared you better if you had just been *patient*—I knew this would happen!" Gradually his words felt more distant. Alice knew what this meant.

She panicked. "No, no — Bishop, don't let me go back. Don't let me go back…"

A thick fog enveloped the hallway. Black branches and a canopy of leaves stretched across the ceiling, hiding everything away until she was completely back in the clearing, alone.

"Bishop!" she screamed.

No response.

Cautious, she slowly stepped forth, heels sinking in the mud. Her legs felt heavy.

The fog cleared to reveal a splintered oak door, paint chipped, hauntingly standing on its own. The sound of rainfall sounded from the other side, but she couldn't see it.

The longer she waited, the clearer it all seemed. If she hoped to return to reality, she had to go through.

Her whole body trembled as she moved closer. She stalled all she could without stopping completely, though once her hand neared the doorknob, fear gripped her and she hesitated. Reminding herself this was her only option, she took a breath and grabbed hold.

Alice's Memory, 1948

7. The Clearing

Alice

The rain was torrential and likely to flood.

She ran through the night, quick as a flying bullet, her skirt torn and tearing further with every stride. Splashing and kicking up mud, Bishop kept pace beside her. He gripped a newly sharpened wooden stake while she held her father's old shotgun, loaded with ironwood slugs.

Bishop allowed a quick glance her way. "How are we faring?"

She never willingly allowed her heart to slow so much. To be so far from Theo… It wasn't right.

Her sentiments must have been apparent in her expression. Bishop responded accordingly; he grimaced, but didn't slow in the least.

Eyes watering, she hoped he assumed it was due to the wind in her face. A sob escaped every few breaths, and she hoped he assumed she was panting.

She could hear the difference between rainfall and footfall, and over the many drops of rain she heard the rustle of branches and underbrush. Someone was running through the distant woods. Despite the distance she could hear his every breath and heartbeat.

"*Alice!*" called his voice.

She froze, mud building around her feet as she suddenly stopped. Bishop stopped some ways ahead, an uphill silhouette when he looked back as if to ask, *What is it?*

"Theo," she whispered, wide-eyed. It shouldn't have surprised her. Of course he would have disregarded the letter she left him. Of course he would have chased her.

There was a moment of silence before Bishop spoke. "You can't. Etsu, if you go back it will make matters worse."

She hardly listened. Theo needed closure. Face-to-face reassurance. What if there was something he needed to say?

Increasingly adamant, Bishop continued, "Can you not feel your own hunger—"

"He will get himself lost looking for me," she muttered, "Possibly killed, with Marius still out there." Nothing Bishop could say would change her mind, so she didn't give him the chance.

She sprinted back from where she came, wind blowing her hair back in the sudden burst. She appeared behind Theo in an instant.

"Alice!" he called again, and her ears rang at its volume. He was soaked, turning his head and squinting through the downpour, spitting water from his lips. His ears, cheeks and nose were red with cold. "Can't we talk about this?!"

She'd never seen him like this. He was hardly dressed — no more dressed than he was to address the neighbors. Red silk pajama pants, slippers, robe and jacket. No shirt. Her stomach squirmed with a certain fear, but not for herself. Theo needed to be as far from her as possible, before he learned what she had become.

"Theo," she finally answered.

He spun about and nearly slipped. "Alice!" He hurried to her, holding her cold, bare shoulders. "You couldn't have at least brought a raincoat?"

She held the shotgun at her side, keeping the barrel pointed at the ground. "You shouldn't have come out here," she whispered, mostly to herself, though of course he took it personally.

He raised his eyebrows, incredulous. "*I*—You should've stayed home! So we could talk about this, in a house, like civilized people!"

"Theo—"

"Do you have any idea how worried I was—still am?!"

The nervous tension she had been holding back found an outlet when she cried, "It's the same discussion! Every time, and it brings us back exactly to where we started! 'I'll talk to them, Alice, they'll leave you alone.' Has it worked yet?!"

"I'm trying my hardest, God damn it!"

"I'm not saying you're not!" Her voice caught its breaking pitch, and now her pain was evident. Theo must've noticed; he took a calming breath, scrunched his mouth and looked away, reevaluating the situation.

For a moment neither said anything. She knew there wasn't anything she could say to get him to go home—not yet. First he needed to say what he needed to say.

He gestured at the rain. "Can we please talk about this inside?"

"I can't go back," she rasped, throat tense.

"You're scaring me, Dollface. You have to come back."

She couldn't find it in her to say it again, so she shook her head.

Forcing some full breaths, he rested his forehead to hers. "Why?" he finally asked.

Gently tracing a line from his cheekbone to his hairline, she pushed his hair back and weighed her options. He nuzzled her palm as it opened. It was surreal. She had never imagined herself in this situation.

"Marius will keep killing until I go to him," she began.

A nervous timbre raised Theo's voice. "That's suicide."

"You know me better than that."

He humorlessly scoffed, "Oh, well, excuse me; explain it, then."

She didn't want this to be a fight, so she kept her words sincere. "For the greater good, I can't say too much. Just please, trust me. I have a plan."

He didn't respond, but stared her down as if to ask, *Are you sure?*

It wasn't a detailed plan, but it was something. "Bishop will be with me. The sooner we finish this, the sooner we can come back."

Theo considered his choices. He didn't have any, but he had to try. He wasn't Theo if he didn't try. "Let me go with you."

She shook her head, and she could tell he knew why this was a bad idea. "You're needed on the home front. The community's lost without you."

His breath shuttered on an exhale and she knew he couldn't argue. "How long will you be out? Days? Weeks?"

If only. "As long as it takes. Could be years."

"Years…" He couldn't be sarcastic anymore, and for this she was grateful. However, now he appeared broken. Drained. His eyes fell downcast, happening upon her hand. She followed his gaze to the engagement ring on her finger. "I'll need that back, then."

Everything went diagonal.

"It was a mistake," he breathed.

Her ears rang. Her fingers tingled.

She handed him the shotgun. She needed her hands free as she removed the ring. She saw it, but felt nothing.

The subtle pulse of the veins in his neck.

He kept talking.

She moved the jewelry into his hand. "You need to go now." She couldn't hear herself.

Still speaking, he held her more securely by the shoulders. The gun was disregarded, then. She tried to pay attention, though the only words she caught were, "Are you listening to me?"

She needed to control herself.

Her stomach was a ravenous vacuum, constantly pulling, but with only her insides to wrangle.

His throat throbbed with an inviting —

She needed to stop looking at his neck; she closed her eyes.

Their hearts beat so fast.

The warm taste of sweet metallic —
Pennies and sweat —

Ears, ringing again.

No, screaming. Theo was screaming.

Her eyes flashed open and she flung herself back. There he stood, wide-eyed and gasping, grasping his neck. Brightly glowing blood trailed past his fingers and down his forearm, staining his sleeve. His heart sang to her with its every frantic beat.

Covering her ears, she faced away from the clearing and shrieked, "Bishop!"

Brightness from the corner of her eye. Fresh blood glowing on her fingers.

She tore her gaze away and screamed with more fervor, "*Bishop!*"

In too deep a state of shock, Theo moved his hand from his neck and held it before his eyes as if to verify, *Yes, I am bleeding.* "Alice?" His knees buckled, but he remained standing.

It was a knee-jerk reaction when she appeared before him, her movements too quick to see, before placing his hand back over his neck to apply pressure. He tore away from her grasp, stumbling backward, never daring to look away.

Again her gaze lingered too long on his throat. She knew it did, and her will to fight it weakened. Perhaps evil was never a conscious intention. Perhaps it was a primal instinct, which had in some cases convinced the mind, *This is permitted*. She was on the brink of starvation, after all. All she needed was one more taste—

With an inward growl, she tore her gaze upward and focused on his eyes. "You'll be okay!" she promised, "We'll find Bishop; he'll know what to do, just stay calm; stay with me."

He made a sound at the back of his throat as he struggled to breathe. "How… How long?"

She knew what he meant — *how long were you like this?* — but it was difficult to answer when she wasn't Alice anymore. She was a combination of concepts: hunger and peril.

"It happened… weeks ago," she managed. "A month or more. And… the way it happened…" Skimming through her memory brought her most of the way back to herself. "I was never human."

"Etsu!" Bishop bursted into the clearing. Theo stumbled backward, knees again buckling but still not giving way. Before Alice could say anything, Bishop addressed him in a manner not to be trifled with. "Boy, you need to get back to town immediately; do you understand?" Theo didn't speak, and though he could barely move his neck it appeared as if he attempted a nod. It wasn't enough, so Bishop repeated, "*Do you understand?*"

"Yes, sir," he managed.

He hardly had it out before Bishop boomed, "Now run! Save yourself!"

"Theo!" Alice called, and Bishop blocked her before she even knew she was headed back his way. Theo's gaze lingered on hers for a second before he took off.

"You can't help him," Bishop scolded, "I tried to tell you — "

"You shouldn't have told him to run," she breathed. Whenever one encountered a beast of prey, they were told to either play dead or scare it. If they ran, there was something to be anticipated.

A predator chased the prey that ran.

Theo wasn't Theo. He was a gorgeous white stallion, bolting past the foliage. It was a shame to see a beautiful creature go, but his neck was already open beyond repair. Alice had to put him out of his misery.

She reached for the horse's back —

Theo's arm was in her grasp.

Bishop gripped her free wrist. "Etsu — "

She flung Bishop; sent him flying over treetops.

Theo slipped down an incline, struggling to keep his neck covered as he scrambled back to his feet. The mud gave way beneath him. He couldn't lift one leg without the other sinking further in. He was stuck.

Their gazes locked and he froze, a dead man on the brink of either accepting his fate or begging for his life. His chin quivered while his voice wavered, "Alice…"

Silence. Cautiously she knelt so they were eye-to-eye. Everything about him seemed so fragile now. She wondered if his bones would snap like dry wood.

She wrapped her fingers in his hair. His breath shuddered and his eyes closed, and all along she watched his face. "Please," he whispered. "Alice, please."

Again she wasn't sure what to do. For whatever reason she was inclined to make him feel better, so she planted a soft kiss on his forehead. Slowly, his eyes opened. He wasn't reassured, but took a breath and managed a little laugh, just for her. "Whatever happens…" After flexing something at the back of his throat, he continued, "Whatever happens, Alice. I will always — "

She yanked his head sideways and snapped his neck, immediately burying her face in the hollow therein. Even as
his heartbeat grew faint and hers failed to rattle her chest,
she couldn't detach. She tore in until every drop was
drained, only to wake when both their hearts came to a
complete

Stop.

The New Reality, 2010

8. It Did Happen

Alice

Ears ringing. No. Screaming. She was screaming.

Alice awoke wailing at the top of her lungs. While her eyes were open, she didn't register anything until many moments later. Gasping for breath, she took it all in. Bare, off-white walls. Windows with thick, floral-patterned curtains. Carpeted floor. White wicker dresser, and matching headrest to the queen-sized bed in which she lay. It was dark out. The only light came from a dim lamp on the bedside table.

"Etsu?"

She jumped and snapped her gaze to Bishop. He had been sitting beside her all along, in a dining room chair.

"Bishop—" her voice was hoarse, and she couldn't stop gasping for breath. "Bishop, what—was that?"

His eyes were wide, and she felt hers were, too.

She tried again. "Bishop? What did… Did that…?"

His mouth opened, and so she instantly quieted. Then waited, holding her breath, and she hoped her mind would quiet, too.

He dropped his gaze as if he would find his words at the corner of the wall behind her. It was a higher timbre he used when he finally spoke. Quieter. Pained. "I've kept it in a place you would never happen to find it."

She continued to stare at him, waiting for this to make sense.

Finally she realized what he held between his fingers, resting over his knee. He held it out to her. Theo's engagement ring.

"I retrieved it once I deduced what was happening," he said. "I thought it would have triggered all this if I had shown you earlier, but… Well, it's all done, now." He kept talking. It wasn't her intention to be rude, but she couldn't pay attention anymore.

She leaned back against the headrest and stared at the wall across from her. She remembered she could've still been under the crypt, or in an asylum. So it was possible this never happened. She couldn't say how the quilt felt over her skin, and although she initially thought it was because she was numb, now she wondered if it was because, in reality, there was no quilt.

With a jello grasp, she pushed the fabric aside. She couldn't feel her feet, so while at first she wondered why she had difficulty moving them over the side of the bed, she eventually realized it was because they were still tangled in the other sheets.

Faintly she registered Bishop ask, "Where are you going?"

"I need to feel something." Her voice didn't sound like it came from her body.

His eyes remained wide, though his brow slightly furrowed. "What do you mean?"

She wasn't sure if there was more to explain. All she knew was there was nothing to feel in here. It was all too soft, or lukewarm.

The muscles in her legs wouldn't remember to tighten, so she stumbled to the door and supported herself with a hand on either side of the threshold. There wasn't a clear distinction between the floor, the walls, or even the ceiling. After moving both arms to one wall, she wondered if she really did crawl across the wallpaper, her feet sliding along the floor only for balance.

"Etsu." His voice sounded trapped in a bubble, somewhere behind her. "I don't think you should be on your feet yet."

"I don't feel normal." She wasn't sure if this was supposed to be a counterpoint, or if she agreed with him.

"You look like you're not back yet."

"Where am I really?"

Silence. She felt him grip her shoulder, and it seemed it was with some urgency that he turned her to face him. Still, it felt like a dream. He hadn't aged. People aged in the world of reality.

"Etsu, look at me," he said, and it was only somewhat more clear than before. "You are here. My cabin."

She shook her head, "No."

"The year is two-thousand ten. You were gone eighty years, but now you're back."

She hiccuped. Her vision blurred, her eyes felt warm, and still she shook her head. "No." Her head hurt. Her voice cracked, and when she realized she was beginning to believe him, everything in her recoiled. "I need… I need to be outside."

He nodded, "This way, then."

If ever before the entire space beyond the hallway felt like the same room, it especially did now. "The stove should be in the kitchen," she said.

"Naturally," he muttered. He opened the front door, and she realized she had been leaning into his arm the entire way.

The chill of the night smacked into her chest and stung her face. The air seemed to freeze at the back of her throat, and it didn't feel right to breathe it, but she did. She could feel it.

She stepped past his grasp and down the porch stairs. While she doubted she appeared graceful in the least, her steps felt light and quick, as if the air was water and she was cutting through.

Once she made it a few paces into the front lawn, she wasn't sure where to go from there. If all she needed was to be outside, she was there. No other space would feel any more like outside than the space in which she was now.

"Is Marius real?" she asked.

Some paces behind her still, Bishop answered, "Yes, Marius is real."

"Is my heart real?"

"Yes, as is the peculiar way it beats."

She pulled her attention inward. If it was beating now, she couldn't feel it. However, if everything which occurred since returning from the crypt really happened, her heart had to have been beating again. "Is Marius back?"

"He...comes and goes"

"Then it can still be Theo."

Bishop sighed. "I know you know better."

Her arms wrapped around her middle and her nails clamped into her sides. Her throat ached, and she felt there had to be something she could do for it, but she couldn't remember. She realized she stood bent just enough for her face to be parallel to the ground, and she wondered if this was her subconsciously preparing to throw up. She didn't feel as if she would, but again, she still had trouble feeling.

A sharp gasp, and her chest expanded. This was it. This was what her throat needed, or something like this.

Arms still tight around her middle, she fell to her knees, the dirt crumpling beneath her. Despite the cold, her face felt hot.

Again she gasped. The air seemed to catch on everything, producing a deeper, more grating sound. As her vision somewhat cleared, the inner sides of her eyes cooled with wetness. "Bishop—" A gasp. "Bishop, I don't understand. I don't understand."

She sensed that he knelt beside her, then felt his arm drape across her back.

Thmp. It was a subtle sensation which pulsed at the center of her chest.

Her eyebrows shot up and her eyes widened. Even more confused, new tears obstructed her vision. "I don't understand. It was him, Bishop—I saw him; they were identical."

"They share similar genes," Bishop conceded. "If you had seen him when he was younger, you might have seen the differences more clearly, but they're not identical."

"But my heart—"

"It wasn't him—"

"*But I couldn't have killed him!*" she shrieked, hurting even her own ears. "He wouldn't take back his ring one day into the proposal! *One day! He wouldn't!*"

"Etsu,"

"*So it couldn't have happened! I couldn't have — !*" She sobbed, then found she couldn't stop. It hurt. Screaming felt better, but she had to stop.

She curled more tightly into herself. Now whatever sound she made, it felt like laughing, and her back shook all the same.

Eighty years' worth of denial finally caught up with her, and it seemed it would be eighty years more before it passed.

Theo didn't wait for her. He died, broken and terrified, at her hands.

9. The Parking Lot Brawl

Jack

Jack should've stayed home. It was dumb; he was supposed to have stayed home to watch Grandma Ruth. Instead he'd asked Gabby to switch chores with him so he could finish in time for his date with Wyn. He shouldn't have left the house. Even with Grandma's *Wisher* bracelet for *protection*, the runes in the wooden beads wouldn't do shit for what he was about to deal with.

It was after dark and painfully cold as he pushed his shopping cart out of the store exit, down from the sidewalk and into the parking lot. His hands were wrapped in black home-knit gloves, a matching hat pulled over his head. Buttoned down his chest was a peacoat, the most expensive thing Wyn had ever bought for him. It didn't look like anything special. It matched the contours of his frame and kept him warm. While he hadn't asked for it, he wasn't complaining.

Like an idiot, he had parked Gabby's car far from the store entrance, isolating himself, making him an easy target. At first he wasn't sure, but it soon became apparent a group of boys was following him; they had no other reason to be headed his way.

"Fuck," he breathed, air coming out in a puff of smoke. It didn't matter how often he'd trained himself with self-defense videos on YouTube; he was outnumbered. And these were the jocks from school.

Except, one of them wasn't. He was an artsy type that'd never usually hang around these douches. He hadn't exchanged a word with Jack in over a year.

Fucking George. When Jack remembered his sister Monica was one of the injured cheerleaders from the Vampire Crypt, everything came together. These assholes were about to interrogate him, kill him, or half-ass both. One thing was certain: Jack was getting his ass beat.

"Hey dipshit," one of them called. This was Luke, Crystal's boyfriend, the beefiest of beefcakes. His sister was killed last year.

If Jack continued on his way and attempted to unload the groceries, they would remember to know which car was his. They would vandalize the shit out of it, and even with Wyn's money, he couldn't afford to fix it or buy Gabby a new one.

Jack slowed his cart to a stop and groaned on an exhale, "I know what this is about."

"Why'd you do it?" This was George, more hurt than assailing, as figured from his widened, bitch-ass brown eyes.

"I literally couldn't have done it," Jack replied. "Monica and the others can tell you that. Crystal's mom can tell you how she stopped me from crossing county lines and followed me all the way back until Gabby dropped me off at the house." Officer Robinson still believed he was innocent, but she still couldn't let him pass county lines. Annoying as it was, he understood she had a job to do.

"Why were you trying to escape to Erie?" George asked, voice rising.

"I was looking for my dog!" Jack exclaimed as Luke cut back in with, "Crystal's mom can't save you anymore, asshole! Smart move with that one!"

Jack went cold. "What do you mean?"

"Come on, don't play stupid!"

One of Luke's taller buff friends murmured to him, "Maybe he doesn't know."

He was hardly finished when Luke snapped, "He's full of shit, Troy!"

Jack turned his attention back to George. While Troy might've had something of a brain, he wouldn't abandon Luke in a fight. But George didn't really care for any of them; he was the weak link. If he could get George to fight his case, it might've been enough of a distraction to at least make a break for it. His last resort was to, by some miracle, take Luke down in one punch and hope the others' morale would be broken enough to discontinue.

"What happened to Officer Robinson?" Jack asked.

George answered, and this was a good sign. "She's in the hospital, throat slit. Happened the same night my sister and them were attacked."

Oh fuck no. Jack had assumed there was only one psycho. Unless the Ripper got extremely busy in one night for no reason —

But Jack didn't talk to any of the cheerleaders, and there was *definitely* not something going on with him and Crystal's mom. Although, the attack on the officer made sense. She was the only one going after the actual killer, and so for now there was no one. The Ripper could get sloppy if he wanted to.

"Guys, I have nothing to gain from any of this; it doesn't make sense," Jack reasoned.

Luke wasn't having it. "Then I have no reason to break your face. But that's not stopping you, so."

Jack saw it coming and bulldozed Luke with his shopping cart before the jock could swing his fist. Luke stumbled back, and Troy took his place at the frontline, also swinging a fist. Jack dodged, and knew a bulk of his chances depended on where he landed his first punch. Before Troy could consider his next move, Jack clocked him square in the face and Troy dropped like a sack of oranges.

Jack ditched the groceries and ran. The two remaining jocks darted after him. They were faster, so they caught up, one shoving him to the side and knocking him off balance, into the other, who readily grabbed his arm. The shover snatched his free arm, and Jack saw George catch up as well. For a moment he was grateful. They were holding him down for George. George wasn't about to hurt him. His face told everything; he thought Jack was innocent.

It had to have only been a second that they stood watching the other, and as that second stretched, Jack's hopes sank. George's bitch-eyes were as wide and scared as before. He wasn't afraid of Jack, though. His gaze flickered between the two jocks, and Jack understood. George had to impress his new friends. Jack was screwed.

"George," he tried anyway, hoarse, "you know I didn't do it; ask your sister when she comes back—she'll tell you it wasn't me."

"She doesn't remember what happened," he replied, seemingly grateful for the excuse to stall. "She said they were drinking beers, and then blacked out." Again, his gaze flickered between the two jocks. "But if you're crippled to shit when the next one happens, we'll know it wasn't you." The moment arrived. George made a fist and swung it into Jack's stomach. Jack let out all his air before it could collide, so the wind wasn't knocked out of him, though he doubled over anyway. It still fucking hurt.

There was nothing he could've done about the next hit, which was to the face. George broke his nose with a horrifying *crunch,* and Jack's breath caught so he couldn't yell even if he wanted to. Blood dripped over his upper lip and he closed his mouth.

Luke made it back to them, shoving George out of the way for his turn at the human piñata. He raised his fist, and

Jack knew to expect his face to shatter on impact. Just before the punch could land, he dropped all his weight, effectively dodging it and nearly escaping the runners' grasp, but the jocks held tighter. Luke tried again, this time punching downward. There was no escape. He got the whole side of his face, and this time, although Jack tried, he couldn't stifle the yell.

His ear felt hot and he saw red. His nose burned, and every slight movement made it worse.

"Quick, his legs," said one of the jocks that held him. Both lifted him enough so his legs would stretch their full length. When he realized what they were bracing him for, he panicked, lifting his knees to his chest. They wouldn't drop him—not this time. Both Luke and George let their fists fly until Jack didn't have the energy to keep his legs safe. He was hardly there anymore when he let them dangle beneath him. The jocks lowered him just enough so his heels touched the ground, the rest of his legs at an angle suitable for chopping lumber. They were going to snap his legs like scrap planks for firewood.

"No," Jack groaned.

"I know, I know," Luke replied, "Can't kill girls if you can't chase them." He lifted his foot, ready to stomp.

"Hey!"

All snapped their attention to the woman who yelled. Jack didn't know this voice—not at this octave, anyway. When he saw her, though, he recognized her. Maybe a year or two older than himself, hair that was arguably red or light brown, thick frame, cute face and sassy demeanor… She waited tables at the diner he and Wyn went to all the time. He remembered seeing her name on the check, but he couldn't remember what it was. It began with B.

"Bhh…" He began to call her name back when he again remembered he didn't know what it was.

A sprinkling of a crowd had begun to form at the storefront. When B rushed in to help, two strangers from the gathering followed. If they knew who he was, he doubted they would've done anything.

Panicked, Luke ran off. Unsure of what else to do, the rest of the jocks and George dashed after him, leaving Jack to drop into a heap on the pavement. He faced the sky, and all he saw was black layered with translucent streetlight-orange. He turned his head and spit blood from his mouth. This was exactly the way he needed his night to start.

"Jack," the waitress said, standing above him as a silhouette with the light behind her head, her dangly earrings glinting in the dark. She knelt to his level. "How bad is it?"

He emitted the sort of groan one would make while stretching and rasped, "I'm fine."

"Can you stand?"

They didn't get the chance to break his legs, so yes, but, "Not yet," he answered.

"Well can you sit?"

Why'd this lady need him to move so badly? The jocks were gone; she should've left him alone now.

After his initial rejection, he found the will, then the strength, and turned to his side. Carefully he pushed the ground away from himself and sat.

"Your nose is broken," she stated, "Gimme."

"What?" He looked her way, and before he knew it her hands were at his face.

"Don't move," was her only warning before she pressed either side of his nose and pushed it back into place with a *snap.*

"*Ahh!*" he yelled, more surprised than hurt. As the shock wore off, however, he noted the dull throb to every point in his body, and everything hurt. He groaned again.

"That should take care of that," she said. "Do you need to go to the hospital?"

"No, I'm good," he insisted, "just gotta get my groceries home." He found his feet and stood, B following him up.

"You sure?"

"Yup. Thanks, Bri." That's what it was, Bri.

She smiled at the mention of her name. She needed to not be seen doing this shit. "Anytime," she replied. Yeah, she needed to stop. Most girls knew by now. If she knew his name, she knew who he was. Why was she dumb?

"Do you need someone to drive you?" she offered.

She hardly had all her words out before he answered, "I'm good. Later," and walked off.

It was lucky everything in his shopping cart was still intact. He unloaded it into Gabby's car, stuffed glove-compartment napkins up both his nostrils to stop the bleeding, and continued with his errands as if nothing happened.

Maybe he should've let them break his legs. George was right. If another girl died while he was crippled, people would know it wasn't him. If the Ripper was smart and knew to wait until Jack was healed before killing again, girls would be safe in the waiting period. If it meant keeping them safe, all Jack would have to do, then, was never be in one piece. Keep his limbs broken.

It was something to think about.

His mind wandered. If he was really about to follow his conscience, he had to do something about Wyn. Somehow she hadn't been targeted yet, unless the Ripper had something special planned for her.

Jack loved her. It was nothing like the way he loved Sarah, but it was love nonetheless. He couldn't let her go through a special hell and death when she was brave enough to be with him all this time. She deserved better. He had to dump her.

He had come to this conclusion many a night.

…

Jack cleaned himself up the best he could once he got home, switching out the napkins in his nose and using his own makeup kit to cover the redness and the bruising. This wasn't his first rodeo.

He wasn't sure what he and Wyn would end up doing after they ate, so he grabbed his fake ID just in case. Gabby had pointed out how strange it was that the fake still worked, now that basically the whole town knew who he was and that he was still in high school. If this was the one bit of luck that would stick with him through this, though, he wouldn't try to read too far into it.

When he made it to the diner a nine, Wyn wasn't there yet.

He waited at a booth by the window, where they usually sat, right by the entrance with the "Wait to be Seated" area directly behind him. Working that night was Bri, who smiled whenever they made eye contact. She was staring at him; the only reason he kept looking at her was because he kept feeling it. She needed to stop. Yes, she had an excuse—she was his server; she needed to look his way to see if he needed anything, and then smile because that's what you do in the service industry—but both of them knew she was flirting, and the Ripper would know, too.

"You clean up well," she teased, dropping off his Coke.

It didn't matter what she said; he was gonna respond with this anyway: "You know I have a girlfriend, right?"

Her head withdrew to her neck as she was quite literally taken aback. "So?"

So she was gonna play dumb. He let out a breath and tried a new approach. "Do you know who I am?"

"The guy everyone thinks is killing girls," she answered. So she really was dumb. "But I know it wasn't you."

He shook his head. "Doesn't matter. Fact is, girls who talk to me die, and I don't need you on my conscience. So please, whatever you're doing, stop."

Her mouth opened as if to fire back, but she never did. Eventually a defensive grin tugged at her lips. "Alright, I'll stop being nice to you." She briskly walked away, and when she returned with his silverware, she let it drop on the table. "And next time you wanna let a girl down easy, don't lie. I was here when you broke up with her."

"That never happened."

"Yeah, okay." She walked away, and under her breath uttered, "dick."

He watched the bubbles in his Coke. That took care of that.

He wondered what she had seen that could have been mistaken for a break-up. Maybe she saw a couple's quarrel? Did he and Wyn have a fight here before? He didn't think they'd ever fought before, unless it was something minor.

When he still felt someone staring at him, he looked up. It was Wyn, curly red hair pulled back in a puffy ponytail. He had no idea how long she had been standing there, watching, but she didn't appear amused. She offered a weak grin when he saw her, then sat across from him. "What was that about?"

He shook his head. He didn't want to get into it.

"What happened to your face?"

He could only clean himself up so well with napkins still up his nose. "Nothing new," he answered, and he knew she'd know what he meant.

She quietly stared at the table, then finally asked, "Would you have given her a chance? If there wasn't a killer?"

He felt guilty. She was right to have felt insecure about their relationship, but for the wrong reasons. "You mean if I wasn't dating you?"

She nodded.

He shrugged. "I don't think about that kind of thing. Don't have the luxury."

She bit her lip. Just as Jack found the words to begin with the break up, she asked, "Did you order anything yet?"

He shook his head.

"Are you hungry?"

He shook his head again.

"Wanna ditch this place and go to the Velvet?"

He shrugged. It didn't matter where they were, so long as they weren't still dating the next day.

Once he paid for his drink, they left the diner and got into Gabby's car, where Wyn presented a new bottle of spiced rum - the *good* kind. He couldn't remember much past that point, but he assumed they drank it and got blackout-drunk.

Doo-wop softly played from the tinny stereo speakers.

He was parked in a clearing that overlooked a cliff, Wyn in the driver's seat, making out with him. He didn't know what he would do without her. She was all he had to look forward to at the end of the school day—his only light in a dark place. He recalled the week she had left town, and how quiet it was. How alone he was. He couldn't go through that again.

With a firm grip on her hair, he brought her face closer. She kissed back with just as much fervor. "Theo," she whispered. That was what she called him. For now it didn't matter that no one else called him any variant of his first name. It didn't matter that he preferred Jack. For now they were teenagers, fooling around as teenagers often did.

"Wyn," he breathed back before she again smushed his lips with hers. She held his face in one hand, the other traveling down his chest and abs. He couldn't help a low moan as she passed his waistband, but then something in his mind jarred awake and went, *Nope.*

He stopped her hand from going further.

She paused, and he had to debate whether or not it was really worth it.

He dropped his gaze, catching his breath as he rested his forehead against hers. "Remember that thing we never do in horror movies?"

Silence. Finally she backed off, neither surprised nor pleased. He felt bad, but it didn't feel right.

"You know your life isn't a movie, right?" she murmured.

"I'm sure people in movies think the same thing."

"I know that's not really it—just tell me what it is!" she cried. He was wondering when she would finally call him out like this. "Is it me?"

"It's not you," he panted as he fixed his shirt. "It's just... I can't."

She peered down at his pants, which apparently indicated otherwise. "I think you can."

"That's not what I meant."

"Explain."

He groaned out the rest of his breath and leaned back in his seat. "I'm not... I'm too stressed, all the time—"

"You know a good way to relieve stress?"

"—and I'm not ready."

She was silent for a second, lips pressed together. There wasn't a way to argue this one. She sighed, then offered a small, sad smile, as if to say, *It's okay.*

"I'll drive you home now," she offered. He nodded, and they were off. Neither had anything to say for the rest of the trip.

Always, when he went into a date with the intention to break up, they'd end up making out and then breaking up wouldn't make sense anymore. Every time, his own selfishness, or cowardice, would convince him to stay. He lost track of how many times this had happened.

Maybe the next day he would have better luck.

10. Breaking Reality

Alice

Alice had been laying like a mummy on the guest room bed for longer than she could guess. Lights off. Curtains drawn, day or night. She wanted to be back under the crypt, but didn't have the will to get there.

She didn't want to do anything. She remembered feeling this way when she first discovered herself paralyzed underground, though back then she couldn't place why. Now she knew. Now more than ever, she wanted to give up, in every meaning of the word. There was only ever one man she loved, and she killed him. How could she hope to accomplish anything if she couldn't do something as simple as keep her hunger in check, or her rage, or whatever it was? How could she hope to function?

Again and again, she went over it in her head. There needed to be some sort of justification. She wasn't truly a monster; she was good. She would never have done anything like this of her own accord. She had just undergone her transition into full-fledged domsuco. She still had yet to seal the transition with blood — *drinking* blood. Perhaps it really was the monster in her, and her true self had nothing to do with it. Perhaps it was the mere fact that Theo was there, with fresh blood pumping through his veins, that set her over the edge.

Yet, the timing of it all lent itself to the nagging notion that she was, still, in denial. He was in the middle of taking back his proposal, more than likely explaining how he couldn't have waited for her; their love wasn't strong enough to have lasted until she returned.

This didn't sound like him, though. He would always say how he had loved her since the day they met, and then just before he died he said, "I will always…" She assumed he would have finished with "love you." It seemed right, but she had to remind herself that her opinion was biased.

Even so, she had never snapped this way before. Since her last and only fight at school, she learned everything could be resolved, or at the very least deescalated, through calm discourse. This vicious, downright maniacal response wasn't like her.

So she decided it was the monster. While this might have quelled some of the guilt, it hardly made anything better. She still wished she could've died with him, or in his stead. She was still the reason he never raised a family the way he had always wanted—the reason he couldn't have a future.

"The stars shine brightest on the darkest of nights," Bishop mused, muffled through the door.

She didn't know how to respond. So she didn't.

He cleared his throat as if to change the topic, then for a moment it was quiet. "You know it's been over a week, now. Since you've left that room."

Her tongue felt heavy, stuck to the roof of her mouth.

He might've waited for a reply before he sighed. "I missed you while you were gone. I wanted so badly to bring you back. Having you back, I... I don't want you to disappear again."

Her eyes moistened. She didn't want to cause him more pain, but still, she didn't know another way to deal with her own.

His voice regained some of its usual strength. "I have to go to work. The hospital. Do as you will, as I know you shall." The floorboard creaked as she imagined he stood.

Now knowing how long she had been laying like this, she acknowledged he had a point; she had to return to the world. It was only a matter of when.

Various scenarios premiered in her mind. If she tried to interact with anyone in public, the littlest things would remind her, or break her, and she had to consider that maybe she would see that boy again. She couldn't burst into tears if she happened across him.

"And don't you worry about anyone recognizing you from the diner," Bishop said from the other room. "I ensured they wouldn't remember you. Including the boy." The front door opened and closed. Bishop was gone. If she hoped to at least leave the room without being seen, now was the time to do it.

She pulled on her new shoes, brushed her matted hair and stepped slowly down the hallway. Still, it felt as if she was floating.

The rooms at the end all shared the same walls, though the kitchen stopped with the end of the black and white checkered tiles. The rest of the floor was hardwood, from the dining area straight down to the living room, which was closest to her.

She wasn't sure how often she was supposed to eat, though to be safe she crossed to the fridge, which was smaller than what she was used to. There wasn't anything remotely normal inside. Just stacks of plastic bags filled with glowing blood.

Grimacing, she pulled from the top of the stack and prepared it the only way she had ever known. She found Bishop's sauce pot, poured the bag's contents within, and put it over the low flame of a gas stove.

She gagged. It still felt so wrong.

With a clean spoon, she occasionally stirred. Once the meal seemed warm enough, she took it off the flame and dined straight from the pot. Eating it with a spoon felt especially strange. And too slow.

She found a mug in one of the overhead cabinets, poured the blood in and drank from here instead. It was still abnormal, but it felt easier.

Once finished, she set the mug on the counter and pushed it away. She didn't intend to use as much strength as she did, but the mug went flying, shattering against the opposite wall.

She pulled her hair back and forced some full, calming breaths. She really needed to learn her strength.

She needed to calm.

She needed

Hand clamping over her mouth, she sobbed. She couldn't function. Moving was too easy; she couldn't feel anything when everything was weightless.

What if it was weightless because it wasn't real?

"I'm sated, therefore I've eaten, therefore this is real," she whispered. "I'm sated, therefore I've eaten, therefore *I won't tear anyone's throat out!*"

She sank to the floor, holding her breath. If she wasn't breathing, she wasn't sobbing and she wasn't screaming. She squeezed her eyes shut. She needed to calm.

She needed to feel something. To prove this was real.

Pain would do it.

One of the ceramic shards of the mug sat on the tile not too far away. She picked it up, touching the sharp end to her arm.

It already bled in her grip.

She remembered this was what Winifred had started doing after Theo dumped her.

Alice dropped the shard and staggered to her feet, gripping the counter for support. The marble crumpled in her hand. A brief examination of her palm showed her cuts were already healed, yet the fresh blood remained.

She had to get out of the cabin.

She burst out the front door and into the night. The wind seemed to lift her; the cold seemed to sooth her.

The boy. If he was in her head, he would act like another Theo, or a warped Theo—a personification of her own fears and insecurities. If the boy was his own person, he was real. If he wasn't, perhaps this false reality would finally shatter when they met.

She had to be ready for the public, then. For the instance this was real. At the very least, she had to shower.

After a deep breath and some time to steady her mind, she turned back to the indoors.

...

It all looked like relatively the same technology. The shampoo bottles had a darker, more masculine design, though this was possibly because it was a men's shampoo which sat there. The design of the room itself seemed more masculine as well—the pastel colors and floral patterns of her time long gone, replaced by shiny and sleek, creme and red elegance. A mirror took up the full square of the wall above the sink.

On it was taped a note.

Dear Etsu,

> *I'm glad you've finally left your room. Here are some things you should know before you leave the cabin, and I will happily answer any questions when I get back.*
> *The country is at war again, going on about 10 years now. The new fear is Muslims—not the Japanese. Contradictorily, we're headed into an era of acceptance—regarding race, sexual prefer-*

ence, and gender roles in society. And we don't say "Negro" anymore.

I have a selection of your old clothes hanging in the laundry room. They're still outdated, but by today's standards they'll do.

Sincerely,
Bishop

She appreciated the sentiment, though overall this raised more questions than answers. Was she supposed to interact with others differently due to this new war? Did Bishop expect her to put on a show of fearing Muslims if ever she met one, so she could blend in? If "Negro" wasn't the proper word anymore, what was?

She found a clean towel and her old robe in a cabinet beneath the sink, then contemplated these questions as she showered. Once finished and toweled off, she found a pen in one of the drawers by the sink and tacked her inquiries on at the end of the note. She wasn't sure when she would run into Bishop again, but she hoped he would answer back in due time.

Wrapped in her old robe, she stepped into the room next door and found it was the laundry room, as she'd expected. There hung her old clothes, which she carried in one arm back to her room. With Bishop's note for reassurance, she chose a simple black A-line dress from the pile, as well as a black blazer. Paired with her new black shoes and dark red lipstick, her outfit was complete. This was darker and harsher than her usual look, but it felt appropriate to her mood.

The time had arrived. Either everything which had happened since the crypt was real, or it was in her head. Meeting the boy would settle this once and for all.

Following the rate of her heartbeat to the best of her ability, she strode briskly passed the strip mall from earlier. Hardly anyone was out, but those who were didn't pay her any mind. Mostly, they were cliques of teenagers and young adults in peacoats and leather jackets, standing at sidewalks and leaning against street lamps, smoking. She overheard some dramatized conversations and learned they pretended to be more than they were, exaggerating their hardships and imagining their lives were tough enough to deserve something better in return. If this boy was anything like his peers, she didn't want to meet him. Nothing was worth the headache.

Her heart beat the slightest bit faster as she wandered further, and a recollection of what this sensation used to make her feel now brought warmth to her face and moisture to her eyes. Feeling this way used to be a good thing. Now it only fooled her for a flicker of a second before she remembered Theo was dead and she'd never see him again.

She had to get a grip of herself.

She wasn't sure when the sidewalk ended and the sticks began. Eventually she came to stroll up a long, uphill driveway. Tall, thick trees aligned either side, forming a heavy canopy overhead. Waiting at the end was an old brick house with a brilliant red door and some off-white siding.

Based on the beat of her heart and a scent she found newly familiar, she knew the boy was inside. However unsure if this was an appropriate hour to approach a neighbor—a stranger, at that—Alice approached the door and rang the bell. Her arm shook. She felt sick.

A brief hiatus before the house creaked on all floors, though the footsteps ascended from what she assumed was the basement. Her heart hastened, and she knew who would answer.

The bridge of her nose tingled. She blinked her eyes clear before anything could come of it. She wouldn't let this boy's new first impression of her be just as manic as his previous, but her breath went shallow and quick at the memory of how similar they appeared. She needed to brace herself, but she didn't know how. There wasn't enough time.

A blind lifted from a nearby window. Her breath caught when she glimpsed his eyes—Theo's eyes, if only Theo was cautious and bitter—and everything went far away. Such a familiarity mixed with something so foreign caught her off guard, and she found herself staring in the hopes of wrapping her head around it.

He observed her for a moment longer before his gaze softened into something to which she was more accustomed, and for this she wanted to throw up. Here he was, a ghost— whether friendly or no, he was here to torment her, and she would willingly let him.

The blinds fell back into place with his retreat. The satisfying scrape of a metal bolt turned, and the door opened. She clamped her lips between her teeth to keep her mouth from stretching in agony.

With his hand to the doorknob, and wearing sweatpants and a long sleeved shirt, he was a surreal imitation of late-teens Theo. But he was thinner and more solidly built, and his shaggy wet hair reached past his ears. Theo never had his hair so long.

His mouth was partially open, and she heard a lack of airflow through his nose. Whether this was due to seasonal allergies or to a deviated septum, she couldn't tell. A crookedness to his face implied he broke his nose and busted his lip often. A faint scar interrupted his left eyebrow. Some mostly healed bruises along his cheek told her he participated in a fight about a week prior.

Her eyes felt especially cold in the light wind, and she wondered if it was because she was wide-eyed or if it was because she hadn't completely blinked out her tears. Her mouth felt left open.

Her gaze fell on his neck and she stifled a gasp. Puncture wounds—some shiny and old, some red and new—formed innumerable pairs of raised semi-circle scars. Not just over the jugular, but both sides of the neck, over the nape and across the throat. No one else in town had it nearly as bad.

Her stomach rose. This was her doing—he was Theo.

But if this was Theo, he wouldn't have been so young after all these years unless he was a domsuco. If he was a domsuco, he wouldn't have a heartbeat. He did.

"It's a little late to be asking about your lord and savior," he grumbled, startling her to the present. The slight difference in his voice confused her ear. His sound was hoarser and tiredly deeper than Theo's, and there was a laziness to his annunciation which Theo didn't have.

She replayed his words. She wasn't sure if what he said was supposed to be a joke, but in any case, she didn't get it.

He stared past her, deadpan. "Is this about Monica and them? Or Officer Robinson?"

She shook her head.

"What, then?"

Knowing how to interact without facing any consequences, she stared into his eyes.

Face falling and arms dropping to his sides, limp, he fell into trance immediately. This didn't seem to work so quickly on the others; she didn't expect this. At the same time, she was relieved to see it so blatantly working.

Words. What were words at a time like this? "Theo?"

No response.

If this was a dream, she could control it. She could make it a *good* dream. She didn't need to be distressed anymore.

She touched his face, and though it might've been impolite, she didn't care. Upon contact, however, her heart leapt and she gasped, withdrawing her hand immediately. This was too painful to have only been in her head—but she'd had these thoughts in a dream before.

Gripping her chest, on a low breath she demanded, "Who are you?"

"Jack," he monotoned.

The girls in the Crypt hadn't talked back, but then again, she hadn't asked them any questions.

"Full name?" she asked.

"Theodore Jackson Van Sloan."

The pit of her stomach squirmed. This was more like it. The dream. But it still felt like a lie.

Squeezing her eyes shut and turning away, she ran an aggravated hand through her hair. If this was a dream, why wouldn't she simply wake up? None of the other dreams lasted this long. "What do you want from me?" she cried when she faced him again.

Still monotone, he replied, "I want you to leave while you can."

This wasn't a generic answer. Nor did it pertain to their history. She didn't understand it, so…this was a fair indicator this wasn't all in her head. He wasn't Theo.

She returned her gaze to his scarred neck. "What happened here?" she asked.

"Nothing."

Bishop said people couldn't lie under trance so, to the boy's knowledge, he was telling the truth.

She crossed to him for even closer inspection, heart rattling her ribcage as she traced her fingers over the marks. The texture was rough, scratchy. Real.

She worked to calm her breath. "For now let's assume everything's real," she decided. She didn't necessarily have to believe Theo was dead and that she had killed him, but if this conversation hadn't shattered the false reality yet, it wasn't about to. If she was stuck here, the best she could do was participate in the ride and hope for a happy outcome.

If this reality had consistent rules, and Young Theo had so many scars and scabs on his neck, it meant… He had a regular visitor, and Alice had nothing to do with it.

She maintained contact for as long as she could before releasing with a pained grunt, stepping away and catching her breath. Maybe saving the boy was the only way her subconscious could redeem itself. Maybe once she succeeded, she would awaken to find Theo had survived after all, or that she had never attacked him. In any case, her experience with the cheerleaders taught her she had to do the right thing, no matter what.

There was more she needed to know, then. She couldn't work with the boy solely while he was under trance. She needed to meet him, the way regular people met one another. But how?

She scanned his foyer for an object of interest. She could smell a dog, though she didn't see or hear one.

A stack of papers perched upon a nearby end table. They read, *Missing Dog*. Paired with the image of a playful chocolate lab.

This was the answer.

After telling Jack to forget their encounter and go back to doing whatever he was doing, Alice removed her shoes, held them tightly in one hand with the flier in the other, and dashed out into the night, into the woods.

11. A Proper Meeting

Alice

Pets wouldn't typically wander too far from home, so Alice slowed to a stop once she reached the woods beyond Young Theo's house. Wetness hung in the air, and she knew snow would soon fall. She had to find the dog before he froze to death, if he hadn't already. For all she knew, finding him could have been a long lost cause by now.

Eyes closed, she listened to the world, one of the Missing Dog fliers rolled in her grasp. She heard the beat of her heart, comfortably steady with this distance. A far-off owl hooted. The northern wind carried the scent of wet dog. Her eyes shot open and she took off, flying past the trees and through the thick underbrush— *wind blowing her hair back in the sudden burst. She appeared behind Theo in an instant.*

"Alice!" he called, squinting through the downpour; ears, cheeks and nose red with cold. "Can't we talk about this?!"

She stopped short, holding her middle as if to keep it in one piece — an awkward feat with the flier and her shoes still in her grasp.

"Please don't," she breathed, squeezing her eyes shut as she hoped to reset. She hated the woods. She hated the woods at night. She hated running through them, and she hated that it was cold and the air was wet. "Don't you dare cry; don't you *dare* cry." She gripped her things tighter and growled. If she was determined, she wasn't cripplingly depressed. She had to focus. She had to function.

Something was off. Not just her emotions. A feeling in her chest; a sound which grew more succinct, *th-thmp-thmp, th-thmp-thmp —*

Her mind quieted; her remembered pain took a backseat. Someone besides the Young Theo was near enough to make her heart beat.

"Marius?!" she called, taking advantage of her bravery while she had it. There was nothing to be afraid of if she didn't care what happened next. She hadn't yet become attached to this new reality.

The unseen creature kept his distance, too far to detect with her other senses. Her heart kept it's same triple-beat, *th-thmp-thmp, th-thmp-thmp* —

"Marius!" she demanded, assuming he was close enough to hear, "Either fight me, or leave!"

No response. The off-beat vanished, leaving her chest oddly empty even with the remaining presence of Young Theo's beat.

She wondered if this actually happened. If Marius was after her, this was his chance to attack. For what purpose would he avoid confrontation? Did he not know she was back until that moment? Did he need to prepare himself, now that she was stronger than she was when they'd last met—when she was still human, for all intents and purposes?

Two choices stood in her mind. Either she could accomplish nothing in fretting over what he could plan to do next, or she could focus on the task at hand.

She growled again, letting it bubble up into a hardboiled cry. She forced her arms from her middle and recommenced her run.

The sound of low, haggard panting.

She slowed to a stop, spotting a chocolate lab which sat uphill. The dog's ears were up and alert as he watched her, perfectly still and no longer panting.

Alice unrolled the missing dog flier, her shoes still dangling from her other hand's fingertips. The dog's name read *Lestat*.

Upon glancing up to compare him to the picture, she learned there was no mistaking; this was him. She rolled the flier back up and kept her pace unhurried as she approached.

Getting Lestat to chase her wasn't difficult. As she was so recently reminded, beasts of prey chased whatever ran, so all she had to do was run back to Young Theo's house at a pace the dog could match. Once he was close enough to recognize his home, he bounded past her, straight for the back gate. She couldn't knock on one's back door upon first meeting them, so she led him around to the front.

All along she heard voices within the house, Young Theo's included. She didn't focus on what was said, mostly because it was rude, but also because it wasn't necessary. All she needed to know was that they were still awake. Hardly an hour had passed, but any number of minutes could've made a difference if it was already close to bedtime when she first arrived at their door.

Faint voices and a musical score sounded from the up-stairs. She assumed this came from a television—one cer-tainly more advanced than the kind she had ever encoun-tered.

Lestat jumped at the door, ringing the doorbell in the process.

"Was that the doorbell?" Jack murmured, muffled through the wall. Alice felt the slight increase in the pace of her heart which meant he was walking towards her.

She couldn't do it. He and his family would see the pained look on her face once he opened the door, she would hardly be able to keep the waver from her voice, and all in all this would become an uncomfortable situation for all parties in-volved. She wanted to flee.

But she couldn't back out now.

She took a breath and finally put her shoes back on.

A young woman's voice sounded from the upstairs, "Someone's at the door *again?*"

"What do you mean, 'again?'" he asked.

Alice's heart quickened, *th-thmp, th-thmp,* and she heard his footsteps just as clearly as she felt them.

"If it's one of the cheerleaders' dads, say you're not here," called the young woman. Alice by now assumed this was his sister.

Just as he had done before, Jack lifted a blind for a peep hole, spotted her, then answered the door. Alice put conscious effort into keeping her air steady.

The sound of the doorknob. The hinges rotated accordingly.

And…

They couldn't have glimpsed the other for more than a second before Lestat burst inside with kisses to the boy's face. Taken off guard, Jack stumbled backwards, the door opening wider so Alice could see a young woman with dark hair and a narrow chin walk down the staircase.

The girl's jaw dropped and her expressive brown eyes widened. "Lestat!"

Alice swallowed the lump in her throat. "I saw your flier," she managed.

The siblings exchanged glances. She didn't know what it meant, but she didn't have the mind to guess.

Before anything else could be said, Lestat recommenced jumping, nudging Jack's elbows and bombarding his face with kisses. The Young Theo tilted his head away. "Sorry, I gotta—I'll be right back, just—Alright, dog!" He retreated back into the house, the dog running ahead and back, as if in a hurry. Alice watched until he was out of sight, her heart fractionally slowing. She and Jack's sister were the only ones left in the room, and neither seemed to know what to say.

The young woman gazed through the open door past her, then grimaced. "You can come in," she offered.

Alice didn't expect to find the notion amusing. The idea of needing an invitation. A breathless giggle escaped as she stepped inside, closing the door behind her.

The teen put out a hand. "I'm Gabby."

Alice took it. "I'm Alice. Pleasure to meet you."

It was an infinitesimal difference, but she felt her heart quicken with Jack's return. She watched as he cleared a wall, an envelope in his grasp.

"Here," he said, handing it over. Without registering what was inside, she took it. He continued, "As the flier promised."

The flier promised a reward. This was money. She snapped her gaze to his when it registered, and she held the envelope back out to him. "I only did what any decent person would."

He made no effort to take it back, but watched her curiously. He seemed to debate whether or not he wanted to inquire, though in the end he asked, "Do you know who I am?"

She didn't want to lie. "Do you know who *I* am?"

Silence. "Fair enough. I'm Jack."

"Alice." Finally she noted his hand was held out. She had no idea how long he waited before she noticed. Her heart was already racing, but she couldn't resist a handshake without breaking the rules of basic social conduct. She took in some air, bracing herself in a way she hoped no one would notice.

She raised her hand to meet his.

Thmp thmp thmp —

And when their fingers met —

ThmpThmpThmpThmp —

She smiled, giving his hand a casual shake, relieved it didn't have her writhing in pain. She did, however, have to tighten her throat to keep from whimpering.

Jack watched her for a moment before dropping his gaze. "Well, uh. Thanks." This was a dismissal, though he didn't seem happy about it. Searching for some form of explanation, Alice peered at Gabby. The young woman looked elsewhere, awkwardly shifting her weight to the other foot, waiting. Perhaps something had happened before Alice entered, and they needed to address it.

In any case, she grasped the hint. "It was my pleasure," she replied, now unsure of what to do with the envelope in her grasp. In the end she tucked it into her skirt pocket. She needed to pay back the boutique for her shoes, after all. "Ta ta for now?"

Jack grimaced, and it seemed as if he disagreed, but "Yeah," he said.

She bit her lip, confused as to what she could have possibly done wrong. However disappointed, she wouldn't let it dishearten her. This was only her first attempt. With this in mind, she crossed back to the front door.

"Actually, wait," he said.

Alice paused, then turned around. First she glimpsed Gabby, who shot Jack a look as if to say, *What are you doing?*

"Are you new in town?" he asked.

"For all intents and purposes," Alice answered.

He nodded to himself, as if he had guessed. "Visiting?"

"I moved back in."

His mouth scrunched, bringing another pang to her chest. This was Theo's same face whenever he was frustrated with something out of his hands—the tighter the scrunch, the more frustrated he was. "You, um. Be safe," said the boy.

Gabby shot her a polite grin. "Thanks for finding Lestat!"

"My pleasure." Hoping to pull herself back to the present, she turned back for the door and replayed his words. What could have warranted such warning? If it was a local concern, she would glean something from the paper. Perhaps she should have read one prior to leaving the cabin.

She stepped outside and closed the door behind her. She doubted they were still watching her through the window, but to be safe she kept walking a human pace. Now when they spoke, she couldn't help but overhear.

"What the hell was that?" Gabby demanded.

"What the hell was what?" Jack asked.

Silence.

"What?" he pressed.

"Girls *die* around you, and you're giving her goo-goo eyes?"

Alice froze mid-step. It would've explained his bruises and most past injuries, if he was killing girls. They would've fought back. But Jack couldn't have been killing girls; he couldn't sully Theo's image. Rather, she wouldn't allow it.

She strode back to their door and knocked.

Jack answered, and before he could say anything, Alice began the interrogation. "Girls die around you?"

His eyebrows shot up. "Whoa, wait—"

Now wasn't the time to build trust. She couldn't risk him lying about this, so she stared into his eyes. Just as with last time, he fell into trance instantly.

Now Gabby was worried. "What are you—"

Alice turned to her. Gabby fell silent once their gazes locked, and although she wasn't as fast to fall under as Jack was, it was still too easy.

Alice turned back to the boy. "Did you kill the girls?"

Unblinking, he stared straight ahead. "No."

This was a relief, though the issue remained. She peered at the marks on his neck and wondered if, or how, this would have anything to do with it.

She wondered if the killer was the same from eighty years ago. Marius. Perhaps, with Alice in hiding, he chose to torment Jack in the hopes of drawing her out. It could explain why Jack carried so much of Marius' scent. Marius undoubtedly knew of Theo, and what he meant to Alice. He undoubtedly saw the semblance in Jack.

She stared back into the boy's eyes. "Dismiss the memory of my accusing you. Invite me someplace. Let's chat." Now

174

she addressed both siblings. "Forget this conversation happened. Awaken."

Both dropped out of trance and continued as if nothing happened. Jack furrowed his brow, as if feeling the intrusion of a new motive. "Uh, do you have plans for tonight?"

"I don't."

"Cool, me neither."

If this was the beginning of an invitation, it was endearing. "Are you inviting me someplace?" she asked.

He paused. "I mean..." His eyebrows somewhat rose when he came to the realization. "Wow, I was, but I mean... Fuck it, let's do it."

She resisted a cringe. Theo would never have sworn like that. Not around a woman, anyway. Not so casually.

If Gabby's look was intense before, it was startling now. Finally Alice understood. Gabby wanted to protect her. "Jack! You—" She glanced at Alice. "You're not even dressed. And the roads aren't safe."

"I can come back another day," Alice offered.

"No no, today works," he insisted, though now it seemed it was mostly about saying no to his sister than it was about seeing Alice. "I'll get dressed and then we'll see if the roads are good to go?"

Gabby's mouth hung open.

Alice smiled. "That works for me."

"Alright," he said. "Gabby'll talk to you while I'm getting ready." This said, he rounded a corner, opened a door and bounded down the staircase, presumably to his room, the basement.

Gabby watched after him, as if to scream, *Are you serious?!* When he was out of sight, she released a breath of frustration and turned her attention back to Alice. "It's nothing against you," she promised, "he just needs to stop being stupid."

Alice curiously tilted her head.

"Well if you're new in town, no one really knows you exist yet, right?"

"I suppose."

Gabby attempted a hopeful tone, though it came across as more unsure than anything else. "You should be good, then." Noting how false it sounded, she tried a more honest approach. "If you've ever lived in a big city, same rules apply. Stick to lit areas at night, travel in groups, and I guess avoid old cemeteries. Who knew, right?"

Old cemeteries. So it *was* her encounter with the cheerleaders they kept referencing.

"Wanna sit down?" Gabby asked.

"Don't mind if I do."

The teen led her deeper into the house. Past the foyer threshold was a linoleum-tiled kitchen and adjoining dining room, a cluttered living room on the other side. A crochet project sat in a recliner. Every hard-backed chair had hand-sewn cushions and covers. Numerous wall decorations featured cats and comforting phrases such as "All we need is love," and "Faith brings happiness."

One particular poster caught Alice's attention. From a far-away view, sitting on posts at opposite ends of a fence were the two felines. Both watched the other from over their shoulder, completely at ease, tails mid-flick. Applied over it was a quote which read, "If you love a flower, don't pick it up. Because if you pick it up, it dies and ceases to be what you love. So if you love a flower, let it be. Love is not about possession. Love is about appreciation — Osho."

"It's a little messy," Gabby admitted before leading her the rest of the way to the living room, "but we never have company, so."

"That's quite alright. This is much more lived-in than my place — more inviting."

"Live in the same four-bedroom house for three generations, and shit just accumulates."

Again with the swearing. Was this the norm? If Alice hoped to fit in with her supposed generation, did she need to give in to this vulgarity? No, she refused to go so far. However, maybe it was time she accepted such words as part of one's day-to-day vocabulary. It was possible they had lost their punch over the years—perhaps with new words to take their place.

There was a flat television screen mounted on the wall— huge at maybe two feet wide, but so thin. Where could it have fit all its wires and lights?

"Nana's stuff," Gabby explained, moving some plush knickknacks from the sofa and onto the coffee table.

This raised a question. "Where are your parents?" Alice asked. "If you don't mind me asking."

"No, it's fine." Gabby motioned for Alice to sit, and she did. Gabby took the sofa space beside her. "Mom works, like, all the time. And uh, our dad died last year. Or went missing. Probably died."

Alice wasn't completely over her own father's death a year after the fact. "I'm sorry to hear that," she murmured.

"It's fine. I mean, it isn't—we could really use his help, but." She paused. "Do you drink?"

"I don't."

"Do you mind if I grab myself something?"

"Not in the least."

"Can I get you something else? Hot chocolate, or…?"

"I am content."

"Cool." Gabby stood and crossed to the kitchen. "But yeah, he was one of the first to go when things around town got dangerous, after Sarah. Jack's first girlfriend. This was before anyone knew anything, but if Dad was still around and knew what we know now, I think he could've stopped it." She grabbed a Budweiser from the fridge and snapped it open. "I think that's why he was one of the first to go; they knew they wouldn't get away with anything if they gave him a chance."

"Was your father on the force?"

"Nah, private investigator, ex-military."

"Ah."

"But the cops have to be on someone's payroll or something; they're useless as fuck when it comes to this killer," Gabby exclaimed, nudging the door shut with her knee.

"What do we know about him?"

Gabby took a swig then sat back down beside her. "The killer? Only that he's obsessed with Jack. Or she—no one knows, and some of these girls, I wouldn't put it past them."

As Alice mulled this over, Gabby seemed lost in her own thoughts. "Actually," the teen finally said, "I'll join you and Jack, wherever you're going. Is that cool with you?"

So far she learned more from Gabby than she did Jack, so, "Yes," she permitted.

"Cool beans, I'll go get ready, then. He should be about done now."

A series of coughs sounded from the basement. Alice wasn't sure if Gabby would've heard.

As Gabby downed the rest of the can and stepped out of the room, Alice realized the cleverness in the girl's decision. In a public setting, if Alice spoke to Jack in Gabby's presence, it was possible she was there with Gabby, not Jack. This could've been the deciding factor between Alice getting attacked or getting home without incident.

Mechanical chimes sounded. Whatever device it was, it came from the kitchen, and it wouldn't stop.

"The machine will get it," Gabby promised as she ascended the steps in the foyer. A door closed and Alice knew the girl wouldn't hear anything that followed.

The chimes eventually stopped, and a tinny voice spoke. "Shit. Hey, it's Crystal Robinson, from school." The girl sounded rushed; panicked. Finally Alice realized these were what telephones were now. "Listen," Crystal pleaded, "they want everyone to think I'm crazy, because I won't believe their bullshit; I know what I saw in the crypt."

Alice gasped, the sound stretching with each notion that pieced together. Crystal was the first girl she put in trance. But it didn't work.

"There was a girl," the cheerleader continued, "Asian or something, our age. The other one—"

Silence. Alice waited for her to finish, but soon realized the machine had cut her off.

This was a problem. Alice couldn't sit and chat with the siblings yet; Crystal had to be dealt with, immediately.

Perhaps a little quicker than was humanly comfortable, Alice stood from the sofa and crossed back to the foyer, just in time to see Jack emerge from the basement door. She jumped, though her heart should've prepared her for this.

"Alright," he said, "let's see what the roads are looking like."

His eyes were red. Dry. He carried a scent which she recognized before, though it was more apparent now.

Smokey cream. Whatever he'd just done, Marius had done it often.

Briefly she lost track of her rush, though when she remembered she blurted it out as if to make up for lost time. "Forgive me, I forgot, I—have things to do."

"Oh." He seemed genuinely surprised. "Well uh, if you're done before midnight, me and Gabby'll be at the Velvet by about nine. If you wanna meet up. If the roads don't look like death."

Gabby and I, she compulsively thought.

"Absolutely," she said, reaching for the doorknob. Jack grabbed hold first and opened it for her. She didn't expect this, and so didn't account for how close they would end up. Both stood within the threshold's confines, facing the other. They didn't touch, but she was near enough to feel his warmth.

He peered out the door and down the driveway as if unaffected, his face turned to leave his neck and chest open. The material of his simple shirt was just thin enough to fall with the shape of his lean muscles, and she wanted to feel if his chest was as solid as it looked.

Her mind recoiled when she put a word to the feeling: lust.

His brow furrowed. "How did you get here?"

"I walked," she answered before considering how bizarre this was.

"For real, though."

She wracked her brain in the brief moment of a second chance that followed, but couldn't come up with a realistic alternative.

Now he seemed either suspicious or on the brink of being impressed. "How far?"

"I can't say." She told the closest, least absurd version of the truth when she explained, "I needed to clear my head, so I went for a walk. When I saw the flier, I was near enough to the address to step up to the challenge, and I haven't been home since."

He eyed her attire. Bare legs, pencil skirt, open neck. "You weren't cold?"

She laughed and shook her head. "Cold never bothered me."

"Damn," he breathed. She liked that she impressed him, even though she had an unfair advantage over most humankind. But he didn't know that; it didn't matter.

But why did she care if she impressed him?

He cleared his throat. "Well. If you have important things to do, I can give you a ride. Faster than walking." He would have had a fair point if she couldn't outrun any vehicle.

"Are the roads safe yet?" she asked.

He peered back down his driveway. In the short time they were inside, it had been plowed, along with the street at the end. It wasn't snowing anymore. "Should be," he answered.

No matter how badly she needed to get back to Bishop, she had to do the humanly realistic thing. It would have only been a few minutes' difference. "Then I will gladly accept," she decided.

"Right, let me grab my jacket."

Simultaneously they stepped away from the door, ending up closer than they were initially, bumping shoulders. This time Alice wasn't prepared for the drumroll that was her heartbeat; she gasped.

"Sorry," he murmured, then continued as if nothing happened and closed the door behind them. Alice stood completely still until Jack was distant enough for her heart to return to a more comfortable rate. There would be a day her heart wouldn't react so violently to him.

That day could not come soon enough.

12. A Highroad

Jack

If he was awkward before, he was straight indecent now —he was so stoned. However, he knew this about himself, so he tried extra hard to make up for it. He grabbed the doorknob to Gabby's car first as he and the new girl neared, opening it for her. He didn't have to. He probably shouldn't have. Just like with the front door, she jumped and sharply gasped when they made brief contact—their fingers brushed.

"Sorry," he mumbled, letting the door go and stepping back. He was so high; he was making it so obvious.

"It's fine," she said, stepping into the passenger's seat. With her blazer, black dress and heels, she looked like a businesswoman. What business did she have going for a nighttime stroll in the middle of nowhere? What office was close? Or, did she live nearby? She said she couldn't sleep and that was why she was walking. What kind of person rolled out of bed and put on business casual to go walking around at night?

He closed the door once her limbs were clear, then let himself in on the other side.

Was she a cop? Was he about to drive stoned with an undercover? No, the feds wouldn't have sent someone who stood out so easily—this girl was so out of place in so many ways. First, there was maybe one other Asian person who lived in this town. Second, she was in business casual. An undercover would try to make herself like him—he wasn't a business casual crowd, he was…younger and significantly less successful. Sending him someone who could pass for a high school girl would've made more sense. This was just weird.

He had to play it safe, though. What could he do now that was playing it safe?

"I don't mean to rush you," she finally said, tight-lipped, "but I do need to get home as soon as possible."

He had his key just sitting in the ignition. He hadn't moved for a hot minute.

"Right, sorry," he murmured, starting the car.

He couldn't pass for sober. All he needed was a Hawaiian shirt and a cigarette in a cigarette holder sticking out of his mouth, and he was Hunter S. Thomson—the epitome of not-sober.

Carefully, he pulled out of the freshly paved driveway, down the newly salted asphalt. While his eyes were on the road, he felt like she was watching him, but whenever he glanced at her, she wasn't.

Was she seriously only there that morning to return his dog? Why did it feel like there was something more to it; like she came in with expectations, or a preconceived notion? She was definitely upset before he opened the door.

He was just being high. Paranoid. Not everything was about him; if she had trouble sleeping, and she was upset before he answered the door, she was probably dealing with her own personal shit. She was in all black; she could've spent the previous day at a funeral.

"Who died?" he asked.

It was as if he hadn't said anything. Then, "What do you mean?" she asked.

"Forget it." He was wrong.

Silence. He couldn't look away from the road, so he couldn't say what expression she wore.

"Is it so obvious?" she finally grumbled.

So then he *wasn't* wrong. "Not hard to guess these days. People dropping like flies."

She nodded, distracted. Another glance caught her arms crossed tightly over her middle like she was literally trying to hold herself together. Her face contorted, and quickly she closed her eyes and forced some full breaths through her nose.

"Sorry," he mumbled again. *Please don't cry, please don't cry.*

"What's your name again?" she asked abruptly, startling him so that for a second he forgot.

"Uh — Jack."

"Jack, Jack," she softly echoed. "Jackson, but Jack."

"Yeah, actually." He couldn't remember if he told her his middle name, but someone must've. Or, *did* she know more about him than he thought she did?

"Jack," she began, loudly, as if this would disguise the waver in her voice, "Do you like Shakespeare?"

"Uhh I can't understand it and I wouldn't pay money to see it, but I don't *dislike* it."

She laughed like chimes. Sad, manic chimes. "Of course; that's exactly how…" She didn't finish, but leaned her head back against the headrest, biting her lip with a strange smile.

"Sorry, was that a dead-guy answer?"

He glimpsed her eyes squeeze shut before he returned his gaze to the narrow, hilly road, the woods growing thicker on either side.

"I'd rather not have that reminder," she said.

"Yeah, sorry. Dumb move on my part." He was fucking up hardcore; he was way too stoned for this. "I've been de-sensitized, I guess. Don't know if Gabby told you yet, but people've been dying left and right."

"So you've both said." She pushed her hair back, seeming to pull at her roots. He wasn't expecting it to be a turn-on, but it was. He liked long dark hair, then. Who knew? Hers reflected the light well.

This was totally the wrong time to be thinking these things. He cleared his throat and focused more intently on the road ahead. He had a lovely girlfriend. Sure, he planned to break up with her, but she was amazing, and if he couldn't risk staying with her, he couldn't risk warm fuzzies with a girl he just met.

He felt the girl's eyes on him again. He felt judged, like she was reading his mind somehow. Like she knew some-thing. "What was your name again?" he asked.

"Alice."

He nodded, hoping he'd retain it this time. Alice didn't deserve a crush from him; she deserved a long, happy life. Not that he was crushing on her; they just met.

He had to stop thinking—just *stop thinking*.

"I don't know where I'm going," he announced as soon as it hit him.

"That's right," she breathed, then more loudly said, "Turn around. We're some acres behind your house."

"Past the strip mall?" He looked at her long enough to see her nod.

"Cool." No one else was on the road, so he made a U-y and continued his drive as if this was all completely legal.

"I'm sorry I'm like this," she said, probably in reference to her mood.

"You're fine," he promised, "Sorry I'm fucking stupid."

"I wouldn't say that."

He grimaced; he would.

"I think I do better without pleasantries," she continued. "People walk on eggshells. I prefer to address the elephant in the room. Clear the air; get it out of the way."

He nodded, though he wondered if she was just saying this to make him feel better.

"Tell me about yourself," she suggested.

He rolled to a stop at a stop sign, looking both ways. He was being careless before, not fully stopping or giving it enough thought. This was Gabby's car, and Alice was in it; neither deserved to get wrecked. "Well," he began, "I'm a real downer."

She laughed, the chimes less manic.

"That wasn't a joke," he said.

"I didn't think it was. But it's good; it's different. Where I'm from, people try too hard to be the envy of the world; they'd never admit to anything so miserable."

"Weird. Most people I know treat pain like a contest. Like it matters who's got it worse, when we're all miserable anyway, so what's the difference?"

She nodded as if to say, *True.* Then she went quiet, the expression gradually dropping from her face. "I won't see any of them ever again." As if realizing she was still in the car with him, she added, "They're, well, in a fixed point in time, so to speak. I doubt I'll ever return."

He wasn't sure how to respond. "Is this a bad thing?"

"I can't say. The people who were left weren't any I'd ever want to see again—except for maybe his sister—but it was all *familiar;* I knew how to navigate it. Here, I don't know what I'm doing."

He assumed 'he' was the dead person. He wouldn't ask for clarification when she was trying not to think about the guy.

Anyway, he couldn't say he knew the feeling, but he nodded in acknowledgement.

Silence lingered before she weakly smiled, staring through the windshield as if she was finally content. "You're real."

He shrugged. "I guess." He had no reason to be fake. It wasn't as if people would treat him differently one way or another.

Her smile widened. "Now we *really* have a problem, don't we."

He didn't know what she meant by that. "Sure." Now he wondered if maybe he wasn't as real as she thought; a more genuine person might've asked for clarification before they agreed to whatever.

She remained smiling through the window, even as her eyes glistened.

13. An Unlikely Alliance

Alice

Jack had waited until Alice made it inside before pulling out of her driveway. While she understood why and appreciated the gesture, she wished he had left sooner. Walking took too long; she needed to find Bishop immediately.

Once the door closed behind her, all the words came tumbling out. "Bishop, one of the girls from the crypt—!"

The doctor strode in from the hallway, unperturbed, casually resting his hands on his hips. "I took care of her."

She fell silent. There were so many things this could've meant.

He observed her outfit. "I'm glad you got out today."

She didn't know what to feel about it when there were more pressing matters at hand. "What did you do to her?"

"She's locked in your room until she decides to hear reason."

She let out a breath, drifting to the dining room table to lean her forearms atop one of the chair-backs. "I'm sorry; I didn't think she was under trance when it happened. I should've said something."

"It wasn't you," he assured her, "I tried it again myself. Interestingly enough, it doesn't work on her mother, either; somehow they're not wired that way. I'm beginning to think all it takes is the will to shut out what you *want* to hear, and to pay attention to the *facts*—what you can physically hear and see."

This was interesting.

Alice didn't have the mind to continue the conversation, so instead led the way back to her room. As she turned the knob and gently pushed, the door wouldn't open. It was blocked.

"Should I bust through?" she muttered.

Bishop shook his head. "I already have to fix the counter."

She remembered she'd destroyed it that morning. "I'm sorry about that."

He dismissed this with the wave of his hand. "I'm happy you left the room. But come, the window should open from the outside." He led her down the hall and out the back door, which opened from the living room.

Looking to the desired window, they found Crystal's silhouette straining to lift it open.

Alice frowned. "Might you say it can *only* be opened from the outside?"

"It's merely stuck. I closed it quite harshly in my haste."

For a moment they only stood a slight distance, watching, never having stepped too far from the back door.

"If she won't listen to you, maybe I should try," Alice suggested. "Alone."

Bishop raised an eyebrow. "And she'll listen to *you*? After what you did to her?"

He had a point. "I don't know," she admitted. "But it's worth a try."

Bishop frowned and waved an arm toward the window as if to say, *Be my guest.*

Alice strode forth. As she neared, the girl's movements slowed. Her narrow brown eyes widened and she screamed, darting to the dresser she'd pushed to the door.

The scream rang in Alice's ears, though she refrained from covering them or recoiling as she lifted the window open.

The dresser scratched the wood paneled floor as Crystal shoved it aside, flinging open the door.

Bishop stood waiting on the other side. "Boo."

She screamed again and slammed it in his face.

"Bishop!" Alice scolded. Crystal might not have heard, but he giggled to himself on the other side.

Bracing her back to the door, the girl held out a desperate hand, one which begged Alice to keep her distance. "Look, I don't know what you got against Jack, but I know his name and that's about it; I don't know him, I swear to God, please, I know nothing! I don't even know you're at all connected, right? Nothing, I promise, please, God—"

Alice noted the stitches over the girl's jugular, the remainder of wounds beyond anything another human could inflict. She could barely focus on anything else. She knew it wouldn't change anything, so she didn't want to say it again, but at the same time she felt obliged to say *something* and she didn't know what else to say. "I'm sorry," she decided.

Stiff and hyperventilating, Crystal watched her. Then, "What do you want with me?"

"Nothing," Alice assured her before considering why the girl was there to begin with. "Only... There are some things you seem unable to forget, and therefore there are some things you should know."

The girl remained unconvinced.

Hoping to ease the tension, Alice stepped closer with painstaking slowness, then sat a comfortable distance before her on the bed. "I can't apologize enough for what happened in the crypt. For what I did."

"I won't snitch," Crystal spouted. Alice couldn't help a slight grimace and Crystal must've seen the issue, for she quickly added, "Trust me, I know better—"

From behind the door Bishop interjected, "You're only saying that so we'll let you go."

Whatever happened to letting me do this alone? Alice narrowed her eyes at the door. "We need to establish trust," she reiterated for him.

Crystal exasperatedly laughed. "That ain't gonna happen."

"We don't care if *you* trust *us*," Bishop scoffed, as if the insinuation of the alternative offended him.

Alice continued as if he didn't say anything. "I understand there's a killer in town. I have reason to believe he holds the same extraordinary abilities as I, and if this is the case you cannot let anyone know you can't be hypnotized."

Still, Crystal didn't move. Panting, she stared as if trying to decide if she heard her correctly. "What?"

Bishop answered, "Remember how your friends in the crypt quieted, then followed our orders to a T?"

Crystal turned her gaze, coming to stare at the wall. "That's... What the fuck is happening anymore..."

"That's charm," Bishop replied, "And it doesn't work on you, nor on your mother. The killer must know about your mother, which I assume is why she was attacked. If they find out about you, you may not escape with your life."

The girl peered back at Alice, staring her down. "If the Ripper ain't either of you and it ain't Jack, who is it?"

Marius. But, the monster could change his form; there was no telling how he portrayed himself these days. And there was still the possibility it wasn't him.

Alice bit her bottom lip, thinking. "Maybe that's where we can help each other." She figured Crystal was already too involved to turn back; it would've been pointless to not make the best of it.

Bishop seemed to disagree. "Don't drag her further into this than necessary."

"Worst case scenario, what could happen?" Crystal asked.

"You die, I die, Jack dies in prison, Alice isolates herself underground again."

The quick rise and fall of Crystal's eyebrows seemed to say, *Oh, is that all?*

He continued, "If the true Ripper learns about Crystal's ability, and hears she's helping us, how long can she withstand torture? Either he learns about us through her—or he has intentionally drawn us out and therefore has nothing to learn—in either case, the girl won't live."

"Okay I get it!" Crystal exclaimed. "Look, if you really didn't do it, why'd you attack us?"

Bishop retaliated, "She wouldn't have let you live if she was the Ripper!"

"I wasn't in my right mind," Alice cut in. "It's no excuse, but it's the truth. I let myself think it wasn't real."

"Not real—are you *nuts?*" While at first Crystal seemed angry, now it seemed she wanted to undo the outburst, eyes wide.

"I…" Alice wasn't sure how to answer. What classified a person as *nuts?*

Silence lingered. Crystal's expression relaxed before she murmured, "That wasn't supposed to be a trick question."

Even so, Alice didn't know how to answer.

Finally Crystal took a calming breath, letting her head fall back against the door. "Shit, and I asked for this too, didn't I. It was my idea to go into the Vampire Crypt, looking for vampires."

Alice's gaze dropped to her feet. "I doubt you asked to be hospitalized."

"Yeah, well…" Crystal sighed. "Look. At least four girls have died in the last year since this all started, and ain't no one's done shit but pin it on Jack and rip him a new asshole. If it's really not you, and there's any way I can help, let me."

Alice wouldn't respond right away, but thought it through. She assumed Bishop was doing the same.

"The deaths," Alice began. "Are there any outliers, or are they all girls who've spoken to Jack?"

"Some outliers," Crystal verified. "Me and my friends— well, I guess that don't count. Then there's my mom, only she ain't dead—"

"I intervened," Bishop explained. "But I didn't see who it was. I must've scared them away."

Crystal's mind seemed to disconnect from her body; her gaze deadened. "You mean to tell me you just happened to be on the road in the middle of nowhere, exactly at the time she was attacked?"

Bishop whined, muffled by what Alice assumed was his hand, "No, I mean to say we were both in Erie, and while she was headed north for the hospital, I was headed south from the hospital; it's a simple matter of travel logistics, if you would think before pointing your perfectly manicured fingers —"

Alice raised her voice just enough when she asked, "Are there no other outliers?"

Crystal nodded. "Jack's dad. If that's actually connected. I think that's it, though."

"So they're all definitely connected to Jack."

"But he ain't behind it."

"We know."

"Because he ain't a vampire?"

Alice wouldn't argue technicalities, but nodded back, "That, and I asked."

Crystal squinted, though before the question formed in her lips she seemed to have answered it herself. "Hypnotism."

"Exactly," Alice murmured, distracted as she came up with the next question. "Can you think of anyone who would have a motive? Anyone you've never seen in sunlight, or who never seems to eat, or hasn't aged since you've known them?"

Frowning, Crystal shook her head. "No one eats or goes outside anymore."

Alice squinted.

The girl continued as if she didn't notice, "Is there anything more obvious to the average normal-person? Like, no reflection or shadow?"

Alice raised her hand to the light and watched its shadow on the wall, then turned her attention back to the mirror on the wall which returned her reflection.

The girl frowned, having followed her gaze. "Alright, so... God damn, if I knew we were supposed to be looking for vampires, I might've paid closer attention to this sh—" She stopped short, eyes unfocusing. Slowly she raised a finger as if to further indicate she had a thought. "I ain't sayin' it's definitely her, but that waitress from the diner they always go to—Jack and Wyn. Think her name's... It's Bri, her name—still ain't sayin' it's her, but... I mean, it would make sense."

"How?"

"I don't know if anyone else ever saw her in daylight, but I haven't. She's almost always there for night shift—only night shift. Jack's there all the time, so maybe she's making him, with that hypnosis bullshit, or making the other food joints turn him away so the diner's the only place that'll take him in."

"Does she want him?" Bishop asked.

"Definitely," Crystal answered. "And she's so obvious about it, like she ain't worried she'll be next—" Interrupting herself, she murmured, "But if she can do whatever she wants, why is she waiting tables..."

"It gives her an excuse to see him every day," Alice guessed. "If they don't go to the same school—"

"She graduated last year," Crystal verified. "He would've graduated with her, but. Well, you know. All this shit going down, you really think he's focussed on his studies?"

"But it's so easy to pass these days," Bishop countered. "I wouldn't be surprised if this was the Ripper's doing, as well. If Jack doesn't graduate, he can't escape to an out-of-state college. It keeps him stuck."

Crystal added, "And I know for a fact Bri's got that marry-your-high-school-sweetheart, never-leave-your-hometown fantasy."

Alice let the information stew. If it turned out they were wrong, they would know soon enough once they established if Bri even was a domsuco. The process would be as simple as Alice standing in the same room and listening out for a heartbeat. It was a start.

"I'm meeting with Jack today," Alice informed the others. "He invited me to the…Um…"

"The Velvet," Crystal figured. She was right. "Again, one of the only places that'll let him in, and Bri's usually there after the diner closes."

All the more reason for Alice to go. She crossed to the door, Crystal stepping aside and keeping a safe distance. After taking a breath in preparation, Alice reached for the doorknob.

"Lose the blazer," Bishop said as soon as she opened, standing closer to the threshold than she'd anticipated.

"What?" she asked before his words registered.

"That's business casual. You need casual-casual."

Her brow furrowed and her head tilted.

Already standing before the closet, Crystal reached for the handle, then paused. "There's nothing weird in here, right?"

"Clothes," Alice replied.

This was all the girl needed; she opened the closet. "Aww whaaaat." Her speech was slow as she flipped through the hangers. "Talk about vintage… When's the last time you went shopping, 1946?"

"Possibly."

"That's right," Crystal muttered under her breath, "Fucking crazy-ass Rip Van Winkle meets Twilight shit going on in this…" She frowned. "I want everything in here. Ooh." She stopped on a dark blue coat—or black. Alice couldn't recall what color it was, nor could she pretend to know how it appeared to the regular folk.

Crystal peered back at Alice as if to double check, then back at the garment. "Lucky for you, vintage is in; check this out." She pulled the hanger from the closet, revealing a cozy, loosely fitted woolen coat. The material was textured like poodle fur. Its single front button closure featured large, plain plastic black buttons, and the slanted hip-length pockets came with a false pocket slot above each. The hem stopped mid-thigh.

"I, personally, wouldn't wear it," Crystal began. "With my frame it'll look like I'm wearing a laundry bag, but you got that model twig figure going on—and, it's wool; it's practical, not work-space specific, and it goes with what you're already wearing."

Alice exchanged a look with Bishop, who now stood at her side, frowning with a thoughtful finger to his lips. "Yes," he finally said.

"Alright, so…" Slowly, Crystal laid the coat out on the bed between them, keeping herself as distant as possible. Now it was silent as she returned her gaze to them, and it was clear someone had to address the elephant in the room: could they trust her?

"I might be nuts," Alice admitted, "but you know how you'll sound if you try to tell anyone any of this?"

Crystal nodded.

Bishop added, "And those who *would* believe you would have an obligation to kill you."

Alice snapped her gaze to him. This was news.

He explained, "Once people know what they're up against and how to fight it, they'll think they can wipe us out and chaos will ensue. But, for so long as we're invisible, we can do whatever we want and they can live in peace. We're betraying our kind just for letting her live."

"That's sick," Alice said.

Bishop shrugged, "Basic code of conduct; I don't make the rules."

"I won't tell anyone," Crystal interjected, voice rising. "Look, I wanna live, okay? I want the deaths to stop, and I want The Ripper to be brought to justice. One way or another."

Alice and Bishop exchanged another look. Alice was already decided, and prepared to fight him if he disagreed.

It was hard to say if he had given in, or if he would have come to this conclusion on his own. "I'll pay for your taxi," he decided, still not having turned from Alice.

Crystal didn't seem to grasp what this meant; she wasn't relieved yet.

Finally Bishop looked at her. "You live. Don't make us regret it."

Her eyes closed as she let out a breath, hand flying over her heart as she halfway turned around, knees sinking before she brought herself back upright. "Thank God, holy shit — I won't, I promise, you won't regret it."

"Good. You'll help me convince your mother to do the same while Alice," he turned to aforementioned, "meets with Jack at the Velvet."

"Go team," Alice murmured, hoping this was a phrase Crystal would relate to.

The cheerleader did not react.

14. The Velvet Club

Jack

Gabby wouldn't let Jack hear the end of it. He had no idea what it was about Alice that convinced him he needed to see her again. She seemed cool enough, and pretty badass with that whole 'cold never bothered me' thing, but this typically wasn't worth risking someone's life over. While he agreed with Gabby when she pointed out how dumb of an idea this was, he wasn't about to admit it.

"Seriously?" she demanded, "Did you suddenly forget girls die around you, or do you just not care anymore?!"

They were leaving the parking lot now. Since his last encounter in a similar location, he put more attention to situational awareness and scanned their surroundings, keeping Gabby in his peripheral so he could adequately follow her lead.

"You hardly even knew the cheerleaders!" she continued, pulling a cigarette from her handbag and stopping beside a lamppost. The Velvet was just ahead, a short line at the entrance.

"Exactly!" he snapped back, and as he made his argument he started to believe it. "If this guy's killing girls I barely know, it's pointless trying to protect them!" Gabby lit her cigarette and took the first drag as he went on, "It's pointless closing all of them out when I don't even know their names —and then they die anyway! It's fucking—" He paused. While Gabby was clearly upset with him, she was only a certain level of emotional about it. He needed to take it back a notch.

His breath came out in a puff of smoke and he dropped his gaze to his feet, pushing his hands deeper into his pockets. He noted Gabby had somewhat calmed as well. She knew something about what it was like to have her friends turn on her, since the deaths started. Even those who didn't consciously ostracize her rarely saw her anymore. She was lonely like him.

"I get it," she murmured. He nodded in acknowledgement, and it was silent before she offered him a cigarette, which he accepted. "I get it, I do," she continued. "This girl, she's new, she's a clean slate. But… How long do you think she'll last if you keep talking to her? And in public, where anyone can see?"

He shook his head. It didn't look promising, but there was no way to know. "I'm just tired of letting this shit control me," he grumbled.

She didn't say anything for a while, finishing her cigarette before flicking it at the pavement. She nodded toward the Velvet. "You ready?"

She had a bit of a head start, so it was a few more drags before he caught up and flicked his cigarette as well. "Yeah." Fake IDs at the ready, they crossed to the back of the line.

Luckily it moved quickly. It was early enough for not too many people to be out yet, though he knew any minute now the crowds would come rushing in. If he wanted anything from the bar, his best chance was to immediately get as many orders out of the way as he could. Start out strong. Two shots of tequila, followed by a long island iced tea to keep him going the rest of the night. If he got sleepy he would have Gabby smuggle an Irish coffee from the pub next door for him. If he blacked out, he'd wake up to Wyn. He'd done this enough times.

He wasn't sure where Wyn was. He'd called her twice to see if she wanted to go with him, but she didn't answer. Usually she would answer within milliseconds. He didn't consider it until then, but him inviting another girl out drinking… Of course he didn't mean anything by it, but with Wyn feeling as insecure as she was, she probably wouldn't like it. Hopefully Gabby being there would help the situation.

The twins weaved through the light crowd and to the bar. At first he thought it was in his head, and that it wasn't anything worse than the usual, but anytime anyone glanced his way, they deliberately turned their backs or walked elsewhere. Closer inspection revealed puffy eyes. Tense jaws. Four or five seemed angry while the other several seemed scared, or some other form of upset. He'd seen this before. He knew what it meant.

You're being paranoid, he told himself, though one look at Gabby told him she saw it, too. She frowned, wide brown eyes both curious and wary as she scanned each face.

"Maybe we shouldn't be here tonight," she suggested, voice mostly drowned in the music. "It's only been a week or so since Ashley."

She might've been right, but they'd made it this far, and he didn't wanna stand Alice up if she did decide to show. And he needed his goddamn tequila.

The bartender was a big guy. If anyone was to make a local film about Zeus, this was the guy to cast. Late thirties, broad shoulders, muscle, little bit of a gut, features akin to the painted faces on ancient Greek pottery. Acting-wise, though, he'd have to convince people he wasn't a big softie.

As per usual, Jack and Gabby waited far past what should have been their turn to be serviced. What wasn't usual was how, once the last person got their drink and Jack and Gabby were the only guests left, the bartender lifted the bar separation, closed it behind him, stalked past the siblings and out the back door.

"What the fuck!" Jack called, clear over the music.

"We should just go," Gabby said, but Jack stormed after him, shoving the back door open so that it slammed the adjacent wall.

"Who died?" he demanded, in case there was anything new since the attack on the cheerleaders. Did one of them die at the hospital?

The bartender had a cigarette to his mouth, fumbling to light it. His chin quivered, but he frowned it out and forcibly turned his features to something more intimidating.

Gabby burst out the door, too, and grabbed Jack's wrist. "Let's *go*."

"Ashley had a lot of friends, kid," the bartender said around the cigarette. Finally he got it lit, taking a long drag before shakily exhaling with, "Dumb move, you know."

So then it was still Ashley. Jack sighed his relief before considering how insensitive it would seem. The bigger man simmered in this for a beat, then slammed Jack into the wall. The sensation was oddly familiar, as if this'd happened recently.

"Hey!" Gabby grabbed the guy's arm with both hands, yanking him with all her bodyweight, but he wouldn't budge.

"I don't need you playing dumb, got that?" dude threatened, the waver in his voice dampening the affect, even as neither twin could push him off. "It's enough that you come here every day—"

"You stop that right now," Jack wheezed around the pressure in his chest, "I barely knew her—"

"She sure liked you—"

"It's not my fault she—"

"She what!?" the bartender suddenly boomed in his face, shoving Gabby off his arm in one easy move. She stumbled backward before steadying herself against the wall.

Bartender continued, "Dropped her neck on your knife and hung *herself* upside down?!"

Jack's vision turned red, as did his face—he felt it. It was a knee-jerk reaction when he screamed and flung his forehead at the guy's face.

A new girl's voice called, "Jack?"

Jack opened his eyes. His head was heavy. He and Gabby stood inside, and Wyn was with them, looking all pretty and shit. He was so shitfaced, he was so fucking shitfaced, why was Sarah dead, why was there another *fucking* murder?

The bartender was also back inside, doing his thing behind the counter. Dude didn't look injured, and Jack didn't feel injured, and neither were removed from the premises, so apparently that situation outside had sorted itself out okay. It didn't feel like a dream, so it wasn't like it was all in Jack's head. Unless it was?

Whatever; if he was drunk, it meant he eventually got his alcohol, and that was all that mattered.

Why was the Ripper so busy all of a sudden. One death, five injured, all in one month?

Jack stared up at the club's balcony lounge.

George and the jocks were onto something, earlier —

"Where are you going?" Wyn's voice. He'd just reached the stairs. He couldn't recall how he got there, but he was impressed with his unconscious follow-through.

"I'll be right back," he slurred. He wasn't lying. It was almost a joke — one he almost could have laughed at —

His vision unglazed and he realized he was gripping the balcony's rail, staring down at the regular dancing crowd. He couldn't be spacing out like this; he had shit to do, before anyone could stop him.

He slowly paced along the railing, peering down until he found an open space. He didn't want to land on anyone.

He climbed the rail, gripping the beam to his side for support once he was up and upright. He got some curious looks. Not a lot, but some. He needed people to see. He needed them to see the proof, when he actually broke his legs. He couldn't think of a better situation. He was drunk, so the physical pain would be numbed. And there was a club of people. Witnesses.

The ground was so far away. He thought he'd find it daunting, but instead it called to him. He laughed. What if, instead of landing on his legs, he landed on his head?

He playfully bunny-hopped off.

The floor came at him fast. He could feel it already, his freedom —

The ceiling went *swoosh* —

He started, nearly knocking Wyn's chin with his head. They were cuddled on the lounge couch. He'd been asleep. Not knocked out. Not injured. Was that all a dream? His body felt sore.

Wyn gently wrapped her cool fingers over his brow. His eyes closed. This felt amazing.

"Good morning, sleepyhead," she crooned, then kissed his hair. It wasn't morning; she was just being cute.

"I don't remember drinking anything," he whined.

How much was a dream? Had the bartender tried to fight him outside over Ashley?

Wyn kissed his head again. He huffed a sigh from his nose and decided that, for now, it was a dream. He'd deal with reality later.

"Where's Gabby?" he asked.

"Smoking." Wyn pulled her face back just enough so she could see him. It was still a funny angle, with her face still so close. "I got your messages."

"I figured," he said. She wouldn't have known to meet him there if she hadn't. He forced himself upright, holding Wyn's shoulders for balance as he stood. "I'm gonna join her, if you wanna come."

Wyn nodded, offering herself for balance all the way from the top of the lounge balcony and nearly to the front entrance when he saw Gabby come back in.

Everything muted out and faded away when he spotted the next person to enter the club. He didn't expect her to make it, and up until now he wasn't sure he wanted her to. Now he realized, he did. He knew it was selfish, but she was the first person in years besides Gabby and Wyn to show up to anything he'd invited anyone to, and it felt good.

Something about her gaze reminded him of a Lord of the Rings elf, majestically scanning the imminent army of orcs, hair like a black curtain down her back.

Gabby squinted at him and spoke once she was close enough. "Who're you looking at?" So she didn't know Alice had entered right behind her.

Wyn tried to follow his gaze, but didn't have the height advantage.

"It's the girl who found Lestat," he said, then to Wyn, "I think you'd like her." He honestly had no idea if she'd like her, but if they could be friends, life would be easier. "Alice!"

The girl caught his gaze. Wyn finally saw her.

And that was all Jack remembered of that night.

15. Winifred Dodds
Alice

The music was too loud. There were too many people, all with the old marks of domsuco teeth along their necks. At least five of the several intoxicated couples interacted in such a way that should not have been done in public, kissing and rhythmically grinding their pelvises together.

Alice reminded herself to stop acting like an old lady before stepping further into the Velvet Club, and a rogue thought stopped her in her tracks.

If Theo was here, he would already be on a first-name basis with everyone.

She twisted her mouth and tuned out the music as best she could, listening in on conversation to conversation until—

"Alice!" There stood Jack, shaggy brown hair reaching past his eyes and earlobes.

A smaller teen girl leaned into him, her curly red hair haloing her head like a lion's mane. Her eyes were green and almond-shaped, outlined in black liquid liner beneath dark, smokey eyelids. A fragility to her features reminded Alice of —

Alice's eyes widened and her mouth fell open. "Winifred Dodds?" she all but breathed.

It couldn't have been. But yet…

A jolt to the girl's overall composure the second she heard her name. Her gaze snapped to Alice's.

It was strange. So much makeup—Alice was surprised she recognized her at all. The girl's freckles were gone. Her hair was *red*. The subtly brushed-on shadows beneath her cheekbones made her face look thin, and so it lost its cute, familiar fullness. Although, looking closer, Alice realized it wasn't all an illusion; Winifred's face had actually thinned drastically. And her chest was notably bigger. She still carried her familiar scent—light, crisp and sweet, like roses and dewdrops.

It was silent between them as they watched the other from afar. At first there was nothing, no sign of recognition—only that moment of shock during which nothing could register. Then Winifred's eyes widened. The music drowned out all else, though still the older friend heard when the girl whispered, "Alice?"

Alice's mouth remained open, and reality proved even harder to trust. Winifred and Theo were back together.

Winifred waved her hands over Jack's and Gabby's eyes, and the siblings fell under trance immediately, no eye contact necessary. Perhaps this was why it was so easy for Alice to put them under. They'd done this so many times, they'd been trained.

The old friend turned back around, still stunned silent, then began her steady approach.

Alice stepped forth as well, heart quickening the closer she was to Jack. Her hands were shaking, and she didn't know what she was feeling. Both of their paces hastened until—

"Alice!" Winifred threw her arms around her. "What have you been doing all this time?! How long have you been a domsuco!?"

"I haven't been doing much lately," she answered, too overwhelmed to know what more to say. Finally she put her hands to Winifred's shoulders and back. She was there.

Simultaneously they withdrew to see one another at arm's length, Winifred beaming when she screamed, or laughed. Alice laughed back, and held her close again, the girl's curly hair sticking up to tickle her nose.

"You've met my boyfriend already, I heard?" Winifred pulled away just enough to gesture back at Jack, peering away from Alice for only a second. "Did you know he's Ruth's grandson? Theo's sister's grandson?"

"I noticed the resemblance," she allowed. "But… You…?"

Winifred waited for Alice to elaborate before smiling wider, taking her by the hand and leading her back to Jack and Gabby. If Alice didn't know any better, the siblings could have appeared too sauced and sleepy to interact. "Look at this," Winifred boasted, pulling down Jack's collar to reveal the bite marks. "My boyfriend and my blood bag. Convenient, right?"

Alice didn't see this as something appropriate to brag about, but her tone remained light as she asked, "You put him under trance whenever you're feeling peckish?"

"I do it whenever I feel necessary. Certain steps must be taken to keep certain things secret, if you know what I mean." Overly playful, Winifred winked and nudged Alice's side. "I don't prefer them screaming, unlike some? Madame Vampire Crypt?"

It must not have been hard to guess it was Alice, if all the other domsuco in town knew better than to make such a scene. Her gaze dropped. The fact that the others drank from live human sources didn't seem to be the issue; it was when they left a trail that it became one.

Winifred gasped, a slight smile still tugging her lips. "You mean it *was* you?"

Now Alice felt foolish. She had given herself away.

Her old friend laughed. "Alice! Goodness, that'll teach them to look for things that go bump in the night! You're not the Ripper, are you?"

"I'm, no, I'm not the Ripper." Alice closed her eyes and shut out her surroundings, aiming to reset. Her mind was clouded and she was on a mission; these two things did not mix well. She needed to think…

Winifred was a domsuco who was connected to Jack.

She was a suspect now.

"Come, let me show you around!" the girl exclaimed. She addressed Jack and Gabby, "Follow me."

They did, and Winifred led them all up a set of steps to a lounge landing which overlooked the club scene below. The couches were all taken. Winifred waved her arm and the people got up and made room as if it was their own decision, then with the biggest grin she turned back to Alice and gestured for the friends to sit. Uncertain and unnerved, Alice took the sofa. Winifred had Jack sit on the adjacent couch so she could sit on his lap, and Gabby took the space beside them.

"I don't know how I survived being mortal for as long as I did," Winifred laughed, planting a kiss on Jack's face for emphasis. This didn't sit right with Alice, though at the thought of this being the result of a strange, lingering jealousy, she did her best to ignore it.

Alice asked, "When did you stop being mortal?"

Winifred tilted her head in thought. "A little before the town buried you."

The town buried her?

Winifred's smile gradually faded. "Bishop didn't tell you?"

Bishop? Alice felt her gaze harden. "What didn't Bishop tell me?"

"Ooh, so he hasn't then." The girl's gaze lowered, gradually losing focus. Whatever memory played through her head wasn't pleasant. She wrapped Jack's arm around herself for comfort. "It was when my family and I supposedly went on that trip—that was what you were all told, wasn't it? We were on vacation?"

Alice nodded.

"Well, that… That wasn't what happened. We were, um. We were kidnapped, and…" Her face went lax, and her voice went dead. "He killed my parents. Right in front of me."

Alice's mouth fell open and she didn't mean to yell, "*Bishop?*"

"Hm? Oh! God no, sorry, not Bishop. He didn't say his name, though I've heard this one tossed around, and I think… I think it was Marius."

Alice's mouth remained open.

"He murdered your parents too, right?" Winifred asked.

"My father," Alice answered, rushing, "What did he want?"

Winifred sadly shrugged. "He didn't say anything to me, not a word. I asked him why, but he didn't answer, and his face was blank the entire time. Completely without reaction. Then it was my turn. I asked him again, and the way he…" Her mouth remained open as she struggled for words. When her eyes locked on the distance, Alice knew she wasn't there anymore. Slowly she uttered, "He looked me dead in the eye and said… God, I'll never forget this."

"What did he say?"

Her eyes remained distant. "'I should rape you, Winifred Dodds.'"

Immediately something rose in Alice's chest and throat. She didn't expect this. "Did… he?"

Winifred shook her head. "I don't know if he really planned to, but… I still don't understand. I've gone through my memory so many times, trying to figure out when we could've met, or what I could've done. But I haven't done anything, to anyone. Have I?"

Alice shook her head.

"Well," Winifred continued, "it was my turn next. He'd already broken all my fingers before he suddenly left. Bishop burst in a few seconds later. He didn't explain anything, just bit his own wrist, then mine, and pressed them together. I was so terrified, I transitioned on the spot, and he pointed out the nearest exit. So I ran."

Alice didn't know what to say. "I… Winifred, I had no idea. I'm so sorry."

"Don't be. My parents… My mother was an alcoholic, did you know? And my dad cheated, all the time. Neither wanted to deal with me, but the times they did, it was because I'd done something to bother them, and… well, I didn't see it then, but their punishments were a bit extreme."

There were too many things to which Alice could react. She didn't know which to address first.

When Winifred figured Alice wouldn't respond anytime soon, she assured her, "Really, don't feel sorry. Marius made me the woman I am. Strong, confident. Powerful. I used to worry about everything: what people thought of me, what most I could afford to eat and to wear while maintaining the facade of wealth, growing old and ugly, being out late by myself. Now there's nothing. He freed me."

Still, Alice didn't know how to respond. She considered that maybe she didn't need to, but then she didn't know how to switch the topic in a way which didn't seem insensitive. She wanted to react in a way that was best for Winifred.

The silence seemed just as uncomfortable for the aforementioned, who shifted her weight and glanced about the bar. Finally she asked, "He was the killer, though. Right? Eighty years ago?"

Alice knew who she was talking about. "Do you think it's him again? Now?"

Winifred shrugged and shook her head. "I've been trying to figure that out myself. It's a little different this time around, and I can't imagine it's the same person after all these years, but… Well, if *we're* both still here, who's to say he wouldn't be? And after eighty years, I'd say it's possible for a killer to change up the routine a little."

"Do you suspect anyone else?"

Again Winifred shook her head. "I would at the very least guess it was a domsuco, but none of the evidence explicitly implies a superhuman. Not this time, anyway. But, if the Ripper's a domsuco, he slices a razor over the puncture marks once he's finished, so that it only looks like a sliced neck. Then, to account for the complete blood loss, he hangs the corpses upside down so it all would have drained. I assume this is the reason, anyway—otherwise it's purely an aesthetic."

Alice frowned. While Winifred understood the killer's process, it didn't mean anything condemning.

"Who do you think it is?" the girl asked.

"I'm still meeting everyone," Alice answered. "Though, do you know of a girl named Bri?"

Winifred tilted her head. "The diner girl?"

Alice nodded.

Winifred let her gaze drift in consideration. "She's human, but… She doesn't seem to care if she'll die. Or, she doesn't think she'll be next…" She nodded to herself. "I don't know how she'd pull it off, but I suppose it's possible."

Now there were three people Alice had to investigate. She and Bishop could keep an eye on Winifred. It might've been asking too much to have Crystal keep an eye on Bri, even though it felt appropriate to pair the human with the human suspect. Just because Bri was human, it didn't mean she wouldn't prove deadly against a human opponent if she really *was* the Ripper.

But if it was Marius…

"I'll know if it's Marius," Alice figured.

"How?" asked Winifred, eagerly curious.

Alice couldn't see how it would hurt for the old friend to know even if she *was* the Ripper, so she elucidated. "Marius has the same affect over my heart as Jack and Theo."

Something about this distracted Winifred. Her gaze turned more somber; defeated. She nodded for Alice to continue.

Alice could guess what this change in mood was about, but she wouldn't address it yet. She continued, "When I was near Theo and my heartbeats turned irregular, I knew Marius was close. If I stay near Jack and notice anything irregular, I'll know Marius is in town. If I feel it and another girl dies…"

Winifred nodded. "You'd know it's him."

Alice twisted her mouth. "Not exactly. It'd prove he's a strong contender. But, on the other hand, if there's another death — nearby — and my heart's unaffected, we'll know it *isn't* him."

Winifred nodded to herself, glum. "So you'll have to stay near Jack."

Alice didn't entirely care for this plan, but…it was necessary. She nodded back.

…

They chatted late into the night, Jack and Gabby under trance the entire time. Alice doubted these precautions were necessary, and the longer the siblings lasted this way, the more uncomfortable she became with it.

"It was cool seeing you again!" Winifred exclaimed as they left the Velvet Club and entered the parking lot. She and Jack walked hand in hand as Gabby trailed behind. As they neared Gabby's car, Winifred turned and addressed the mortal. "Here, you drive Alice to her place, go home, sleep it off and forget about tonight."

Without a word, Gabby walked ahead, opened her door, sat in the driver's seat and waited.

Alice glanced between Winifred and Jack, and Winifred knew what she meant to ask.

"I'm going to drive Theo home," she answered.

Alice's breath caught and she played the words back in her head to be sure she heard correctly. "You mean 'Jack?'" she suggested.

Winifred shook her head. "I call him Theo. Anyway, I might get myself a midnight snack, if you know what I mean." She playfully winked, but before she could nudge, Alice blocked and gently lowered her elbow.

"Enough, Winifred," she murmured.

At first the girl was wide-eyed and still, like a startled kitten. Finally she attempted a laugh, as if to make everything okay again. "Enough what? What do you mean?"

Alice bit her lip and considered whether to continue or to drop it, though in that short moment when neither spoke, the sound of her heartbeat became more apparent. Winifred had to have heard it.

The girl's chin quivered and she lowered her gaze before Alice could know for certain if her eyes had watered. Voice even, though strained, she muttered, "Will you take him from me again?"

Alice's gut dropped and her mouth fell open. She didn't know how to answer. It was such an off-the-wall question, and she didn't expect the friend to be reduced to this point so suddenly.

When she took too long to respond, Winifred's chin quivered again and she shielded her eyes, as if this would mask her tears. "Please. Please, let me have this—only this, if nothing else. I've waited so long, and I'm working so hard to make things better for him."

"I'm not trying to take him from you," Alice finally said.

For a second the girl didn't respond. She might've calmed the slightest bit before she asked, "What about your heart?"

"You don't suppose I'm in love with Marius, too, do you?"

The girl sniffled before she raised her head from her hand and watched the stars, waiting for her tears to filter out. "I'm sorry, I'm... It's been stressful. I'm lucky the Ripper's too afraid to confront me, but I still have to wonder how long it will be before he sets some sort of trap. I know this worries him, too—Theo, I mean—or, Jack—I don't doubt it, but..." She emitted a low sigh. "We're working through some issues right now. It's been rocky. He retrogresses to a dark place every few months, and I constantly have to reset the timer, so to speak — so he won't kill himself. I don't know how faithful he's been, and I — I can't have him ending up with you again, I can't."

"I've never been with Jack."

"You know what I meant."

"I'm sure, but I'm beginning to think you consider them interchangeable."

Winifred didn't respond. Alice wasn't wrong, then.

"I only ask a few favors," Alice said.

The girl sniffled again, dabbing the last of her tears away. "And they are?"

"First, don't let him be your blood bag."

Winifred's jaw dropped, and while Alice understood her exasperation, it drained her patience. "Open wounds are detrimental to the mortal immune system. If you care for his well being, you would stop."

Again, Winifred couldn't respond. "And the other favors?"

Alice pressed her lips together, wondering if it was wise to address it. "Do they need to spend so much time under trance?"

"That was just today," Winifred assured her. "I knew we had catching up to do, and they can't know we've already met—not unless we convince them and everyone they know that you grew up here. Well, you know what I mean—that you grew up with them and not their grandparents. Believe me, I did that, and I do *not* recommend it."

Did this explain why *everyone's* neck carried scars? Was it the mark of one who had seen too much hypnosis? Was the connection better when blood was involved?

"He knows I used to live here and that I moved back," Alice said.

"That's fine, I just... If he knows you're from my childhood, I can't predict what sort of inconsistencies he'll catch, you know? It isn't as if he'll ask me about them every time, so I won't know to fix them."

Alice nodded her understanding.

Winifred wiped the last of the remaining tears from her face. "Anything else?"

"That's it for now. I'll investigate Bri. In the meantime if there's another death in the area and my heart doesn't react, we'll know it's not Marius."

The girl absently nodded in agreement.

"Until next time, then?"

Winifred pressed her lips together, thinking. "Maybe not yet." Still, she kept thinking, and slowly she smiled then laughed to herself. "It's funny. I'm so used to humans and their early bedtimes, I almost forgot we can easily keep this going until the sun comes up."

It was a moment before Alice grasped the implication. "What did you have in mind?"

"There's something I want to show you." She pushed her hair back, glancing back at the car. "We needn't take the *mere mortals*," she playfully added, gradually coming back into her sprightly self. "They're good to drive. Well, Gabby is."

Alice frowned. While she was itching to get started with Bri, she couldn't find it in her to say no. "Alright."

"Alright? You'll go with me?"

"Yes."

"You're not mad at me?"

"No, I'm not mad at you."

The girl's smile widened with a combination of relief and excitement. "Gabby!" She glanced back over her shoulder. "Change of plan! You drive Theo home. You know the drill."

Gabby only stared straight through the windshield. It would've been impossible for her to not have heard, though nothing in her face implied she did.

Winifred peered up at Jack, gently holding his face between her hands. "Go home with Gabby and rest. I'll see you tomorrow." She kissed his mouth, and it seemed out of habit that he kissed back, lips barely moving. "I love you," she muttered.

"I love you, too," he replied, monotone.

She grinned. After ushering him toward the car and watching as he climbed into the passenger's seat, she turned back to Alice. "Shall we walk?"

Alice's gaze lingered as the boy closed the door behind him. "Yes," she replied when she remembered she was presented a question, though still she was too concerned to drop it. "Have they driven like this before?" Somehow this only scratched the surface of what she found wrong with this picture, though she couldn't place what the more grand issue was—if it was something aside from a remembered envy.

"Oh, yes. I wouldn't worry about it," Winifred answered. "I daresay it's safer than driving sober. I know they look half-asleep, but they're focused entirely on their goal, no distractions, just 'drive home.'"

Alice didn't find complete solace in this.

Winifred tilted her head toward the road. "It's not a long walk. This way."

Alice nodded and kept pace beside her.

The girl was right. It wasn't a long walk at all, though it was still difficult for Alice to gauge what was relatively short or long anymore, time-wise.

They had traveled beyond the sidewalk, following the road up a hill. Alice recognized this area. The road had widened since last she saw it eighty years ago, and the trees had grown taller and the terrain more worn, but finally there was an iota of recognition to be had in her hometown.

There was an old red church exactly where she remembered it. One room large, with a tall, narrow steeple. Fenced in at its side yard was a modest cemetery, its many tombstones eroded and cracked.

Winifred's pace slowed as her mind apparently drifted, and gradually she paused. "I realize this may be a morose gesture, but I meant it with the best intentions."

"What?"

Winifred grimaced, then continued the walk toward the church. "By the time Bishop saved me and I returned, you were both gone. Theo had a grave, and I looked but you didn't, though I heard you had died as well. No one would tell me where your body was, so…" She opened the gate into the cemetery, gesturing for Alice to follow. As she closed the gate behind them, she finished, "I did what I could with what I had."

Curious, Alice continued to follow her down the thin, muddy path up the hill. First she recognized her father's granite gravestone. Beside it stood a marble slab Alice had never seen. Winifred pointed at it with her nose, encouraging Alice to have a closer look. It read:

ETSU "ALICE" AISURU
1928-1948

"NEVER DID TOMBS LOOK SO GHASTLY WHITE. NEVER DID CYPRESS, OR YEW, OR JUNIPER SO SEEM THE EMBODIMENT OF FUNERAL GLOOM. NEVER DID TREE OR GRASS WAVE OR RUSTLE SO OMINOUSLY. NEVER DID BOUGH CREAK SO MYSTERIOUSLY, AND NEVER DID THE FAR-AWAY HOWLING OF DOGS SEND SUCH A WOEFUL PRESAGE THROUGH THE NIGHT."

"I heard what happened," Winifred explained, voice strained. "Stories and rumors. They said you were the monster. That you confessed to killing him, and laughed. I didn't believe any of it. They buried you unceremoniously, and I couldn't let that be your last impression on this world. Mortals are here for a blink in time's infinity, before they're dead forever. So in the end, all that will be left of us is our memory, and..." She took in a calming, staggering breath. "I wanted you to be remembered for who you really were, deep down. And for all your reading."

It was a moment before it clicked, though by the fourth quoted word Alice knew the epitaph sounded familiar. "This is from *Dracula*," she realized.

Winifred's grin slightly widened. "I remember the year we read it to each other, maybe twenty pages a night, for every day leading up to Halloween. We saw ourselves in Lucy and Mina—their kinship."

"And Lucy, with her three boyfriends."

"Not boyfriends!" Winifred laughed, and Alice laughed as well. Although both understood it was merely a joke, still Winifred defended it, "It wasn't her fault—or mine—that three men wanted her. There was only the one who she loved."

"And so that made me Mina."

Winifred ambled across the dirt to another tombstone, sighing in a near sing-song, "With her less dramatic, and overall more romantic situation."

Alice felt like an awful person every time she thought of him, but there sat his grave. *Eugene Hickory.*

Winifred nodded, staring downward. "That man adored you." When Alice followed her gaze, the death date struck her. September 15th, 1948. Their anniversary — the day she and Theo kissed in her kitchen.

Gene's father, Abe Hickory, pounding his fists on the front door before Bishop answered. "Where is he?" demanded Mr. Hickory —

Alice returned to herself just in time to glimpse Winifred grimace before peering back at her. "Was it too morose?" the girl asked, " Bringing you to your own grave?"

"Morose, maybe. I wouldn't say too much so. Just enough."

"Just how you like it?"

"Just how I like it."

Winifred smiled, and her lips quivered before she sobbed, then covered her mouth. "I'm sorry. I never expected I'd see you again, and it's just hitting me. You're here. You're really here." Again she sobbed, then squeezed her eyes shut.

Without a thought, Alice held her, and immediately Winifred's arms wrapped around her back. "Where have you been all this time?" she wailed, however muffled into Alice's shoulder.

"I've been—"

Theo, sitting beside her on the bed in her room one night while Bishop was at work. "You never did tell me how that date with Gene ended."

She wished she could tell him. "I don't want to talk about it." She wished she could at least come up with a half-truth.

"If you don't start talking, the evidence will, and you won't like what it has to say about you."

"Evidence?" This wasn't the direction she anticipated this to go. Finally she saw it—Theo's arms shaking. Barely holding himself together. "What are you saying?" she asked.

His voice was strained. "You were the last to see him."

"No, he took his car in after it crashed—someone at the lot would've seen him."

"So you were still there for the crash."

"Yes! Theo, what—"

He stood, eyes distant, pacing away. "There was no driving that car after the crash, Alice; I want to believe you, I really do—"

"He's... dead." Everything went distant. She meant it as a question, but her voice wouldn't go up that way.

He stopped with his hands on his hips, hanging his head, his back to her still. She caught his reflection in the window. Stone cold. "I want to believe you," he said, "but I can't let myself be stupid."

"You think it was me."

"Give me something. Anything."

"I don't know what happened!" she finally cried. She wasn't sure when she stood, but she crossed to him as if she would turn him around. She stopped with her arm mid-reach. She couldn't touch him when she was like this. She'd only transitioned yesterday; she didn't know her strength yet. "Look at me and tell me I'm lying!"

"I can't."

"Look at me and say I could so much have left his body if I knew he was..." She couldn't finish.

Still, he wouldn't turn around. "The second I look at you, I'm blinded," he uttered. "I can't do that."

She wracked her brain. She still wanted to tell him the truth, but he wouldn't believe it even if she did. "He was taking me out of town. My heart slowed, and I thought I would collapse again, so... I jumped out of the car." This much was true.

Now he found her gaze in the reflection.

"I'm fine," she assured him, holding her hands up as if inviting him to check. "Clearly. I didn't mean for it to distract him. I heard his voice after the crash, so I knew he was okay, but...I was so mad at him for not listening to me... I kept walking."

"From the spot of the crash? That would have been... ten miles?"

"I didn't know it would kill him."

He shook his head. "It wasn't the crash that did it."

Gene, wide-eyed, throat open and body mangled over the pavement, slumped against the car's front tire.

"Alice, talk to me, what's happening?"

She gasped when she returned to the present, her eyes level with the surrounding tombstones. Winifred kept her upright by the shoulders all along, watching her, wide-eyed. Both were kneeling.

"*Marius* killed Gene, right?" Alice asked, "Not me?"

Still clearly concerned, Winifred narrowed her eyes. "That's what I've heard?"

"But it happened the same day I transitioned. I blacked out, so I don't know."

It seemed to be a moment before Winifred grasped what it was that concerned her. "Was his blood on your mouth when you woke up?"

She gave it some thought, then calmed. "It wasn't."

Her old friend slowly nodded. "Now can you tell me why your eyes rolled back and you started convulsing like a possessed woman?"

Alice felt her eyes widen. No wonder Jack had appeared so concerned when she had flashed back to Theo at the diner.

She explained her situation as best she could. She wasn't prepared to share who truly killed Theo, but now Winifred knew Alice hadn't resurfaced until recently since she was first buried; and her memories of anything that happened since the day of her transition had been coming back in sudden, vivid bursts since the moment she first saw Jack. This was all clearly news to Winifred.

In turn, Winifred filled her in on what relevant information she could of the events between Alice's transition and burial. As Alice had gathered, the deaths didn't stop after Gene. At first they seemed random, but the community began to recognize a pattern after the fifth. They were all people who'd exhibited strong anti-Japanese sentiments, from signs in their shop windows to the countless vandalisms of Alice's own home. While Gene didn't quite fit the bill, she was the last to see him alive.

Alice did remember having come to these same realizations about the deaths before she and Theo kissed, but she didn't recall the town turning against her. It made sense for them to believe she was their Ripper. She was the intended scapegoat then. Now it was Jack.

Defining Choices,
2011

16. Playing Hooky

Alice

"Just like that, she's a harmless teddy bear?" This was what Crystal had to say when Alice told her how the previous night went. Because Crystal was out of school indefinitely (as far as the school knew, she was still at the hospital), they didn't have to wait to meet up. It was relatively early as the teen sat on Bishop's couch, Alice on the nearby sofa. Bishop leaned against a wall in the kitchen, undoubtedly too tired to trust that his eyes would stay open if he sat someplace comfy.

In response to Crystal's criticism, Alice grimaced. "I'm not saying Winifred's in the clear. I'll continue to watch and work with her, but in the meantime she's innocent until proven guilty."

Finally she noticed her own heartbeat. She must have been rebuilding her tolerance, for lately it would pulse at a regular rate even when she and Jack were in their respective homes. Before, it would only beat once every several minutes while maintaining such distance.

It was doing something especially unusual at the moment—this, or Jack was coming closer at inhuman speeds. The beats pounded exponentially faster and more intensely, *thmp-thmp, thmp-thmp*.

"I think it's time—" Bishop yawned, finishing his thought on the exhale. "—we wrapped this up?" It wasn't a question, or a suggestion. It was by mere chance his tone landed this way; Alice knew him well enough to know this.

Crystal shook her head with a slight shrug. "If that's it, that's it, I guess. I don't trust it for a second, though."

Now Alice heard the car as it pulled up the driveway and realized how foolish she was for not figuring it out sooner. Jack wasn't running at inhuman speeds; he was driving.

Crystal stood. "Well, Dr. Winston, as much as I love your super-piggyback rides, I'mma call me a cab."

Although the doctor nodded, it was clear it didn't register. He opened the door for her as if she was leaving immediately.

There stood Jack, about to knock. Bishop's grip on the doorknob hardened, denting the metal.

~Jack, Previously~

Jack awoke as if to the sound of screaming. It sent a spear through his skull, so he groaned and slapped at his nightstand until the alarm clock shut off. His head throbbed every second that followed.

Fuck school today.

Closing his eyes, he hoped that, by the time he woke up again, his hangover would be a non-factor.

How did the night with Alice end?! Jarring himself awake, he checked and saw it was 9 AM. If first impressions meant anything, Alice was a morning person—that's what he got from the business casual attire, anyway. He didn't have her number, but he knew where she lived. He had to verify for himself if she had made it home in one piece.

While his hangover had dulled to a numb cloud, to be safe he reached into his nightstand for the ibuprofen, popped three pills and washed it down with his flask-liquor. As was part of his morning routine, he packed a quick bowl and smoked, taking stupid-large hits in his haste. Once his head felt like a more peaceful cloud, he pulled on some clothes and hurried out the door to Gabby's car. Mom always dropped Gabby off at the community college on her way to work, which allowed Jack his own mode of transportation so he wouldn't need to deal with the assholes on the bus. He almost felt like he was abusing Gabby's generosity, but that didn't matter right now.

He strapped himself in the driver's seat and sped off. Alice didn't live far, but still he felt like he needed to be there five hours faster.

He wondered if he was taking weird, unnecessary measures to ensure her safety. He hadn't done the same for a lot of the others, though his reason for this was because they all should've known better. Alice still had no idea what he might've dragged her into.

But, on the other hand, maybe he was making it worse by trying to see her again. Maybe he was the stupid one this time.

With a frustrated grumble, he pulled over. The road was narrow and, with the trees so close, there was hardly a shoulder to sit at. He had to think quickly before some asshole could careen around the bend and smash into his side.

He let his forehead drop against the steering wheel, closing his eyes in the hopes of calming his head. Maybe it was only because he was high and paranoid that he doubted himself now. His sober decision was to check on her, and it made the most sense to trust his sober-self.

Compromising with fate, he decided he wouldn't need to be in her presence long. He would knock, see if she was alive, then leave before the killer could notice.

As reassured as he'd ever be, he turned back onto the road and finished the trip to her house, pulling up the driveway. It felt strange, jogging up the porch steps. A certain apprehension intensified as he neared the front door. People didn't just show up at people's houses unannounced anymore; this was weird.

He rose his knuckles to the door —

It opened. "Whoa," he said, hand still raised.

There stood a man, maybe forty years old, black. Jack felt like he had seen him before, this close.

The man's eyes widened. He had to blink once, hard, before looking at Jack again as if to reevaluate the situation. Finally he peered behind himself.

Jack followed his gaze, and —

"Good morning, Jack." There stood Alice in the living room, a few paces back. If she was surprised to see him, it didn't show.

He looked like a slob in her presence. The hems to his pants reached under his tattered shoes, and his graphic T was a size too big. His peacoat only gave him so many fashion points. Meanwhile, she wore a teal, billowy blouse tucked into a pencil skirt. With her hair half-up so her ears showed, her bangs curved over her forehead and the rest of her hair fell like black silk over her shoulders. Indigo jeweled flower-heads were pinned to her earlobes, and a short matching necklace hung just past her collarbones. Wherever she worked, she probably made more than both his parents had combined.

He didn't realize how little hope he had for the situation until he let out a breath he didn't know he held. She was there; the Ripper didn't get to her already.

"Hey," he finally greeted back. "I, uh, don't have your number, so…" He trailed off when he saw who stood beside her. "Crystal Robinson." Luke's girlfriend.

"That's me," the girl replied, shifting her gaze before any level of eye contact could linger. This was the effect he had on most girls lately. Most knew they weren't supposed to interact with him.

He stared, silent as he tried to wrap his head around it. "You're alive."

She allowed a small smile, and he knew she didn't fear him. "For sure," she said.

"Any chance you saw who it was?"

She glanced between the man at the door and Alice, then shook her head.

This wasn't a surprise, so he couldn't be too disappointed. The important part was that people were safe, and this was already far better news than he expected.

Clearing his throat, he shook his head, put out a hand for the man, and introduced himself. "Jack."

"Dr. Bishop Winston. Pleasure to meet you." The man's voice had a musical quality—deep, but soft enough to easily work for a woman.

Bishop motioned for Jack to step inside. It was only after the door was closed behind him that the doctor put out his own hand. They shook.

Now Jack had to think. He didn't need to be there anymore, so he had to go. This was the deal. He wondered if there was a way to do it without being weird, or if this was even a thing that mattered.

"What do you need?" Alice finally asked.

"I…" He scratched the back of his head. "I don't remember last night, so it was a good time?"

"It was a… Yes," she decided.

"Awesome. We should do it again," he offered, like an idiot.

"Something more memorable," she suggested.

He saw what she did there, but couldn't summon even a quick grin. "Yeah." Dropping his gaze, he shoved his hands in his jacket pockets. He had to stop acting like a fucking moron. "Yeah, uh… Yeah. Okay." He backed into the door, trying to find the doorknob without looking. After failing so many times, he turned around and let himself out like a regular person.

He hissed to himself as he jogged down the porch steps, "Why are you so fucking stupid?"

The creak of the front door. He spun around maybe too eagerly.

It was Crystal. Quickly she closed the door behind her. "Hey," she said as she neared. "Yeah, look, these guys don't drive cars, and a taxi's hella inconvenient. Think you can give me a ride?"

"Uhhh…" If he was a halfway decent person, he would've said no.

"It'd take maybe five minutes. No one will know, if you don't tell them."

Still it felt risky. But then, it looked like Crystal had already made it to the Ripper's list. Maybe it was too late for her and it didn't matter what he did anymore.

"Yeah," he finally said, gesturing toward his car.

"Awesome, thanks." She let herself in on the passenger's side.

He slowed as he mirrored her, thinking… This didn't feel right. Crystal in the car—sure, that was fine—but something was off. In a sense he felt he was leaving a job incomplete. He couldn't shake it.

He had sat and closed the door by the time he reached this conclusion. He put the key in the ignition, started the engine, but paused before he could put it in gear. "I gotta go back," he concluded.

"Why?"

He didn't get up yet. Now there was the guilt which crept up on him, and he wondered which sensation would be more easy to bear. It was difficult to measure, because he wasn't entirely sure what he intended to do once he got back there. Maybe set a date to this someday-plan they mentioned?

But this would have her killed.

"The Ripper attacked you for no reason, right?" he finally snapped, more flustered than intended.

"Uhhh yeah, pretty much," Crystal answered.

He nodded to himself. "So it doesn't matter what the fuck I do." Decision made, he opened the door and stepped out.

"You sure about that?" Crystal called through the window, voice rising an octave.

He almost paused, but it was too cold to not be moving.

He hadn't talked to the cheerleaders before they were attacked, so yeah, that was the only thing that made sense. It gave him a selfish freedom—selfish, because there was still the risk factor whether he liked it or not.

Closing his eyes and quickly shaking his head, he decided he didn't care anymore. If there was nothing he could do about it, what was the point in acting like there was? All he could do was live for the temporary friendships, mourn his losses, rinse and repeat.

He knocked on the door.

Again, Bishop answered. Alice now stood a few paces closer, and it was clear he had just interrupted a conversation.

"Hello again," she greeted.

"Hey," he said, every subsequent word tumbling out on the same breath, "So you're playing hooky too, right?"

She stared at him for a second. "What?"

"Not going to school? Or, work?"

"Oh." She looked away and squinted.

"And I'm playing hooky," he hinted.

"…Yes." She glanced at Bishop, as if for help, though all the man did was fight a grin and turn away.

Whether she understood his implication yet or not, Jack cut to the chase. "Wanna hang out?"

She smiled, though gradually it faded, her gaze falling on the window behind him. Finally she exchanged another look with Dr. Winston.

"A little sunlight wouldn't kill you," he said.

She watched him as if she didn't trust it, but when she finally returned her gaze to Jack, she nodded.

He mimicked her nod. He thought he'd be happier with his decision, but the guilt was overbearing—she still didn't know. But he couldn't back down now.

"Alright," he said. "I gotta drop Crystal off first, so we can go and figure the rest from there, I guess."

She subtly grinned, and this made him feel a little better. Upon grabbing her woolen jacket from the nearby dining chair, she said, "I'm ready when you are."

"Alright." He opened the door for them, remembering this time to turn to her dad and say, "It was good meeting you, Dr. Winston."

"And you as well, Maverick. Sorry, Jack. Jack."

Was this her dad? Or, was this her boyfriend? Roommate?

Alice squinted, adding a level of confusion to her farewell grin to Bishop. With the proper pleasantries exchanged, they were good to leave the cabin and hurry through the cold and to the car.

~Alice~

Sunlight. It had been so long, Alice had forgotten how bright it was, even when the sky was overcast. The fourth color of night was less noticeable, but still present. She used her hand for a visor. Even through the autumn chill, she felt the day's warmth bathe her skin. She didn't think she'd ever experience this again.

Crystal's muffled voice grumbled, "*Stupid*, stupid-stupid fucking cute-ass motherfuckin' Justin Bieber-lookin' death-bomb gonna get us all six feet under."

Alice spotted her in the passenger's seat to Gabby's car. The teenager's eyes widened with a combination of shock and frustration when she saw Alice approach, and when she spoke Alice knew she wasn't meant to hear. "Stupid-ass-bitch, why'd you say yes?"

The domsuco shot her a discreet look in the hopes of re-minding her of her hearing ability. It worked, though the girl wasn't intent on taking anything back. She didn't speak any louder, but more purposefully directed. "Why'd you say yes?!"

Jack walked around to the driver's side, Alice taking the seat behind him.

"Alright," he said, "which way are we going?"

"Head toward town and I'll tell you when to turn," Crystal answered, elbow to the door with her head in her hand.

He nodded, and before shifting it in gear he pressed the button to what Alice assumed was the radio—

Static, screaming and feedback, all at once, and she didn't know what was happening, but she gasped and gripped the door handle. If there was a such thing as monsters besides the domsuco, it was this, and in a shrill, grating voice it shrieked of its own suffering

More screaming.

No. Laughing.

Crystal was cracking up.

A low, "Sorry," from Jack's direction, and as he turned the dial the satan spawn quieted. He pressed a button and the noise cut out as soon as music began to play.

"Girl thought she was dying!" Crystal howled.

Alice knew what she wanted to ask — *What in the world was that?* — but if it was common knowledge, she didn't want to date herself. Was that meant to be *music?*

She lowered her arm from the door and released the handle, which fell in her lap. It was a moment before she realized what this meant. "I'm sorry, I…broke your door."

He peered back, and his eyebrows rose when he saw. "Well, damn." He stared for a second longer, lacking a response. "Uh. Don't worry about that, I'll…deal with it; here, put it wherever."

She placed it on the seat beside her.

He put the car in gear and began the drive. They had only made it past the driveway when he glimpsed Alice through the rearview mirror and asked, "So you know about the Halloween dance, right?"

"Yeah," Crystal answered.

He glanced at her, then back at the road. "That's… Cool. Alice?"

She shook her head and didn't think to verbalize it for him. She had forgotten about holidays. They seemed like a thing of the past; they were human. While she missed participating, she doubted society had room for her. "I don't," she finally answered aloud.

"I don't think she even goes to our school," Crystal added.

"You get one out-of-town guest, though, right?"

"I don't know, I don't think so."

It didn't matter; Jack was quite certain. He glanced back at Alice and directly stated, "Right, well it's tomorrow. You should stop by."

This was the third thing he invited her to. When he initially invited her out for the day, she assumed it was because he was still trying to fulfill her trance-order, and if she denied him it would drive him mad. Now she was unsure. Her only commands were to *invite me out someplace,* and *let's chat.* Technically, he had done both.

But he had to have still been following her orders; she couldn't have left so great of an impression as to warrant this.

She bit her lip. She wished there was a way to know if he was acting of his own free will; she hadn't yet learned the extent of her power. Was she so strong that, even after her orders were fulfilled, a lingering urge to fulfill them would remain?

If he was any other person in a regular situation, she might've put him back under trance and told him he wasn't obligated to do anything for her anymore. However, after seeing how Winifred took full advantage of this ability, she doubted more tampering with his mind was the answer.

In any case, the thought of a high school dance made her anxious. If it was anything akin to the Velvet's atmosphere, she wasn't sure she could participate without coming across as an old lady trapped in a young girl's body. Winifred saved her the embarrassment last time, though she couldn't depend on distractions forever. She needed to learn the culture.

"Hello?" Jack glanced at her again before returning his gaze to the road, and she realized she had been quiet for a while when she should have formed a response.

Crystal replied for her, "Girl can't dance for shit."

"More importantly," Alice began, "wouldn't you go with Winifred?"

His brow furrowed, but then, "Oh! Wyn, yeah, I'm going with her; just extending an invite. Bring whoever; we'll get them in." He looked both ways before taking the road left, muttering, "Winifred."

Alice further considered his invitation. Perhaps he wasn't acting under anyone's influence. Perhaps he did genuinely want to see her again. In which case… It felt nice to be wanted.

"I'll go," she decided.

Jack nodded. Crystal, however, was not satisfied. "You mind stopping at a gas station real fast?" she asked.

He checked his fuel. "Sure." There was a station just ahead, which he pulled into.

"I need cigarettes," the girl explained, then turned back to Alice. "You should come with me."

Jack pulled up to a pump and parked. His motions slowed as he distractedly unbuckled his seatbelt, then peered back at Alice through the rearview mirror. She wasn't sure what her face might've betrayed.

With a solemn nod which said, *I should've seen this coming,* Jack stepped out of the vehicle. When Alice reached for her handle, she remembered she had broken it off. Jack opened her door before she even considered asking for help.

"Thank you," she muttered as she stepped out.

He nodded and closed the door behind her. He wouldn't look at her; he was cutting her out from his thoughts and she despised it.

Alice followed Crystal into the convenience store. There was a small, but slow line at the register, which gave them ample time to chat. The mortal teen began her rant in a low hush the second they stepped inside. " 'Hey, wanna play hooky?' 'Sure!' 'Wanna go to the dance?' 'Okay.' 'Hey, let's catch a movie and make out at the back of the theater.' 'Alright.'"

"I just met him," Alice intoned.

Crystal darkly laughed into her hand. "Well it's a good thing we're not dealing with a psycho-ass bitch!" She was apparently convinced Winifred was the Ripper.

Alice turned her gaze to the front of the line. She only had that much longer to deal with this.

"I just met him," Crystal mimicked, and she captured Alice's character surprisingly well. It was clear when she reverted back to herself. "Really? You just met—You think *she* cares?"

"We don't know who it is," Alice reminded her.

"Right, and that totally invalidates everything I just said."

"Assume the Ripper *does* come after me, what difference is it to you?"

"As far as I know, you're the only one who cares and who's strong enough to deal with her, and you're going in blind. What if she's stronger than you, or smarter than you? She takes you out, and then who's left to take care of this? Dr. Winston? For some reason I don't think he's all about that life."

Alice acknowledged this with the bite of her lip. But she didn't want to reject Jack's invitation. She genuinely wanted to get to know him. Whether it was because he looked like Theo or not, she… She enjoyed his company.

But Crystal had a point, and while Alice had to be near him for the sake of having a tell on whether or not Marius was close, she didn't have to interact with him to do it. He didn't need to know she was present.

Alice peered out the window and found Jack sitting against the car, his back to her, waiting with his head bowed and his hands in his pockets.

"Think of the bigger picture," Crystal pressed.

"I am," Alice snapped back. "This whole ordeal has dictated so much of his life, now he barely has one. Winifred has to break into his mind every few months just so he won't kill himself—no one deserves to live this way—"

"That's not the bigger picture," Crystal interjected, but Alice wasn't finished.

She hissed, "If I'm the only one who can hold up against the Ripper, I'm the only one who can be his friend without facing consequences."

"No, see, that's the *problem!*" Crystal hissed back, "You're thinking like a hero with a damsel in distress; you care about one life versus the several that would suffer, because you're choosing to ignore that once this bitch feels threatened, she's killing us all."

Alice crossed her arms over her chest. "How do you figure that?"

"She kills whoever's flirting with him—or can be perceived as flirting with him—which would be all fine and good if she could kill you easily—and I mean 'you,' specifically—because if she can't, what do you think she'll do? Try and fight you anyway, fair and square? Not fight at all; let you get away with it? Or, I don't know, take it out on the rest of us because we're easy targets and killing makes her feel good?"

Alice pressed her lips together, thinking. Because she didn't know who the killer was, she couldn't pretend to know how he or she would react. If it was Marius, none of this would matter.

Crystal glanced back at the front of the line. They only had so much time left to discuss this. "Alright. Jack's gonna drive me home first. Make up some shit, ditch your hooky-date, and quit the flirting."

~Jack~

Jack could hardly focus. When he first attempted to put the gas pump to the tank, he missed. He missed on his second attempt, and raised the pump high in preparation to slam it against the side before he reminded himself this wasn't his vehicle. It was Gabby's, and she didn't deserve this. He already had to fix the door handle.

His breath was shallow. He needed air, but he was already outside. His hands shook. It was cold, though he barely noticed.

He was so close. He might not have been so upset if he wasn't so close to building something new. Fresh. The close circle of people he'd been left with since all his old friends had died or shunned him, it was too tight—suffocating. Alice was like fresh air, and while he was more ready to call it a fleeting sensation before, he wasn't now. He'd gotten his hopes up. Like an idiot.

Who was he kidding, though, who was he fucking kidding. Yet, of all the ways this could've ended, this was probably the best. Crystal would tell Alice what the deal with him was, Alice would avoid him, and that would be the end of that. Her chances of getting out alive would be that much better. He should've been happy for her. If he had any sort of conscience, he would've been.

But *fuck* everything.

He finally got the nozzle in and pulled the lever. Shit was too shitty for him to be sober. The second he got home, within ten minutes the flask in his pocket would be empty. It wouldn't *numb the pain,* as the cliché went, but at the very least it would muddle his thoughts so that he literally couldn't think about anything anymore. He could hope to black out and forget how shitty he felt when he started. It was the closest he could get to being dead without actually killing himself.

He took a few deep breaths and squeezed his eyes shut. His head hurt. His breath shuttered on an exhale. He had to pull himself together before the girls came back. This was assuming they wouldn't call a taxi and ditch him.

He leaned his back against the car while he waited, shoulders up and chin lowered to keep his neck warm, hands balled in his pockets. Slowing his breath, he took the part of himself that made him human and buried it in the deepest recesses of his mind. The intention was to have a scarecrow in its place: blank yet cold on the outside, nothing on the inside. Nice and numb.

His breathing was back. When the gas was done, it was a steady hand that withdrew the nozzle and placed it back where it belonged. Alice and Crystal approached just as he turned to let himself back in the car. "Got what you needed?" he asked, deadpan.

"Yup." Crystal took back her spot in the passenger's seat.

He peered Alice's way, and it was so obvious Crystal had told her. Alice was quiet, eyes distant, mouth rigid in preparation to deliver bad news. It seemed to have been an accident when her gaze met his, and in that moment both knew they read the other perfectly—her face said it all: *I'm so sorry.*

He let out a breath through his nose. So was he.

Alice sat behind Crystal this time. Possibly because it was most convenient, since that was the side closest to the convenience store. Or, possibly because it was furthest from him.

He wasted no time in recommencing their journey. He didn't think to ask Crystal which way to exit the gas station; luckily he'd guessed correctly. She gave him directions here and there, though aside from this, no one said anything.

It wasn't until after he parked and Crystal made it up her porch steps and into her house that Jack and Alice exchanged any words. This didn't mean he looked at her, though.

"Want shotgun?" he asked.

No immediate response. As he peered back, she unbuckled her seatbelt, then stepped out. She took the seat beside him before he could get too tangled in his thoughts. Again, she seemed distracted—perturbed, jaw stiff as she gnawed her lip and stared intently through the windshield. He waited. He knew what was coming, and the more she stalled, the more he wanted to skip this conversation, drop everything and drown in a flask.

Maybe he was being paranoid. Maybe Crystal was trying to discreetly ask for a tampon or something—whatever girls needed other girls for. Maybe Alice still didn't know.

In any case, it was too quiet for too long. "So, um." He gestured toward Crystal's house. "How do you know her?"

"I took her to the hospital."

He was about to adjust the heat, but paused. "You mean... Recently?" If this was the case, then she knew all along. Although, maybe not. All that was certain was she knew the brutal shit the Ripper was capable of—not the targets or the accused.

She nodded. She took Crystal to the hospital recently.

Now there was only one more question to ask. "Then—" His voice cracked, so he stopped it right there. Breathed. Tried again, although his throat hurt. "So then you know how all the girls..." He didn't want to say it, so looked at her and hoped she would get it without further prompting.

Again, she nodded. She wouldn't look at him; her eyes fell on his fingers as they hovered over the air dial. He followed her gaze and noted how his hand shook. However embarrassed, he wouldn't wallow in it for long. He finished adjusting the heat and firmly planted both hands on the steering wheel. Knowing how his voice would continue to crack if he relied too heavily on it, he instead spoke in a grumble, using the back of his throat. "I can drive you home, if you want."

She bit her lip again as if she wanted to reject the offer, but instead closed her eyes and said, "Yes."

He nodded. Just as he suspected. He wanted to beat the steering wheel and drive as fast as he could, windows down and music blaring, but he was too aware of how reckless this would be. He wouldn't have minded crashing, but this wasn't his car, and Alice was with him.

He needed his own car.

He pulled himself out of this fantasy with an attempt at a deep breath. "Alright," he said, shifting them from parked to drive. He pulled the car around to avoid using the reverse, then carefully took the rocky driveway downhill.

Neither said anything all the way back to her place, and it was still deathly quiet as he painstakingly pulled up the long driveway to her remote cabin.

Once he parked, she didn't immediately try to get out. "I'm sorry," she finally muttered, softer than the hum of the engine.

He nodded in acknowledgement. He wouldn't risk speaking right now.

Still, she didn't leave. He heard her breath stutter on what to say next.

Last year when his female friends decided seeing him was too much of a risk, most of them clarified, *You're really cool, I just value my life.* This never made him feel better, so he spared himself the pitying look on her face and kept his attention on the windshield.

"Listen," he grumbled, "this doesn't need to be a whole thing. You can just go. I get it."

Silence.

"Alright," she said, just as quiet as before. "This will end soon. I'll see you then."

While the optimism was refreshing, he couldn't pretend he felt the same. Again, he nodded. Finally she stepped out and pushed the door shut behind her.

He looked to his pocket where his flask resided. He was still in Gabby's car, so he still had to at least wait until he got home before having at it.

He put the car back into gear and left. While it only took a few minutes to get home, the wait was an agonizing mental loop of needing alcohol, needing pain, and needing to die. Even once he reached the loose gravel of his driveway, the wait was unbearable. This was a safe enough distance, he figured; he pulled the flask from his jeans pocket.

"Jack," called a sharp, authoritative male voice.

Jack jumped out of his skin, heart pounding as he fumbled to stuff the flask back. *Fuck fuck fuck fuck fuck —*

Sarah's bio-dad stood leaning against his police car at the top of the driveway before beginning his approach. Jack slowed to a stop as the detective neared his window. Unfazed by Jack's obvious distress, Lloyd glanced at the teen's pocket and proceeded as if it didn't matter. "You need to come with me."

"Says who?" Jack snapped, adrenaline rushing. He was hopeful he'd had the flask away before the detective could've seen it, but he couldn't be sure.

"Says Miss Briana Benson," the older man answered.

Bri. The diner waitress.

Jack clenched his jaw, closed his eyes and inhaled deeply. This wasn't a surprise. Today was just the day for the universe to shit on him. "What's the connection this time?"

Detective Lloyd nodded back toward the police car with no obvious intention to answer. Yet, there was also no sarcasm. No aggression. Just focus and determination. This was…different.

Curious, Jack parked Gabby's car in its spot and followed the detective's lead.

17. Briana Benson

Jack

Cruising through the woods away from the general public, it didn't look like they were headed to the police station. Slinking low in the back seat to avoid chances of unwanted attention, Jack asked, "Where are we going?"

Detective Gerald Lloyd's hardened blue gaze found Jack through the rearview mirror, then scanned left and right before carefully making his turn. "Robinson was right; this isn't adding up," the detective grumbled to himself. "I owe her an apology and a spa day."

Jack's attention was piqued, but he wouldn't get his hopes up yet. This could have been a trick. That same familiar tactic of lulling him into a false sense of security, except now they were doing it outside the confines of the interrogation room.

"What did you find?" Jack asked anyway. "When did Bri die?" If the cops were at least pretending to be on his side, this gave him the opportunity to know what they knew, and to freely mention his own thoughts on the case.

"Okay, easy there," Lloyd chided with an annoyed grimace. "Just because it doesn't add up doesn't mean it wasn't you."

Exasperated, Jack all but yelled, "How the fuck—!?"

"Stop and just listen, okay?" the detective whined before apprehensively sucking his teeth. After some hesitation, he glanced back through the rearview mirror again and asked, "When was the last time you saw Briana Benson?"

"Uh, last time I was at the diner with Wyn. About a week ago. *Is* she dead?"

The detective nodded to himself, not in answer. "Right, and you're an observant kid, aren't you?"

Dude wouldn't stop dodging questions. Annoyed, Jack did the same back. "Can you tell me *anything?*"

Lloyd stuck to his script, unfazed. "Since Robinson's been in the hospital, has *anyone* been watching you?" Maybe he wasn't trying to be a dick. Maybe he was too focused to be distracted with questions that wouldn't help him.

Despite his lingering bitterness, Jack focused on what was asked. He didn't think Officer Robinson was even officially watching him. It seemed more like she was taking it upon herself during her free time. But what was Lloyd talking about; was there supposed to be an unmarked van stationed outside Jack's house every day?

"I'll answer that for you," Lloyd continued. "No one has. You're under investigation, yet no one is actually looking into you."

"But everyone thinks it's me."

"That's the difference between looking and thinking, and that's what makes this all so...freaky." The detective pulled over as far as the woods would let him. "You know where we are?"

Jack did know. It was Maple Street, before it turned into Maple Lane. Where Sarah used to live. "I'd still like to know *why*," he replied.

"This is where your dad's car was found, but on the other side."

"...Okay?"

Lloyd squinted and twisted in his seat, indignant. " '*Okay?*' Fucking punk — I'm giving you the benefit of the doubt; the least you can do is show some respect!"

"I didn't mean any disrespect!"

"Moving on." Not at all satisfied, Lloyd pulled back onto the road and pointed back at the spot where Jack's dad's car was found. "Remember that." They resumed the drive.

"So, everyone's convinced it's the obvious suspect: you," Lloyd continued. "Yet no one's investigating you. On paper everything looks right, but in practice—*somehow*—*everyone* dropped the ball, assuming someone else was taking care of it. That doesn't just happen, kid — that's someone tampering with the system, or — or — just, not the kind of thing that happens in a town like this, and not the kind of thing that happens for just anybody. I knew this already, but I looked into it to be sure, and it's just as I'd suspected: you're not anybody."

"Thanks," Jack said flatly, knowing full well the jab was intentional.

"No one in this town is," Lloyd added as if it wasn't. "We don't have celebrities, or millionaires, or high-standing politicians. So just *how* are you getting the same technical leniency as a crooked cop?"

Jack twisted his mouth in thought. While his day-to-day experience didn't *feel* like special treatment, it apparently was. But why was he special? Someone with connections, or some kind of pull in the police force, seemed to think he was. But if they were really so powerful, why was Jack still under investigation in the first place? Was this legal limbo supposed to be a blessing, or was it supposed to be torture? After all, if no one was investigating him, it meant there wouldn't be anyone to see for themselves that Jack wasn't going around killing girls.

"Investigate me, then," Jack offered.

Detective Lloyd shook his head. "Too obvious. Due to clear personal ties to…the first victim…"

Jack nodded. They were in the same boat, not wanting to say her name, especially when it was in relation to her death.

Sarah's bio-dad cleared his throat. "I'm barred from working the case, which is why I'm investigating Miss Briana instead."

"Is she still alive?"

"I'm getting there."

They pulled up to Sarah's old house and Jack's skin crawled the opposite direction. Seeing this place used to put him at ease, but now the oak tree stole his focus and put him back in the horror movie scene from last year, even in broad daylight.

A cheap plastic sign with bright red vinyl lettering stuck out of the lawn to say, "FOR SALE." It had been there for over a year now. The vacant house had two counts against it, being that there wasn't much of a demand for property in Sabertown, and someone had died there.

"Do we need to be here?" Jack managed around the growing lump in his throat.

"In a minute." Detective Lloyd put the car in park and turned off the engine. "Based on the Ripper's most apparent MO, Miss Briana Benson is next. She hasn't been to work in a few days. Did you know that?"

"I haven't been back to the diner since last week, so no."

"Well, I noticed and asked the other waitresses about it. Sorry, 'servers;' you kids like that gender neutral shit these days, don't you." Not allowing Jack a response, Lloyd plowed ahead, "The servers looked at me like I had two heads, like they didn't know what I was asking. I had to find three different ways to ask if they knew where she was, and finally it's like they woke up and realized they hadn't seen her in a few days."

Jack's brow furrowed.

Lloyd saw. "It gets stranger, right? So I go to her house to see if she's there. Her parents answer and say she's fine, she's just in bed with the flu. I'm not satisfied; I need to see it for myself, so I ask if I can see her anyway and just ask her a few questions—about you, so they wouldn't worry and think she's in trouble with the law, and so maybe they'd talk some sense into her and see how risky it is, being a girl and talking to you."

"I tried to tell her—"

"That's fine," Lloyd said dismissively. "So they show me her room, and I see an empty bed. I ask where she is, and they're confused—*they* look at me like I have two heads, even though they're *right there with me* and can *easily see she isn't there.*"

Jack stared at him blankly. "I don't get it."

With a manic chuckle, Lloyd inclined his head, waved a hand from the steering wheel and cried, "You're telling me! I had to *argue with them* for five minutes before they admitted she wasn't there! But they acted *surprised* about it. But then…" The detective pressed his lips closed in a tight line before uttering, "If it was only them, I could say they were committed actors, but with the servers, too… They looked scared. They looked genuinely surprised that she wasn't there — like they really believed she *was* there, even while all of us were in the room and she wasn't. They said her car

hadn't left the driveway in days... You ever done psyche-
delics?"

"No." Jack didn't have to lie for this one.

"Right, like you'd say anything different." Lloyd turned
his gaze out the window, still antsy with his different
thoughts. "Well, *I* haven't. I don't know if it's possible they
could've been under the influence, and that's why..." He
grimaced. "But the servers, too?"

While the detective silently mulled this over, Jack did the
same. He almost wanted to ask if mind control was a real
thing, but he kept that dumb idea to himself.

Finally the detective stepped out of his car and said, "I
came here to see what I could see with this new...perspec-
tive." He opened Jack's door, too, but the teen was reluctant
to step out.

"I'd rather not," he said.

Impatient, Lloyd argued, "If I can do it, you can, too."

Jack grimaced but obliged, even while his whole body
felt weak and shaky. He needed to know what else the detective knew.

"Abandoned vehicles are a rare thing, when the paper-
work's fine and the machinery works," Lloyd began. He
closed Jack's door behind him and led the way through the

lawn. "Seeing your dad's the way it was, I always suspected foul play, but I didn't have enough to piece it all together. I also remember he was a PI, right?"

"Yeah," Jack answered, miffed but keeping it to himself. He'd already figured his dad was probably dead, but he still didn't feel right talking about him in the past tense.

"Right, so I figure he was on my same train of thought, coming here for perspective—rather, he was on his way back *after* finding perspective, just before he went missing. So now I gotta think, did he find something? What did he find? What *could* he have found, that none of us had?" Lloyd stood dead center of the lawn, under the shade of the oak tree, hands on his hips as he surveyed the surrounding houses. "I kicked that thought out of my head because, again, I had to remember this case isn't being handled right, from the very beginning. What could a guy do without clearance? He can talk to people who are willing to talk; he can find a witness. Lucky for me, I've known all the neighbors for a while now, and they all know me."

Jack nodded. "Since you used to live here."

Lloyd lifted a hand for silence like he was swatting a fly. "I checked in on all of them. Casual conversation. I learned the grandpa across the street died. 'Oh, I'm so sorry to hear, when did this happen?' 'Oh, about seven months ago. He died peacefully in his sleep.' Who else died seven months ago?"

Jack couldn't keep letting it go. "Who the fuck said he died? Did you find a body?"

Lloyd sighed through his nose and closed his eyes. Although annoyed, he knew Jack had a right to be, too. "Sorry. Missing. But do you see what I'm saying?"

Jack turned away and tried to objectively replay his words. By casually looking up, his gaze happened upon the stub from the tree that used to hold a longer branch. He couldn't look away. He forgot what he was supposed to be thinking about.

Lloyd continued, "The grandpa was a witness. I'd bet my life on it, and I'd bet my life that the Ripper killed him, and… I'm sorry, kid, but I'm pretty sure he killed your dad, too. And somehow this maniac is, I don't know, drugging everybody into believing nonsense stories, so it's likely he's killed more than just the girls you talk to. And for whatever reason, those are the only deaths he wants anyone to know about."

Jack nodded. He heard him, but he couldn't bring himself back to the conversation fully enough to form a response.

"What are you looking at?" Finally Lloyd stepped closer to the tree and followed Jack's gaze.

"You weren't there," Jack muttered. He had to believe this was why Sarah's dad wasn't responding the same way he was to just being there. The man hadn't seen her body until after she was moved.

When Lloyd seemed to see what Jack was looking at, he softened. "Was that...the branch?"

Jack didn't want his voice to keep betraying him, so he didn't voice an answer. At the same time, he was angry enough at the detective that he felt justified in withholding a *little* something, so he wouldn't even nod.

"Why did we have to come here?" the teen managed with the back of his throat. He didn't need this today. He'd already lost Alice; he didn't need to relive losing Sarah, too.

Lloyd nodded to himself and motioned for Jack to head back to the car. Jack went ahead without question, grateful to dip into the backseat.

The detective began the drive back the direction they came. Some minutes in, he made a noise at the back of his throat in preparation to speak, though he hesitated. Finally he grimaced and got it over with. "It was a test."

Silence. Jack let it register. "A test?"

"Yup."

"Bringing me here…was a test."

Lloyd's grimace deepened. "Yee-ah."

Silence. Jack squeezed his eyes shut, and anytime he recalled Sarah's vacant gaze, he'd instead imagine busting through the separation to the front seat and throttling her bio-dad. This calmed him enough to keep his voice low and even when he asked, "Did you think I wouldn't care?"

"I didn't know what to expect one way or another."

"You were there when we started dating."

Lloyd's face softened with what could've been guilt, and he tried to cut in with, "Alright — "

"I got your blessing before I bought the ring."

"I know I — "

"She said yes!" Jack couldn't help his voice rising as he violently gestured toward the direction of the school. "Someone saw it in the courtyard! The cameras would've seen it!"

Lloyd's tired gaze found Jack's through the rearview mirror. The security footage had a history of prematurely erasing itself, and no one stepped up to being the person who saw them. "Jack —" the detective began with the intonation of someone who was about to follow with, *we've been over this.*

"So why the fuck would I kill her?!" Jack's voice cracked, and after this telling sign of his emotions getting the best of him, he gave in and beat his hands against the separation, yelling, "*Why the fuck would I kill her?!*"

Lloyd sighed through his nose and leaned his head back, cruising with professional attention.

Jack continued, "Even if she did break up with me, do you know what I would've done?" He waited a beat to pretend to give her dad a chance to respond, then bellowed, "*Not fucking kill her!* Yeah, I would've been heartbroken!" he screamed, hoarse already. "I would've cried, I would've been confused, I would've wanted to know why, I would've done all I could to change, to get her back! But I didn't need to because *she fucking said yes! We could've been happy!*"

"Alright, are you done?" Lloyd finally yelled back.

Jack sat back in his seat, still fuming, but fully aware that shouting wasn't helping his situation. His arms were shaking.

Breathing heavy through his own stress, Lloyd eventually added, "You passed the test. Flying colors. Now chill out."

While the thought was loud in Jack's head, it came out mousy. "Why wouldn't you believe me?"

Lloyd's gaze softened again, even as it was still focused on the road. "I was angry, and you were there. Even if you aren't the Ripper, she... If you were dating someone else..."

ack saw where he was going with this because he'd had this thought, too. If Jack wasn't dating Sarah, she'd still be alive.

Neither said anything until they were most of the way back to Jack's house. "What now?" the teen asked.

"Now I look for Briana Benson and investigate any other deaths or missing persons in this town," Lloyd grumbled, having his work cut out for him.

Jack nodded in acknowledgement. "You won't tell anyone you think I could be innocent, right?"

"That'd be the smart thing to do, wouldn't it."

"If you don't wanna end up like my dad or Officer Robinson."

The detective nodded, grim. "That means if you find any-thing, you can't contact me. You contact the station, under-stand?"

Jack nodded.

Lloyd absently nodded back. "Anything else?"

Jack doubted he'd have an opportunity like this again, so he racked his brain. "Do you know anything about a new girl in town?"

"Another Kimberly Michaels?"

"Basically, but she's not dead yet."

"What's her name?"

"Alice."

"Last name?"

"Don't know."

"Does she go to your school?"

"Don't think so."

Detective Gerald Lloyd twisted his mouth, thinking.

"But I know where she lives," Jack offered.

"Well if that isn't all the information a serial killer would need."

While Jack knew he wasn't being serious, he couldn't help shooting the detective an agitated look which said something along the lines of, *dude.* "We decided to stop hanging out and it's kinda fresh, so can you not?"

Lloyd chuckled with sick pleasure. "Okay, where does she live?"

Jack rolled his eyes and told him as they began up his driveway.

The middle-aged man squinted through the windshield. "Is that her?"

Jack jumped up. "What?"

Sure enough, there she sat, waiting on his porch steps. While Gabby and his mom were still out for the day, Grandma Ruth was home to let her in. It was possible Alice hadn't knocked.

"What the fuck," Jack breathed.

Alice's eyes pinched with concern as she took in his mode of transportation, and she said something to herself that could've been, "Oh, no."

"Should I take her in for questioning?" Lloyd offered.

"No. I don't know. I don't know why she's here — we *literally* just said she shouldn't be near me. She initiated it!"

She hastily stood and approached, even as the car continued up the driveway. Her strides shortened comically as she slowed to keep herself at his window. "Jack," she said as if she had been holding it in all along, muffled through the glass.

"I'm fine," he answered, over-articulating so she would read his lips easily.

"What happened?" she asked.

"Why are you here?" he shot back.

"*What happened?*" She didn't seem offended that he didn't answer her question; just too worried to give a damn.

The detective chuckled. "She's as stubborn as you are."

Jack slapped the back of his seat then looked Alice square in the eye. *"Why are you here?"* He didn't care that she was worried; she had no right to flip flop with him like this.

She held his gaze long enough for him to see she was accepting the challenge—to see who would cave and answer first. Her eyes were dark gray, like mirrors. He saw himself and everything around him reflected so clearly in them, even through the glass of the window.

Lloyd put the car in park and, with that same sick pleasure, stepped out and offered Alice a wide, friendly grin. "Good afternoon, miss. I hear you're new in town?"

"What happened?" she asked him instead, attitude unchanged.

"Oh, nothing new," he answered, dripping with sarcasm even while there was not a lie to be found. He patted the hood above Jack's head and added, "Just checking in on Sabertown's own Jack the Ripper. He kills girls, you know?"

She narrowed her eyes at the detective, unwavering. "So they say."

Lloyd grimaced through the grin when he peered down at Jack. "What is it about you, kid? The boyband haircut? Your stupid face?"

"You *can* just let me out now," Jack offered.

"Yeah, yeah, in a minute."

"You and your fucking minutes."

Lloyd redirected his attention to Alice. "What makes you think you're not next?"

"Nothing."

Lloyd's head tilted and his eyebrows rose in genuine surprise, taken off course from a conversation he'd likely rehearsed. "You mean, you don't think you'll die?"

"I've answered all I care to answer. Can he go now?"

He let out his air on a low whistle as he turned back toward his car. "Oh-kay." He returned to his front seat and turned toward Jack, lowering his voice so only he would hear. "She's more of an Ashley Baker. Good luck getting rid of her."

Jack scrunched his mouth. He was thinking the same thing. Ashley was brave and thought she at least had a chance. It didn't matter how many times Jack tried to warn her.

Lloyd opened the door and Jack spilled out without a second to waste. The teen slammed the door shut, began the uphill incline and motioned for Alice to follow.

"Just don't be following them home, alright?" Lloyd called after him. "We talked about this!"

"Very funny!" Jack called back.

Lloyd cackled and drove off.

Alice glared back at him, silent until the police car was out of sight. "I never liked cops."

Taken aback, Jack observed her. She didn't seem like the type. Too professional; too clean. "You've had run-ins before?" he asked.

"It was 1948 — practically," she added. "Where I used to live." Jack didn't know enough about history to know what she meant by this, but he let her continue.

She set her jaw. "Cops everywhere, they're just a reflection of the town as a whole, but with the power and self entitlement to do whatever they want about it."

This didn't answer the question, but was something to chew on.

Jack waited. When Alice looked away from the road and found his gaze, her eyes softened. "I'm sorry. What happened?"

"Just questioning. Nothing new. Why are you here? Did you leave something in the car?" That had to be it.

She examined him briefly, eyes flitting as if scanning his soul for any tells. Finally she accepted his answer and looked away. "This…" She gestured broadly to imply the whole situation. She bit her lip, then sighed, eyes lowered. "This has scared everyone else away, hasn't it?"

"Or killed them." This wouldn't help his case, but he had to make sure she understood. Finally, he was trying to do the right thing.

The struggle raged in her faraway eyes until she nodded subtly to herself and asked, "What did you have planned for hooky?"

Everything went still. He didn't know he was staring at her until she returned the gaze. If ever she seemed uncertain before, now was not one of those times.

"You know how quick this killer is, right?" he asked. "A whole year, and still no one has even the slightest idea who it could be?"

"I'm aware."

"Girls who go out of their way to talk to me end up dead within the week."

"I'll be careful."

"You don't think they were? Sticking to lit streets and traveling in packs—means nothing when this guy's killing you in your sleep."

Alice looked to the woods, thinking.

"You're not the first girl to think she's invincible," he continued. "The last one was Ashley. She worked at the Velvet. Then there was Lana, Luke's sister. She almost made it into the cheerleading team. Maybe that's why the cheerleaders were attacked in the first place, but not killed—I don't know, whatever! Point is, shit's real and it's not worth the payoff." The second he felt the weight in the truth of his words, his throat tightened and his voice went nasal. Now was as good a time as any to stop talking.

Alice remained silently thinking. He needed to keep quiet and to let her go, but it was like being presented with his own self-destruct button. It was torture to convince himself he needed to push it.

Finally she muttered, "I know you have no reason to have hope, after how many times this has happened, but…" She looked at him, eyes pleading. "I don't mean any disrespect toward the others, but I may be more capable."

"You flinch whenever I happen to brush against you," he grumbled. "So excuse me if I doubt that."

Her eyes hardened and her jaw subtly set. "You're right," she purred with a surprising venom. "I flinch. It's been so long since I've had physical contact that it shocks me every time. My fight or flight instincts kick in and I choose not to fight you, so 'excuse me' if I fail to see my flinching as a hindrance."

This was a better response than he had anticipated, though he still wasn't inclined to get his hopes up. At the same time, he still wasn't keen on letting her go.

As her words replayed in his head, he wondered what exactly happened to her before she came back to town, and what conditions she had lived in.

She stepped just close enough so he'd hear when she muttered, "I need you to understand that you don't know me. I've starved. I've been buried alive. My heart's stopped beating for far longer than what most people come back from, and I'm still here."

"The fuck?" he breathed.

Slowly she stressed, "I—can—handle—myself." Finished, she waited. But he didn't know what to say.

"Think of what we can do," she added on a more encouraging note. "The Ripper has adopted a pattern; we can use it to our advantage, identify the next target—"

"You."

When Alice inclined her head and stared him down, he realized this was the point.

"You'd use yourself as bait?" he asked.

"Happily."

Alice, hung by the ankles, a thick trail of blood flowing up her face and long black hair—

"No," he asserted over the subtle wave of nausea in his throat.

She tilted her head away as if to say, *Oh, come on.* "Jack—"

He continued up the driveway. "I appreciate the gesture, but you don't have to do anything."

She laughed, aggravated like she knew he wasn't about to let her inside to continue the conversation, but it wasn't like she was gonna force him *not* to go home. "Fine," she called after him, hands in her skirt pockets. "I plan to do what I can regardless. If we work together, we can cover more ground and act more quickly, but I won't argue with you."

He scrunched his mouth and, again, stopped walking. If she really was about to go after the Ripper herself, was there a point anymore in denying her company?

He yanked off his hat in one hand and pulled at his hair roots with the other. He had some thinking to do.

"What would you like to do?" she asked when he apparently took too long.

Anything was better than standing around, warring with himself. "I don't know," he said, "take a walk? I gotta think."

Silence. Finally she nodded and turned away. "Let me know what you decide," she said over her shoulder, the wind lifting her hair so it appeared to be waving underwater. "You know where to find me," she finished, turning her face away.

Was it just him, or was everything she did seductive?

He had to stop thinking these things.

"Whoa, hold on," he called. "I didn't mean—I'm not telling you to leave!"

"If you're most comfortable with me elsewhere, why, I'd hate to impose!" she yelled over the wind.

"Wait though, just… wait!"

She glanced at him, frowning, but she waited.

A decent human being would've stressed how bad of an idea it was for her to help him. Taken her home, no matter what she said. But he didn't want to be a decent human being. It never made a difference in the past. *Live for the temporary friendships, mourn the losses, rinse and repeat.*

He looked back to the road. Why did she want to help him? Could it really have been a genuine hero complex? There had to have been something else to this, but if it all came back to bite him in the ass, he didn't want to think about it.

He stepped in front of her, into her view. She caught his gaze, unreadable—intimidating, whether she intended to be or not.

"Wanna, I don't know. Drink?" He wasn't looking to get shitfaced—just a little something was all he was thinking. There was flask-liquor to share.

Alice looked to the sun, then back to him. "This early?"

He remembered normal people weren't alcoholics. "What about weed? Do you smoke?"

"I haven't."

"Do you…want to?"

After a thought, she shrugged with just her expression, if that was possible.

"Alright," he said, nodding, distracted with the increasingly apparent thought that this was new, and it was happening. "Yeah, okay. Let's go, then. Can't do it here." He unlocked Gabby's car with the button from where he stood. "I can pack it, if you can drive."

Alice offered him a weak grin before taking the rest of the way up the incline with him.

This was strange. There was a feeling in his chest, and he didn't know what mood to attribute it to. Stress? Anxiety? Yet, somehow…relief? Was it possible to simultaneously feel like a guilty sack of shit and…lucky?

In any case, a decision was reached, and there was no turning back now.

18. Stoned And Spooked

Alice

Wacky weed was what Theo's father had called it. Before her transition into being a domsuco, and the horrors which followed, Alice might have barely tolerated Jack for such a vice as smoking the wacky weed. However, with trauma to put things into perspective, she felt the stigma attributed to it was arbitrary. What made one mild sort of intoxication any better or worse than another? People drank coffee and alcohol, and smoked cigarettes, and no one would bat an eye but Theo's long-dead grandmother, who supported Prohibition in the '20s.

Alice recalled how ingesting human food would make her nauseous. She hoped that because she wouldn't have to eat or drink the herb, her body wouldn't have a reason to reject it. If it took effect, splendid, if not, it didn't matter. At this point participation was more for the sake of bonding than it was for her own personal gratification.

"You've never been high before," Jack said flatly from the passenger's seat. It was as if he didn't believe it, but she knew in truth he did. "Wow."

She smiled and waited for him to quit playing around. They were still parked at his house.

He checked his pocket with his free hand, then nodded toward the glove compartment. "Let's get on the road. Too public here." It was still illegal, then.

She nodded, then noted a pedal missing, as were a couple levers. How was this vehicle operational? "Where's the clutch?"

"No clutch," he answered, already with a baggy of green on his lap. "Automatic."

"Automatically grinds your gears?" She couldn't help the sarcasm; this wasn't making sense. "And where's the parking brake?"

"Calm down, Grandma, you're obviously more used to stick—"

He called her Grandma. She dated herself.

He continued, "but this is actually a whole lot easier. All you need to worry about is steering, going forward and backward, stopping and going, and look, this is your parking brake."

"It's just in park."

"Exactly. Easy, right?"

She didn't trust it. However… it did seem simple enough. "I've only driven old cars," she muttered.

"I figured," he said. "It's okay. Just, you know, don't kill us."

She wanted to give him the death glare, but she smiled too soon.

He pulled what looked like a Flyin-Saucer toy from the glove compartment—the sort of plastic disk the kids would fling back and forth in the park. With it, he retrieved a small glass smoker's bowl, then placed the toy like a dish over his lap. "Drive like you're on your way back to your place, but then instead of turning left at the fork you go right. It's more scenic, and it'll circle you back around to my street." Manually he began tearing his product into smaller pieces, all collected within the makeshift dish.

Now was the time to test her ability.

It was a rocky first few miles. She hit the break with her left foot every time she would have usually changed the gear, and each time she reached for the shift she was reminded this was a different beast. Jack only complained once when the car jerked and he nearly dropped the dish, though since then she made herself more conscious of her actions.

The road led them past old, large houses. They might've looked nice at some point, though now their paints were chipped, vines growing up the walls and completely obscuring some of the windows. For a moment Alice was distracted by the beauty that was nature, with its vibrant fall colors in contrast to the newly fallen snow. Then gradually she began to recognize something familiar. A scent? A scene?

Jack raised his completed project: a fully packed pipe of finely torn reefer. "If you want you can park. No one's lived this way since forever. Unless you'd rather multitask."

He read her well; she didn't want to multitask. She couldn't shake the sensation that she'd been here before, and she didn't want to distract herself further.

Finally it hit her. So much foliage and trees had grown in, it was amazing she figured it out at all. This was Theo's old neighborhood. She knew it was close, but she didn't realize it was *here*.

She pulled up his old driveway and parked. Through the broken down fence she spotted the pool, dried out, a quarter-way filled with dirt, ferns growing within.

She wasn't sure how much her face gave away, so she explained, just in case, "I… I remember my father told me this used to be where the mayor lived."

Apparently she beat him to it. "I was about to say, yeah. My great-great granddad or something like that."

"Something like that," she agreed.

He paused mid pocket-reach, and she knew his next question: how would she know?

"'Van Sloan' isn't a common last name," she answered. "When you said your family's been here for generations, I put two and two together."

"I told you that?"

"It was either you or Gabby." In actuality, she couldn't remember if either of them had.

He frowned, then returned to his pockets. "So you like history, then?"

"Some aspects I find interesting, but no, not necessarily." She could've done without Pearl Harbor, and Hiroshima. If all of World War II was wiped from time, that would've been most perfect.

She peered back out the window. "I remember the… stories I'm told."

"So you've heard about the vampires."

She started, but was slick enough to keep it out of her voice. "Vampires?" There was no way he knew.

When she looked at him, she was comforted to see a sly grin; he mocked the very idea of it. "Yeah," he replied in a faux attempt to convince her. He pulled a lighter from his pocket and held it out, pipe included. "Bunch of grown-ass men, not even a hundred years ago, went all Van Helsing on this one Asian girl because people were dying and somehow it was her fault. Because you know, if there's a vampire in town, it's gotta be the foreigner."

"Naturally," she replied.

"But yeah, my grandma was there when they did it."

Ruth, only a few years older than herself, watching from a distance in shock as the neighbors picketed outside Alice's house.

Alice blinked. Then froze. It was happening again.

"She still thinks it was bullshit," Jack continued —

Theo through the window, convincing the neighbors to go home. Alice left her farewell note on the table and joined Bishop at the back door.

Theo, dead in her arms.

The wet of the forest floor on her knees as it continued to rain.
"Kill me," she sobbed as Bishop approached, "Just kill me."
"You know I won't," he replied.
She held her lover close and ran back into town. Once she arrived—

"'A bloodcurdling scream cut through the night,' is how she put it," Jack related. "All the men in town rushed outside to save the damsel in distress, only to find that girl with blood on her face and Grandma's brother dead at her feet."

But she wouldn't have let him go—

Alice took a breath and forced herself present. "That sounds an awful lot like she did it," she said.

Jack nodded. "That's what I said. She apparently had a whole villain's monologue, too, laughing and everything—"

*A scream from her core through a tightened throat, "None of you are safe for as long as I live! Look! Your precious golden boy! Dead! Gone! **And he was kind to me!**"*

The neighbors only stood wide-eyed with their mouths open, like fools. They had all seemed so certain it was her before, yet they were so surprised now. So genuinely she laughed, or cackled, or sobbed —

"But Grandma Ruth wasn't convinced," Jack continued. "It was like what's happening now, apparently; it's easy to blame the scapegoat, but the actual factual evidence didn't add up. So when the girl was saying all these things, Grandma was just confused. I mean, horrified — probably horrified — but really confused, because it didn't make sense —"

Her laughs finally stirred them into action, and so her work was done. She wasn't sure who pried his body from her fingers. She couldn't say who shot her close-range with a revolver, or who threw salt in her face, or who ran her through with a kitchen knife. All that was clear was the moment Theo's father, with a face of stone, plunged the wooden stake through her heart. It burned like a red-hot curling iron. Her throat caught, so she couldn't scream —

She gasped.

Jack jumped, snapping his gaze in all directions. "What?"

"Nothing," she assured him, and she cursed her voice for betraying her.

He turned his face back to hers and silently observed. "Doesn't look like 'nothing.'"

A stake through the heart was supposed to be one of the few things that killed a domsuco. She knew she was special, but… Could she *never die?*

Knowing Jack wouldn't rest without an explanation, she pressed her hand into her side as if she had a menstrual cramp. "I'll live."

Observing for a moment longer, he seemed to grasp what she was hinting. "Nothing a little weed can't fix?"

"You tell me."

He let out a relieved breath and sat back in his seat, holding the pipe out to her again. "Nah, you hit that and tell *me*."

It was endearing, how he worried. She couldn't help a small grin before she lifted the pipe to her mouth.

The scent of earthy burnt cream became more apparent. Now she understood where it came from. Marius must have also smoked, then.

The smoke was so plentiful they could barely see through the back windshield. Jack's eyes were red, and Alice imagined hers were, too. She felt sluggish. Relaxed. It was difficult to think about anything for too long, almost as if she was in a dream state. She smiled when she concluded this was what she was meant to feel. It was working. She didn't think it would.

Jack's thoughts seemed to have gone elsewhere. Alice followed his gaze back to the old Van Sloan house. He muttered, "I wonder if this is all some kinda karmic generational payback."

"Hm?"

"The mayor scapegoated a foreigner. If he knew she was innocent, I don't know, but I doubt he cared either way. Fast forward to now, and here I am. The new scapegoat."

Both were silent as Alice took in his words. When he seemed to realize she had stopped coughing, he again offered her the pipe.

She didn't need it. His face distracted her. So cute, so sad. Such a sad pup, all the time. He needed a distraction. A *happy* adventure. "Do you want to go in?"

He raised an eyebrow. "Pretty sure that's trespassing."

Theo, frowning as he leaned against her porch. "Are you suggesting we break in?"

*"It's not breaking in if no charges are pressed." By now they knew Winifred and her family weren't on vacation, and **someone** had to investigate their house.*

He opened his mouth as if to counter, then closed it.

Her throat closed. This wasn't an intense flashback, or a memory she had forgotten. She was reminded, however, and her chest felt full.

She cleared her throat and responded before Jack could note her change in mood. "No witnesses."

He gazed back at the house, then shrugged. "Alright, let's do it." He put the pipe in his pocket and together they stepped out and crossed the open front yard and spacious front porch. Jack tried the door and it opened with ease.

The ceiling and back wall had caved in seemingly some time ago, leaving in its wake a wide, gaping window to the outside and an ever-floating cloud of dust. The sun fell through in such dramatic rays, they reminded her of old Romantic paintings.

"Wow." Lips parted, Jack nodded his approval at what one could've construed as the home's former self. He laughed. "How can a guy go from having all this, to nothing." Alice understood his frustration. If her own grandfather hadn't made some poor business decisions, her father wouldn't have had to start a new life here, and as a result she could have wanted for nothing. Instead she had to be poor and *foreign* in an environment which despised both.

It was as if to speak to a ghost when Jack looked up toward the second floor hallway and sighed, "Bence Van Sloan, why'd you have to be a prick?"

She couldn't agree more, though she couldn't entirely blame the man for being a product of his generation.

Ever the curious adventurer, she climbed the rubble to the upstairs. Jack followed. She had faintly detected a scent since before they pulled up—rain and something floral. It wasn't entirely out of place for the setting, so she didn't think anything of it until she remembered pairing the scent with a person. If no one lived here, how could a human scent have still lingered?

The floor was intact, though for Jack's sake she tested each board before deeming it safe for him to follow. There was no banister to stop them falling over the edge, so carefully they kept to the walls and crossed to Theo's old room, for no other reason than it was his. The door had been removed, though the room was built in such a way that a wall was the first thing anyone saw upon entering; there was a corner to round before seeing the rest of the space.

She expected to find not even a plank to stand on, or at most a dirt-covered room with the walls blown in. However, when she rounded the corner she saw all the walls were intact, as was the floor and the ceiling. There was furniture, too, and closer inspection showed it was all new. Clean. Someone visited often enough to make this space their own.

There was a large, fluffy rug spanning from the wall to the end of the bed. Clothes sat atop the comforter, and jewelry on the dresser. The necklaces, rings and earrings each carried small stains of old blood, the glow varying in accordance to freshness. She wondered if Jack would notice, or if the blood wasn't nearly so visible to those who wouldn't perceive it as glowing.

Just as she was about to consider what else she saw, she remembered to whom the scent belonged. It was so obvious, she could've kicked herself. Of course Winifred would have made herself a home in Theo's old room.

Before Alice could consider if this wasn't something Jack should see, he stood beside her and took it all in.

"Whoa," he breathed, wandering some steps forward. "Is this what a crack house looks like?"

"We should go," she suggested, hoping not to come across too concerned.

He laughed, "What? This just got interesting."

"This has become intrusive." This was the first excuse which came to mind, but on second thought she wasn't sure if it was a good one. Thinking was difficult, but even a more sober-minded person would see bloody jewelry as a bad omen. Wouldn't they?

Jack crossed to the bed, then was still, his back to her. Alice waited, desperate to come up with something better. They needed to leave.

"This… feels like a deja vu," he murmured, holding the bed frame. Frowning, he looked up at the ceiling.

"Jack," she warned.

"There's no one here," he promised, and while he most likely meant no disrespect, she couldn't help but feel slight-ed when he looked at her and added, "You're high; you feel like someone's gonna walk in and catch us, but it's just paranoia."

"If that was ever my issue, I wouldn't have suggested we come in."

If he had a comeback, it was gone the second his gaze fell on the dresser and his eyes widened. Immediately, he paled.

A new fear gripped her. She was missing something; she didn't think anything here could elicit such a response from him. Or, did he notice the blood? "Jack?" she asked.

He seemed only present enough to take some hesitant steps forward, holding out a hand as if to touch one of the rings, but he didn't. When he laughed, she knew it was because he didn't know how else to process it. "Sarah's ring."

It was dainty with a delicate band of interwoven, white gold leafs, and a centered, sparkling diamond with so many facets. As he reached closer, Alice hissed, "Don't!" but it was too late; he picked it up. Arms shaking.

"Did I tell you we were engaged for a few hours?" he asked.

Her throat tightened. She wasn't sure if he was waiting for an answer, but finally she shook her head. "Me and... Us, too," she said. "Before he..." She couldn't finish. She didn't want to lie, but she wasn't sure how to tell the truth — or anything close to it.

Jack nodded. He understood as much as he needed to.

His voice wavered up a pitch, and it was an unstable hand that pushed his hair back. "What the fuck is this fucking shit?"

"We need to go." She didn't know how else to answer.

"I need... I need to find some answers." Nodding with some certainty, though still too scared to be in his right mind, he pocketed the ring and crossed to the closet. She approached him slightly faster than was humanly comfortable, for what he really needed to do was stop taking things, and stop touching things. The weed smell would only cover so much if he decided to rub his scent over everything— Winifred needed to not know they were ever there.

When she paid closer attention, however, she realized his scent was already present. Although he apparently had no conscious memory of it, he *had* been here before.

She listened carefully to her surroundings. If worse came to worst and anyone came back, Alice would throw Jack over her shoulder in a fireman's hold and run them out of there. She wasn't sure if she wanted to put him under trance, though rather than consider it now she decided she would do it later if it proved necessary.

She wasn't sure if this was a rational response to the situation.

He opened the closet, immediately recognizing some of the things within. "My flannels." He only allowed himself a second to be surprised before pushing these aside and fishing through dresses and other female clothing until he recognized a blouse. "Wyn's shirt." His movements slowed as he processed more information. "A lot of this is Wyn's."

"Jack, *please*."

"I thought you said you could handle this?"

"Not my first time high! And completely unprepared, when the Ripper can be back any minute?!"

Jack seemed to recover some sense when he looked back at her. As far as he knew, she was in grave danger just for being alone with him. If this was the case, this was the worst place she could possibly be.

He nodded, then led the way out. She followed close behind. Her heart rattled in her chest, and it was hard to hear anything else. She held her breath, and for a short while this helped—that was, until he noticed.

"Breathe," he reminded her, and for argument's sake she obliged.

Going down the rubble proved easier than going up. Jack slid down as much as he needed, then jumped and cleared the rest. If Alice had gone her full speed, her escape would've been flawless, regardless of her footwear. Instead she learned the hard way that her heels weren't made for this sort of thing. She couldn't move fast enough when the debris loosened beneath her; she gasped and slipped most of the way down. She couldn't give herself away, therefore she would fall.

Jack took her arm before she could, guiding her back to balance while maintaining a decent speed. Both darted out the door, Alice pushing the edge of humanly possible and Jack keeping pace to the best of his ability. They flew down the porch steps and all but skidded to a stop once they neared the vehicle, Alice fumbling with the keys as she claimed the driver's side.

Why did Jack have so many keys? There was his car, then there was his house; why were there more than two keys? Why was she high? This wouldn't have been nearly so difficult if she wasn't so high.

"Black candle," he whispered harshly from the other side.

She squinted, then figured he'd actually said *black handle*. This made it easier. She pressed the "unlock" button, opened the door and sat, closing herself in with one hand and starting the engine with the other. Jack moved in perfect synchronization, the door slamming shut beside him.

"I'm so sorry!" he cried, squeezing the back of his head between his hands. "I wasn't thinking! I wasn't—"

She meant to say, "It's okay," but instead, "Uhhhhh!" came out. Too overwhelmed for words, she put the car in gear and drove forward to turn around. She couldn't sense Winifred yet, though if at any point the girl decided to be there, she would arrive within seconds—an instant was all it took for her to catch them.

While speed was important, sound was also key—they had to keep it down. If she revved the engine, or skidded over the asphalt, it would draw attention.

Neither let out a breath until the old neighborhood was miles behind them, though still it was quiet. Alice glanced at Jack and saw he had been staring dead ahead the whole time, on edge. It wasn't until they had pulled up his driveway and parked that he mumbled, "I gotta go back."

Her movements slowed as she powered down the engine. "Don't."

"Why not?"

There was a reason. It was so obvious, though she couldn't find the focus and remember what it was. "It's... dangerous."

"Yeah, I get that. I'm not asking you to come with me."

"That's not what I'm worried about."

It was becoming increasingly probable Winifred was behind everything. If Jack arrived at this same conclusion, it would lead to a series of circumstances she couldn't predict.

If Winifred *wasn't* the Ripper, Jack would needlessly isolate himself from one of the few good people he had in his life.

"What are you worried about, then?" he asked when she didn't elaborate.

Winifred couldn't be the Ripper; she was *Winifred*.

Alice let out a bewildered breath. Now she had to come up with something. "You aren't—qualified." There was a better way to put this. "The police know how to...evidence." She put her palm to her head. She never wanted to be high again.

"The police are useless!" he snapped, then, "Sorry." His frustration maintained a low simmer, and she knew he had more to say. He frustratedly scrunched his mouth and looked away. She let go of the steering wheel and hoped the finger indents had been there all along.

"But they're useless," he said. "Either I tell them what we saw—or, what *I* saw; no one needs to know you were there—and they assume I set it up; or, even if they do believe me, they'll die once they get there or 'not find anything conclusive.' It'll be another dead end. I can't send them, and it's not like I can send anyone else, so who's left?"

"Better someone else than you," she mumbled, then she realized she said this out loud. Yes, she cared about him, but at someone else's expense?

He paused. Then looked back at her. His rage was gone, distracted. It seemed as though he wasn't sure he heard her correctly. When he looked away, he still seemed uncertain.

She wanted to protect him, but she also didn't want to keep him in the dark. She'd told him they would figure this all out quicker and more efficiently if they worked together, and she was right. She needed to tell him something. He needed to know what she knew, and vice versa. But how much could she let on? And without sounding crazy, or strangely jealous?

"Wanna go inside?" he finally asked, "Chill for a bit?"

She nodded. He nodded back, and both took a moment to collect themselves before stepping out.

19. Skyrim Bracelet

Jack

There were some things to consider in the silence that took Jack and Alice past the gate and through the back door. The simple fact that she cared about him made him feel as though he shouldn't put himself in danger, but something had to be done and the police were incompetent. It didn't matter how he looked at it; if he didn't inspect the abandoned house himself, no one else would do it properly. He couldn't call Detective Lloyd directly, but he couldn't call the station, either — they wouldn't take him seriously. If Alice called the station, the Ripper would find out and she'd *definitely* end up like the other girls.

He considered Officer Robinson. It wasn't like she was suddenly off the Ripper's hit list since she was attacked, so if he spoke to her now it wouldn't be the difference between whether or not she made it out of all this alive. She wouldn't be able to do much physically in her current condition, but she might have a better idea of what to do. He doubted the hospital would let him see her, though if Crystal went with him it would make things easier. But then that meant asking *Crystal* to risk her life.

He opened the sliding glass door and let Alice in first.

Eyes half closed and brow slightly furrowed, she held the door frame for support and she stepped inside. If he wasn't so preoccupied, he could've been amused. Usually she seemed so well-spoken and composed. To see her this confused and faraway was reassuring, if ever he felt like a bumbling fool around her before.

The backdoor opened into a small, beige-tiled sunroom. The double doors leading into the dining room-kitchen combo would always remain open; no matter how often the humans closed them, Lestat would nudge them open for access to the windows and dog-door.

Alice passed like a ghost through the sunroom and into the dining room.

Sliding the door shut behind them, Jack recalled what it meant to be a host. "We can sit somewhere, if you want.

Living room, my room, here…" He joined her in the dining room.

The decision seemed harder for her to make with each option he presented, and he didn't know what more to suggest, so he stopped. She let out some tension on a breath. "Jack, I hate being high."

After a quick look toward the foyer, he leaned toward her and lowered his voice to say, "I won't make you smoke again, don't worry, but my mom should be back any minute now, so let's not talk so loudly about it?"

She followed his example and quietly replied, "There's only one other person here, and it's not her."

He almost countered, but then wondered, "How would you know?"

"I heard a cough, and there's no other cars in the driveway."

He didn't hear a cough. But he knew Grandma Ruth was here. She rarely left.

Alice turned to the dining room table and placed her hand on a chair. He thought she would eventually pull it out and sit, but she didn't.

His gaze fell on the antique hutch against the wall, and he couldn't help a humorless laugh. When Alice looked at him, he pointed his chin to it and said, "It's full of witchcraft."

She tilted her head, her curtain of black hair sweeping from her shoulder to fall past her chest.

He figured maybe this needed further explanation. "My grandma thinks we're, like, witches. Except she says we're *Wishers.*" He snickered, shaking his head, not chancing a look at whatever face she could be making. She probably thought his grandma was crazy. First vampires, now this? "Now whenever my mom's home and she's awake at the same time, I smell the incense and hear them both do their little chants for peace, or protection for the girls, or banishing whatever dark spirit attached itself to my life, all depending on the phase of the moon or the day of the week." While it was embarrassing, he wanted her to get the full scope for how ridiculous it was; he pulled up his sleeve to reveal his rope bracelet with runic wooden beads. "This is how desperate we are."

She squinted at it. "What is that?"

"Proof we're running out of options." He looked it over himself, and it was as Skyrim-looking as always. "It's supposed to make evil creatures writhe in pain."

She curiously observed, but didn't make a move to touch it.

He pulled down his sleeve and leaned back against the table, the side closest to her. Hands balled in his pockets, he let out a breath and hoped to blow the hair out of his face. It half-worked.

As if at the formation of a new thought, she squinted, her gaze gradually dropping. Finally her lips parted with a question, but she hesitated.

"What?" he asked.

"Do…" She looked at him, mouth still rounded in *oo*-formation. "Do you love Winifred?"

This was a more personal inquiry than anticipated. He didn't know how to answer. "Where'd this come from?"

Peering from him, to the table, then to the rest of the room, she answered, "I'm curious."

She thought Wyn was a suspect.

"You know it can't be her," he said. "Right?"

"I only know what I'm told. I don't know most things."

"There's no way she could've lifted any of them."

"Humor me." She found his gaze, and he found sympathy in hers. Like she also didn't want Wyn to be the Ripper.

Like she also thought it was a ridiculous lead; like she was apologizing for even thinking it.

It was weird to admit aloud to another person, but here he was. "I... care about her. I think about her a lot, and I wanna be around her more often than not, but... It feels more like an addiction than like what I had with—" His throat closed before he could say her name. "My last girl-friend," he finished. He felt her ring in his pocket.

Alice nodded to herself as if she knew it.

Feeling righteously judged, he grimaced and added, "Look, I just... She's the only good thing in my life right now. I don't know if I love her by default because there's no one else, or if there's something more to it, but in either case I know—" His arms were shaky. He was letting on *way* more than he thought he would, and he was upsetting him-self. He cleared his throat, scratching the back of his neck. "I know we're not gonna make it. She's gonna die, and then that's it—I'm done."

She nodded, lost in a thought again before she took in his face, gaging him. Once she seemed to have made a decision, she said, "While I was in high school, there was a boy, Eu-gene. Kind enough. Handsome enough. Like you, I lacked options, and the only boy I had ever wanted was taken, indefinitely. So—" She hesitated, dropping her gaze back to the table, and he knew why. Whatever followed wasn't something she was proud of. "When Eugene suggested that we started going steady, I agreed. I thought it was the right thing to do. There wasn't a reason not to, and I didn't want to hurt him, or humiliate him."

Jack's initial reaction was, *Yikes*, but quickly he noted this set-up wasn't so different from his with Wyn.

She continued, "We were together for a little over two years. It might've been bearable at first, but…" What she said next, although quieter, was more heavily articulated. "Always, he would call me by my traditional name, in an accent he was certain I had." Despite the weak laugh that followed, Jack knew she low-key despised the guy for this.

"So your boyfriend was racist?" he asked.

With a sideways grin, she squinted and laughed, "Racist?"

Now he was unsure. He thought this was an example of racism, but if Alice didn't see it that way, maybe he was wrong.

But then he remembered a definition. "Stupid assumption based on race. Racial prejudice. Racism."

She tilted her head in thought, gaze drifting. "I didn't feel attacked, or oppressed. Annoyed, definitely, but…" She peered back at him. "Do most people see it that way?"

He shrugged. "I know about as much as anyone else in this area, if not less. Probably less."

With a weak sympathetic grin, she inclined her head as if to say, *You don't mean that.*

But he did. "I talk to maybe five people on the regular: my mom, my sister, my grandmother and my girlfriend. Shit, four. No one talks to my mom unless they have to, Grandma Ruth doesn't leave the house, most of Gabby's friends have shunned her, and Wyn just chooses not to talk to anyone. You, I just met you."

"And I was a hermit for…a while," she murmured in agreement. As curious as he was, this was a question for another time.

"Rrright," he continued. "Any bit of social knowledge I have comes from the most out-of-touch people I know."

Although she nodded, she seemed distracted now, and for a second she didn't say anything. "Right." She grimaced. "Anyway, because of the way Eugene… treated me, I felt no guilt for…" She started over. "The boy I wanted—let's call him 'Ted.' I'd had a, well, severely rough morning, and it turned out he hadn't slept in days, and…" A flicker of a smile, though the grimace quickly returned.

She didn't need to finish for him to guess what happened. "And you cheated?"

"It wasn't planned. And it was only kissing."

"Still cheating."

"Well I never claimed to be perfect," she snapped.

He raised his hands in surrender, leaning away. "Not judging, just saying." He lowered his hands and, to further prove himself, added, "It's not something I haven't thought of."

Now when she looked at him, it was with a guarded curiosity.

"Not with anyone in particular," he explained. "I mean, sometimes, but mostly it's the idea I think about—my chances of getting away with it. Without the Ripper knowing."

"And Winifred?"

"It's not about her, it's about… I get a little freedom if I could get away with it. But, honestly, if I cheated and she caught me, we'd finally have a reason to break up."

"The fact that you want to should be reason enough."

"I'm not the one who cheated with Ted because I couldn't dump my weeaboo boyfriend, so."

Her brow furrowed at *weeaboo*, like she didn't know what he meant by that, but then after a quick thought she offered a small frown and subtly nodded as if to say, *Touché*.

"Why'd you tell me all that, anyway?" he asked.

"Fair exchange," she answered simply. "I'd asked a personal question, after all."

Seemed legit.

"So," he said. "Did you get what you needed from that? My answer on Wyn?"

"I got the truth, so yes. But it doesn't prove or disprove anything." Then, as if it were an afterthought, "It offers plausible motive. A girl can tell when she's losing someone. Paired with what we saw back there, it doesn't look good."

"What did you see back there that says it was Wyn?" This might've come out a tad too aggressive.

"I'm not saying it's her," she promised.

"What did you see?"

She gnawed her lower lip. Then, "The girls' clothes were all the same size. All hers. Right?"

They might've been. He only recognized some, but he didn't pay attention to what she was wearing all the time.

"That could mean anything," he countered. "That could mean the Ripper's obsessed, and she's next."

"How did the Ripper come into possession of your flannels?"

"I don't know, snatched them while I wasn't looking!" He saw where she was going with this. Girls take their boyfriends' clothes, and Wyn wasn't any different. There were many flannels he'd let her borrow that he'd never seen again. Some of them were there. If not all of them.

Alice raised a hand as if to tell him not to worry. "I don't mean to accuse her. Believe me, I would rather not, and you're right. What we saw can mean so many things. This is why we're talking about it."

He closed his eyes and let himself calm on an exhale. "Sorry I got defensive."

"It's fine. It's natural."

Finally he pulled out his chair and sat, and she followed suit. Unprompted, both angled their seats so they could face each other.

She sighed, voice low. "I have more. Not about the Ripper, but… It's relevant."

"Go for it." He pulled his flask from his pocket. If ever there was an occasion to drink, this was one of them. "Want any?"

"I can't process alcohol properly."

Must've been a shitty lesson to learn. "Sorry," he murmured, twisting off the lid. "Do you mind if I do?"

"Knock yourself out."

He nodded and took his first swig. He wasn't sure if he would've restrained himself if she *did* mind.

Silence as she searched for words. She leaned closer across the table and murmured, "I know you want to run."

"*Hohhhh.*" This felt like cause for another swig. He helped himself to it.

She continued, "You wouldn't be human if you didn't. It doesn't make you a coward, or selfish, or anything like that. Or if it does, I don't care. But running doesn't change anything, and it doesn't make you feel any better. Whether the Ripper follows you or not, the deaths will continue."

He stared quietly at the flask in his grasp, pensive. This bothered him more than anticipated. While escape seemed impossible regardless, it was a fantasy he'd always revisit. But now, hearing this, he couldn't even have that anymore.

She raised her hand as if to reach him across the table, then paused mid-go.

"What?" he finally asked.

"I was going to… Well, I don't know what I was going to do, exactly. But then I wasn't sure if I should." Yeah, she was stoned. It looked like she wanted to offer a comforting touch of some kind.

"I'll allow it," he replied.

Still she hesitated, staring at her hand before finally landing two awkward pats on his grip around the flask. He snickered, and with a bashful grin she lowered her hand back to her side of the table.

"I'm glad to have met you," she said. "Regardless of… whatever may happen."

He nodded, but didn't know how else to respond. Her words lingered in the air, confusing him. "Why?"

Now it was her turn to be confused. "Why not?"

"You know you have more to lose than to gain here, right?"

"It isn't about what I can gain. And I won't die."

"Should I list you off the girls who thought the same thing? Again? Having a boyfriend doesn't stop this guy, if that's what you're thinking. Or, girl. Whoever's doing it."

She went dead. Cold.

He remembered her dead guy and felt like an idiot. That was her boyfriend. It had to be.

"I'm not seeing anyone," she finally muttered.

"I'm sorry," he mumbled. "That was dumb."

She said nothing, though it seemed more likely because she couldn't speak than because she didn't forgive him. Eventually she nodded in acknowledgment.

If he let the silence linger too long he'd retreat back to his dark place as well. He wanted to start a new conversation, but wasn't sure how to leave this one.

Maybe it was best to address the elephant in the room. She liked that, right?

"How did he die?" he asked.

She met his gaze, and her agony hit him like a tidal wave to the chest. He knew it too well. She was him, a year ago. Hell, she was him *now*, whenever Sarah came up and caught him unawares.

She bit her lip and dropped her gaze.

"Cancer?" he asked, "Murder? Drunk driver?"

"Let's go with that last one."

"What was it actually?"

"Something I'd rather we didn't discuss."

He scrunched his mouth. He'd crossed the line. "Sorry," he mumbled.

Again, she didn't respond. Instead she clamped her lips between her teeth, sat stiff as if she wasn't breathing, then stood and paced to the kitchen island.

He didn't want to upset her further, but at the same time he didn't know how to drop it. Maybe he needed to be the one to open first—maybe then she would reciprocate. Fair exchange.

"Someone murdered my last girlfriend," he called, then considered how he could've walked up to her and not yelled it across the room.

Putting a hand to the counter as if for support, she muttered, "I'm sorry." She might've meant it, though nothing suggested as much.

He wasn't after her pity anyway, so, "That's not why I said it." He stood and hid his flask back in his pocket.

Now she peered over her shoulder at him. In her look he knew she finally understood the gesture. Her gaze drifted, and he watched the gears turning as she sought her response. "A monster ripped my father's heart from his chest," she said. "Right in front of me."

Holy fuck. Not the reveal he was hoping for, but *holy fuck.*

As she took in his expression, she deemed it necessary to add, "Take it as you will." She let out a breath and returned her gaze forward, away from him. He didn't think it was her intention, but he felt cut off. He didn't want to be cut off; he wanted to be with her in her head for as long as she had to suffer through it.

He didn't yell it this time, but spoke just loudly enough for her to hear. "Mine's probably dead, too. Haven't seen him in almost a year."

She didn't turn around like he'd hoped she would. Either she wasn't surprised, or she was still so stuck in her head that she didn't hear.

Finally she leaned back against the wall-counter, arms over her middle, holding herself again. He crossed to her side, and once he was close enough she muttered, "Well, you already know the separate wounds I've endured and survived."

"And you know I'm a sad, lonely murder suspect."

She huffed a quick laugh through her nose, expression unchanged. He wanted to comfort her. Somehow.

He lifted a hand level to her bicep, but paused before he could decide where to land it. When he felt he was taking too long, he laughed. Alice had just done this same thing. He didn't think he was this high.

She peered at his hand, a weak smile gracing her lips when she undoubtedly figured what was up.

He explained, "I was gonna… I don't know, but you always, like, jump."

"I'll allow it." Yeah, she knew what was up. She was teasing him.

He still wasn't sure what he wanted to do. He wanted to offer more than an awkward arm-pat, but he wasn't sure how much contact was too much for her.

Hands were safe. Right?

He lowered his hand, opening his palm and angling it out to make an obvious invitation. He would know if it was too much if Alice decided to not go there.

It apparently took her a moment to register the gesture, but after staring at his hand for a good second, she took it.

A sensation in his throat and chest overwhelmed him, like everything was okay yet he wanted to cry. The last time he felt that was —

"No! I mean — keep going, let's do this right."

His smile widened. "Alright, Sarah Becker." He opened the box. Her eyebrows rose in the middle and he reveled in it —

His body went numb. Everything felt far away. He couldn't tell what he was looking at. "I… Uh…" He didn't know what to say. He let go of her hand. "I'm sorry."

"Hm?"

It felt like they snapped their gazes to each other simultaneously. As if she'd been distracted up until then, too. She looked surprised. Borderline scared.

He answered, "I know I initiated, but… I…" There wasn't anything intimidating about the way she stared back at him, unblinking, eyes still wide with shock, yet somehow it messed with his head and he still didn't know what he was saying. Not knowing what else to do with his hand, he shoved it in his pocket. "Sorry."

Gradually she looked away, eyes flicking with each passing thought. "I should go," she finally decided.

"Go?" He'd fucked up; he'd made things too weird. What kind of high motherfucker thought hands were safe? Or was he completely misinterpreting everything?

"Was it something I said?" he asked.

She shook her head, turning around for the back door. "I just — I…have to." She'd made it out the kitchen, continuing through the dining room.

He didn't know what to do, but he needed to do something. If she already didn't plan to see him again, what more could it hurt for him to try any dumb thing to change her mind?

But what kind of asshole would try to make her stay?

"Wait!" he called, panic spiking the second she touched the backdoor handle.

She turned, wide-eyed. Her fingers never left the handle, but she waited.

He still didn't know what he'd say. The fact she stood there waiting did nothing to alleviate the pressure. He only had so much time to find his words.

Both were silent for too long. He was losing her.

Gradually her eyes returned to their usual narrow shape and she raised her chin. "You'll see me again," she promised.

He didn't expect this. He believed her.

He nodded. She nodded back, then left.

20. Another Beat

Alice

There was a reason Alice left Jack's house the way she did.

From her spot beside him, both still leaning against his kitchen counter, stoned as witches, her heart raced as it usually would in this proximity. But then there was an added, off-beat syncopation. As if...

Her eyes widened when it hit her.

Her heart beat as if there was another source.

Theo was her senseless first thought, for despite everything she was an optimist at her core. Reality quickly gripped her, however, and when the next off-beat turned her gut, she thought, *Marius*.

As cloudy as the weed already made everything, her senses went even more muddled. Why, of all the days she could have tried weed, did it have to be this day?

"I should go," she managed. The words, like thick glycerin—more solid than liquid—felt stopped at her lips. She wasn't sure if they made it past.

"Go?" So he did hear.

She nodded. She wanted to tell him why. Maybe he deserved to know. But if there was a right way to do it, she couldn't conceive of it in this condition, and she didn't have the time. Either Marius was coming to her and she needed to be out of Jack's presence as soon as possible, or Marius was the Ripper and Alice had to intervene before another girl died.

"Was it something I said?"

She shook her head, turning around for the back door. *One foot in front of the other,* she told herself. "I just—I…have to." She'd made it out the kitchen, into the adjoining dining room. The back door was only some feet away.

Closer now. Her fingers met the door handle.

"Wait!" he called, panic raising his voice.

She spun and faced him. He stood wide-eyed, shaggy brown hair half in his face to have him appear even more distressed, arm outstretched as if to physically pull her back though he'd only made it as close to her as the dining room table.

She had to hurry, but she couldn't leave while he was like this. Why was he worried? She hadn't let anything slip about Marius, had she?

As she replayed the events leading up to the moment she said she had to leave, she finally understood. Despite her saying it wasn't something he'd said, he still thought it was his fault she was leaving. He still thought she was abandoning him the same way his past friends had.

"You'll see me again," she promised.

He stared back. It seemed he believed her when he lowered his arm and nodded.

She nodded back, then left. Now all there was left to do was find Marius. But she wasn't that brave. She wasn't strong enough; she wasn't sober enough.

If he was on his way to her regardless, this didn't matter; she had to put as much distance between herself and Jack as possible.

The first thing she did once she reached the woods was rip a sizable limb from a felled branch and tear the splinters at the tip to fashion a makeshift stake. In the hopes of bringing the battle to a place wherein she'd have help, she took off her shoes and ran to Bishop's cabin.

"Bishop!" she cried as she bursted through the front door, careful to keep it from swinging into the wall, "Marius!" She dropped her shoes inside the door.

Bishop appeared in an instance, hair lumpy in its pre-styled morning stage. "What'd he do?" he yelled, dazed and with a shotgun at hand, not fully awake but startled into action. He wore gray plaid pajama pants, no shoes, no shirt, and a dull green quilted robe, its belt undone and the length dangling predominantly from one side. "Where's he?" He bounced back when he'd unwittingly put his shoulder into a sliver of sunlight which the curtains didn't catch.

He scanned the environment, stiff and cradling his burnt shoulder, only letting his tension out on a full breath when he figured they weren't under immediate attack. He let the shotgun rest along the nearby dining room table.

"I don't know," she replied, "but I feel him—I felt them both, so I know it has to be—"

"Marius," he affirmed. "Can you tell where he is?"

"Near. Just… near."

345

A distant scream—so distant it seemed to only reach them as the tail end to an echo, but loud enough that maybe even a mortal could have heard.

"A girl," Bishop noted. He and Alice exchanged a look.

"So then he *is* the Ripper," she muttered, though she still wasn't sure. What business could he have with Jack, or any of the teen girls? If it was to call her out of hiding, why would he only have started a year ago?

Bishop shook his head as if to say he didn't know. "The attacks are usually at night."

Another scream.

Alice reached back for the front door, stake still at hand.

"I can't follow if you leave," Bishop warned, stepping as close as the shadows would allow. His recent burn illustrated why.

"If the girl isn't dead already, I can't let her die," she argued.

He bit his knuckle, though before she could twist the doorknob, he picked the shotgun back up and reached with it across the sun's rays, putting the handle to her torso, the barrel aimed safely down at the empty space between them. "Wooden slugs," he offered.

This surely beat her makeshift stake. With a somber nod, she accepted the new weapon, exchanged a last look in farewell, and left, tossing the torn branch as she neared the woods.

She followed her heartbeat closer to the area wherein she used to live, and her thoughts went back to Theo's old room. Deciding she would test this thought, she altered her course to bring her straight there, and her heart responded accordingly — quicker.

So Marius was the Ripper. If the Ripper was a domsuco, he didn't need to be present for his kills — he could have someone else carry them out for him. Yet, she still couldn't fathom a sensible motive.

A heavy scent saturated the air, sweet and metallic; familiar and again reminiscent of pennies and sweat.

When the house came in sight, she slowed to a stop. Anyone who knew her, knew hers was the only heart to ever beat so fast. Marius would hear it from wherever he stood, and so he would already know she was there. She couldn't go in through the front door, if she wanted *any* element of surprise.

A teen girl cried from within, muffled through the walls. But there weren't any heartbeats. So they were both domsuco.

The scent of rain and roses faintly rose from the smell of blood. *Winifred.*

The sobs quieted. Then Winifred shrieked, *"It's him, Alice! He's the Ripper—!"* Her cry was interrupted when something sizzled, and her response was a horrifying mix between a howl and a high, throaty scream.

With technique she didn't know she had, Alice launched herself up into the canopy of a tree. She tossed the shotgun upward, freeing her hands so she could slingshot herself with a branch on either side. She swung her legs forward, snatched the shotgun from the air, and crashed straight through Theo's old second story window. Shattered glass showered the room as she landed with a cat's grace, taking aim with the shotgun over her forearm the second she spotted him—the figure in all black. While he was too backlit to distinguish specific features, she knew it was him. Felt it.

His weapon was drawn as well. A crossbow. Wooden bolts. A teen girl's body hung behind him from the ceiling fan, gently swaying by the ankles, throat slit and skin shallow, drained. Her shape and attire were familiar. Heavyset, dangling earrings.

—maybe eighteen, nineteen years old, with pretty features arranged in such a way that did not flatter. "We don't have any seats available right now," she began, "but if you'd **wait** to be seated, we'll have one ready in about fifteen minutes."

Alice met her before. At the diner. "Bri?" she whispered.

Somewhere behind Alice, Winifred sobbed between catching her breath. "He knew—to find me here—He planted their things—so it'd look like—"

Never relenting in her aim or looking away, Alice removed her woolen coat, handing it back to Winifred so she may drape it over her head for shade. "Run."

"I had no way to trace it back to him," the girl cried, hoarse, "or to stop him from bringing everything here—and Bri—"

"Winifred!" Alice snapped, "Run!"

Finally Winifred took off, and Alice glimpsed burns on her face. Smoke rose for every spilt instance the girl touched sunlight.

Once she was gone and there was only silence left save for the accelerated beat of Alice's heart, Marius grumbled, "I should've shot through you to get to her." Again she heard his strange accent—the same he'd used when they last met in 1948. It didn't sound so out of place in these times. The lazy articulation was similar to Jack's and many of the other teens' nowadays, yet there was still an otherworldliness to it.

She kept her aim.

He kept his position at the opposite end of the room, a silhouette before a wall of unharmed windows, the dresser with the bloody jewelry behind him. Bri's body continued to sway, and it was all Alice could do to not let it distract her from her true target.

"You won't shoot me, will you," he finally said. It was more of a curious statement than it was a question. "You're too *good*."

Her father's blood running down the cracks of the yellow kitchen tiles—

Gene, wide-eyed at the wheel of his car, head bleeding—

Alice blinked the memories aside. They weren't new; she was past this.

But her arm was shaking. She cursed her arm for shaking. He noticed. If there was a worried stiffness in his posture, it could've been simply due to the possibility that she would slip and shoot him by accident.

Finally he laughed, a bitter edge cutting into his dark timbre. "But no one's that good. It's because I feel like him, isn't it? That you won't shoot me? I look like him?"

He could've looked like Theo. The last time she saw him, he was slightly too old, with a heavier brow and hooked nose, for her to see this connection. He would've changed his appearance by now, then. To distract her. "Make it stop, and let's find out," she dared.

Again he laughed without mirth, now shaking his head as if this was a foolish request.

She waited. Nothing changed.

"If you allow Wyn to live, you will lose Jack," he warned.

"What do you know about Jack?"

"Everything."

She scowled. This told her nothing and he knew it.

"I won't shoot you," he promised. He was trying to play nice.

As if he hadn't taken away the only living family she had.

Everything went loud and her ears rang, blaring—she couldn't hear Marius yell, but watched as he staggered back, gripping his bleeding shoulder, mouth gaping.

She'd shot him.

With a strange steadiness, she reloaded the shotgun and again took aim. His crossbow lay at his feet. He'd dropped it.

The silence was eerie when he stopped screaming. As the ringing in her ears subsided, she heard his haggard breaths. "I won't shoot you," he said again.

Not with your crossbow on the ground. She fired another round.

He was quicker this time. With a shocking puff of black smoke, he disappeared. More black smoke materialized behind her, and the rate of her heart spiked to signal he was at her back in an instant. She didn't know how he could do that, but of one thing she was certain: this was not a domsuco ability.

Like a fool, she froze, and he had both her wrists bound in one hand, his hand over her mouth. But it wasn't his hand. It was a hard plastic mask, or lusterless metal, which covered her nose and lips. It was familiar.

He'd done this to her before.

A new fear gripped her, her scream muffled through the contraption as a gas released within. Though she fought to free her wrists, her arms gradually went limp as everything went dark, as if a sudden cloud obscured the sun. She hated herself for the tears which rolled down her face. As was a common theme in her old nightmares, she couldn't move. It was like she was paralyzed underground again — or, as if she never left. He was all that kept her upright.

She calmed, though it wasn't by choice. The tears remained rolling.

"A nitrous oxide derivative," he explained in her ear, voice warped, the closeness raising the hairs on her neck and tickling something in her lower back. "Laughing gas. I won't shoot you, but I won't let you shoot me again, understand?"

Her head lulled forward; she couldn't lift her neck.

He continued, "Let me kill her. You'll only protect her for so long, and under your protection she will get away with it, again and again. Then when Jack finally does what I should've done a long time ago, you'll look at him like he's the monster. Don't force his hand, Alice. Let me do it. Let *me* be the monster."

She hadn't completed transition the last time he'd drugged her. She was stronger now, though it didn't currently feel like it. She'd be damned if she couldn't best an old trick.

She closed her eyes and forced a coherent thought. If she held her breath, the drug wouldn't continue into her system. She didn't need to breathe to live, so she could hold her breath indefinitely without any consequence.

So she did. Already she noticed her surroundings becoming brighter and clearer again. If he could assume she was helpless for only a half minute more, she would have her strength back.

"Alice?" His voice was still warped. She could've imagined the touch of concern which entered.

He removed the mask from her face, and she fought the urge to inhale fresh air. "Breathe," he said. This time he sounded exactly like…

"Theo," she breathed, then cursed herself. She didn't mean to say this aloud. While the drug wore off, clearheadedness still didn't seem within her grasp. She wondered if she was still high, or if this was a lingering side affect of the drug, or an affect of shock.

More of her strength returned, and while she wanted to peel herself from his grip, she let her wrists remain limp in his fingers. Shifting her gaze from the drug-mask in his grasp, she noted the rope bracelet he wore. Like Jack's, with the wooden runes, but with more of them. She wondered what they all did.

"I died when he did," she mused. Now she was aware of her back to his chest. No warmth.

He sighed. "You're breathing."

She laughed. He really was depending on her to have all of the same fallbacks she'd had before she transitioned. "Breathing," she whimsically echoed. "Who needs it?"

He pulled the mask away, and there was the ruffling of material as she assumed he put it in a pocket. "Sleep," he told her.

"Do you nee-eed breathe?" she slurred. "Do you sleep? What do you eat?" If he wasn't a mere domsuco with handy potions and chemicals, she honestly didn't know what she was dealing with. Even humans had managed to get their hands on age-altering potions, and if there was one thing they knew about Marius, it was that he loved any narcotic he could use to his advantage. But *how* did he magically appear behind her?

Silence. He took some steps toward the wall, and she let her legs drag accordingly. He adjusted her weight until her back was to the wall and she faced him in full, his hand to her shoulder to keep her upright. Through the shadow of his hood, she found the whites of his eyes, then the hypnotic black of his irises. Despite the subtle wrinkles on either side, the shape was familiar. He was right about who he looked like, now with his softer brow and smaller nose. Even if he still appeared slightly too old, always, he had the same narrow jaw and wide, expressive eyes.

"Why does everyone look like him?" she whispered.

"Sleep," he whispered back.

"But you're younger than when I last saw you," she whined. "How?"

He stared her down, silent, then knelt with her until she comfortably slumped against the wall, leaning so she no longer needed his hand to remain upright. "Aren't you just full of questions," he grumbled, pulling a fabric case from his pocket and letting it unfurl on the floor beside him. She eyed the collection of glass vials, syringes and canisters within.

"Why not kill me and be done with it," she murmured.

"You're the only one who can help me."

"Help you?" It didn't look like he needed helping.

"Rumor has it." He attached a needle to a syringe, and with it withdrew some liquid from a vial. "I don't see why you would, but we want the same thing." He turned her wrist so the soft side was up. "There isn't a name for this chemical yet, but it will make you sleepy. It's likely you won't remember these past few minutes."

"Would it work the same for you?"

After a pause of consideration, he relented with a nod. If he was telling the truth, he was an idiot for doing so. If he was telling the truth, she, then, had a few options. Without outright looking, she spotted his crossbow in her peripheral vision. "Are you sure you heard the rumors correctly?"

"Sleep tight, Alice."

The crossbow was too far away. She grabbed the syringe from his hand, pushing it straight up to avoid catching the needle on herself, and sent him flying off balance.

She was upon him in an instance. With her hand to his throat, his body squirmed beneath her, his back to the floor and both his hands occupied in keeping the needle from his jugular. While he carried Theo's maturity, it looked like Jack's hardened gaze and gritted teeth beneath her, mixed with the confidence and irritability of one who had experienced one too many rodeos.

She shook the thought from her head and instead wondered, why was she using weapons when an animal should use her teeth?

His neck shined with so many old scars—more scars than Jack—only half hidden beneath his cloak.

Her canines elongated.

"Don't do it," he warned, hoarse and strained.

In her mind, instead of a devil, she had a Jack on her shoulder who laughed at Marius and retorted, *"Fuck yourself."* The memory of her voice told her she'd said this aloud.

He threw his weight sideways, and she was on her back, peering up at Theo's old ceiling. She still had the syringe.

But, some feet away, Marius had the crossbow in one hand and Bishop's shotgun in the other. His hood was a heap over his shoulders.

She stood crouched at the ready—

A flash of black smoke, and a new needle stuck in her arm. She tore away from Marius, and the needle tore her arm, but she got free and her hold remained tight on the initial sleepy-time needle.

Senses fishy in her thoughts furbled like a whimsical jabberwocky poem she once staid. Words and fears all corbled, and if his irises swirlen yestertime, they spiraled todatime, moving inways covers otherways never. Outside turned inside, up and down, leaf and write, back and shoulder, knees and toes—head, shoulders knees and toes—

Marius. Marius was—

Her mouth and chin were wet. "Wart—did yew—*give… me?*" It was saliva, thick as a bull dog's. She was a bull dog?

"LSD derivative," he gasped, catching his breath. The sound echoed from everywhere, hissing softly from the outside and down her back. She snapped her gaze to his direction, and while she wasn't blind, she couldn't see him. Everything was cool colors and vague shapes—no means of conceiving where one object ended or another began.

He continued, "A small dose would make you open to suggestion. If you hadn't broken the vial in your arm like a damn savage, it wouldn't have come on so strong."

This explained nothing. Nothing explained anything. But Marius was bad and she'd been trying to stick this needle in him, so that was what she had to do.

The thing in her hand didn't look like a needle. There was a long point at its end, but it was mostly a glass tube.

She had to trust her former self—this was a needle, whether she believed it or not.

She took a step. She wasn't sure if it was ahead or to the side, or if she merely stepped in place.

"You're tripping balls, aren't you?" he grumbled.

Balls balls balls balls

"Alice?" The voice was younger now.

She turned her face. She wouldn't believe it until she saw it, but then she saw it. No subtle wrinkles, no gray hair. He was as young as she'd remembered. Her heart reacted accordingly as he cautiously approached, as if she was a skittish cat. *Thmp-thmp, thmp-thmp.*

"Where are your shoes?" he asked.

She looked down and remembered she was barefoot, though she couldn't remember why this would be seen as strange. She was indoors; people didn't have to wear shoes inside.

"We should get you to Bishop," he offered. She wasn't sure what expression she saw in his face, warped as her perspective made it. Nothing was static long enough to be observed—everything shifted in constant motion with the wavelengths of her consciousness, like running water. She imagined great concern, but she still wouldn't let herself believe it.

"Yornut Theo," she said.

While the maybe-concern remained, he seemed partially confused. "Uh. Okay, sure."

Jack? She tried to listen for heartbeats, and while she heard so many, it was impossible to distinguish what was hers and what could have been his.

"How long… here…was I?" she managed.

He stepped closer. "Your pupils are like *saucers*. God damn, if it wasn't smart for me to come out here on my own, why did you?"

It had to be Jack—Marius couldn't possibly have overheard this conversation. She would have felt him.

When it seemed clear she couldn't form a response, he let out some tension on a sigh and asked, "Did you see who did this to you?"

"Marius."

"Is he the Ripper?"

She thought it would be evident with Bri's body hanging from the ceiling fan, but when Alice peered that direction, there was no body. It was moved.

"I… I don't know," Alice decided. Had she ever told Jack about Marius? Did it make sense that he didn't have more questions about him?

He scrunched his mouth, gaze lost to the distance as he grew deep in thought. "Alright," he decided. "Come on, we should go."

"You won't—search for clues?"

"I did already."

This didn't sound right. And he wasn't wearing what she'd left him in. Granted, he could've changed, and it wasn't as if he wore what Marius wore.

Her gaze fell to his wrist with the runic bracelets. There were more runes than what Jack ever had, and her breath caught, but the longer she stared, the more the runes seemed to be dancing, and replicating, and dwindling. She couldn't rightly say how many there were.

Bishop would know.

"Alright," she agreed. "Bishop's."

He nodded, gesturing toward the door as if to say, *After you.* But she couldn't have her back to him.

She held out her free hand. Warily he eyed it. Then, once he took it—*Thmpthmpthmpthmpthmp*—

This wariness could have been due to Marius debating her trust. Or it could have been Jack hesitating because of what happened last time. Either way, the thought nagged at her consciousness that she was hand in hand with her father's killer and she wanted to be free of whatever of her own skin had ever touched him.

"You're that out of it, huh?" he asked.

She didn't answer, but focused on her footing as they crossed out of the bedroom and across the dilapidated second story.

"What's that in your other hand?" he asked.

At a glance she saw she still held the full syringe. "Mystery," she answered.

The grains of the hardwood floor were really tiny bears, or twig-men, 2-D yet layered, stretching and squatting and overall forming an image which wiggled as one.

As the floor became scarce, Jack-face hinted, "It's gonna be hard to balance with no hands." Still, she held tight, and they maintained vertical the rest of the way, even as they skidded down the rubble back to the first floor.

If he was Marius and he was suggesting that they go to Bishop, why was she playing along with his game?

She slowed to a stop and considered new options as they crossed the threshold onto the front porch.

"What?" he asked.

Deciding she needed at least a mild element of surprise, she forwent an explanation, threw him over her shoulder in a fireman's hold, and ran.

"*Alice, what the shit?!*" he cried, and while it made a convincing Jack impression, she still wasn't convinced. She continued her run, feeling the different palpitations in her heart as she brought them both closer to Jack's house. If Jack was still at his house, the Jack over her shoulder wasn't Jack.

As if realizing her plan, Jack-face swore under his breath and pushed off. While it hurt her shoulder and threw her off balance, her pride swelled for having anticipated this—despite her falling to her back, and despite his great strength, he didn't get free. With the syringe still in her grasp, she stabbed it into his thigh without hesitation, ensuring all of its contents were injected in full.

"You're making—a mistake!" He clawed at the earth and dragged them both some feet backward, and still her grip remained tight. She felt the muscles in his side and thigh lose their tension, and within the minute she bared his full deadweight.

"She'll kill again," he wheezed. "She knows you'll believe anything she tells you. She… She…"

All was silent, save for her odd heartbeat and staggered breathing. She never thought she would be in such a situation. It was laughable. But now she had to decide what to do with him before he woke up.

Bishop would know.

21. Hosting a Hostage

Alice

"Is this a lot of runes?" Alice called, holding up Marius' limp wrist before considering how Bishop wouldn't have had any context for how many runes was too many to have belonged to Jack's bracelet.

Having bursted in through the front door, she finally took in the situation. Bishop and Winifred both bolted up from the couch, Winifred with a soft felt blanket over her shoulders. Something about this was absurd. But, everything was absurd. The shadows of the light fixture on the ceiling were like bent spider legs, slowly moving and crawling and expanding to take up the full top portion of the room.

"What do you mean?" Bishop asked, diverting her attention so the ceiling-spider was no more.

At the same time Winifred breathed, wide-eyed, "It's him." Then, gathering more volume, speed, and a higher pitch, she cried, "Why did you bring him *here?*"

"I didn't know you'd be here," Alice answered simply.

Eyeing Marius all along, Winifred stepped back until the couch was between them. Her burns had healed, though some holes remained along the arms of her blouse.

Bishop seemed to finally grasp who was who when he cautiously approached, pulling Marius' slumped form up by the shoulder, leaning him back against the nearby wall of the kitchen counter for a better look. The killer still looked like Jack, though his face bubbled and melted the longer she stared at it. No one else seemed to notice, so she considered this was another hallucination. She already had difficulty deciphering what was real; this—all of this—certainly didn't help.

"Is everything real?" she asked.

Distracted, Bishop answered, "As far as I can attest." He opened one of Marius' eyes with a finger, waving a hand over and watching the man's pupils react to shadow. "How did you... *How?*" Bishop asked.

"Mystery syringe," she replied.

Bishop frowned. "Maybe a sleep potion. I'm assuming he hasn't slept much throughout the last several decades, so it's possible he'll be out for days."

This felt like new information, though Alice couldn't say for sure. Were potions real? Domsuco were real, so why not? Were dragons real?

Off of her look, Bishop assured her, "It's science we don't understand, but science nonetheless. Until we do, it's a potion."

Alice laughed, then noticed the strange look Winifred gave her—as if the girl had figured something out. "What did he give you?" her old friend asked.

"LMNOP-like." *LMNOP, LLLOP, Ellen melon tree, yellow-mentary ...*

Winifred squinted while Bishop stiffened. Suddenly he stood back at Alice's level, staring into her eyes. "My God, your pupils!" he cried. "LSD! My God, he *dosed* you!"

This was a grand degree more disconcerting of a reaction than she'd anticipated. "Will I be allkay?" She heard the voice of her child-self instead of her current-self.

"Yes!" Winifred interjected, and while she left the couch behind her, she was still careful to keep the others between Marius and herself. Gently she took Alice's hands, leading her back to the living room. "You'll be okay. The walls are breathing, belongings are strange, and it's hard to remember if bagpipes exist, right?"

Alice gave it some thought, and as she watched the walls loom closer and further and closer again, she giggled, "You're right."

Winifred smiled back, and suddenly smiles were everywhere, and that was the extra comfort Alice needed.

"He did that to me, too, while I was still human," Winifred explained. "I didn't know you could still be drugged after transition." She led her back to the couch, and so they both sat. "It doesn't last forever, the, what's it called, LMNOP—"

"LSD," Bishop muttered.

Winifred continued, "It takes a while to wear off, but it always does."

"How long?" Alice asked.

"Eight hours," Bishop answered. "Depending. How much did he give you?"

"I broke a vial in my arm."

Silence. Alice peered between Bishop and Winifred, who exchanged startled glances.

"That isn't how regular LSD enters the bloodstream," he said.

"LSD-*like*," Alice reiterated.

Bishop nodded dismissively. "Benzodiazepine nonetheless."

"What?" Winifred and Alice asked in unison.

"Trip-stopper." He all but vanished before she heard his voice from his room, under his breath, "A *vial*—How are you *functioning?*" At the same time Winifred screamed, "Don't leave us alone with him!"

Alice put a comforting hand along the girl's arm. "I'll protect you."

Winifred only glanced at her for a second before staring back at Marius.

Alice stood from the couch.

"What are you doing?" Winifred's voice went so high, it came out more as a whisper. A funny connection occurred to Alice as she recalled how her old friend always had a similar reaction to a spider in the room—she'd sit on a surface as far from it as possible, with her legs up so her feet wouldn't touch the floor. Was Marius only as threatening as a spider, then?

Alice glanced up at the ceiling-shadow spider and decided, yes.

Speaking was difficult, so she didn't bother. She knelt before her father's killer, slumped against the wall of the kitchen counter as he was. While asleep, he might as well have been a harmless bug.

She pushed his head back by the forehead. His eyes were closed. He still looked like Jack. "He's right," she grumbled. "I'd kill him if he didn't look like them."

"You couldn't kill him anyway."

"I got this far, didn't I?" Alice couldn't help her voice rising.

"That's not what I meant."

All Alice saw of Winifred was a sliver of the back of her head from over the couch.

The girl continued, "Nothing kills him. Fire, stake through the heart, none of it." Silence. Winifred turned her face along the top of the couch until she could see her one-time captor. "We should restrain him before he wakes up, though. In case he wakes up sooner than later."

"I'll take care of that," Bishop offered as he returned with a fisted hand. He crossed to the kitchen, removing a spoon from a drawer and emptying a white powder into its bowl. "I didn't think this through," he muttered under his breath. He all but disappeared, then materialized before them again, now with a prepped syringe. "Typically you'd swallow the pill, but if you reject anything that isn't blood, you'd only regurgitate it if you tried." With the syringe, he added small amounts of water to the powder in the spoon, then mixed it all until it fully dissolved.

"You're going to stick that in me?" Alice asked.

Bishop nodded, eyes still on the solution. He squeezed the remaining water from the syringe into the sink, then with the newly empty syringe he sucked up the contents of the spoon. "Unless you'd rather be downright bonkers for the next fifty-two hours?"

What was fifty-two? What constituted an hour? Was it a feeling, or a measure? Was a measure a feeling? If time was arbitrary, did any of this matter?

"You're still recovering from your time underground," Bishop insisted. "Now is not the time for you to have a psychedelic experience."

Bishop knew what he was talking about. She could trust him. But... "Why did Marius want to bring me to you?" she asked.

"To keep you safe, I imagine."

She was still missing something. Marius could've kept her safe, if he wanted. Why give her to Bishop, an enemy in his eyes? "He trusts you," she figured.

"I suppose he does." His intonation indicated he hadn't thought of it that way before.

"Why does he trust you?"

Bishop's lips parted with the wish of an explanation, but nothing came out. He was holding something back. *Could she trust him?* He had a pill in a syringe for her. She was learning too much. He was going to drug her into forgetting.

She stepped back, steadying herself against the counter, awkwardly reaching over the space Marius occupied so her legs wouldn't touch him. "Why does he trust you?" she asked again, backing further and into the wall so she no longer reached over the body.

Bishop turned to Winifred. "She's not going to let me do it." He was avoiding the question.

"*Bishop!*" Alice screamed, louder and more manic than intended, and now everything felt loud—she had to yell just to hear herself. "*Why does he trust you!?*"

"Maybe if you answered her question, she *would* let you," Winifred suggested. Alice couldn't read her face. Her expression changed with the imaginings of melting eyebrows and twisting mouths. It was as if everything was liquid smoke, which didn't rise but sank, swirling and distorting any which direction depending on how anyone moved.

Bishop sighed, and Alice couldn't read the intonation in this, either, but somehow she watched the sound float to her on a vertical bridge through the melting smoke. "He trusts me to keep you safe, the same way I trust him to cloud your judgment," he said.

This wasn't enough. There was still something he wasn't telling her.

He read her well, glancing at Winifred to say, "She still doesn't trust me."

Now Winifred stepped closer to Alice; it was her turn to try and sway her. Her crystal-blue gaze fell to Marius and she stopped when she was on Alice's other side. "Don't you think this conversation would be easier when you're sober?"

"He won't make me sober—he'll make me forget," Alice countered.

"I won't let him," Winifred promised. "And even if he does, I'll still remember. I'll remind you, and then we can both ask him, together. I'd *also* like to know his history with Marius."

Winifred was too calm. She was in on it. She didn't mean anything she said; she said it all only to assuage her.

The old friend's gaze dropped back down to the killer. "Would you mind stepping closer to me? I know he's asleep indefinitely, but... I'm sure you understand?"

Maybe she wasn't in on it. Maybe she only thought Alice was being crazy, and that Bishop was being the good doctor. This hardly changed anything. Alice was still on her own here. Perhaps if she played along for just long enough, she would make it to the door and be able to outrun them both. *I'll keep my memory intact and wait out the drug.* The memory of her voice had her wonder if she had muttered any of this aloud.

When Bishop issued a simple, "Nope," she felt a sting in her shoulder. Suddenly his voice was at her side, "We've already had one out-of-touch domsuco on the loose."

The pang of betrayal hit her deep in the chest. She couldn't fight Bishop the way she fought Marius—she simply couldn't do that to him. Yet he would drug her on a whim. The same way Marius would. "You're no better than him," she uttered, eyes warming with tears. Already her throat hurt.

"Aww, Alice!" This noise from Winifred sounded like a mix between a laugh and a cry, as if Alice was being cute for being sad. "You don't mean that!"

"We'll see when she sobers," Bishop grumbled, pulling back the needle and stepping away. He ducked out of her view, and when he stood he had Marius draped over his shoulder. "In the meantime, I'll be in my office."

Alice felt sunken into the kitchen floor—engulfed in its checkered tile as she sat against the counter, wild-eyed and gripping the wall for support. While Winifred spoke from a spot beside her, Alice had given up on trying to understand her a long time ago. For a while Alice assumed the girl was yanking her chain, speaking in gibberish as if it was English all for the sake of watching Alice struggle to keep up. When Alice realized she mentally and physically couldn't ask Winifred for clarification, she considered the more likely possibility that it was her own perception which was bonkers—not Winifred's monologue.

Many moments later—it was impossible to discern if it was minutes or hours—, after what Alice realized was a stretch of silence, Winifred spoke and Alice understood. "I should have never left him," her old friend said.

Alice turned her gaze to the girl, studying her expression as best she could. While she finally grasped language, faces were still difficult to read and Alice still couldn't form words. Thankfully nothing was melting anymore.

Winifred glanced at her, and off of what must've been an inquisitive look, she dropped her gaze and explained, "Marius. He wanted to kill me those decades ago, when he had me. But he kept me for so long, I'm not sure he ever would have. But now he will. I feel it."

Alice didn't understand, though she wasn't sure if this was still due to her perception of language or to Winifred being strange. "You would have rather stayed with him?" As soon as it came out, it sounded ridiculous.

Winifred grimaced. "I… I don't know," she sighed. "While he barely said a word, I could still sense his…pain." The last word was uttered with a subtle squint, as if she was still unsure if it was the right word. "Not at first, but gradually, and when he finally said *something*, as disturbing as it was, it was still—progress, in a way. Wasn't it?"

Alice couldn't say.

Winifred continued, "Of course, I'm afraid of him—and I hate him—but I also... I pity him. And I wonder if I hadn't left, if I could've gotten through to him. Maybe he wouldn't be so angry with me now if I... But now we're back to square one and I don't think he'll hesitate again."

Alice frowned. "You blame yourself for the way he treats you."

Winifred drew her knees to her chest. "There has to be something I did. There has to be a reason he chose *me* to... I still don't understand."

Alice watched Bishop's door in the hallway open from where she sat, and he strode nearer. "That should keep him down indefinitely," he muttered.

Winifred glanced from him, then stared down the hallway at his door. "What should?"

Bishop stopped at the edge of the counter, fists on his hips in a stance he often took when he felt finished with a job well done, but was still 'on.' When he explained the situation to Winifred, it seemed as if he was talking to himself. "He's on timed doses of a tranquilizer, which will increase over time to counteract his estimated tolerance as it builds. In the unlikely instance it should wear off a brief moment before it's re-administered, he's bolted down in such a way he won't have the leverage to break free." A flicker of a smirk came and went across his face. "The bastard's not going anywhere anytime soon."

Winifred remained staring at the door. "How do you know him?" the girl finally asked.

Bishop bit his lip, then turned his attention to Alice. "Can you understand me?"

Alice allowed a beat to let her comprehension sink in before she nodded.

Bishop peered at the couch in the living room, then muttered "Oh, what the hell," and sat on the floor across from her, legs crossed. He glanced at her eyes briefly before dropping his gaze, possibly to the space where the counter met the floor. Alice wouldn't look away and check. She felt stuck in position, and she wanted to observe Bishop uninterrupted.

"I know Marius from…centuries before I came here," he finally said. "Back when I was still human. At the time we had the same goal—to maintain the power balance between mortals and Domsuco. For a time we were unstoppable, until…" He pressed his lips in a hard line. "Chaos whispered too seductively to him. He believes death and violence are the means to true peace. And now we're here."

"You're still not telling me everything," Alice accused.

Bishop glanced at Winifred. "Some secrets are not mine to share." The glance told Alice the more honest issue. He didn't want Winifred to hear.

He continued, "Both of us were miserable people when we met, so we understood one another—spoke the same language. He's a master of manipulation; I didn't notice what path he lead me down until…" He cleared his throat. This was a story he wouldn't share, and Alice wouldn't press him for it yet. "Well," he said, looking her in the eye. "He trusts me because he knows me. He needs you alive, for whatever reason, and he knows I'd do anything to keep you safe even if it meant consequently doing him a favor, which I would rather not."

"He says I'm rumored to help him."

In a flash, Bishop's brow was furrowed and his eyes were wide with concern. "Help him? How?"

She shrugged with the shake of her head.

Bishop bit his lip, looking away. "But you know better than to do that. Don't you? He thinks the only way to end pain is to rid the world of all humans."

Winifred dropped her jaw, equal parts confused and upset. "If he wants to end pain, why did he torture me?"

Bishop sighed. "That's one thing I never understood."

As Alice replayed the last conversation she had with the monster, she found there was only one thing which made sense. "He sincerely thinks you're evil."

Winifred started. "*Evil?*"

It was strange to think of Winifred as evil, especially when one considered how she was too timid to even harm a fly, before she had turned into a domsuco. Before Marius abducted her.

"Bishop?" Alice asked, hoping he could fill in the gaps.

"Either this, or he thinks that torturing her—or killing her—will serve a greater purpose," he suggested. "Since his plan will result in death regardless, who he harms along the way ultimately won't matter, in his eyes."

"But what purpose?" Winifred cried.

Bishop explained, "If he needs Alice to help him, he needs her to be on his side. If he presents her friends as villains, one by one, she will become isolated and vulnerable to his advances—she would go to him when there is no one left, simply to not be alone, as is the human condition. And he would convince her it is the right thing to do." He glanced at Winifred. "If he paints you as the villain, he needs to respond to you the way he responds to villains. He hurts you to make his story convincing."

Bishop exchanged his next look with Alice. "He was convincing, wasn't he? Did you nearly believe him? Or...*did* you believe him?"

"I believe he believed himself," Alice muttered, already seeing where he was going with this.

Bishop nodded. "That's already more trust in him than is safe."

22. Insights At The Mall

Alice

"Finally, we can go to the mall and be a couple of girls!" Winifred squealed.

The full effects of the LSD seemed to have worn off by the time she and Alice ended their super-human run and stepped out from the scarce woods beside a busy street, though some traces of the existential wonderland still lingered in Alice's mind. Even in this wave of a come-down, she saw the strangeness in this turn of events. Going shopping, after everything that had just happened. But Winifred wasn't comfortable being under the same roof as her one-time captor, nor was she yet comfortable returning to the world without a safety blanket—someone who could protect her in the event anything should happen. None of this was said, but Alice read her old friend well, and she had to be here for her.

And, even if Marius really wasn't the Ripper, a night out to celebrate his capture still felt appropriate. By process of elimination, they were one step closer to learning the truth.

Winifred decided the mall was the place to go, remembering Alice hadn't yet had this experience. Alice didn't know what to expect, but she also didn't think much of it. It was only shopping, after all—what real difference would the venue make? Winifred had a tendency to exaggerate the greatness of new, material things—much in the same way Alice had in regards to automobiles. Back when they were beautiful and made sense, anyway.

As Alice observed the structure across the busy street from her, and could more clearly see the immaculate squares of buildings with light-up logos attached to even more grand squares of buildings with similar such signs, it began to dawn on her that maybe this would be a newer experience than she had anticipated. The parking lot was an ocean of bland monochromatic cars, all shiny in the orange streetlights and the eerie non-blue of the static from power-lines —a static she would not have perceived prior to transition.

"Is this what you do with your girl friends?" Alice asked, too dazed to ponder if this was a silly question. Girls went shopping—it was in their blood. She should've known. Some things would never change.

"I haven't yet, but I've gone by myself," Winifred answered, beaming. "It isn't the same." While this seemed like a lonely experience, it was as if Winifred couldn't be bothered spoiling her good mood over this.

"All this time, and you've only gone by yourself?" Alice asked.

Winifred sighed, though her grin was mostly unchanged. She nodded for Alice to follow before dashing across the street—effortlessly dodging the speeding traffic to practically materialize at the other end of the road. No one slowed or swerved or honked; no one seemed to notice. If they had, they would have only registered a glimpse of movement before it was gone, and by that time they would have no reason to give it a second thought.

Alice followed suit, just as effortlessly. Leading the way through the parking lot and to the mall's entrance, Winifred explained, "I've had Th-*Jack* take me a few times, but it's clear he doesn't want to be there. His sister's sometimes there as well, but I don't think she likes me. Or, I don't know if she likes what I like? I don't think she *dislikes* me, I just don't know how to *be* around her. If that makes sense."

Alice nodded, though became distracted. This all seemed to hint at a disturbing notion. "Did you do anything with anyone before you met them? Gabby and Jack?" As they neared the entrance, Alice reached to open the doors, only for them to open automatically as they had done in the hospital. This time she had the sense to feel foolish for reaching.

Winifred didn't tease her as she expected she would. Now the old friend's grin had faded, a remembered pain haunting her eyes as she focused her stare straight ahead. "I had a lot of time to myself," she said. "I don't know if anyone's told you about the internet yet, but that's where a lot of my time went, once it came about. It was stiflingly lonely before that. "

"I don't know what the internet is."

Winifred laughed. "My goodness, it's like *Blast from the Past*—and a dream, all in one! You're here, and I have to explain to you what—" Again she laughed, covering her mouth.

When Alice took in just enough of her surroundings so as not to walk into anything, she found an interior as stark and bright as the hospital in Erie, but with wooden accents and colorfully decorated shopfronts which contributed an element of life and excitement that only a retail center could. It was like an indoor strip-mall—or two indoor strip-malls, face-to-face along either side—and two stories up. There was a sunroof—or, a moon-roof—and so many people.

Winifred had stepped some paces inside, also peering up at the glass ceiling. She only glanced back at Alice for a second before further leading the way down the wide tiled floor. Alice kept pace beside her.

"Okay," Winifred started, "imagine a television screen with typewriter keys at the bottom. With it you can…" She laughed, "My goodness, this is going to sound so bizarre and amazing, and here we all are, taking it for granted—"

"What?"

With a carefully articulated enthusiasm, Winifred peered into her eyes and stressed, "We have access to practically every*one,* and the knowledge of every*thing* in the world at our fingertips—a library, a directory and a telephone, all in one."

Alice couldn't grasp how this was possible. She couldn't be impressed yet; for now, there was only confusion.

Winifred spent the next several minutes trying to put it all to words. Without the context of having the internet right in front of her, Alice wasn't sure if she fully understood before she gave in and said she did—if for no other reason than for Winifred to get on with her story. Perhaps Alice would gain a better grasp of how it all worked within the context of a narrative.

Winifred continued, "I talk to friends in cyberspace every day. Having only this certainly got old after a while, and there was the occasional dick-pic to deal with—well, there still is—but overall it wasn't so bad; I wasn't nearly as lonely as I was *without* the internet—"

"Wait just a minute, *dick-pic?*" Alice wasn't sure if this was internet-slang, or if it was…exactly what it sounded like.

Winifred laughed out a quick breath through the nose. "Oh, the teens of our times were so innocent, weren't they?"

Alice and Gene weren't entirely innocent. She'd *seen* a… She'd seen his on occasion, but… "You mean *pictures* of…?"

"Yup."

"All—all of a sudden?" She stammered, "No, um, personal— Or, no, no sort of…?"

Observing Alice's face, Winifred's laugh renewed. "Sometimes it's utterly out of nowhere, otherwise it's because they see an excuse of an invitation."

"*Why?*"

"I don't think anyone really knows."

After the silence which followed, during which Alice tried to wrap her mind over whatever sort of mentality could allow this to happen, Winifred sighed, "That's the internet for you. All the power this world can offer, and boys use it to send dirty pictures to unsuspecting girls."

"That *is* bizarre."

They hadn't been walking fast to begin with, so it wasn't too jarring when Winifred slowed to a stop. Alice stopped a few steps ahead of her, and when she glanced back she found the girl halted before a boutique. Closer inspection revealed it wasn't the items which caught her attention, but the blown-up poster advertisement which featured three young women in sporty winter coats, smiling in the snow, the sun shining at an angle to produce a fantastical lens flare.

"You're lucky, being able to be out in sunlight," Winifred murmured. "In a small town like this, not many people are out after dark."

Alice's heart swallowed itself. It hurt for Winifred's hurt, and for not knowing what she could do to fix it.

Winifred grimaced. "Or, okay, enough people are, but they're not... We're not quite cut from the same cloth, if you catch my drift? They're the sinners and outcasts we've been told to avoid all our lives—and after trying to chat with a few, I understand why. They're awful—even the few other domsuco who stayed here. This, and most things are closed after dark, so… Take *people* out of the question, and there's not much left to do besides art and video games. And books. I've read *Twilight* so many times—it's a real gas."

"I'll add that to my reading list," Alice muttered.

Winifred allowed a small, distracted grin, but it was gone as soon as it came. She had more on her mind; more to say. "Any conversation I had, for the longest time it was in my own head." She concluded, "With the internet, I could speak with people all around the world—the good people who're awake during daytime hours, whole timezones away."

So Winifred had been completely on her own for decades. This shouldn't have been a surprise, given the girl's shy, introverted nature, but… *Decades?* She couldn't find *one* other person, besides Jack—before Jack—all this time?

Winifred continued their stroll. Alice noted that most of the displays in the shop windows were for women's wear, and Winifred seemed to be thinking the same thing. "When was the last time you got clothes?" the girl asked.

"I bought shoes the day I came back," Alice answered, then amended, "Well, I meant to. I still have to pay the girl back."

Winifred smiled. "You really are so good, aren't you."

"What do you mean?"

"You know you don't have to pay her back, right? Do we or do we not have special mind powers?"

"Just because we *can* use them doesn't mean we *should*."

"That's exactly what I mean!" Winifred laughed, teasing, "You perfect square, you!"

Alice smiled, knowing this was all good-natured, but she never thought of this as being an especially good or kind thing, paying for things at the store. It was simply the thing to do. She wasn't a thief.

Winifred sighed, "We'll do it your way today; don't worry. I have enough to cover us both. It isn't as if we need the cash for food. Come on, let's try Hollizombie."

And so they went. Alice was surprised by how dark it was in there. While she could see perfectly fine, she noted how others squinted at the tags and lifted shirts into the light to adequately tell what was navy blue versus what was black — she wasn't the only one with this issue. When she checked a tag for herself, she was relieved Bishop had given her extra cash; she couldn't ask Winifred to spend fifty dollars on what should only have been nine or ten at most. Because Alice needed more than one new thing, however, they left for someplace less expensive and sought the clearance section therein. Alice found her preference was business casual, though she had to dress blouses down with jeans—or skirts down with light denim or leather jackets—to fit in with her supposed age range.

Winifred clapped her hands in appreciation as Alice stepped out of the dressing room. The latter wore a black faux-leather coat, fitted most flatteringly to her slim frame, and a dress made of a heavy winter fabric, the color of red wine, the hem stopping just below the knees. Paired with already-purchased black woolen socks and black suede boots, she was unstoppable.

A new plan apparently sprung to Winifred and erupted in the form of a sharp gasp, "Hair!"

Alice tilted her head, her curtain of raven hair slipping to obscure a portion of her face and shoulder.

Then, with a different enthusiasm, Winifred asked, "Does your hair grow back?"

"I don't think so."

"That's okay, I was just wondering. Mine doesn't, but I know you're different—anyway! Wanna dye it? It can always be dyed back if you don't like it."

The notion felt like a perfect combination of daring and safe. Alice's hair was generally the same throughout her life, and a bold, immediate change felt right somehow. She nodded.

Winifred squealed, and once Alice's new outfit was paid for, the bubbly ginger led the way up the magical escalators and to a salon. The atmosphere wasn't anything like the classic barber shops Alice was used to. It felt more like a zen garden, all earthy greens and yellows and browns, with the lights a warm gold.

At Alice's insistence, the barber allowed her to keep her hair's length. At the barber's insistence, Alice got "layers," so her hair didn't fall in one solid sheet, but in several. Winifred and the stylist talked colors, and by the time they were through, Alice had what they called "lowlights." It was subtle, but she noticed the new burgundy color whenever her hair touched light, and she liked it.

The stylist for Alice was available for some time before Winifred's, so now as Winifred sat with her head beneath the metal oven helmet, Alice waited in a spare barber seat before her.

Still observing her new color through the mirror, Alice chuckled at a thought. Off of Winifred's inquisitive look, she explained, "Your mother would have said this was the Devil's salon."

Winifred responded with a silly grin. "I'm spitting in God's face for altering what He gave me. You remember she thought Ruth let a demon possess me when I was under trance that first Halloween?"

The old memory resurfaced as soon as it was said, and Alice was taken with an unexpected laugh, "Yes!" Ruth wasn't a domsuco, of course — but even humans had methods for working their magic. And Jack did mention they were *Wishers*. Alice wasn't sure if a Wisher was its own being in the same sense that a domsuco was. In any case, Ruth's hypnosis wasn't nearly so strong of a trance that Alice or Winifred could produce now, but it still was very real.

Winifred's grin gradually faded from her eyes, though remained left over on her face. "Do you still believe in God?"

Alice shrugged, not recovered from the tickle of nostalgia. "I don't know. The concept's absurd when you think about it, but then, how did we all get here?"

Winifred pursed her lips to the side, thinking. "Jack keeps wanting to end it all."

Just like that, all of her humor evaporated; they passed a point of no return, and this conversation wasn't going to lighten up anytime soon.

Winifred continued, "I keep trancing him out of it, but the more I do it, and the more I listen to him, the more I wonder if maybe he's onto something."

"What do you mean?"

Winifred grimaced. "I'm stuck here. I don't know how or why—I know I *can*, theoretically, leave whenever I want, but I just *can't*. I'm here every day, doing the same thing, every day, and even with the little variation time naturally offers, it all still feels the same. *I* feel the same. I'm trying to break the cycle and try new things, but I still don't feel any different. I wonder if I was supposed to die when Marius had me. Or, before that, even."

Alice knew to what she referenced, sighing. "You weren't meant to bleed yourself out—"

Winifred, though her gaze was distant and she seemed deep in her thought, didn't miss a beat; "Nothing felt the same after Theo broke up with me —"

Alice cut in, hoping to provide comfort in her sternness, "You're meant to die when you die." With a gesture toward the heavens, she added, "You're spoiling His plans for you if you take your own life, right?"

The muscles around Winifred's eyes tightened with a subtle squint. "I thought you didn't really believe in Him?"

Alice couldn't disagree, but she also couldn't pretend she knew anything for certain. "In any case. I think we gals are made of something stronger than heartache. We're built to survive it, even if it doesn't feel like it."

Winifred continued to stare her down with a burning question, or an accusation. Alice understood why. If what Alice said was truly what she believed, why had she let the town stake her once Theo died?

Alice dropped her gaze and answered, "Well. If it wasn't true, would we both still be here?"

At this, Winifred eventually deflated. "It's been so long, though. Maybe I got better since Theo came back. I mean, Jack. And you're back now." She offered a forgiving grin. "There's still so much I have to show you."

Alice grinned back, though her throat hurt. Curse it all, she could have cried. "I'm sorry I wasn't here. I should've been here."

Winifred shifted her weight, uncomfortable with this sort of attention. Alice understood it by now; even after all this time, Winifred still wasn't used to power. Someone apologizing to her gave her the power to forgive, or to not, and so she felt put on the spot. "I don't blame you," she finally offered. "Theo just has that affect on people, I guess."

Alice laughed, hoping this would ease Winifred back to her comfort zone.

Winifred shyly grinned back.

The Day of the Dance, 2011

23. The Green Notebook

Jack

Class was in session, and this time Jack was present. The fluorescent lights seemed to white everything out. Posters were a sad attempt to cover the nausea that was the thickly painted white cinder block walls.

He figured he needed to maintain some sort of passing grade, so there he was, taking notes, or at least trying. Their teacher lectured, and his classmates seemed to pretty much already know what he was talking about. Jack considered raising his hand and asking for clarification, but the last time he did this, all the man had to say was, "If you were here yesterday, you would know." Students were expected to copy the notes of their peers for any day they were absent, but seriously, who was about to help Jack the Ripper?

Fifteen minutes in and he gave up. He had a more important project to work on. Fishing through the backpack at his feet, he pulled out his green notebook and skimmed through the pages.

He'd hardly situated himself before the door at the front opened. Pencils ceased their scratching, and as the door opened further the teacher seemed distracted enough to pause as well.

"Crystal!" a boy exclaimed. A few others echoed in suit, and about five students stood when they saw her.

There she was, a bandage over her neck, though the last time Jack saw her she didn't need one. The stitches were a bit scary, though, so it was probably for the best she kept them hidden.

The boy and the five others swarmed to the front, wrapping around her in a jumping amoeba group hug. The teacher, the same Mr. G-opoulos who had been subbing a year ago, smiled and seemed happy to let the moment linger. There was hope in his face, and when Jack allowed an indiscreet look from left to right, he found the sentiment reflected in the majority of the other students as well.

"Hey guys!" Crystal wheezed, all of her air having been lovingly squeezed from her lungs.

She caught Jack's gaze. At first he figured she was looking at someone behind him, though the more detail he discerned, the more he doubted this was the case. As soon as he became unsure, her smile warmed, and he knew it was for him. Of course now she wouldn't be afraid of him; she survived the killer and learned for herself he had nothing to do with it. He doubted this meant they would become friends, but just knowing he had at least one other person on his side was refreshing. Smiling didn't come naturally to him as of late, but he tried the closest thing he could muster: a lopsided mouth-stretch.

"Alright," Mr. G-opoulos said, "find a seat, and we'll get back to it. Crystal, it's good to have you for the next thirty minutes."

"It's good to be back," she replied, and as the group hug dissolved, she finally had a good look at what her seat options were. A hush enveloped the room as it dawned on the others. The only empty seats were around Jack. Their faces fell; it was as if they thought he'd finish the job on the spot.

"Ooh noo," Jack mutedly sing-songed, knowing how especially morbid it came across to anyone who wasn't Crystal. "Not *that* seat."

This was met with indifference for some, more fear from others, and anger from the rest, especially the first boy who stood. "Here," that boy offered, striding to his own desk and clearing the space for Crystal, "you don't gotta sit by that."

"Don't be stupid." She crossed to Jack before the boy could finish. Jack couldn't help smirking at the responding stupid look on the kid's face.

When everyone else seemed baffled, Crystal explained, "Guys, it ain't him. Come on already." This said, she sat in the nearest open seat.

The only face Jack could see clearly now was Mr. G-opoulos'. He seemed confused. "Right," said the teacher. He cleared his throat and continued, "Now, everyone, partner off. Discuss the reading; you know the drill."

Most of the students already sat by their friends, so not many had to move to find a partner. Jack didn't bother with any of it; he returned to his notebook, flipped to a blank page and wrote, *Alice*. He wasn't great at guessing ages, so she could've been anywhere between eighteen and twenty-five. He wrote this in, too, then added some other character-istics off the top of his head, as he had done with the others. *Quiet. Kind. Composed. Amish and doesn't know it.*

A voice close at his back, "Are those all suspect profiles?"

He jumped and spun in his seat, pulling something in his side and bashing his elbow into the desk. There sat Crystal, behind him now, watching over his shoulder.

"How long have you been there?" he asked.

"Long enough. Listen, it ain't Alice."

"So you saw who it was?"

"Couldn't see shit."

"Thought so." Holding his side, he carefully turned back to his notebook. "All we know is Alice was in the area when it happened, but then she found you and brought you to the hospital, right?"

Crystal bit her lip as if she wanted to argue but couldn't. "God damn, I wanna live, but I wanna help."

"Don't worry about it."

She strode around and sat at the desk in front of him, backwards so she could face him. "Fuck that, just…" Again she bit her lip, thinking.

He waited.

She found his gaze, decided. "If I tell you anything you don't know, it could kill me. So what do you already know?"

"Could it kill *me* if I told you?"

She rose an eyebrow like he was dumb, and waited.

"Yeah, you're right," he groaned, "I don't care." He pulled old homework from the notebook's built-in folder, put it in as a bookmark and flipped to the first page. He showed her, *Personal relation to target. Personal relation to me. Connections to corrupt officers. No drugs used to subdue victims—superior fighting skills? Victims all girls who spoke to me—killer jealous?* He gave it some thought and made some adjustments, writing upside-down. ~~*Victims all girls who spoke to me — killer jealous?*~~ *Didn't know cheerleaders.*

Crystal frowned. "Forget me and my friends; we're still alive." She pointed to where he wrote *jealous.* "I think that's what you're looking for."

This, paired with what he and Alice had found…

"Do you know anything about an abandoned house hide-out?" he asked.

Crystal shook her head, leaning closer with intrigue.

Considering how anyone he knew could've been the killer, including Crystal, he kept Alice out of his story when he told her what he had stumbled upon at the old Van Sloan place.

Her mouth dropped open with a high, muted, "Whaaaaaat?"

"Alright, class," Mr. G-opoulos announced, "Back to your seats, and let's see how well we do on these quizzes."

Jack snickered. He would bomb it.

Before Crystal returned to her first desk, she told him, "Meet me after school, outside by the basketball courts. I have an idea."

He nodded, accepted a quiz that was handed back to him and placed it in his notebook with the rest of the tests he didn't bother with. To pass time, he continued filling out Alice's profile. All nice things. He paused when he realized he was acting like a tween girl, writing about his crush in a not-so-secret journal. He couldn't be thinking like this. There was a bigger picture to consider, and he didn't have the luxury to go changing things, or even wanting things. He had to focus.

Finished with Alice's profile, he flipped the page and worked on Dr. Winston's. He hardly had anything substantial down before he felt he was wasting his time. It wasn't Alice and it wasn't her dad — or roommate, or whoever he was; the Ripper was someone Jack knew all along.

He flipped back through the other profiles. Crystal verified his initial instincts; he was looking for someone jealous. What girl would be jealous enough to kill so many other girls? If he was a competent officer on the case, who would he question first? He already knew the answer. He always knew.

Wyn. And she was there for the first two deaths.

He flipped to the page he thought she'd be. Then back further. Then forward. Confused, he started his search from the beginning, painstakingly turning the pages one at a time. Everyone he knew was in there—his own sister was in there. As he came to pass Alice's page, he frowned, leaning back. He could've sworn he'd made a page for Wyn.

He remembered Detective Lloyd's narrative about the servers and Bri's parents. Their minds had been fucked with.

It couldn't have been Wyn, though. It wouldn't have made any sense; she was so sweet and innocent, all the time, and scared, and she was also actively looking for the Ripper. And she didn't have the physical might.

Still, he found a clear page and wrote her name.

. . .

The last bell of the day rang. As Jack strode down the halls, he hitched his backpack further up his shoulder and buttoned his jacket closed. Hands balled in his pockets, he shouldered one of the doors open and stepped into the October winter wonderland with the hundreds of other students. While the majority swarmed to where the busses would stop, Jack rounded the corner and found the basketball courts.

"Hey!"

He turned to the voice. He knew it was Crystal, though she wore her hair hidden beneath her hood, eyes behind dark sunglasses, and mouth and neck under a scarf. From afar it was hard to tell she was even a girl, and this was likely her intention.

"Hey," he called back, waiting for her to catch up before continuing to their destination. There were some things he'd thought about since they last spoke, and it all combined to make him feel not quite right. He couldn't even pretend to pay attention in class—the rest of the school day had been spent getting these thoughts down on paper, debating what was plausible and crossing out what wasn't.

He'd never been to Wyn's house. She was insecure about their relationship. It wasn't a crime, but it was something to think about—like Alice said. It created an obvious motive for slaughtering anyone who caught his prolonged attention, and displaying them so the others would know to back off.

Crystal put down her backpack once they got to the basketball courts.

"Why here?" Jack asked, leaning against the metal-netted fence.

He had to go back to the abandoned house and see if he could find anything else of Wyn's, or if he could find a murder weapon. He needed something more telling than her clothes and his missing flannels. Did the rest of the jewelry belong to the other girls?

"I figured it'd be easy for the others to find," Crystal answered.

His train of thought froze mid-formation. "Others?" As soon as he said it, from the corner of his eye he saw them approaching. Five boys. The same fuckers from the parking lot—Luke, Troy, the other two, and even George. So he'd been initiated to their sports-cult, then.

Jack stood straight and slipped on his other backpack strap. Hoarse, he demanded, "What is this?"

"Calm down," Crystal groaned as if he was foolish for acting all on edge, "I heard what happened between you guys, but it ain't like that anymore. I told Luke it wasn't you, now they have something to say, and then we can all share the power of knowledge and actually do something."

He didn't trust it. He wouldn't run yet, but he was ready if he needed to.

The boys weren't in any rush to get there. When they finally did, they stopped with about two feet left to go before they were even a comfortable handshaking distance. While they were chatting amongst themselves before, none of them said anything now. One of the runners and George stared in his general direction, while the rest stared at their feet. None would meet his gaze.

"Soo," Crystal hinted, verbally nudging her boyfriend to proceed.

Luke grimaced. "Soo," he echoed, then didn't seem to know what more to say.

"For the record," George began, "I never actually thought it was you."

Jack didn't hesitate to reply, "That's what makes you an even bigger fucker."

"Hey!" Crystal scolded.

"He's right, though," one of the runners snickered. The thinnest and fastest of them, he wore his hair just past shoulder length, and for this reason alone Jack assumed he was a fellow stoner.

Jack looked back to George and gestured toward the others, "Yeah, at least these guys thought they were doing the right thing, but you knew and you did it anyway. *Fuck you.*"

George's face reddened and his articulation went sharp. "Not for nothing, but if we got to break your legs, your name would've been cleared by now. Can't kill girls if you're on crutches."

"That's not why you fucking did it, and you fucking know it!"

"Oh my God, guys!" Crystal yelled, "Bigger picture!"

Jack locked his fingers behind his head and paced away. By the time he paced back he was calmed enough to admit, "I get where the rest of you were coming from." To Luke he said, "You thought I killed your sister and nearly killed your girlfriend. After Sarah, I…" He trailed off, dropping his gaze. His arms followed soon after.

Luke's look softened.

Jack finished, "If I had a target, I'd actually be a murderer."

Luke nodded. Finally the other runner looked at him — the one who hadn't said anything yet. He seemed especially quiet. Ashamed. He was probably feeling guilty the second that parking lot encounter was done with.

"Okay," said Crystal on a glove-muffled clap, "Honestly, guys, we don't even all need to like each other for this to work. Just civil. Do we at least know everyone's names?"

Jack was the only one shaking his head. "You two," he said, pointing at the runners.

The stoner offered a friendly grin and a handshaking hand. "Adam." He and Jack shook.

The quiet one's grin was more humbled. "Michael." They shook as well.

"Right, progress, good." Crystal was rushing this, but no one objected. "So here's what I'm thinking. Whoever we're dealing with has eyes and ears everywhere, so we gotta be super-paranoid in how we go about this. If there's anything you wanna say that you don't want the killer to hear, write it down, then burn after reading, or eat it, I don't care."

Adam's eyes were uncertain, and his mouth offered the amused counterbalance. "Remind me why special ops is killing high school girls?"

"Ain't saying it's special ops," she answered. "A real psycho's behind this shit, and clearly they got some influence in high places, because seriously, one year, five deaths—And the police have *nothing?* I call bullshit; someone knows something, but someone's got them turning a blind eye. Seriously,

I bet there ain't even police tape up around the Vampire Crypt, and that's not even our jurisdiction. Jack," she addressed him, "I hope it's cool that I already told them what you saw yesterday?"

"Nothing I can really do about it now," he replied, glad he never mentioned Alice. "Also, a reliable source told me there're other deaths, besides the girls. Just the girls are the ones the Ripper wants people to know about."

Troy lowly whistled.

"That's fucked," Luke grumbled, and Crystal nodded.

"Right," she said. "So here's my plan to get Jack into the hospital to talk to my mom without getting us killed. You guys all gotta come with us, and Jack, if you don't own anything a jock would wear, you gotta borrow something." She planned to camouflage him with a crowd.

He looked at the others. Intact sneakers were one thing. Clothes that weren't a size too big. Shorter jacket. But was this necessary?

"And a hat," Crystal added. "Basically wear anything you'd never actually wear. If anyone sees you and recognizes you, we want them to assume they're wrong and that you're someone else. And while you guys don't actually have to like each other, it'd help if you pretended."

"I think it's Wyn," Jack blurted when this plan seemed too convoluted to work. While the guys seemed curious or confused, Crystal appeared startled, checking over her shoulder. As if he was right.

"Your girlfriend?" Adam whispered. It was as if he meant to remind Jack, *You're dating that girl; are you sure that's who you meant?*

"What makes you say that?" Crystal asked, still recovering from the derailment.

"From an objective standpoint, she's the only one that makes sense," Jack answered. "Firsthand experience, I know she's the jealous type. We've been together for a year, and I still don't know much about her—no idea where she even lives. She doesn't hang out with anyone else, so that means whenever she's not with me, she's the only person I know who can't be accounted for whenever another girl dies."

Crystal gnawed her bottom lip. The others silently mulled it over as well.

Finally Luke shook his head, "No, can't be her."

Troy agreed, finally contributing his two cents. "She's too tiny, and Ashley knew kung fu."

"Tell me what good knowing kung fu does when she's killing you in your sleep," Jack replied, remembering he'd told someone this recently.

Troy grunted in acknowledgement.

Crystal hugged herself for warmth and commented, "I was really hoping to be at least in a car by now."

Jack nodded; it was cold and they needed to speed things up. "You guys go to the hospital; don't worry about smuggling me in." He swung his backpack around, opened it from where it rested beneath his arm, and withdrew his green notebook. He handed it to Crystal. "Give this to your mom, let her look at it, whatever. I don't need it anymore."

She tried to hand it back. "You don't *actually* know it's Wyn; you might need this later."

"It's all memorized," he replied. "And if there's one thing I learned recently, it's that other perspectives help, so. Let her look at it." He closed his backpack and got ready to leave.

"Wait." Whatever she had to say must've been important; she broke away from Luke just to catch him. "What are you about to do?"

This was a good question. He didn't have a plan. "Confront her," he answered. "Somehow."

"So best case scenario, you accuse her, she's innocent and you cause an unnecessary rift in your relationship." There was already a rift, though she didn't need to know that. He let her continue. "Worst case scenario, it's actually her. What do you think would happen then? She'll admit it and accept jail time? This person has real influence, Jack—she could do anything she wants and get away with it."

"Yeah, I get it." It was annoying that she was right, but he still had to do something. As he thought it out he told her, "She's still Wyn, though. She won't kill me for talking to her."

"It ain't you I'm worried about."

That's right, only the girls are at risk. And the only girl besides Wyn he'd ever invited anywhere, who was still alive, was... "Alice," he muttered.

"Or literally any girl who even looks at you," Crystal conceded. She was also at risk.

While Jack bit his lip to consider his options, he noted the guys all exchange worried glances.

"You're damned if you do and damned if you don't," Michael mumbled. "But if you talk to her and it turns out you're right, you're one step closer to stopping this."

415

Troy nodded. "Get uglier before it gets better. Like a bruise."

Luke nodded as well, having nothing else to contribute.

Jack looked away, blocking everything out as he tried to think. They were all right. If he confronted the killer, whoever it was, shit could hit the fan in all sorts of fun new ways. But, if he did nothing, nothing would change. If it meant finally putting an end to all this...

He turned back to them. "I gotta do it."

The guys were grim, but all on the same page. When he looked at Crystal, however, he noticed her face had lost some color. He knew this face. It was the look they all had when they knew they were next. The notebook shook in her grasp. There was a flicker of a smile, as if in the hopes of keeping this light, but it was gone as soon as it came. "I ain't getting out of this alive."

"You don't know that," Luke insisted, maybe too quickly.

Jack's simultaneous response was a bit more morbid, but realistic to say the least. "None of us do."

Crystal peered back at her boyfriend, then to Jack. Her breaths were shallow, her adrenaline up. After taking in their surroundings again for reassurance, she hurriedly whispered, "You have no idea how — how fast this person is. There were four of us. One of her."

"Whoa, wait," George interjected, eyes widened, "Monica said you guys just had a few beers and blacked out —"

"None of us drink!" she screamed, scarf slipping from her mouth to her chin. After forcing some full, deep breaths, she panted, "They don't remember anything — one of them maybe had a drink, I don't know — then I guess assumed we all drank — so now — now that's what they all believe — but I saw what happened — I remember — this — shit! Vividly! Fuck," she fixed her scarf back over her lips. "I'm not supposed to remember nothing. No one's allowed to know I remember anything, okay?"

After Luke and George exchanged a glance, Jack remembered a rumor he'd overheard. Once Crystal had recovered enough to speak, she kept going on about vampires, she was attacked by a vampire. Considering she wasn't currently in a mental institution, she must've stopped insisting this was the case, though it was beginning to seem like she did still believe it. A vampire would have enhanced hearing, which would warrant writing everything down and burning after reading.

When no one answered right away she pressed, "Guys? Okay?"

All nodded, and Luke said "Okay," while some of the others mumbled, "Yeah."

While it probably wasn't vampires, Jack also didn't think Crystal was crazy enough to make it all up. Would hallucinogens have shown up in an autopsy?

It was strange, thinking it was Wyn. "I'll… hold off on accusing my girlfriend," he offered, "until we have a plan. Still, you guys know everything you need to know; go to the hospital without me."

"What are you gonna do?" asked Luke. This was also weird. Jack never would've guessed he'd end up solving murders with these guys.

"I'll draw attention away from you," Jack answered. "While you're all getting shit done, I'll keep her distracted."

"What if it's not Wyn?" George asked.

Adam gestured George's way as if to say, *That's what I was thinking.* "Yeah, what if you're just chilling with her for nothing, while the actual psycho's watching us?"

Crystal glanced over her shoulder, again assuring herself this was not the case. "Unless she's watching us now and sees we're clearly planning something, she'll have no reason to. She's always either watching Jack or whatever girl she thinks is hitting on him, which now would be Alice."

Jack nodded. "See you guys tomorrow."

"Tonight," Crystal corrected. When Jack seemed confused, she asked, "You're still going to the dance, right?"

Oh shit, he forgot about that. It was Friday already? Wyn would be nice and distracted for a good two hours prior, then. She and he would arrive back at the school at around eight, and—fuck, he'd invited Alice. Why did he do this?

Crystal added, "We should pretend everything's normal, so we don't raise suspicion."

"Yeah," he answered absently.

"Right. Later." As Crystal rejoined Luke, they all stepped past him and headed toward the parking lot.

Before completely passing, Adam addressed him, though stared ahead, never making eye contact. "Unofficial peace offering," he mumbled. At first Jack didn't get it, but when he looked down it all became clear. Cradled in Adam's hand at a crafty, though seemingly uncomfortable angle was a fresh, hidden joint. Jack was right, dude was a stoner, though nowadays most people were. The real game was to guess who wasn't, and if Jack had to bet, he'd put money on Michael. He was too clean-looking.

419

"High-grade medical shit," Adam continued, "And Crystal doesn't know, so don't tell her." So then Crystal also didn't smoke. He wouldn't have guessed, but he wasn't surprised.

Subtly nodding, Jack accepted, also keeping it hidden. He wanted to think Adam was just being a chill dude, trying to make up for their bullshit, but as had become Jack's habit, he wouldn't get his hopes up. He wondered if the guy was a dealer trying to reel in more revenue. "Thanks," he said anyway.

Adam patted his shoulder, said "Later, man," and returned to his pack. Once they were out of sight, Jack wondered if any of this actually happened, then decided it was too cold to think. He headed to his car.

Peered down at the joint.

He knew what he was doing before he got home.

The second he situated himself in the driver's seat, he put the joint to his lips and lit it up. Adam was right. He felt it in his ears and in the instant cottonmouth. This was high-grade medical shit.

The regular ride home would've been too quick, so he headed for the scenic route. All he planned to do was drive through, just as he normally would when he needed the time to finish a joint or a bowl, so he didn't think anything of it.

The thought of the abandoned house had him on the verge of an idea when—

Suddenly he was confused and questioned everything, and he was distressed for some reason. His heart was palpitating. Both of his hands were on the steering wheel, and he realized he didn't have the joint. So it was burning in his lap or in the car somewhere.

He turned on his blinker to pull over, then, shocked frozen, stared out the windshield. He was already parked on the roadside, somewhere between his house and his great-grandfather's house.

There had to have been an explanation. He had to think, but he was too high to focus. He wanted to assume he had just spaced out for a minute and that it was nothing to worry about, but this didn't seem right.

As he gathered his bearings, he glanced at the time. It was almost five o'clock. Two hours had passed.

He couldn't panic yet. He would check the time when he got home. Maybe Gabby had done something weird with her clock—whatever—there was always an explanation.

As he pulled back onto the road, he had to wonder what the fuck Adam had laced the weed with. In any case, it was difficult to drive when his arms were shaking, so he commenced dulling his senses with the rum from his flask.

24. Trust

Alice

Alice didn't know what to do about having seen Bri's body. It was moved, so she didn't know how to report it, or if reporting it was a good idea in any case. At the very least, she had to tell Jack. If they were working together, he needed to know what she knew. While she wanted to believe Marius was the Ripper and that everything was solved the moment she captured him, she knew there was still the possibility it was someone else. Someone she hadn't considered, or met yet, or…Winifred.

With Jack still in school, she used the eight hours' waiting period to bring herself as up to date as possible. Bishop lent her more money, so she finally paid back what she owed for the shoes, then walked from shop to shop in the plaza. She skimmed through all the tabloids, noting all she observed. While she hadn't dated herself too badly yet, she grew more reassured as the day progressed. There were some words of phrase that, while popular in her day, seemed goofy now. And "give me five" no longer referenced the invitation to a handshake, but instead to a two-person clap. Hipsters used to be a thing young people strived to be, though now it seemed those who wished to be one were, and those who weren't not only never wished to be, but loathed the very idea of hipsters.

She would, however, occasionally still hear a familiar saying, like a Bugs Bunny catchphrase, for instance, and it felt like home.

Remembering how Jack had invited her to a dance, she felt she had to prepare for this as well. Bishop suggested that she rent a few movies from the Red Box. A good way to tell if a movie reflected today's teen life would've been if it starred a 20-something year old actor portraying a teen, preferably in a high school setting. She did her best to find a film in which a dance would take place at some point, and once she settled with three, she took them back to Bishop's place and watched with him until he fell asleep, continuing alone until the last one ended at five.

Not only had society changed drastically, but cinema! The image was so clear! And some of the scenes, she noticed, were no longer than ten seconds. She had to finish marveling before she could truly study the content.

Hardly any dancing occurred at dances. This was a shame; Alice knew many dances, and when she went to school everyone made it a point to be-bop better than the couple beside them. Now participation seemed more optional than ever, with students huddled about and maybe hopping in place if the beat felt inviting. It would've been easy to assimilate, however disappointing.

Upon checking the time, she deemed Jack would be home now. Slipping into her new faux leather jacket, she let herself out and ran the distance until she met the edge of his property, where she slowed to a leisurely stroll. Her heart told her he wasn't there, though she cleared the porch steps and knocked on the door anyway. If he wasn't there yet, she would wait and be social until he arrived. She could handle it now.

A string of startled barks sounded from within.

An out-of-breath middle-aged woman answered in a black and red work-shirt. Alice hadn't met her before, but when she saw Gabby in her deep brown eyes she knew this was Jack's mother. "Can I help you?" the woman asked, keeping the door mostly closed between them so Lestat was trapped behind her.

Alice nodded. "I'm looking for Jack."

Mrs. Van Sloan's eyebrows shot up, and it seemed as though she wasn't sure if she'd heard her correctly. "Are you sure?"

At a loss for how else to respond, Alice nodded a second time.

"Oh." It was as if this was the wrong answer, and the woman didn't know how to break it to her. "Well, um. He's not here anyway, but... One second." She closed the door. While Alice would usually deem this sort of behavior rude, she understood why she acted this way. Like Gabby, Jack's mother hoped to keep Alice safe.

"Ma!" The woman mutedly called, only slightly muffled through the door.

"Mh?" an older woman responded from what Alice guessed was the living room.

"There's a girl here for Jack, and I need to get to work."

"Mh. Who is she?"

"I don't know, but she's outside still, and I don't know what to—"

"Have you seen her before?"

"No! Seriously, Ma, why does it matter?" Silence. She sighed. "Really?"

"You get to work. Let me handle this."

A brief hiatus before the rustle of hurried movement. The creak of the back door sounded, closing as soon as it opened. As the woman's footsteps crunched through the snow about the side of the house, the couch squeaked and the older woman groaned with what sounded like a stretch. She sighed, and the sound of slipper-clad feet shuffled across the floor, closer and closer.

The door opened and there stood the old woman herself, Lestat sitting obediently behind her. The woman smiled and asked, "You're here for Jack?"

"I am," Alice answered. Her words were hardly out before she noted the old woman's smile fade, lips parted as her mind seemingly raced. Finally the woman grinned and stepped aside. "Come in. He should be home soon."

Alice smiled back and accepted the invitation.

"Such a light jacket for a cold day," the grandmother commented, closing the door behind her. Tail wagging with the same excitement as always, Lestat stood and sniffed Alice's hands and the hem of her skirt, but didn't jump on her.

"The cold never bothered me much," Alice replied.

"And what did you say your name was?"

"I didn't. Alice."

"Ruth." The crinkles in her face multiplied as her smile widened. "I knew an Alice, once."

A sudden jolt flashed through Alice when she realized this was Theo's sister. Consciously she knew to expect her here, yet to actually see her again, like this, was so... She was so old now.

Alice remembered she needed to retain composure and attempted a casual, "Is that so?"

Ruth nodded, then paused as she looked at her again. "You look similar."

She didn't know how to respond. "Is this a good thing?"

"I'd say so." Ruth laughed, leading her back to the living room. Lestat followed the action. "I'd say it's a good sign," Ruth added.

"How so?"

Still smiling, Ruth shook her head as if to say, *I don't know.* As she sat in the recliner and pulled her crochet project from the coffee table, she said, "She always did right by Theo and me."

Alice, tearing out his throat in the woods. This didn't fit Alice's description of doing right by Theo. She could think of nothing else, so refrained from a response.

"So what are you visiting Jack for?" the old woman asked.

"He invited me to a dance, and I don't know where it is." Alice sat nearest to her on the adjacent couch, and Lestat lay down on the floor between them, practically atop both their feet.

Ruth squinted. "Is he still with Wyn?"

"As far as I know."

The old woman frowned, then shrugged. "Kids these days. When I was in high school, everyone knew everyone's business, and if they didn't know, they jumped to conclusions. No one would dare do this sort of thing. Too much attention."

Alice agreed. Crystal had already jumped to the conclusion that she and Jack were flirting. "I found Lestat," she offered, "Perhaps he still feels indebted?"

"Or perhaps he's tired of seeing Gabby and that girl all the time," Ruth replied, and both knew this was the more likely scenario. "I couldn't blame him," she added, and it was clear she meant it. "He and Gabby, they're too different, like... like..."

"Cats and dogs?"

"Fire and air. And then Wyn." She paused. "You know, I haven't met the girl."

Winifred must have kept it this way for a reason.

"Still," Ruth argued, "if he needs new company, I don't understand why he doesn't find another *boy* to uh, 'chill' with."

Alice did. "No boy wants to be associated with someone who supposedly murders girls; it would ruin any social circle he could hope to maintain. But if a girl is seen with Jack, no one would assume anything of her. All they would think is she's the next victim."

Ruth frowned, giving it some thought. Apparently something struck her as odd, for she came to squint her way. "So you do know of the darkness which surrounds him?"

Alice nodded.

"And you're still here? For him?"

Again, she nodded.

Another pause. It wasn't a demand or a means to call Alice crazy when the old woman slowly leaned forward, elbows on her knees, and asked, "Why?"

Alice skimmed through her many reasons, hoping to find one which was both accurate, non-incriminating, and brief. "He blames himself. Cuts himself off. It doesn't sit right with me; it's unwarranted. I know I don't seem at all intimidating, so I figure if I, as unimposing as I appear, can confidently stand by him and say it isn't his fault, maybe... I don't know." She dropped her gaze, doubting she had conveyed anything right thus far. It was difficult, mixing white lies with vague truths.

She tried again. "He needs reassurance. Hope. And... I think once his peers see he's nothing to be feared, he can have a social life and be happy again."

Ruth didn't respond right away. While Alice could tell the old woman appreciated the sentiment, doubt still overcame.

"Has it not crossed your mind that you may die as well?" she asked. "What sort of example would you be then?"

There wasn't an easy answer for this. "I've... handled my share of monsters," Alice decided. "This one's grown cocky; slipping up. I doubt he'll be able to kill again and get away with it."

Ruth frowned, gradually coming to lean back in her seat. A tiny laugh bubbled up, then with some uncertainty she let it happen. Smile quivering as it came to cross her face, she once again peered at Alice. Never breaking eye contact, she took her hands in hers, arms shaking with rickety excitement. "You are a godsend, dear child. I believe you will help him."

Alice appreciated the confidence and the enthusiasm, though at the same time she couldn't understand where it came from. If she was herself Ruth, she would've remained cautious—much in the same way Jack had.

"Thank you," Alice replied when she remembered it was more appropriate to respond than to not.

"Thank *you*." Ruth waited a beat to let it land before setting her hands free. "Have you told him your experiences with monsters?"

"He knows we've crossed paths."

She shook her head; this wasn't enough. "Tell him how you did it. Spare no details."

For Ruth's sake Alice smiled as if to say *I will,* but to say this aloud would've been a lie. She had considered telling Jack about domsuco and Otherkind, but Jack would believe she was crazy before he would believe *her*. They wouldn't make any progress if he could dismiss her advice for the ravings of a lunatic.

Ruth stood and crossed to her antique hutch. "There's something I've been meaning to give the girlfriend. I never see her, so I've never been able, and regardless of how many times I've asked Jack to send it along, it always ends up back here." She pulled a bracelet from a drawer, the accessory similar to the one Jack wore. Knotted rope and wooden runic beads. She crossed back and motioned for Alice to hold out her wrist. "These things don't happen by accident. I believe you were meant to have it."

Remembering how Jack said it would make evil creatures writhe in pain, Alice replied, "I couldn't possibly rob Wyn of a gift."

Ruth shook her head, "No no, I insist. I can always make her another one."

Alice stared at it. If it burned her on contact, it would be easy enough to tap into Ruth's mind and have her forget it ever happened.

Reassured, Alice held out her wrist.

The old woman grinned, explaining as she tied it on, "It's intended to feed off of your energy. If evil is near and you don't feel threatened, it will do nothing. If evil is near and you *do* feel threatened, it will empower you." It did nothing to Alice, but if it worked the way Ruth said it would, this added up.

All the while, Alice's heart beat faster. Based on the rate at which it accelerated, she knew Jack would arrive within seconds.

The front door opened, and a draft carried a scent of faint amber, weed, something subtly floral, and—

Pennies and sweat.

Fresh blood. The floral scent usually meant Wyn. Marius' scent was too similar to Jack's, so she wouldn't have been able to detect the monster if she tried. Why was Jack bleeding?

"That should be him," Ruth said without looking up. She finished tying the rope, then called, "Jack!"

"Yeah," he called back from the foyer. This was a distracted *yeah*. Not the sort which implied, *What is it?* but the sort which stated, *This is a response.* There was the rustle of his jacket as he took it off, and Alice could hear the wood settle as he placed it over the coat rack.

"You have a visitor," Ruth finished, still not looking up.

All fell silent in the foyer. She had his attention now.

"It was good to see you again," Alice said to the old woman. She knew she slipped as soon as the words came out, but by then it was too late. Ruth paused, and Alice had already begun her walk back to the foyer. The old woman would sooner doubt her hearing than realize they had met before.

Alice rounded the corner, throat tightening when she saw him. Due to her acute hearing she knew when to stop walking, though she didn't account for the fact that he wouldn't. Their noses nearly touched before he stopped short and staggered backward.

"*Jesus*," he hissed.

"Jack," she said. Leftover blood made his neck glow. The teeth puncture wounds were fresh as of today, but somehow already scabbed.

"Hey," he answered, finding his balance. She didn't need to be a domsuco to smell the alcohol in his breath. His eyes were red, though this could've been the result of smoking. If he was inebriated and nothing more, her only concern would've been that he drove home this way. However, there was something in his posture—the unsettled way he kept shifting and pacing—that made her think that, not only had something happened, but he remembered.

He peered past the threshold into the living room, and while he didn't have a view of Ruth, it was clear she was for whom he was checking. Safe to murmur without being overheard, he told Alice, "She's usually upstairs watching her shows by now." He retreated back to the foyer, hissing, "Shit," under his breath. "There's no way I can pass for sober."

Alice felt better knowing he at least knew this about himself.

"Wanna go for a walk?" he suggested, already pulling his jacket back from the coat rack.

"It isn't too cold?" she asked.

"Thought you were a winter goddess."

"I meant, for you."

"Oh, I didn't notice." He nodded toward the exit. "Come on."

Eager to learn what he knew, she followed his lead. Did he find Bri's body?

He closed the door behind her. "I've been drinking that liquid fire," he added, reaching into his pocket.

"I noticed," she replied.

He pulled out his flask, though just as he was about to put it to his lip, he paused. Shook it. "God fucking damn it."

"What's wrong?"

"I'm out." He shoved it back in his pocket and walked the stone path ahead. Alice kept pace.

"No," she clarified, "what's wrong?"

Still distracted and hurried, he glanced her way then back ahead. His movements slowed when her implication hit him. Halted, he snickered as if to mitigate the weight of the situation. "It's that obvious?"

She didn't need to answer. It was.

He let out a breath, tilted his head back, then found his words. He murmured, as if to himself, "Feel like I'm losing my fucking mind."

"How so?"

His voice tittered on nasal when he answered, "I can't remember shit that happened after I left school! It's like, one second I was hitting the joint, the next, I… I was still in my car, but there was no weed, and it was two hours later."

So he didn't remember, but whoever made him forget was sloppy in their methods.

"And I've blacked out before," he added, defensive, "I know what it means to 'get too high' or 'get too drunk,' and that's not what happened, I legitimately—I was on my way home, smoking a joint, three-thirty, then I was on my way back from the scenic route—you know, the one with the old houses and…" He trailed off, eyes unfocused as something occurred to him. "I'm sorry, I know you didn't want me to go in, but… I think I did."

"What?!" she demanded before she could ask the better question: why?

He heard what was implied and rushed, "I don't know! I didn't think anything would happen—I was only gonna be in there for a few seconds—"

"What happened after that?"

Frustrated, though trying to focus, he gritted his teeth. At the end of the day, though, he clearly already knew his answer. "I can't remember."

Someone had put him under trance and tampered with his mind again. Things couldn't continue this way. She silently vowed never to do this to him again, regardless of what was safe or convenient.

"Was I drugged?" he asked, "Is that how roofies work?"

Still somewhat distracted, she shook her head. "You would've remembered waking up or snapping out of it, and you wouldn't have been driving."

He gnawed his lip and dropped his head, his knit hat keeping his hair from falling over his eyes. "Did another girl die?"

"Not between two and five today. Not to my knowledge." She would tell him about Bri later.

He stared silently at the ground. "This feels familiar," he said finally. "I've forgotten something this way before. And then with Sarah—" His voice cracked and he stopped, then shook his head. When he started again, he spoke lowly from the back of his throat. "I was asleep for the few minutes it would've taken to…" He found Alice's gaze, pleading, and something in her flipped. "What if it *was* me?"

"It isn't you," she promised. Perhaps Ruth was right. Maybe he did need to know more, like what he was up against.

Alice peered over her shoulder, as if this would prove any use in detecting a creature who wished not to be noticed. "Can we talk someplace private?"

"That's why we're outside."

"Someplace confined would work better. Underground."

He gave her a long, silent look, as if suspicious. "Who do you think's gonna hear us?"

She couldn't answer unless they were underground, therefore she didn't.

He didn't seem surprised. "Did you hear that when Crystal first woke up, she wouldn't stop screaming about vampires?" This was news to her, and it must've shown in her face. "Yeah," he continued, "Vampires. They said she stopped and that's why she's out now, but then today she warned us about communicating carelessly, like someone was listening in on our every conversation. Like they had super hearing."

All of this was worrisome, but first she needed to know, " 'Us?' Who's 'us?'"

"Me and some of her guy friends."

Her mouth fell open, as if to protest, but there were no words. She and Bishop had given the girl explicit instruction: she couldn't tell anyone what she knew. Yet Crystal felt *Alice* was acting foolishly? Frustrating though this was, dwelling on it wouldn't help them now.

She let out a breath and closed her eyes. "Please, Jack," she said. "I'll feel much more comfortable saying what I have to say if we were someplace else."

"What do you have to say?"

She crossed her arms and waited.

However skeptical, he eventually sighed, "Fine, I'll bite." He led the way back inside, then to a door in the foyer which opened to a descending flight of stairs. He must've known it would be cold there; he kept his jacket on. "It's not very clean," he warned.

She nodded. Already she detected the distinct musky scent which accompanied most boys' rooms.

Satisfied, he led the way and she followed. The stairway opened into a decently sized room. Cement floor, with a geometrically pleasing rug. The only available light spilled from two windows near the ceiling. Snow and underbrush from the other side kept the light mostly obscured, and with how late it was getting, there wasn't much to be shielded.

Despite the dark, she could see to what mess he referred. When he slapped his hand to the wall and flipped the light switch, he undoubtedly saw for himself as well. Clothes and snack wrappers shared the floor and most surfaces, and the bed was unmade.

She absently noted his interests. The walls were layered with rock band posters and comic book heroes, while the worn paperback novels in his bookcase were mostly in the deep-fantasy and science fiction genres. A guitar leaned un-ceremoniously against the wall.

"Alright," he prodded, turning his back to the room. The steps he took backwards might've been unintentional. "Doors are closed, we're underground..." He stood at the foot of his bed. "Privacy." When he felt the bed at his leg, he seemed confused as to how it got there.

Still she hesitated. How could he have driven home this way? But this was an issue for another time. "Can you play music?" she asked.

He squinted. "I… can? Where are you going with this?"

"I'd like to know what you listen to." It was another way to mask noise.

Although confused, he crossed to his nightstand and pressed the power to a small machine which sat on the surface. While the invention was new to Alice, it couldn't have been new to the times. It was scratched, luster lost long ago.

The device only had a second to whir before he suddenly slapped the *eject* button, remembering, "You already know what I listen to; you don't like it."

"Is that all you like?"

If he was listening, he could've fooled her; he hadn't looked back when she spoke, but shuffled through the stack of discs which also sat on the night stand. One gave him pause before he replaced the other disc in the player, skipped through a few songs before they could start, and stopped at one which opened with a dreamlike guitar sequence.

"Boom. Music." Now he faced her.

There was nothing left to address now, save for why they were here to begin with. It was a daunting notion, for how could she bring up domsuco in a way he would believe?

She bit her lip, then muttered, "The attacks never happen in the sunlight. No one cares to investigate —"

He closed his eyes, dropped into his mattress and groaned, "I *know* —"

"I'm reminding you," she insisted, raising her tone just enough.

Elbows on his knees, he sank his head through his fingertips, pushing his knit hat off and his hair back. "Why?"

She hesitated, but gave him her most honest answer. "Because once I say what I need to say, I don't want you to dismiss it."

He stared at the floor for a moment longer before meeting her gaze. Detecting the vulnerability in her countenance, his features softened. He patted the bed space beside him, flinging aside a sock that would've otherwise been in the way. "Talk to me."

She took some steps closer, though hesitated to complete the journey. "I don't need you to think I'm insane."

"What if I kind of already do?" He ducked and reached beneath his bed.

Oh no. She didn't think she had acted too out of the ordinary. Where had she gone wrong?

When going in blind failed, he leaned further to see what was under his bed — or, what wasn't. "Fuck." He came back empty handed.

Noting the change in her expression, he offered a small, reassuring grin and explained, "Come on, you're hanging out with *me*."

While this was a relief, she couldn't be calmed yet.

He pulled open a drawer in the nightstand. "Thank fucking God." After withdrawing a flask, he pulled his empty one from his pocket and put it in its place. "Want any?"

She shook her head.

"Sorry, yeah, that's right, you don't do that. Sorry."

"It's fine." She bit her bottom lip, still unsure of how to proceed. Even with all the facts splayed out, if he had already ruled out 'vampires,' 'domsuco' would prove a more trying concept for him to accept. The better option would've been to show him, but she didn't need him to be afraid or suspicious of her.

Suddenly it clicked. She found the perfect middle ground. "Let's try an exercise."

"Exercise?"

"If you trust me," she added.

"Trust you to what?"

"Act in your best interest."

He waited for her to elaborate.

Remembering she had been invited to sit beside him, she wavered on the notion of actually doing it. The bed could've been read as an intimate setting. There was no room for a woman on the mattress of a man who was spoken for. But then, times were different. And Alice knew neither held an impure intention.

She stepped the rest of the way to the bed. "I can get you to a calm state," she explained, gauging what the most comfortable, appropriate distance for herself would be before she took her seat. "After that I can ask you a series of questions. If this works, you'll remember what happened before five o'clock today." When she peered back at him, she thought maybe she had misgauged. They were much closer than she had intended.

"You're gonna hypnotize me?" he asked.

However hesitant, she nodded. She didn't want to use this term specifically—it always sounded ridiculous to skeptics—but it was what it was. "I'm quite good with it," she promised.

He snickered, but didn't reject the idea. "Well hey, if you're good with it."

She knew he only agreed because he didn't think it would work. This wasn't good enough.

"Neither of us know what happened back there," she warned. "The nature of what I'm about to do is already quite intrusive; there's a good chance this may become deeply personal. Are you sure you want to continue?"

Thankfully, her stern tone took effect. His head tilted, though whether he believed she was capable or not, she wasn't sure. At the very least he gave genuine consideration to the hypothetical. "So," he murmured, "you're saying what, exactly; I'll say something I don't want you to know?"

"It's a possibility," she conceded.

He nodded, gaze dropping to his hands over his lap. "You know, it's funny. I feel like I could tell you anything and you wouldn't judge."

"It isn't my place to judge," she agreed. "I'm too flawed."

He smirked. "Sounds like the sort of thing a perfect person would say."

She didn't expect the compliment. It threw her for a beat before she flickered a grin. "But, um. There's a chance you will hallucinate and relive your memories, more or less. Depending on what happened…"

"Things could get weird," he finished for her.

She nodded.

He took a breath. "Let's do it."

25. Remembering The Nightmare

Alice

"Somewhere in the back of your mind, you know what happened before five o'clock," Alice promised. She wasn't sure if a domsuco could expose one to a less potent trance, but this was her hope. She remembered how Ruth had done it for her party tricks those years ago, when she was still a teen. "First, I need you to look into my eyes."

Jack did as instructed, and again she was aware of how close they sat on his bed. She felt the warmth radiate from his chest, and upon catching the sound of his shallow breaths and accelerated heartbeat, she knew he, too, was aware.

"Your eyes are like mirrors," he slurred in a near grumble. "What color is that even?"

"Gray," she answered. She still couldn't believe he had driven home as intoxicated as he was.

He shook his head. "Mirrors aren't gray, they're... metal...?"

"Focus on what you see in them. Try to identify every detail."

He stared, and when his pupils dilated she knew it was working.

"Trust your instincts," she coached. "Which of these details stand out?"

He only stared silently on. She was unsure if he would answer.

"The windows," he replied. The conviction with which he stated this was reassuring; it meant he wasn't wildly guessing.

"Why?" she asked.

"I was outside."

"Where?"

No response. His eyes unfocused, and she knew he didn't see her anymore. "Jack," she warned, "I am your tether to reality. Do not lose sight of me. Do you understand?"

"Yes."

"Any question I ask, you must respond, even if the answer is 'I don't know' or 'I don't want to answer.' Do you understand?"

"Yes."

"Where outside were you?"

Although he didn't answer, she knew it was because the answer had yet to form. His words fell out slowly when he finally spoke. "We were outside, leaving the old Van Sloan house."

"Who were you with?"

"Wyn."

She had guessed this much, though having it verified worried her. "Was anything said?"

He was as still and silent as an alert woodland creature, listening. "She said she was looking for me. I don't know why she would think to look there."

"What did she want?"

"…I knew something. Something about when I talked to Crystal, we figured it out. We figured out… It seemed so obvious, but I can't…" He was breaking himself out of the trance.

"You're getting ahead of yourself," she said. "Everything you need to know will come out in your exchange with Winifred. What did she want?"

A pause before his eyes flashed wide and he looked away. "I went back to the Van Sloan house to see what else I could find, and Wyn's the only one who fits the profile for the killer. That's what me and Crystal were talking about, the profile."

Oh no. What she feared would happen was happening. If Winifred was the Ripper, and he found out—

But it wasn't Winifred. It couldn't have been. She was *Winifred*.

There was still the rest of his memory to unfold. Perhaps Marius had escaped, and he was the reason Jack was as shaken as he was—not Winifred.

Jack continued, speech accelerating with every word. "Wyn knows me, she's jealous, she doesn't connect with other girls—or anyone, really. And... There's more. I know there's more; how did I forget?"

"You're getting ahead of yourself," Alice repeated.

"It's not gonna work. I can't focus; there's too many questions."

"If you want it to work, I can make it work. Is this something you want?"

"Well sure —"

"Then look at me."

He let out a frustrated breath, but did as he was told. "I'm looking at you."

She knew it wasn't his intention, but it felt as if he stared into her soul. It took her a second to recover. "Right. We're about to go deeper. You'll find it easier to focus, though you may find it more difficult to differentiate between what's happening right now and what happened before five o'clock. Is this something you're comfortable doing?"

"Yes." His was an unflinching, determined stare into her psyche.

She remembered a key step to the hypnosis Ruth would always do. "This time, I need you to take a deep breath in. Pace yourself slowly, take in as much air as you can." She waited for him to proceed, and she continued when he did. "When you can't take in any more, breathe out, just as slowly. Imagine all the stress leaving your body. Feel the weight in your limbs. Release the tension." There was a few seconds of delay before he took this next step, slowly breathing out.

"By the end of this exhale, you will hardly be able to lift a finger, and that is fine."

Once he was out of breath, he apparently felt it. "Whoa…"

"Do you still see the windows in my eyes?"

"Yes."

"But they're not the windows to your room, are they?"

He squinted, though his face remained mostly unstrained. "No," he agreed, mildly surprised.

"Where are you?"

"I'm… I'm in the room with—" His throat tightened. "Sarah's ring."

"Who's standing beside you?"

He didn't answer. His eyes unfocused. He was losing his sense of what was in front of him; he didn't see her anymore.

"Jack," she warned.

For a split second his eyes refocused, and she saw the struggle he fought to keep them that way. "I'm… I'm with… Wyn's there, somehow, I…" He might've had a thought, though he didn't immediately finish. "If I deeper… I mean, if I… won't see you…deeper."

It was a moment before she understood, but she should've seen this coming. His visual attention needed to be directed inward if he hoped to see the memory.

"Can I?" He sluggishly broke the gaze and moved his hand some distance across the bed, fingers sloppily dragging along the comforter. She knew where he was going with this. Anticipating the rate of her heart at its most amplified, she met him in the middle, taking his hand in hers. The feeling in her chest gave her the idea this was right. He squeezed her fingertips as if to test the connection, and she squeezed back. This would be his new tether to reality.

His head slowly lifted, as if he meant to nod but then forgot midway. Without the need to see her, he let his eyes close and flitter as they needed, head dropping.

"She asked me what was wrong," he continued. "I couldn't tell her. She asked why. I wanted to leave, just in case it wasn't her and the killer came back, but she didn't care, she wanted to know what was wrong."

"What did you tell her?"

" '...I don't know what to do.' " The way he said this was all-encompassing, as if he referenced more than that one situation. He was so without hope that it made her melt.

"Fuck," he breathed, turning away but still holding her hand, "I'm too high for this."

"You're doing just fine," she promised, though she hardly had the words out before he continued.

"I was... I swear I'm not just saying this to be nice, Wyn, but... You're an amazing person—and ridiculously brave for sticking around as long as you have."

Alice felt her eyes widen and her mouth open. He was completely immersed. She didn't think it would happen this effortlessly.

He let out a breath and with his free hand pushed his hair back. "But... With everything that's been happening, this shouldn't... Let's be real; I shouldn't be in a relationship right now." There was more to be said, but then it was as if he was a recording and someone had powered him off. All emotion fell from his countenance, and he sat perfectly still.

"Jack?" Alice squeezed his hand. He didn't squeeze back. "*Jack.*" He was breaking up with Winifred. He was interrupted.

"We're walking to the car," he continued, monotone. However delayed the reaction, he squeezed her hand. She squeezed back for good measure. "She has me open the trunk. I can't move or say anything, but I can do that." Long pause.

Winifred had stopped him from breaking up with her. Alice wondered at this before, but now it seemed more likely—he wasn't with Winifred by choice. This was wrong, but it didn't make her the Ripper. There was still time for Marius to show up.

"What is she doing now?" Alice asked.

"She's looking for my notebook. We've done this before; I've… I've added her page before. I can't move or say anything. …Crystal has it."

"Is Crystal there?"

"No." Long pause. "Yes."

"So she is?"

He turned his head toward her. "Not you. I added Wyn to my list. I've added her before, but…" He trailed off, distracted. "I'm not leaving you for Crystal. …I'm not leaving you for Alice. …She's not making me say this." Long pause.

"What's happening?"

"She's freaking the fuck out. Trying to catch her breath. Screaming, crying. She says she wasn't losing me so badly until you showed up. I'm sure you helped, but this thing should've ended before it began. …She's saying something."

His brow furrowed, as if he intended to decipher ancient text. "There's a fix for this," he read, "There's always a fix." Gradually his muscles began to relax, but then he jumped, and although his eyes flashed open, he wasn't awake. "She's making me forget. She's putting thoughts in my head."

"Stay with me. Listen to what she has to say, but stay with me." She squeezed his hand. He squeezed back. His hold never loosened. "Word for word, what is she saying?" she asked.

He shook his head. "I'll forget again. I don't just hear her; I *feel* it—She's *there*, her voice is—it's burrowing under my skin, in my skull, in my back, like fucking scabies—"

"I won't let you forget," she promised. "Trust me." She remembered Winifred had told her the same thing, *I won't let you forget.* Maybe this wasn't a real memory—Winifred wouldn't make him forget something unrelated to the existence of Otherkind. This wasn't real.

His eyes squeezed shut. Knowing he needed to make his decision fast, he emitted an exasperated groan then decided, "She's saying…" He blanched. Now when he spoke, it was through a strained throat, stuttering on the first strangled syllable, "'Ah-I'm not killing girls anymore. You have no reason to suspect me. Whatever you see in her, I can be that.

The more you learn about her, the more it can make sense that she did it.'"

Silence. His breath staggered as he stared straight through her.

This wasn't Winifred. Alice was one of the few friends she had. Winifred wouldn't turn on one of the only friends she had—especially not after being so alone for so long.

"Do you still remember everything?" Alice asked.

"She was the one good thing I had," he whispered, and it struck her like a strike to the gut.

"Are you ready to wake up now?"

He stared ahead, lips parted. She squeezed his hand. He remembered to loosen his hold. "There's more," he finally said. "She wants me to... But I don't mean it. She knows it doesn't mean anything this way. I'm still there, but I can't... It's like I'm possessed." Then, "I love you, Wyn." It was monotone.

He and Alice were still holding hands, and she could've anticipated what happened next. It stood to reason, if Winifred held his hand in the memory, and if he could easily mistake one reality for the other...

He dropped Alice's hand and pulled her into an embrace. He was so warm. His strength was nothing compared to hers, but his hold was firm, and she couldn't think. She was a mannequin.

He lifted her face with his thumb on her chin until her gaze met his—and for a second she was back with Theo in the candlelight in her old kitchen. He tucked her hair behind her ear and into it whispered, "I love you, Wyn."

She considered pulling away, or putting up a hand to stop further advances. He didn't know what he was doing. But she was frozen, stuck on just envisioning the steps.

He concluded with a gentle kiss to her lips.

Her chin quivered while her stomach churned. This—all of this—it was ugly, and sad, and…wrong, just wrong. Her eyes teared, but she couldn't let this get the best of her—not yet. Jack said there was more, and she needed to hold herself together just long enough to wake him when it was over. Just long enough.

"What happened next?" she croaked, turning her face away.

No answer.

"Jack." She found his hand again and gave it a gentle squeeze.

He didn't squeeze back.

She sighed, dabbing her eyes with her free hand. "I'm waking you up now."

"We're... Don't," he managed, then was silent for another long moment.

She waited.

"We're back in the room," he said.

She paused, unsure of what would motivate Winifred to do this.

"It's cold," he continued, "but I'm just standing there. She's still crying, sitting with her back to the wall. Singing along to doo-wop. Calming herself." Silence. "A happier song's playing now. She smiles. Has me dance with her."

Another silence. He let go of her hand. The way he did it had her assume it was to perhaps scratch his wrist, though what he did instead was untie the runic bracelet. If Winifred went so far as to have him remove it, Alice wondered if this meant their magic was real. If their magic was real and she had him take it off, what was she preparing him for?

He set the bracelet down on the bed to his far side. His heart beat faster. His breathing shallowed and his brow began to bead with sweat.

"What do you see now?" she muttered, unnerved.

Face blank, he didn't answer. Before she could ask again, he gasped with a wince, showing his teeth and scrunching his nose. She waited for him to explain, though in the end it didn't seem as though he could. Slowly he lowered himself, laying back. He squeezed her hand. Only somewhat relieved, she squeezed back.

He remained where he was, back flat with his sheets, body square with the ceiling, arms tense and chest heaving. His expression pinched as he stifled a yell, and his hand flew to his neck as if to stop the bleeding. So Winifred was draining him.

The next song played on Jack's electric music player.

Upon opening his eyes, though his gaze wandered, it was clear he saw nothing. The rest of his body seemed bolted in place, restrained. He peered as close to the wounded side of his neck as his position allowed, as if he couldn't move his head.

"Wyn?" he rasped, "What—" His eyebrows rose in the middle, eyelids squeezed shut. Finally he cried out a quick, strangled call, still bolted in place.

Alice couldn't sit quietly anymore. "What is she doing to you?"

461

He took in a sharp breath. "I don't—" His throat caught, as if he was choking. "I don't want to answer," he managed before gasping.

There was a chance he would yell again, and she didn't want to worry Ruth, so Alice turned up the music. The volume dial was the same as it was for a record player, so she knew what to do.

Jack's face contorted in the worst of ways, agony etched into the stretches of his mouth. His breath staggered, and he sounded on the verge of tears when he rasped, "I'm dying. I'm dying."

"Let me wake you," she said, just loudly enough.

He shook his head. "I need to know. I need to—know." He forced a breath in through his nose.

She pulled his trembling form from the bed and immediately his arms wrapped around her, his fingers gripping her back and his face wetting her blouse where she let it rest. She pushed his hair aside his ear, offering what comfort she could in her touch. She remembered that while he was still under trance, his subconscious was hugely open to suggestion. "You've survived this already, Jack," she whispered, just a kiss away from his temple. "You're strong, and you will feel strong again." Pausing to breathe, she hoped this would ease the tightness in her throat. It hardly helped. "This nightmare ends now."

It wasn't long before he seemed to go limp, though still his breaths trembled and he held her. Occasionally he would wince or moan, but that was it.

The song ended. No music followed.

Many minutes passed.

He choked out, "She was the one good thing I had."

26. Comfort In Denial
Alice

Finally Jack's breaths calmed. "She's finished," he said, monotone again, his breath warm on Alice's collar bone. "She tells me to forget what happened, eat a cookie, then get myself together and wake up before I drive home." Silence. "It's five o'clock now."

"Are you ready to wake up?" Alice asked.

"Yes."

It was a simple enough procedure. Still holding him close, she pushed the hair away from his ear again and murmured, "Wake up."

He blinked. While he was no longer in trance, she knew for a second the vision was still all he saw, until his gaze flicked about his surroundings, his bedroom, and how he still clung to her as if his life depended on it. "Sorry," he murmured, pulling away.

She shook her head. "Don't be."

Catching the waver in her voice, a mixture of concern and confusion widened his eyes the slightest bit more. "Are you crying?"

Wiping her tears before they could fall, she knew she didn't need to answer.

It seemed as if he was about to push his hair back, but paused mid-motion when he saw how badly his arms shook. "What did I tell you?"

"Nothing you didn't want me to know. You were vague."

"I don't mind you knowing, I just... I don't know how..." He paused, letting his thought come together. "All that was real?"

She couldn't say. She didn't want it to be. There was still the chance Marius had planted the memory. She didn't know if this sort of thing was possible, but she didn't want to think... *Winifred*...

"Even if it wasn't," she answered, "it's evident something Otherworldly is afoot. The Winifred in your memory is something beyond human. Those like her have certain abilities."

"She can control people."

"To an extent. Once a person knows to look out for what's real... Well, now that you know, I doubt it will be so easy for her to do it again. If it's a true memory."

He nodded. If this was a relief, it didn't show.

"This may sound strange, but... did she bite you?" she asked.

He hesitated before he put his arm down and nodded, eyes lowered; not looking at her. Ashamed. "My neck. She drew blood. I got dizzy and lightheaded, but she didn't stop, and I couldn't... I woke up just enough, and still there wasn't shit I could do. I tried to push her off. I should've been able to, but I couldn't move. And..." His mouth stayed open, knowing what he would say, and finally he muttered, "I might as well have been roofied."

She couldn't comfort him, so she didn't know how to respond. "At least that was all she did. To you, anyway. I've heard stories of others like her—"

"That wasn't—" Again, he paused. His following words were slow coming out as he tried to find them. "You don't... I didn't tell you everything. She, uh..." Closing his mouth, he let his head drop, eyes flitting as his different ways to continue seemed to flash through his mind. Finally he laughed, though it almost sounded like a cry. "Yeah, fuck. I might as well have been roofied."

Her eyes narrowed. He was trying to tell her something without saying it outright.

Suddenly he stood and stumbled for the exit, grabbing everything along the way as if for balance, but knocking most of them over in his urgency. He needed help.

Just as he shoved the door open, she pulled his arm over her shoulder and rushed him up the stairs. She wasn't sure where they were headed after that, but he looked sick. Bathroom?

"Outside," he managed, and she nodded. Once they reached the top of the steps, they fled through the front door and into the night. He broke away and took the lead now, retching and running on jelly limbs to the trees aside the property.

Theo, shaken and desperate, sprinting through the mud and underbrush —

She never wanted to see Jack in the woods. Especially not like this. However, she didn't want him to go through this alone.

Her pause was brief before she followed past the first tier of bushes. He stood with his back to her a few yards ahead, gripping a tree for support, doubled over and letting it all out. She couldn't see through the underbrush, but heard the wet splash into the snow and dead leaves. When she noted the sensation of air building in her throat and forehead, her ears warming, and how her hands shook and chest heaved, she turned away and concentrated on her own breaths. Jack didn't need her to be sick as well.

She sat on an upended tree root. The longer she listened to him spill his guts—the longer everything festered in her mind—the more worried she became. Of all the things Jack could've meant, none of them indicated Winifred had done anything remotely redeemable. And nothing in her own experience indicated it was possible to plant a false memory—not one which could be reached through hypnosis. Not like this.

But Winifred was good. Out of touch, most certainly, but of course that's what would have happened. No one was left to keep her grounded. She was lonely and she didn't know how to connect with people. Now she had imagined a barrier between herself and humanity, and…

The girl had no reason to feel anything for them. In her mind, she could do whatever she wanted and feel no remorse. Would it be such a surprise if she was the Ripper—?

Her stomach rose and she rejected every thought until it settled. Winifred wasn't the Ripper; she was Winifred. She would get away with whatever she knew she could get away with, but she wouldn't intentionally hurt anyone, let alone kill anyone.

She had to find Bishop; she had to see if Marius had escaped, and if it was possible for him to have planted the memory, or if it was possible to put another domsuco under trance. If the memory was real, perhaps Winifred's part in it wasn't genuine.

Jack sobbed for air between coughing and gagging. Alice didn't hear anymore splashes, though this didn't mean he was done.

He spat whatever was left in his mouth, then quieted, still catching his breath. The wind gently whistled in the bare canopy of branches overhead.

"What is she?" he croaked.

"This is a conversation better held in private."

"Even if she had super-hearing, she's getting ready for the dance now," he sputtered, hoarse. "We're alone." He spat more.

Upon listening harder, and smelling the surrounding scents in the air, she decided he was right. They were alone.

Now she considered his question, then bit her lip. She felt ugly for outing her friend like this, but Jack already saw what he saw, and he needed to know what he was dealing with. She knew she was lying by omission in not admitting she and Winifred were more or less the same thing, but she didn't want to overwhelm him. "They're called domsuco. Only half a part of this reality, relying on blood for life-force."

He shook his head, still doubled over, still struggling for full breaths and still holding the tree for support. "Please. Don't fuck with me, I can't... Not right now."

She unhurriedly stepped ahead and around to face him. Ducking just enough so she might look him in the eye, she muttered, gentle but resolute, "Is this what I sound like when I joke?"

He looked like death with his face sunken and pale, lips somewhat purpled and wet, neck still scarred, scabbed and smeared with glowing leftover blood. When his widened eyes met hers, she saw just how dazed and scared he was, back heaving with every shallow breath. His pupils were large, deep pools of black. His face glistened with tears or sweat; she couldn't distinguish which was what.

Still breathing heavily, he shook his head.

"You know I mean what I say," she continued, "and you know I'm right. It all makes sense, doesn't it?"

"If she's superhuman, there's nothing I can do. There can't be nothing. I can't be stuck like this."

"Maybe you couldn't do it on your own, but you have help now."

He hadn't stopped shaking his head. "No, she's not a... She's just a girl."

"You think anyone could do what she did in your vision? Without drugging you?"

Without the words to respond, he continued to collect himself, then let his head drop again. His eyes closed, and gradually as he mulled it all over he calmed. "You're right. You're right, it doesn't make sense. It couldn't have happened."

He wiped the corners of his mouth on his sleeve and stood straight. Some color had returned to his face, and while he might've still been in shock, it allowed him the calm which was necessary to proceed. "My mind's a dark place, Alice. Lot of freaky, subconscious insecurities, all deeply rooted in some fucked up psychological shit—none of that was real."

He could've been right, so she didn't know how to respond. Still, she at least had to tell him, "In the instance you decide to believe me, you should know the runes in your bracelet work."

He softly laughed, though it seemed more like a frustrated whine. "What?"

"Once you view a threat and feel the need to defend yourself, the runes will feed off of your energy."

He shook his head, but didn't seem to have the energy to retort. Hoping to diminish their chances of stepping in puke, she led the way around and to a safe distance. He kept pace beside her, still wobbly on his legs.

"Are you still going to the dance?" he asked after a silent moment.

"I am if you are."

"You know where it is?"

She shook her head.

He checked his watch as they reached the front porch. "Wyn could be back either any minute or an hour from now."

"Will you be alright? Alone with her?"

He nodded.

She twisted her mouth, doubtful. But, whether he answered in denial, or to emptily reassure her she didn't need to worry about him, she couldn't stay here. She wouldn't be able to control her expression when Winifred arrived; she mustn't make her suspicions known. She needed to learn what she could from Bishop. "Okay," she finally said.

When they returned to the indoors, Alice was only there long enough for him to write her the address to the school, wave goodbye to him and Ruth, and leave. She had to be sure that Winifred was the Ripper, and she would know before the night was over.

~Jack~

He couldn't get it out of his head. It was too absurd to have actually happened, yet it felt too real to have been a lie.

Jack's walk to the first floor bathroom was a slow and distracted one. Fortunately no one was in the kitchen or living room, which he sluggishly passed. No one needed to see him this way.

Hands in his jacket pockets and eyes adjusting to the dark, windowless hallway, all he saw were loops from the vision.

The confusion when he broke out of trance to someone else's ceiling. The weight of a body, light on top of his. Recognition to his grip, tight on her hips —

The sheets blocked his nose and most of his mouth. He flailed against her more desperately —

Ears loud with hysteria, screaming; he couldn't do anything —

Floating. Sinking. Pain became a non-factor. Breathing became easier, or unnecessary — he couldn't tell which. He wasn't there.

Maybe dying was the answer. He drank all the time. He drove under the influence. He walked alone in places he knew he wasn't welcome.

Maybe dying was the answer. Maybe he could finally let it happen —

Snapping back to the present, he realized he made it to the bathroom door. He couldn't say how long he had been standing there. He turned the doorknob and stepped inside. The scent from his mouth only made him want to puke again; he had to brush his teeth. More than likely, he needed mouthwash as well.

Hands numb with cold, he couldn't hold his toothbrush the way he normally would. As if in the restraint of mittens, he wrapped his fingers around the handle, then put it down. He had to open the toothpaste first. His hold would only go so tight.

But this wasn't a real memory; it was a dream that Alice talked him through. She might've believed it, but he couldn't be so sure. This side of Wyn—cold, controlling and powerful—it contradicted the Wyn he knew.

He turned on the water, caught his reflection in the mirror—and noise filled his head. The toothbrush slipped past his fingers and clattered on the tile floor. While he gathered the air to yell, he didn't. He wasn't sure when he staggered back, but he extended his hand as if to check the mirror, then decided the more accurate procedure would've been to check himself.

He hesitated. Fingers trembling over his neck, he traced over the scabs. There were countless puncture marks, as if over the course of the last several months someone had repeatedly stabbed him with a barbecue fork. How did he not notice this sooner?

He wanted to write it off as imaginary, but it was there. He saw it; he felt it. It was real.

His breath hastened. He knew what he was about to do, but he wasn't sure how to go about it; nothing translated right.

"Ah?" he began. Still staring through the mirror, he kept his hand over his wound. His limbs felt weak, and he continued to stagger backwards before finding the wall and melting against it.

It had to have happened. All of it. Wyn had the ability to make him see what she wanted him to see; his neck was like this all along, and somehow he only saw it now. She forced him to do as she pleased, and now what was done was done. There was nothing he could do to change it, or just—make it so it *wasn't*.

His head rested against the wall, his gaze finding the edge between the ceiling and the lights above the mirror. He pressed his lips together, clamping them with his teeth as he took a staggering breath in through his nose. The pace of his breaths quickened, and no matter how hard he tried to calm them, he knew he wouldn't be able—not this time. The second his mouth opened, he sobbed, so again he pressed his lips together. His throat hurt from holding back. Everything blurred as his eyes watered.

Not only did what happened really happen, but it happened countless times, and at this rate it would continue to happen, again and again, because really, what could he do to stop it? If Wyn wanted him, it didn't matter what he did—one way or another, she would have him, for as long as she wanted him. He had the illusion of options before, but now there was nothing.

He raised his knees to his chest, another sob ripping from his back as he came to wrap his arms around his ribs. But he couldn't let himself cry too loudly. No one else could know—not while he needed Wyn not to know he knew. From this point forward he only emitted a rasping series of quick, staggered breaths. He buried his face in his knees and remained like this for an immeasurably long time.

...

He stared at the cabinet across from him, finally calmed enough to steadily breathe. He had to get ready.

Wyn was the only reason he was going to this dance. She wanted him to go.

The noise in his head began to return, but he groaned and stood, bringing his toothbrush up with him. He couldn't think this way and get all emotional again; he had things to do. He still had to brush his teeth. She would be at his door any minute.

Finding the toothpaste again, he recommenced the process, fingers still numb. Through the mirror he saw his eyes were still red, but if anyone saw him it would've been easy to assume he was just high.

Finished brushing and mouth minty fresh, he opened the bathroom door and stepped out. Upon rounding the corner, he froze.

There she was in her pink, short-skirted costume. It hugged the waist, and the sleeves were poofed at the shoulders. He assumed she was supposed to be some kinda fairy princess; she kept a wand on the counter beside her, and she had a tall silver crown on her head.

She stood by the phone, waiting, then smiled and peered up his way. "Hey, you."

Response. She expected a response. "Hey," he managed.

Her smile widened and she stepped away from the counter, gesturing toward her dress. "Well?"

"Uh. Cute. When did you get here?" He should've been more enthusiastic.

"About five minutes ago." Now she waited, legs together and cutely dancing in place. He knew what she was expecting. He had to deliver. Forcing a grin he hoped seemed natural, he finished his cross to her. She rested her forearms along his chest and every inch of his skin crawled. He wrapped his arms about her waist. It was as Crystal had said; he had to pretend everything was normal.

"Happy Halloween," Wyn greeted.

"Happy Almost-Halloween," he corrected. It was cheesy, but he knew it would work. They brought their faces together, touching noses.

"Oh, you," she crooned. His stomach became a clenching fist in his throat, and they kissed. The noise in his head screamed and begged him to run. His head felt hot, yet the nape of his neck was cold.

She glanced back at the phone. "You know you have an unchecked voicemail from, like, three days ago, right?"

"No." He really didn't, though he couldn't fathom the concept of giving a shit.

She pressed the button for him. The message played. Crystal's voice emitted from the speaker. It was an urgent message. He realized he hadn't been listening to any of it, only tuning into, "There was a girl. Asian or something, our age. The other one—"

Silence. He waited for her to finish, then realized she was cut off. "You said this was from three days ago?" he asked.

"Three or four, yeah," Wyn answered, concerned now.

He couldn't concentrate. He couldn't recall a word Crystal had said, so he played it again.

Three days ago was when he and Alice met. Crystal would've still been in the hospital.

"Shit," the message started. "Hey, it's Crystal Robinson, from school. Listen, they want everyone to think I'm crazy, because I won't believe their bullshit; I know what I saw in the crypt. There was a girl. Asian or something, our age. The other one —"

The message finished its second play-through. Neither would break the silence.

This… This was a different perspective. If Wyn was the one killing girls, Crystal would've recognized her. Wyn also wasn't Asian. But then, Crystal didn't have a chance to describe the other person, or what the Asian girl's part in it all was.

Wyn furrowed her brow, as if thinking. "That girl who found your dog."

He nodded. He remembered the part in his vision when Wyn told him, *The more you learn about her, the more it can make sense that she did it.* This could have been her order put into action, or the memory could've been completely fabricated. If it was possible for even Wyn to be a monster, it was possible for anyone else as well. If it was possible for Wyn to shape his reality, the same rules applied to anyone else.

Alice said his runes worked. She flinched whenever they made contact. Was this the runes at work?

How well did he know her?

Jack jumped when loud wind roared from the foyer. The sound stopped once Gabby shut the door behind her, unwinding the scarf from her neck and slipping out of her jacket in one hokey motion to let them both fall sloppily on the coat rack.

"Jack!" she called.

"Yeah?" he answered.

Her eyes rounded when they zoomed in on him in the kitchen. "Oh! You're right there. Hi, Wyn."

Wyn weakly grinned back, glancing at Jack as if to read how he would proceed. Were they about to tell Gabby what they knew? What they'd just heard?

In four quick pats Gabby checked her jean pockets, then reached into her jacket on the rack and grabbed her phone. "Sarah's dad called me today."

"Bio-dad?" Jack asked. It would make sense for the detective to try to reach Jack through her. Jack didn't have a phone, and Gabby was typically good about who she revealed information to. But how was she supposed to know that Wyn might not have been the best person to have in the room for this? How could Jack tell her?

Focused on her screen, Gabby approached. The closer she stepped, the more clearly Jack saw...

Marks on her neck. Both sides, recent and old, semi-circle scars.

Whoever had attacked him, had attacked her as well. While it wasn't as bad as his, it was bad enough for him to forget he wasn't supposed to know anything, or see anything—he wasn't supposed to react, but he stared, pulse racing, arms shaking, ready to fight without an outlet.

He noticed Wyn watching him, pouting with concern or curiosity. "What's wrong?" she innocently asked.

He had let on more than he'd intended, but luckily he had an excuse. "Did another girl die?" he asked Gabby.

She gnawed her lip, grimacing. "Yeah. A girl from the diner?"

Bri. Jack nodded, not surprised. It was only a matter of time.

"Ohh," Wyn muttered, "that's what this is about."

Gabby continued, "They found her outside her house. Oh, and he said, 'tell that punk we're watching him—really watching him now.'" She was always too good at mimicking his cheesy, 90s kids' show villain tone.

Jack nodded in acknowledgement. Lloyd would keep his alliance to Jack a secret even from Gabby, then. And it seemed like Jack was actually being investigated now. He wasn't sure how good of a thing this was.

He stole a look at Wyn's neck. He hadn't noticed anything before, but now he had to check. She didn't have any scars. But he couldn't remember Alice having any scars, either. Her neck wasn't covered before she left; he would have noticed.

While Wyn did always seem innocent whenever they were together, he was ready to turn on anyone who could be the actual Ripper, whether it was her, Alice, his mom—*whoever*. While he wasn't sure to believe what he saw, he was ready for the truth.

And he was ready to kill someone he loved if it meant ending this horror movie.

27. Respect Your Kind

Alice

When Alice urgently called to Bishop from the foyer, as had become a pattern whenever she returned to the cabin, he didn't respond. Catching her breath, she figured he must have still been asleep; it was far past his bedtime when he finally slept that afternoon, and all in all she had been keeping him up like this for days. Of course his body would get the better of him now. Of course he would finally be sleeping like the dead.

She all but materialized before his bedroom door before she knocked. "Bishop!"

His sleep-self whined, and that was all. He wouldn't wake.

Finally she noted the rate of her heart. It wasn't entirely different from when she was at Jack's house, which meant

Marius was still here. Or, returned. If Marius was really free, he could've drugged Bishop with Bishop's own concoction. He could have returned simply to trick them all into believing he'd been there all along. This would fit the narrative of his wanting to frame Winifred for anything—logic would say he couldn't have done anything if he'd been here all along.

She opened the door.

Bishop slept wrapped in the cocoon of an elegant red and gold comforter upon a large four-post bed, a heap of laundry still at its foot. His antique writing desk at the window was the same that he'd always had, notes and journals sprawled across its shelves and surfaces, though it seemed there was finally furniture to match its charm—a mahogany wardrobe and two night stands, all with elaborate hand carved accents.

This room was from where she saw him emerge when he said he was finished with Marius. She didn't see the demon in plain sight. He had to have been here, though unless he was bound in the wardrobe, the only place left to check was...

There was another door.

Unworried about making noise, Alice stepped over boots and shoes, and a pair of heels which she wasn't sure to whom they belonged. The rate of her heart increased accordingly, *Thmp-thmp, thmp-thmp.*

Opening the door, she found what, on first impression, was a master bathroom. Pale-gold tiled floors, marble-like countertops, beige walls and bright, clean lighting. A prepared wooden shank sat beside the sink, and she snatched it up. He was in here, though she didn't look and see him yet.

No toilet. In its place was a mahogany unit of shelves and glass doors, bolted to the walls and floor. Within she saw a series of tools—vials and bottles, and means of application—like an expansion of Marius' fabric case of narcotics. Some items looked ancient—barbaric—while some appeared utterly advanced and out of this world.

The bottom shelf was open. The item within was strapped in place, boxlike, compact with cogs and gears which rotated once per second. A crystal blue light signaled it was on and running. Plastic or rubber tubes spilled out, leading Alice's eye to a tub which sat elevated by a step from the rest of the room, before a thickly curtained window. It was a heavy basin upon clawed dragon-like legs, the whole seemingly etched from one solid stone. Swirling accents in the legs formed small holes through which straps looped.

Alice stepped closer. Her heart accelerated.

Marius lay within, looking more haggard than peaceful, sunken eyes closed, hunched with his chin to his neck. He still had Jack's body—his face and his youth, and while Marius' hair was a significantly darker shade of brown, it was cut to roughly Jack's same shaggy length, just past his eyes. He was wrapped in a white straitjacket, the collar to one of Jack's flannels sticking out from the neck. The tubes from the machine latched in at his inner elbows, and one seemed to attach at the nape of his neck.

Bolts within the tub held even more straps, strung taught across his body. With his fingers covered in the confines of the straitjacket, she couldn't conceive a plausible method of how he could have escaped—let alone of how he could have gotten back in.

Which meant Winifred…*actually*…

Her head cleared of everything. She couldn't think.

"Alice," he grumbled.

She jumped, throwing a step back and her stake up.

His chest expanded with a quiet inhale, and his exhale was a noisy groan as he stretched, arching his back from the basin and pushing his legs out. The groan turned into a pained rasp as the straps tightened, loosening only when he set himself limp back into the tub. *"Bishop,"* he growled, then let his head fall back in frustration. It collided with the tub with a solid *thunk*. "What day is it?"

As Alice considered if she should dignify this with an answer, she wondered if she had the means of figuring this out, herself. All she knew was what year it was, and that it was October. And Friday.

His eyes opened and he observed her—her attire, her new hair, her face. As if this would tell him how much time had passed. "Did he kill her yet?"

His gaze had her frozen at first, though finally she clenched her teeth. It was better to be angry with him than afraid. "You put that memory in his head. You matched it with half-truths so that when I guided him to it, it would feel believable."

His eyebrows shot up and his responding laugh sounded maniacal. This didn't feel like a Marius response; this felt very much like Jack, and she hated it—he still looked so much like him, and she hated seeing him distressed and restrained in a bathtub. *"Why* would I do that?" he asked.

"You tell me."

Again he let his head fall back to the basin, with another solid *thunk,* and there it stayed. Now she saw more of his clean shaven chin and neck than his face. "Why bother asking if you won't believe me?" he asked.

"Bishop says you can't be trusted—"

"This, from the man who lies in his own journals—"

"But if you give me a reason, I might believe you," she finished, raising her voice just enough.

His gaze at the ceiling deadened. "Easy." Slowly he lowered his chin and leaned as close as the straps allowed, hair in his face to appear even more distressed as the straitjacket had him hugging himself. "She will kill, again and again, as she rapes him, again and again—"

Something rose in her throat. "She doesn't—" She silenced at the subtle cock of his eyebrow; a look which further dared her to doubt him, paired with something more pleading. Desperate. As if it was Jack who needed her to believe him, not Marius.

"Ask her, if you don't believe me." His teeth showed in a partial snarl as he articulated, "Ask her if she has to put him under trance—*every*—*time*—before they do it." He held Alice's gaze, and she stared back, searching for a lack of conviction. But there was nothing save for that same desperate plea layered beneath what could have been a threat.

Still, something wasn't adding up. "Why do you care?" she asked. "You want to kill off all humanity. Why does it matter who dies first, or who gets hurt along the way?"

"Just let me kill her, before he does."

She tried again, slower and more loudly, "Why do you care?"

"Let me kill her!" he suddenly cried, spit flying as he threw himself against his restraints. Alice screamed, and he screamed as well, the straps digging tighter with his every flail. "Let me kill her," he gargled. "None else will die if I kill her before he does; just *let me kill her!*"

Panting through her adrenaline, Alice only responded when she caught her breath and reevaluated the situation. "I'm sure you've delivered that line before," she figured. "Good show, by the by."

A new scream tore from his lungs—not of pain, but of frustration. *"You fucking hypocrite!"* he cried, voice reaching a new octave; one only pure, unadulterated rage could fuel, "You'd kill me if you could, but *damn the boy if he kills the bitch for worse! Fuck you and everything you stand for!"*

The compact machine in the shelf unit chimed once, then whirred. The curl of its plastic tubes expanded, and she knew this meant the drug was being re-administered.

"You stand there wide-eyed like you're so pure and innocent! You —" His eyes lost focus, and he shook his head to bring himself back. "You…" Still his gaze strayed from hers. The straps around his body loosened as his limbs went limp, and the glare gradually melted from his face.

"Damn this—brain chemistry," he panted. "Teenage angst…no—filter… no… tact…"

While her arms still shook, and she couldn't say when they started shaking, she felt it was finally safe to lower her stake. "Sleep tight, Marius," she spoke through tight lips.

His body sank back into the basin, and while his eyes danced, it seemed it was easier for them to stay locked on her with his head rested back against the edge. "I'm sorry," he rasped. "I'm so—sorry… Alice… *everything."*

"I'll show you where you can stick that apology."

He weakly chuckled, eyes closing. "Bet you won't."

Damn him for looking like Jack, and speaking like Jack. She wanted to hit him, but she couldn't do it for so long as he was like this.

He was completely limp, breathing deeply, and she knew he was fully under again. Never daring to look away from him regardless, she stepped backwards to the door and let herself out, grip still tight on the stake even after she slammed the door closed behind her.

Bishop sat on his bed, feet to the floor, fully dressed, waiting.

"I know," she panted before he could say anything, "I shouldn't have seen him without you."

He shook his head, grim. "He wouldn't have said nearly as much if he thought I was listening."

She peered back at the door. "You believe any of that?"

"I wouldn't be surprised. It would explain… It wouldn't be surprising. Take what we know of Winifred, continue the pattern—"

"What pattern?" she snapped.

Bishop stared through her, then met her gaze. "I'm sure you've noticed how she calls him Theo, even while he prefers Jack?"

"That doesn't make her the Ripper, and that doesn't mean she's—"

"In itself, no, it doesn't," Bishop conceded, "But it's a telling hint. It's a disregard to who he is as a person. Adding her obsession with, and her dependance upon, Theo... If Jack ever tried to leave her, do you think she would let him?"

She wouldn't. Alice already suspected she wouldn't.

"What memory did you guide him to?" Bishop asked.

"She's the Ripper and she won't let him leave," Alice mumbled.

Bishop's jaw clenched while his eyes closed.

"Could Marius have planted this in his head?" she offered before any convictions could land. "Or could he have put her under trance—made her do this?"

Bishop peered at the door, as if to the demon himself. "Hypnotism is an interesting art. If Jack had a recollection of it before you put him under, it's possible it was planted. If you had to work the memory from his trance-self, chances are it was real. Regardless, it isn't possible to put another domsuco under trance; if Marius asked you to confirm with Winifred, and she admits..." Finally he met Alice's gaze, and his own eyes seemed to apologize for the very thought. "He may be telling the truth."

Her stomach rose and clenched her throat more tightly. Her fingers felt numb. "You said he couldn't be trusted."

"Which is why you must check in with Winifred."

"She knows better," she insisted. "She may be many things, but she's not—" Her throat tightened before she could finish. The back of her neck felt simultaneously hot and cold. "She knows better!"

Bishop kept his gaze locked with hers, waiting. As if she was being ridiculous, or unreasonable. She couldn't stand it. "She's just Winifred!" she asserted.

"I know," he promised. "Winifred, plus unchallenged power, plus time." Now it almost felt like he was pleading back, "Think about it, Etsu. A born victim, suddenly with more power than everyone in the community combined. What do you think she'd do with it?"

"Trance her way into the VIP section and steal clothes from the mall! Not—" She struggled for the words. "Not…" She flew a hand up as if to gesture to the situation.

Bishop stared through her again, thinking. "You don't think she'd try to bring him back?"

She couldn't answer. Both knew she would, though this didn't help her argument.

His face gradually pinched. "I meant to tell you sooner, but everything happened so fast."

She knew he spoke ahead of his train of thought, so teased him with his unintended implication. "You mean she brought Theo back from the dead?"

He grimaced. But it wasn't his *don't be ridiculous* expression.

It was... Which meant...

"What?" she finally asked.

"Well... This is going to sound so barbaric, but she's marked him, Etsu — there's not much we can do without disrespecting our kind — "

"What do you mean; what did she do?" Her words were low, with a forced coherency.

"She brought him back."

Her legs felt weak. Her body felt...weak. It felt like gliding when she crossed to Bishop's writing desk at the window.

She missed some words as Bishop continued, " — I don't know who taught her to raise a wakker slaaf — "

"Wakker slaaf?" Her throat was tight. She wasn't sure if she said this aloud, but Bishop went silent as if she had.

"'Awake slave,'" he translated. "He is an everlasting source of fresh blood; he'll never bleed out or run dry, and for this reason they're… The men, especially, they…" He diverted his gaze. "They're a domsuco's ideal sex slave."

She placed the stake atop the desk. Everything in her peripheral seemed to shift as if the room was slowly spinning. Something solid felt suspended against the base of her throat and her gut turned.

In through the nose; out through the mouth.

She sank into the nearby chair. "She brought Theo back? And now he's…?"

"Jack," Bishop corrected. "Theo's still very much dead."

She looked at him. "But you said…"

He scoffed, shaking his head. "I was wondering if you were listening; that answers that. Jack died sometime last year. I don't know when or how, all I know is he's now a wakker slaaf."

Jack…died? Even while he wasn't gone from this earth, it still felt tragic. So young, with such a depressing life. "How did he die?" she asked.

Bishop shook his head as if he didn't know. "He wasn't dead long enough to have made it to the papers or to have his own gravestone. My guess is Winifred drained him to excess one night, and commenced the resurrection process as soon as she noticed."

This, or he had once successfully killed himself.

Her throat tightened. "Now he's her... slave?" she croaked.

"For all intents and purposes."

She wasn't sure when she started shaking her head, but it was shaking now. "People don't belong to people. People don't..." She stood and paced to the other side of the room. She didn't know what to feel, but everything bubbled up, overwhelming her, until she spun on Bishop and cried, "Why would you sire her if you had no intention of being there for her!?"

He kept his stare through the wall and growled, "I told her I was here if she needed me — it is not my fault she never reached out."

"You could have returned her to town as a mortal!"

Finally he snapped, "Forgive me for thinking you might've wanted a friend once you came back!"

"Well aren't you just a saint!" Alice shot back, not caring how good of a retort this was.

"I am no saint!" he yelled as he found her gaze, standing. "I know I'm not! I don't know how to take care of you—" He flung a hand her direction. "—or make you feel better! Housing you for nine years, wouldn't you think I knew this?" He laughed, as if the alternative thought truly was humorous. "Of course I knew! The second I found you sleeping at Hisao's tombstone, I knew I couldn't be the parent you needed—nay, I couldn't be the *person* you needed, but *someone* had to try! *I* had to try! You wouldn't have made it much past childhood without your friends, but I tried!" He scoffed, "And what sort of a report is that; 'I tried?' We can't rely on me trying here, Etsu; either you have people who help you survive in this world, or I spend eternity knowing I've failed you."

Alice stared at him, then past him. She never knew how insecure he was about how he did in caring for her, growing up. It was touching, but…it didn't fix anything.

He calmed in the brief silence which followed. "I didn't know you'd let the town bury you," he concluded, setting the conversation back on track. "I didn't know you'd refuse to come back to us once I pulled the stake out. She was depressed and I wasn't making it better by staying with her. I kept saying the wrong thing until she left and expressed she preferred to handle herself alone."

Alice reevaluated her emotions. As aggravated as she was with the situation, blaming Bishop for the past wouldn't fix anything. It wasn't as if either he or Winifred had acted out of character; this outcome was... inevitable. She had to focus on the present.

"How do I stop this?" she asked.

"There's not much we can do without disrespecting our kind." He'd said this already.

"Our kind," she echoed, then surprised herself with a quick laugh. "Weren't we... No, of course, *I* wasn't, but *you* —all of *you* were... Yet *I'm* one to think this is all so..." She turned to the window and tried again. "You were all human first, weren't you?" In her core she felt a certain overflow of energy, and she wasn't sure where it was meant to go. She breathlessly laughed. "'Respect our kind.' If that isn't the most *asinine*—*!*" She covered her mouth as if to stifle any further disrespect, but as she laughed again she realized this wouldn't work. "That same asinine rhetoric!" she cried through her hand, then set her lips free and sang in her best impression of a bourgeois housewife, "'Respect your kind,

Bradley! If your fellow American hurts that foreigner, you do nothing! Watch! Laugh! Join, if you like'—*And I dare you to argue!*" she yelled before Bishop could interject, "I dare you to tell me it isn't the same—*damn*—*thing!*"

Finally she found his face. She couldn't say yet if she got through to him. "Or worse!" she added.

There was still a general sadness in his expression—a look of hopelessness—which let her wonder if maybe her opinion meant nothing.

She hadn't finished catching her breath when she demanded, "Well, say something."

"You… swore."

She cocked an eyebrow and inclined her head. This better not have been all he took from this.

He cleared his throat, coming to stare back at Marius' door. "Forgive me. Sometimes I… I like to think I do what I do because it must be done, but then you make me wonder… do I have my priorities straight…"

She wondered if they were talking about the same thing anymore, but still, there were more pressing matters. "How do I free Jack?"

Silence as Bishop gave it more thought. "By words, by force, or by death, is my guess." He gnawed his lip, then offered, "Talk to Winifred. Go from there."

28. The Halloween Dance

Alice

Alice heard the music back from Bishop's cabin, and she wondered if mortals heard the same. Before nearing the high school parking lot, she slowed to a human pace. Her heart hastened with every step, and this was a relief. It meant Jack was here — not alone at his house with Winifred.

The building was easy enough to find, though it was so huge and there were so many entrances, she wouldn't have known where to go if it wasn't for the costumed crowd. She had learned from the movies what to expect. Most of the young women were scantily clad, despite the cold. She didn't understand it, but in the grander theme of lost innocence, it wasn't so appalling. Here her childhood friend was...

Nothing was verified yet. Until she spoke to Winifred, it was still possible Marius had made everything up. In the instance Jack's memory was faked, all it meant was…

Alice gnawed her lip. This scenario wasn't much less disturbing. Regardless of if Marius was to be trusted, or if Jack's memory was to be trusted, Winifred owned Jack with the intention of keeping Theo. Jack was her Theo-shaped doll. One way or another, it had to end.

The scattered teens led the way to the back entrance, which was apparently closest to the gym. Here the music was so loud, she could hardly hear herself think. She wondered if it was louder than the Velvet. It would only get worse once she was inside.

At the doorway, the school faculty waited behind tables, collecting money and stamping ink on the back of all the students' hands as proof they had paid their fee. When it was her turn, they paused. One of them asked, "Do you even go here?"

"I'm a guest," she replied.

"Who are you with?"

She was about to tell them the truth, but wondered if this was a good idea. She knew she didn't look like the sort of person who could hold her own against a monster. She didn't need any of them to turn her away from Jack all for the sake of saving her from "The Ripper."

But without the truth, she needed the time to consider a lie. It must've been obvious; she felt like she was taking forever. "I'm with…"

A thought occurred. She didn't need to deal with this. The faculty hadn't been abused the way Jack had, and she didn't intend to have them do anything they'd regret. She borrowed one of Winifred's moves and it worked; she waved an arm across both their faces and they immediately fell under trance. If any student behind her saw, they didn't think anything of it. The whole town really was trained.

Despite it all being for the greater good, she still felt ugly for doing it. "You've already let me in," she said, raising the back of her hand for them to view the stamp they hadn't given her. "See?"

There was a brief hiatus before they blinked in succession. "Welcome back," said the one, and the other grinned and let her pass.

She realized too late she could have said she was there with Crystal.

With an ill smile back, Alice stepped through the threshold and into a lobby. There was a buffet set up along the back wall, and stretched cotton decorated every corner like cobwebs. Skeletons and pumpkins sat on haystacks which bookended the major doorways, and along the walls hung blinking orange and purple lights.

The gym doors were open. It was dark in there, save for colored pinpoint lights, occasional flashes, and a spinning mirrored ball on the ceiling. The space was packed. And so loud.

She stepped out of the way of the students who filed in behind her, but this was as far as she would venture. She had to focus. As she began to close her eyes and tune everything out—

There wasn't a need. Not far ahead, she spotted him striding toward the gym.

Jack glanced her way and continued. When he registered who she was, he paused. As if afraid of what he might see when he looked again, slowly he returned his gaze. Something was off. She noted the fear in his eyes, and his overall posture screamed how he wanted to flee. While this seemed to be the only natural reaction to what he had remembered, it didn't seem directed correctly.

Alice took some steps toward him. His gaze lowered before he took a breath and began his approach. She was right. He was afraid of her. She couldn't help it; she walked faster. She needed to know why this was happening. What could have transpired while she was gone? What could Jack have done to provoke another memory-wipe? Or was she guessing too wildly?

"Hey," he said when she was near enough.

"Hey," she replied, as if out of breath. She wanted to begin the questioning, but if his memory was cleared and she tried to talk to him about anything, how could she go about it in a way which didn't make her sound crazy?

He might've been waiting for her to form her words, but when the silence lingered too long he commented, "So, you're the Wicked Witch."

She glanced down at her costume and remembered what day it was. She wore a witch hat, one of her old black dresses, and Bishop had done her make-up so that her face was green, but subtle—ethereal. It was a light, dull green base with darker greens to contour her cheekbones and shadow her eyes, and dark green lipstick.

She nodded and gestured toward his attire. "And you, you're..." She didn't know what to guess. The black cloak could've made him anything, and that was the extent to his costume beyond dark faded jeans and a coal black long-sleeved shirt.

He lifted his plastic scythe, and that was the hint she needed. "Death," he finished for her. "I bring death."

She acknowledged with a nod. "How are you feeling?" she asked.

He took a breath and scanned past her head. "I don't know. Weird. Still not sure if it happened."

So then he did still remember. "Trust your instincts," she reminded him.

He nodded, though she wasn't sure how much he heard. He was distracted.

"Is she here?" she asked. He nodded. She knew she was. Perhaps she hoped he would reveal this was the true source of his discomfort, but nothing changed.

Finally he leaned closer and asked, hushed, "Do you see it, too? Everyone's got…" He rested his hand along his freshly scarred neck, glancing at everyone else's. So he finally saw it, now.

Alice nodded. "It's like this everywhere in town."

He didn't respond. Didn't react.

The ginger head popped in past the crowd, her tall plastic crown briefly catching the glow of the gym's disco mirrors. It was strange, seeing her now, having heard all that she had done. Winifred still appeared smiling, fragile and sweet, and Alice stared and wondered how much was a facade, or if she was truly clueless to her own darkness. How much darkness could such an innocent face hold?

Winifred shrunk back slightly when their gazes locked, then managed a polite, though unnerved grin. "Theo!" she called, turning her gaze. After weaving through the crowd to Jack, she took his hand and said, "Here you are."

He lifted his other hand as if to peel himself free, but instead dropped it back to his side. His chest heaved with the reminder to breathe. "Yeah, hey," he replied, staring at her for a second before peering over his shoulder, back into the gym. "I gotta go, um. Bathroom." What he said next seemed addressed to both of them. "Don't go anywhere; stick to crowds. I'll be right back." He was escaping and it was obvious.

Winifred bravely took a breath and whispered, "Okay." This would fit the narrative of her hoping to convince Jack that Alice was the Ripper. Although, for all Alice knew, the emotion could've been genuine. The old friend had always been easily intimidated. Alice might not have done as much to mask her displeasure as she had hoped. She worried that perhaps this made herself look bad in comparison. She hoped maybe as perturbed as she was was as worried as she needed to appear.

When Jack allowed one last look her way, it seemed to reassure her, *Don't worry; we've got this.* It was strange. He simultaneously trusted and distrusted them both.

Alice nodded back.

After offering Winifred one last look, he slipped out of her grasp and into the crowd.

Now Alice took in the other woman's costume and couldn't help a quick surprised laugh. "You're Glinda The Good Witch."

Winifred's gaze dropped, though eventually Alice's implication hit her and she dazedly laughed back. "Wow. Um. Here," the girl offered, gesturing to one of the rented plastic tables, "Let's sit."

Alice glanced at what would've been her chair. Sitting to idly chat didn't feel right. It didn't matter that the worst wasn't verified yet. Jack was Winifred's replacement-Theo. This wasn't right.

Alice gnawed her lip. If she hadn't trapped herself underground for so long, she would never have had to even consider that her old friend might've been even worse off.

"What is it?" Winifred asked.

Alice allowed a quick glance at her before letting her gaze drop back to the chair. "I never wanted to be in this situation."

"What situation?"

She didn't know how to answer. She peered through the crowd toward the direction Jack had left. He wasn't in sight any longer.

Winifred followed her gaze. "Oh," she muttered, as if she should have seen this coming. She sighed, a pained apology clear in her face. "You at least got to have him for a short while."

"We're not thinking about the same thing."

"Aren't we?" This wasn't as gentle as it could've been. Though it seemed Winifred tried to keep it light, Alice saw her struggle to keep it that way. "I can only imagine what it must've been like," Winifred said. "All those years we were together and yet you both... It drove me crazy; you complimented each other so perfectly, and I was only in the way."

"You weren't—"

"No, I was. It's okay. At the time I even knew I was being selfish, but I didn't care, and now… I'm so sorry I didn't let you have your turn."

"No, Winifred—" Still, she didn't know what to say. Sucking her lips between her teeth, she gave it some thought. "I spent the better part of the last eight decades thinking Theo was still…"

While Winifred must have known where this sentence was going, she still waited for an elaboration.

"I'm not over him." Alice's throat tightened and she hated it, but she needed Winifred to hear this. "I don't know if I ever will be. They may look alike and sound alike, and while it hurts in the best of ways to look at him or even be within a mile's distance, Jack is not Theo. As much as I would love for him to be, he isn't. So please don't assign to me feelings I don't have."

Winifred frowned, gaze lowered as she let everything process. Again, she gestured for the rented plastic chairs. This time Alice sat. Her hands shook as she dabbed at her eyes, and she hated it.

Winifred took the spot across from her. "Then why don't you want me to be with him?" She sounded like a hurt and confused child.

"It isn't about what I want," Alice promised, then searched for her first point. She remembered Marius' suggestion. *Ask her if she has to put him under trance—every—time—before they do it.* "What does Jack want?"

"I don't know," Winifred all but whined, as if this was irrelevant. This wasn't a step in a comfortable direction.

Alice shook the thought from her head. "Please, humor me. I assume you've had…" *God, how do I phrase this?* Perhaps it was best to ask outright.

"Sex?" Winifred asked, confused, though clearly having read the question in Alice's discomfort. Alice nodded, and Winifred nodded back, still obviously confused as to what this had to do with anything. Something squirmed in Alice's gut, though she worked to settle it. There was more still to unearth; nothing was verified. However, there was no settling her stomach as she considered her next question.

Winifred waited patiently, albeit with mounting anxiety.

Finally Alice murmured, "Does he remember?"

Winifred's gaze gradually lowered. "Not yet. He's never in the mood when he's awake. I don't understand why."

Jack's memory was real.

"And then today, he…" Winifred's chin quivered. "I've never had this happen before. Ever."

Alice didn't want to hear anymore, but "What?" she asked.

Winifred tucked the corners of her mouth, as if trying to steal her face. "I had him under trance," her voice wavered. "He broke out. I put him back under, and… He was… *crying.*"

The tables were a sickly white—or yellow.

Winifred was a whisper over the music from the gym. "I didn't know what to do. I needed him to stop crying; I needed him to feel better—"

A bubble rose in Alice's throat.

"—so I told him to do just that. But he still… He's acting strangely and I'm afraid to ask him why."

She had to breathe. She had to focus. "You should ask him," Alice managed.

"What if he remembers?"

Alice moved her hands under the table, clasping them tightly over her lap and hoping the girl hadn't noticed the way they shook. "You tell me," Alice replied.

Finally she took in Winifred's expression. Tears glistened in the girl's eyes, and her gaze was lowered as she gave it some thought. "I suppose I could put him under again," she said.

Alice shook her head. "That isn't working anymore."

"I could go deeper. Completely rewire his concept of hurt."

"Alice?" Winifred asked.

Alice had a hand over her own mouth. Her fingers were wet. Her face was wet. Her eyes were hot. The bubble remained suspended in her throat. "You really are so clueless, aren't you?" she rasped.

Winifred drew back, eyes wide. "What do you mean?" she pleaded. "He wouldn't ever know pain again."

Hand still over her mouth, Alice shook her head. Her back shuddered with her every breath.

"Please, Alice, say something—you're scaring me. What's wrong?"

Alice shook her head. "I didn't want to believe it."

"Alice." Gently, Winifred lowered her friend's hand from her mouth. "I can't help you if I don't know what you're talking about."

Alice's gut turned more violently at the feel of Winifred's fingers over hers. Feeling like a ghost, she slipped away and stood. "I need air," she explained.

Winifred eagerly followed, the concern etched clearly in the lines of her face. "Did I say something wrong?"

The girl had him trapped in county jurisdiction and isolated from his peers, presenting herself as the only light in a dark place, just so that he would be with her. She killed the other girls so she had no competition. She would restructure the very core of who he was—wire him to endure more hurt —just so he wouldn't leave her.

Alice crossed back to the double doors through which she had entered, and Winifred kept pace beside her as they returned to the crisp October night.

"What did I say wrong?" the girl fretted as soon as they had paced along the grand cinderblock walls, rounding the corner so they were out of sight and earshot from the regular mortal crowd.

Alice breathed deeply of the frigid air. It seemed Marius was right about everything so far. Had he seen the future? Would Jack eventually kill Winifred?

Alice removed her witch's hat and pulled her braided hair by the roots. "I should have never let them bury me," she started, "I should have been here for you; none of this would have happened—"

"What are you talking about?" Winifred cried, still concerned, as if she truly was so clueless.

"You can change, can't you?" Alice yelled back, pleading. "You're not *evil;* you're — you're just—"

"*Evil?* What—"

"You're just *Winifred!*" Alice shouted, knowing she was babbling. "You just need—someone to talk to, to keep you grounded—!"

"Alice, I'm not *crazy—* !"

"Look at us, Winifred, two nuts," the older friend insisted, "completely bonkers, with all the time and unchallenged power this world can offer; we can do anything—We can go to France!" she exclaimed, hearing how manic she sounded, but she couldn't stop. "Would you like to go to France? We'll leave Jack be—let him have some semblance of a normal life, and you and I, we can move past this, okay?"

She nearly reached to take Winifred's hands in hers, but still her throat rose at the thought of touching her, and this added a new welling of tears to her eyes. "We can make this work!" she continued, "We can start a new life in France, a fresh slate, only we'll do it right! No one could touch us—not Marius, not Jack—*no one* has to..." She knew she lost her steam as she caught herself, recalling all those who had died so far, but she had to keep trying. "No one *else* has to..." Her throat closed and she clamped her hand over her mouth again.

All the while, Winifred stared back at her, wide-eyed. "You're...*worried* about me."

Alice's voice was a high rasp through the strain when she asked, "How did you *start?* How did you... justify it?"

Silence. Winifred dropped her gaze. It was out, now. They both knew the other knew. Winifred was the Ripper.

"I knew you wouldn't approve," said the girl. "But it's who we are now. What's the point of being a domsuco if we can't do what we want? The guys in New York are *ten* times worse; it's probably not gonna be much different in France."

Alice shook her head. "This is insane."

"It's the way it is."

"That same asinine rhetoric," she whispered, then leaned with her back to the wall, allowing herself some time to breathe.

Winifred's face was pleading, but it wasn't enough. It was as if she pitied Alice for not understanding; for being so naive. "I didn't want you to think less of me. You think less of me now, don't you?"

Alice shook her head—not in disagreement, but in dismissal. "Don't. Don't."

"You do!" Winifred warbled, "What do I have to do? To change your opinion?"

Alice breathed for a moment longer, thinking—or, trying to. "Don't think of him as something you can control," she managed. "It can only work for so long anyway; it's clearly starting to fall apart, isn't it?"

Winifred's mouth pressed in a line, but still she waited.

Alice leaned her head back so her gaze landed more easily on the black sky and distant evergreens. "Erasing his reception of pain sounds good on paper. But that's not the answer; you've introduced domsuco solutions to a human issue."

Still Winifred, no less worried than when they had first stepped out, only watched and waited for Alice to continue.

The older friend sighed. She had to explain this. Why did she have to explain this? "Imagine you can't interfere with his thoughts. What do you do?"

Winifred's gaze flicked to the side with a quick, exasperated thought, and she whined, "I don't know, I—carry on as if nothing happened. Shower him in gifts. Love him until he forgets naturally."

Alice felt her expression pinch as she shook her head.

Winifred stared past her as she gave it more thought. When she apparently caught on, she mumbled, "It really feels like you don't want me to be with him."

Alice lifted her head only to let it fall back and hit the wall. "Dash it all, Winifred, my opinion doesn't matter. If he wants to stay with you, let him. If he wants to leave—"

"But I can't!" Winifred cried. "I-I don't know what to do without him! I'll lose my mind if he ends up with anyone else; if he ends up with you, I'll snap! I see the way he looks at you—like you're this magical being—the answer to his prayers."

"He's merely relieved I haven't died like the others yet."

"What exactly are you suggesting I do; just tell me!"

Alice let out a breath and gave it more thought. While it might've made Jack uncomfortable, perhaps it would actually be best for him, as well as for Winifred, if they spoke.

"Be honest with him," Alice finally said.

"About?"

"Everything."

"But he's human. It's against the rules."

"And leaving neck-scars on an entire county isn't going to draw attention from any out-of-town visitors?"

"Only other domsuco can see bites — !"

Not caring for the answer, Alice finished, "He needs to know." It didn't matter that he already knew. The important factor was for Winifred to tell him.

Winifred sighed, dropping her gaze. In the silence, Alice knew she was letting the conversation play out in her head. "I don't know what I'll do without him," she finally murmured.

"We'll deal with things as they come."

The girl nodded, taking a deep breath. "Okay. Fine. I'll talk to him once he's out of the bathroom."

Alice let her gaze drift back to the distant horizon of moonlit trees. Now she didn't know what to say.

Winifred offered a small giggle. "Silly humans and their bathrooms."

Alice couldn't fathom smiling back. Winifred undoubtedly noticed. Her grin faded.

29. Confronting The Monster

Jack

Jack couldn't stay in the bathroom forever. He knew he couldn't, but this was the only place Wyn wouldn't follow him. Or, Alice. Whoever was the Ripper. Either way, somehow, he still needed to get in touch with Crystal.

To free his hands, he had his plastic scythe hanging on one of the stall doors. He leaned against the sink, staring through the mirror at his scarred-up throat.

The punctures were just above his neckline, clearly visible. As if to double check, he ran his fingers over the scabs. He could still feel them. He picked at an older one, and he felt that, too. He checked his nails for proof, and there it was. Dead skin and dried blood. He flicked it away.

It was a strange feeling he had. Numb. Everything in him denied anything that could've happened, so he could still laugh, or talk to someone and forget about it. But then the feeling was always something which nagged at the back of his mind. He still spaced out every other moment, standing stiff and forgetting to breathe full breaths. It never mattered what he was in the middle of doing.

Then there was whenever he saw one of them. Wyn or Alice. It was like trying to balance on a ten foot pole. If he leaned the slightest bit in any direction—sick, scared, contaminated, dizzy—he would fall. His thoughts would manifest into him either throwing up again, crying again, fleeing, passing out, or washing his hands and splashing his face again.

He turned on the faucet and commenced. He really needed one of Crystal's friends to come in already. She was friends with everyone, so it shouldn't have taken long. Literally, *anyone* had to enter the bathroom, and he would ask to use their phone.

He stepped away from the sink, dried his hands, then paced to the back wall. The door opened and he didn't care to register who it was before asking, "Hey, are you friends with Crystal?"

The boy froze in the threshold, neck clear of bite marks as far as Jack could tell. Kid had to have been a freshman—he had that scared-freshman vibe. And he looked like a child. The boy didn't say anything, but then he cautiously stepped backward, then darted back into the hallway.

Jack's mouth fell open. "Dude, really?" All that remained to hear him was the slowly closing door. "The Ripper doesn't even go after guys!"

The door finished closing.

He kicked the back wall and, "Fuck!" he screamed. That was all it took; he leaned off the pole. He wasn't sure which direction, but he was falling. His heart raced and his lungs constricted so he could only breathe with his upper chest.

The door opened again, and again he spun around. There stood Luke, tall and beefy enough to take up most of the doorway, dressed as a gladiator and confusedly staring down the hallway. When he peered back into the bathroom, it all seemed to make sense. "What'd you say to him?"

"Nothing." It didn't matter. "Is Wyn waiting outside?"

Luke glanced back out to be sure, then shook his head. "Last I saw, she was outside-outside with the Wicked Witch."

Jack squinted. If either of the girls was the Ripper, why would one go outside alone with the other?

Luke stepped in fully, letting the door close behind him. "Are you alright?" He had a couple old bites along his jugular.

"I'm—yeah," Jack managed.

"Did another girl die?"

"No. Not that I know of."

The jock wasn't sure what to think, but he apparently got the message Jack wanted to talk about something else. Beefcake removed a flask from his satchel. "Crystal's mom was pretty impressed with your notebook. Said it would take a while to go through." He took a swig, grimaced and continued, "We told her what you saw in that abandoned house. She already had a feeling it was Wyn. She wants to talk to you about it tomorrow."

"Did she say anything about what I should do in the meantime?"

Luke held the flask to him. Jack was about to ask what was inside, but realized he didn't care. He took it, and Luke answered as Jack put it to his lips. "Keep treating Wyn like a princess until she's released and can progress with a real plan."

Jack nearly coughed as he swallowed. This shit burned. He remembered Wyn always got him the good stuff; this had to have been cheap shit. "I can't do *nothing*," he managed once he got it down. He handed the poison back to Luke, who readily accepted. "She's so much more dangerous than you can imagine."

Luke scoffed, "You're beginning to sound like Crystal. *Before* they figured she wasn't crazy."

Crystal knew what she saw. "I have to talk to her," Jack said, "but the second I get back out there, Wyn's gonna be all over me, and then I can't say anything."

"Say no more." Luke reached back into his satchel, this time pulling out his smartphone. He hit a few buttons, then handed over the device. "It's ringing."

Jack looked at the screen just long enough to verify it was calling Crystal, then put it to his ear.

It kept ringing. Jack pulled at his hair through the hood of his reaper cloak. "I don't think she's picking up."

"Give it a few tries. It's loud in there."

It rang more. Then went to voicemail. Jack hung up before the mechanical lady could do her spiel, then tried again.

It rang. Then, a click. "Hey, boo!" The sound of the dance was so loud on her end, when she shouted to make up for it, Jack had to pull the device back from his ear.

"It's Jack," he replied.

"What? Oh! Awkward, hi! I guess Luke told you how it went with my mom?"

"Yeah, listen, do you remember a message you left me? About three days ago?"

"Hold on, I can't hear you. Walking to the lobby now." For a second all he heard was the music and random chatter. If it quieted, he couldn't tell. Then, "What message?"

"Come on, I know you remember."

Luke grumbled, "Easy, there."

"I'm not—" Jack trailed off when Crystal began her response.

"If it was three days ago, I was still at the hospital. Do you know what kind of drugs they had me on?"

"Don't believe it was just the drugs. Listen, I saw some shit, too. I remember something, but I don't know... I don't know how much of it was real."

Now Luke was concerned. "What do you mean?"

"What did you see?" she asked.

He looked back at Luke. "I don't wanna get into the details, but... Wyn's strong. And I wasn't supposed to remember any of it."

Luke tilted his head back in preparation to call bullshit. "How do you remember it, then?"

"I had help."

"Who helped you?"

Crystal cursed under her breath. Apparently she could hear them both. "Fuckin'—Alice?" she asked.

"Yeah," Jack answered. "How'd you guess?"

Another pause on her end. This could've meant so many things, though all that occurred to him was one. Again, Alice was the one Crystal saw in the Crypt. Once it was proven possible for one person to fabricate another's reality, it opened up a frightening world of possibilities. It was possible everything Alice showed him was a lie. If it was Alice in the Crypt, she could've wiped Crystal's memory, and Wyn was innocent. If it was Alice—

"You should talk to her," Crystal finally answered.

"And say what?"

"Ask her what happened in the Crypt, and tell her you'll know if she's lying."

Jack didn't think he had Crystal on speakerphone, but Luke seemed to hear perfectly. He asked, annoyed for some reason, "Why does it sound like you're talking about actual vampires?"

His girlfriend sighed then grumbled, "The Ripper can do so much, she may as well be. Anyway, I gotta get back to the dance; it probably looks like I'm up to something."

"Fine. Bye." Jack hung up and handed the phone back.

Luke huffed out a laugh and shook his head. "You'd think she was talking about actual vampires again." He put the phone back in his satchel.

Jack paced away, mostly distracted. How could he approach Alice with this? If she turned out to be the Ripper, she would've been the one constantly wiping his memory. But if Crystal thought Alice was the Ripper, she wouldn't have sent him to her. Well, he would've hoped not.

He remembered Luke said something. Crystal and vampires. He replied, "I think I would believe her."

"Come on, if this is some elaborate joke —"

"But it wouldn't make sense, would it? To take a joke so far?"

Beefcake shook his head and again tried to laugh. "You're not gonna get me, man."

"*Get* you? Are you fucking listening to yourself?"

This time when Luke laughed, it was aggressive. "Are *you* fucking listening —"

"No—*you gotta get you priorities straight!*" Jack roared, finding an outlet for his distress. "What's the worst that happens on the off chance I'm lying about the darkest of dark shit, all for a fucked joke?"

"Okay! So you believe yourself!" the other teen yelled, not backing down, "Doesn't mean you're not fucking nuts!"

"Then *how do you explain—*" This next decision Jack had to make quickly, before he finished his sentence. Did he care if Luke thought he was crazy? How much did it matter that he received some form of verification for his vision?

" *—this!*" Jack tugged down his collar. The wounds should've been clearly visible before, but if people were trained not to notice, he figured he would bring attention to the whole thing.

Luke squinted. "What are you…" His words faded away the wider his eyes grew. "Holy shit, man," he breathed. "What happened?"

The noise came back in his head and his stomach squirmed. "So you see it?"

An eyebrow was raised for confusion. "Yeah?" The jock remained staring. "Shit, how long has it been like that? Looks like—"

"Months? Years?"

Luke's hand wrapped around his own mouth. "How did I not see this earlier?"

Jack felt his breaths rasp from the back of his throat, and he could hear them, too. He fixed his collar back. "You didn't see it because she didn't want you to see it."

"That doesn't make any sense."

"But you see it now, so it's there." Jack was mostly speaking to himself now. He absently nodded. "And now I have to talk to Alice."

"Whoa, wait a minute, you can't drop that on me and walk away!"

He opened the door. "Yes I can." If the jock said anything more, Jack wasn't listening; he was already halfway down the hall.

So his neck was actually fucked. It could've been Wyn, but it also still could've been Alice; there still wasn't any definitive proof his vision actually happened. He had to talk to her. He had to come up with a way to do it safely. In a crowd would've probably been best. Witnesses. But then, if they were all under her control, would that have actually helped?

Maybe he should've thought of something before he entered the lobby, but without the head to stop and think, he weaved past the crowds. Maybe he didn't care to know the truth. If he came to her and she wiped his memory, maybe it would've been for the best. Or maybe he trusted her not to do this. For whatever reason.

"Theo!"

He jumped and spun about. Not far from his side was Wyn, fast approaching. His legs nearly fell beneath him, but he stood firm. "Hey," he answered.

Alice stood a few paces behind her. She watched him all along, and when their gazes met, she nodded his attention back to Wyn.

He peered back at his girlfriend. "Having fun?"

Now she stood close, both his hands in hers. She let out a deep sigh, eyes falling to his chest. Her eyelashes glistened with leftover tears, and this confused him.

"What's wrong?" he asked.

After glancing Alice's way, Wyn turned back to him and said something. He couldn't hear, so squinted as if this would help. "What?"

She stepped closer and stood on her toes. He flinched at the sudden movement, the closeness of her mouth to his neck tickling something in his lower back.

"Let's dance," she offered. It was hardly louder than a whisper.

"Yeah, we can do that."

Still with his hands in hers, she led him into the gym, past different cliques until they found a spot of their own—a gap in the crowd. Her elbows rested over his shoulders, her forearms dangling over his back. Her brow dropped into his chest.

"What's wrong?" he asked again.

Her back expanded with a sharp intake of breath. If this was intended to calm her, it had the exact opposite effect; she burst into sobs. Muffled through his shirt, she wailed, "I can't!"

It was as if he was supposed to feel bad for her, but he didn't know how. "Uh. Can't?"

More sobbing. "I can't lose you, so I can't—say it!"

If she was coming clean… If it really was her all along…

He jumped when she tugged on his collar, but she rose her lips to his ear, not his neck. "I'm…" She released a quick, shuddering breath. "I'm a monster," she whispered.

The noise in his head now clouded all else, bellowing at him, *I told you so! Run, idiot!*

"What do you mean?" He wasn't sure who he was trying to convince when he added, "You're not a monster."

She kept sobbing. It almost sounded like laughing, though he knew it wasn't.

He stood his full height and caught Alice's gaze from afar. She was watching him, and when he noticed, she didn't look away. Crystal was at her side, and he realized the crowd she stood with were the jocks from the parking lot and the other cheerleaders from the Crypt. The girls still had their necks covered. The jocks all carried old scars, and George's seemed newer. He had a few on either side.

If Alice could control people… This might not have been a real confession.

"What do you mean?" Jack asked again.

Stoner-jock Adam nudged Alice's arm. She jumped and snapped her eyes to him as he asked her something. After her signature initially-confused face, she offered a polite grin and exchanged some words back. She kept glancing at Jack between phrases.

"I'm not human," Wyn finally managed, and the music quieted just enough for him to hear.

He remembered he wasn't supposed to know anything already. "Well then what are you?"

"Basically a vampire."

He could've laughed if he was still clueless. Now he didn't know how to react, so he said nothing.

"Do you believe me?" she asked.

He shook his head. It still could've been Alice.

She bit her lip, thinking, eyes still glistening as she withdrew her arms and searched her hips for pockets. Finally she pulled the plastic crown from her head. "Try crushing this in your hand."

"What?"

Impatient, she cracked the prop down the middle, handing him half. Bracing her half between her hands, she pressed them together. The pieces snapped, some flying through the air.

"Uh, Wyn?" he asked.

The pieces she had left, she closed in her hand, clenching her fist as tight as it would allow, no strain in her face. When her fingers unclasped, all that was left in her palm was white and silver dust.

She pulverized the plastic pieces. Effortlessly.

He braced his own half in his hands the same way she had. He didn't have to follow through to know he couldn't do the same.

Still, he didn't know how to respond. He had to think. "Bri said she saw me break up with you."

"Bri?"

"Then you found me today, and…"

Wyn was what Alice said she was. She could control people.

Something about her seemed more tense than usual. "Today?" she whispered, voice gone with the noise and the return of music. He didn't need to nod or otherwise respond. She knew what he said, and it took all he had just to stand there.

"You remember?" she asked.

"I… I think so," he managed.

"The old Van Sloan house?"

Everything seemed to go dark and fade. He recalled this meant he was close to fainting, so concentrated on his breath. Deeply in through the nose, slowly out through the mouth. He continued like this when he should've been answering.

"Theo?"

"Did you kill Sarah?"

Silence. He found her gaze. She was wide-eyed.

"I did," she answered.

The world slipped far away, tilting.

Arms numb.

"Let… go," he managed.
She might've.

He staggered backward. He needed his head. "You killed my dad." He heard nothing. Just noise. "Sarah," he breathed.

He'd danced with her before, in this gym. They looked like complete dorks, but they didn't care. George took their pictures for the yearbook.

He turned from the center of the gym. Walking, or floating. He needed to be outside.

No, he needed people. Witnesses.

Bleachers.

"Why?" he asked.

Wyn might've answered.

He needed his head. If he was his dad, he would've been much more collected about this.

"Why?" he asked again.

"She was in the way," Wyn croaked. Fading back into his body, he noted tears still streaming down her face. But the way she said it was too matter-of-fact. As if any sane person would've done the same.

His voice rose, "In the way of what?"

She stared at him, slowing to a stop. It was as if it should've been obvious, yet the news was still hard to break. "You," she finally answered.

Sarah died, because…

If he had been single, she would never have…

No. He wasn't the one killing girls. All this time, it was… *I thought you were the one good thing I had.*

He needed his head. Deep breaths.

Feeling gradually returned to his fingers. He could feel his heart in his chest. "I wanted to die this past year. Is that what you wanted?"

Wyn stared ahead as if she didn't hear. Just continued their walk to the bleachers.

"None of my old friends look at me anymore. I don't have a phone because I'd only get hate mail and death threats." More volume and fervor, "I get my ass handed to me every other month! *Is that what you wanted!*" he roared. Wyn jumped, and he stopped walking.

"Please, Theo — "

"Who's Theo?!" he screamed, "Who the fuck is Theo?! That's not my name! No one calls me that!"

"Please," she begged, "I can explain everything, please, just stop yelling."

The bleachers were closed, pushed into the wall.

She screamed as he slammed her into them, hands to her throat. He squeezed the tightest he could—

His back was to the wall and her mouth was pressed to his.

While she ended the kiss, he remained pinned. He couldn't fight. Couldn't move. Couldn't try. He stared past her, enraged and shaking.

Into his ear she pleaded, "They already think you're the Ripper. Hurting me here will make it worse."

Past her head, he noticed some people were looking, left-over concern clear on their faces as they turned away, back to their own lives.

She released, finally allowing him to step away from the bleachers. When he only stood and said nothing, she led his hand to one of the ledges, encouraging him to climb. While the bleachers were closed, there were still a couple rows of seats open at the top.

He welcomed the visual distraction, looking at his hands and footholds to go up. Wyn followed, her skirt poofy enough not to hinder her legs. Whereas he remained standing when they reached the top, she sat, waiting for him to join.

"I've made you a pariah," she began. "I know, and I can fix that. I promise, I can do it in a heartbeat—you'll have all your old friends back."

He couldn't look at her yet. He pushed his hair from his brow, knocking back the hood he forgot he wore as he continued to consciously breathe. "You slit their throats and hung them upside down," he managed. "You can't fix that."

Silence.

Finally he sat, close enough for her to hear but otherwise as distant as possible. He still wouldn't look at her. "Back at that abandoned house, there was… You had me on that…" His throat went dry. He had to disconnect his mouth from his head just to finish. "You made it so I couldn't say no."

She didn't say anything. Now he had to look at her; he had to know if she got it yet. While her eyes were still wide with worry, her brow somewhat furrowed as she waited for him to spell it out. Then her features softened. She got it, but… something wasn't right. "You were smiling. And you made such pleasant noises."

His stomach rose and again he looked away.

"It wasn't about power for me!" she insisted, "I just—I wanted you, and I wanted you to want me back! So for just *one moment*, I would make it that way—"

"What the fuck—"

"But I never hurt you!" she cried, "You wouldn't ever remember, so it was like it never happened! We'd both got what we wanted!"

"Wyn!" he shouted, "No! No, that's not… No! How is that…?"

She looked away, hands to her temples. "I didn't do anything wrong, I didn't…" Desperately she shook her head, but while she might've been so blind before, she couldn't kid herself anymore.

Now she just sat there, sobbing. Becoming the smallest version of herself, she hugged her sides and bent so her forehead met her knees. He probably looked like a real dick, just sitting there while she was bawling, but there was nothing he would have rather done than wring her neck again.

While he was more than ready for this conversation to be over, there was still one thing he needed to know. He waited until she quieted to a sniffling calm.

"Why me?" he finally asked.

Defeated, she stared over the gym, tears still rolling down her face. She would still sob, but not as much. Finally she replied with her only concrete answer. "You were made for me. Only me."

So there was no real reason, then. Just a whim attached to the childish idea that obsession was love, and love was fated.

With the sort of nod that said, *Story of my life,* he stood. "Right." He stepped down to the next bleacher, beginning his descent.

"Wait."

He paused then turned back around. They stood at about the same height now.

She pressed her lips together and closed her eyes, bracing herself. "There's something I need to know. One last thing, but I need to know it's the truth, otherwise I'll..." Her eyes opened as she searched his expression. He wasn't sure what she found. "It will fester," she finished.

"What is it?"

"I need to know it's the truth."

"What do you want; what are you asking me?"

She stared at him until he got it. There was only one sure-fire way she could get an honest answer from anyone. He sighed, "You wanna put me back under trance." He should've seen it coming.

Chin quivering, she waited for him to decide.

"Do I really have a choice?" he asked.

"Yes. This time, yes."

He doubted this, so proceeded knowing this was possibly the last conscious conversation he would have with her. He laughed, though it sounded like manic crying. "After this, I don't want to see you again." She nodded, but he wasn't done. "I don't want to still be dating tomorrow, and I want to make this next part especially clear: I don't want you to ever touch me again. Understand?"

"Yes."

"Good, because now if you end up pulling this shit again, you can't pretend you've done nothing wrong. Now you know."

She didn't respond, but waited until he was finished. When he clearly had nothing more to say, he realized she was still waiting for the go-ahead.

He turned around, scanning the gym until he found Alice again, staring at him wide-eyed. He wasn't sure what would happen next, but it felt like something he wouldn't escape. He would have wanted to say goodbye to his family, though for now there was only Alice. He hoped she would tell them what she knew, if he didn't make it back that night. He hoped she would find him and help him remember again.

He turned back to Wyn. "Alright."

This was the last he remembered of the dance.

30. Entitlement

Alice

Although the boy with shoulder length hair kept speaking, Alice hardly listened anymore. From their spot at the gym's center, she watched as Winifred waved her hand over Jack's eyes, the girl a bleacher row above him for height convenience. He was back under trance.

If it wasn't clear before that Alice wasn't invested in her own conversation, it was now. She openly stared past the boy's head.

His name was Adam. When he followed her gaze, he understood. "So you know about all that?"

She nodded. Luckily he was too high to immediately continue the conversation.

Winifred kept her word to Jack so far; she didn't touch him, despite how clear it was that she wanted to melt into him again. The girl hesitated to get on with it, breathing deeply until enough of her voice returned. "How do you feel —about Alice?" she finally managed. "Romantically?"

Alice's stomach dropped. She honestly had no idea how Jack would answer, though somehow none of the possibilities seemed favorable.

His lips parted as if he would speak, though nothing came out. "I shouldn't think about it."

"Think about it, then tell me."

Silence. "I can see it working." His mouth remained open, as if there was more. Then, strangely, he smiled, eyes coming to squint and teeth coming to show. He laughed, "I can definitely see it."

Alice's chest swelled and her eyes watered. The thought made him smile under trance—while he was his most honest self. Now nothing good could follow.

When she looked away from Jack, she found Winifred had been staring her down all along.

Alice kept her voice steady, though her words came out too quick for one not panicked. "I won't stay in town long enough for anything to come of that!" she called. "You and I, we can both leave—"

Adam peered over his shoulder to follow her gaze. "Are you *talking* to her?"

Winifred disappeared from sight. Alice glimpsed her stop before the DJ booth, pulling the plug so the music muted and left a cloud of silence which rang in most ears. The next second, the girl was gone.

All the lights went out. Some students emitted surprised screams while others laughed.

"Up here, everyone." It seemed to echo from everywhere. The comforting treble to the voice was gone, leaving a low, hoarse alternative in its wake.

Curious and confused, most of her audience looked. A spotlight turned on, wobbling across the room before it found her at the stage. There was Winifred, microphone at hand.

"What are you doing?" Alice whispered.

"Sleep," the girl told the crowd.

Without delay, everyone's shoulders slumped, and their heads fell forward. When Alice took in the effects of her immediate group, she was relieved to see Crystal had gone along with it. Now it was silent.

The old friend paced to the back of the stage, microphone dangling from the wire in her grasp. With her breaths coming and going in staggered sobs, she watched the ceiling and blinked away any remaining tears.

Alice began her weave through the zombie crowd. "Winifred, what are you doing?"

Winifred turned her head as if to look back, but her face only went so far. "I don't have to answer to you, or anyone." When she decided this was all she felt to say, she returned her gaze to the back wall. By now Alice had made it to the front of the stage, though didn't find the need to close in further. She couldn't think of a way to comfort her back to her senses.

Winifred took in a deep, shaky breath before she continued, "I don't need permission to be happy. And for a second I let you make me feel guilty for that. For a second I panicked and thought I would let him leave me."

"You need to, Winifred. It may not seem like it now, but —"

Now she spun about, raising the microphone to her lips, distorting the speakers with her yell, "Stop saying my name as if *I'm* lost!"

"Please, I'm begging you —"

"I'm a domsuco! He's a mortal — he's *my* mortal! He's not even human!"

"Not human? Look at him, Winifred! He's human!"

But the old friend wouldn't listen. *"I brought him back from the dead, and it's within my right to do whatever I want with him! We were fine until —!"*

Too appalled to stop herself, Alice roared back the loudest she had been in decades, *"You were never fine!* The entire year of your relationship—from beginning to end—it was *never* fine; it was the most pathetic excuse for *fine* I've ever seen!"

A snarl was glimpsed before Winifred vanished from the stage.

Alice spun around. It was hard to see—all mere shapes before she placed faces to people. Like a rag doll, Crystal was flung, airborne.

"No!" Alice shrieked, but it was all one fluid motion. Crystal's head snapped skyward and her throat tore open to the blinding glow of her blood. Her eyes had widened and her mouth seemed to have made it mid-scream before the bones in her neck disconnected. Although her skin held everything together, as her body fell, her head seemed to drop separately from her spine.

Alice ran before thinking, putting out her arms as if to catch her. This was her mistake; she wasn't looking at

Winifred anymore. Crystal landed into the cheerleader Alice remembered was Monica, who fell with her on impact—

Alice's eyes widened as she doubled over, momentum pushing her down and forward, taking some of the boys down with her. Remaining in trance, they didn't attempt to get up.

She couldn't breathe. Her heart stopped. And Crystal...

Crystal laid directly before her. Her hand was closest to her.

Still struggling for breath, Alice reached forward and touched her fingertips. Still warm. This meant nothing.

I'm sorry, she wanted to say, though she knew it wasn't enough. What the girl was afraid would happen, happened. If only Alice hadn't snapped, Crystal could've...

She couldn't think this way. Not now.

She knew what to expect when she checked the bleachers, but still she had to look. Grimacing through the pain, she lifted her chin and with shaking arms she pushed from the ground, just enough.

Jack was gone.

She still couldn't breathe. Her heart still wasn't beating.

He could've been anywhere. He could've been dead.

Crystal was dead.

Someone had to wake up. Someone had to do something — anything.

Thmp.

She took in whatever air she could in a sharp, elongated gasp. Careful not to leave lasting damage, she slapped the nearest leg. "Wake up!"

A quick gasp. It was Adam, one of the people she had knocked over. He scrambled off of the others, still on his hands and knees. "What — what just — Crystal —"

"Call the cops."

"I couldn't do anything —"

"Do something now!"

Although in shock, this seemed to jolt him just enough. He reached for his pocket. He reached for Crystal with his free hand, shaking and weak. "She can't… She can't be…?"

"Deal with dispatch, then wake the others."

"Yeah. Yeah." He dialed. "How do I even… What did I see?"

Now it was her turn to be useful. She stood. She didn't want to leave Crystal, but there was nothing she could do for her now. She had to put her energies elsewhere.

"Where are you going?" asked Adam, voice rising with a slow-burning panic.

By the time the question registered, Alice was gone, out of the school and into the night.

Frigid air smacked her nose and cheeks. She wasn't sure when she lost her hat, nor when so much of her hair fell out of its braid.

"Jack!" Wind-chilled tears made her face cold. She listened to her surroundings. As more of the high schoolers awakened, more of their voices masked those of the outside world. It frustrated her, but she knew she had to calm herself and listen more carefully.

Nothing in her heart changed.

She continued her run, entering the woods, now far past the first tier of trees. Beyond the reach of civilian technology, the moon was all that was left, casting the world in an eerie purple-silver glow. Evergreen needles and grass alike glistened with frost, though through the speed of travel it all became a gray-blue blur. Everything stung.

Crystal was dead.

She stumbled and skidded to a stop amidst the thickest of underbrush. Tucking some loose hair behind her ear, she looked over her shoulder, checking, as if it was possible Jack would be there. "*Jack!*" she screamed again.

Nothing. Just the clear path she had made to get there. She noted her clothes were torn. If she healed at the rate of a mortal, she imagined she would still have scratches on her arms and legs. She checked her hands for leftover blood and she was right; she had scraped herself repeatedly.

However loud her mind was, and however intensely she shook, she needed to think. Again she listened, closing her eyes and forcedly calming her breath.

Owls hooted. Wolves some miles away howled. In the more immediate woods was the trickle of a stream.

Teens in the high school were in hysterics as more and more woke up, adding to the noise.

She had to think. Jack was alive somewhere. Where would Winifred take him?

What was she doing to him?

No, Alice couldn't think about this. The longer she stood there, the further and more impossible to find they would become.

Winifred would pack first if they left town.

Panic subdued, she determinedly sprang forth, deeper into the woods. It was strange, going to Theo's house to find her. Strange, but not surprising.

"Etsu!" It was a distant call, though she recognized it immediately.

She skidded to a halt. "Bishop!"

"Etsu!" he called again. When she picked up on the rustling of twigs and leaves, sounding louder by the instant, she knew what to expect. Leaning back to slow his stride, he grasped a tree for help, wrapping around and swinging to the side. "Etsu," he panted, facing her, "I know what's happened, and I know what you're thinking—"

"How—"

"I know things, Etsu, I just do. Listen to me, what happens next, I've known the story down to the last detail, please trust me on this—"

"What is it?"

"Don't interfere. Please, I know what she's doing is wrong—everyone knows what she's doing is wrong—but trust me, he's better off this way—"

"Better off, how?"

"In the end, everyone wins!" He was wide-eyed, verging on manic. "Everyone can win—Winifred gets her Theo, Jack gets to start fresh, and you can move on, we can both move on."

"No, I can't walk away from this."

"But you can."

"What happens if I don't?"

Bishop bit his knuckle and looked away, still fully agitated, but he was stuck. "This can't end well. No matter how I look at it, all the possibilities— Simple probability: it won't end well. After tonight, I don't know what will happen, to— to Jack, to you. If something were to happen, I... Please don't hide again. You don't have to stay with me, but... Whatever happens, you can be happy again. If you don't hide."

So this was what this was about. He would miss her. However touched, time was wasting. "I won't hide," she promised, "But please, Bishop, I need to find them."

"He'll be happier this way—he won't know anything about his old life, feeling hated, guilty or isolated. He'll have a fresh start."

"You keep saying that, what do you mean?"

"You must have seen it coming. Etsu..."

She was too rushed to consider what it was, though something in his demeanor had her think it was important that she knew. "Tell me."

He bit his lip. Then told her.

All or Nothing,
2011

31. A Midnight Walk
Theodore Jackson Van Sloan

While he couldn't remember paying for it or ever seeing the inside, the house that stood before him was surely his. Run-down as it was, it was a beautiful home, and he was blessed. He laughed to himself in Peter Pan-stance, fists on his hips and everything.

After a calming sigh he began his cross to the door. He must've just gotten back from the office. He was a hard-working American—he couldn't think of where else he would've been. All that was obvious was the direction he strolled, down the path and up the porch steps.

A breeze reminded him it was cold as fuck—

He cringed. He wasn't supposed to swear. He couldn't place why, but this was the feeling he got. So fudge, then. It was cold as fudge.

Mostly melted patches of snow rested atop the lawn and roof, yet he only wore light, red silk pants, a gray-blue quilted robe, and slippers—not even socks. And he was shirtless.

It must've been Casual Friday. Wherever he worked, it sounded dynamite. He couldn't stop smiling.

When he reached the door, he almost knocked. Then he had to think, he did live here, didn't he? More certain, he opened the door and stepped inside. Even if this wasn't his house, he knew his wife would be waiting inside, and that was all that mattered.

"Darling," he called before taking it all in. Music played —doo wop. Along the wall were lit oil lamps. The floor was swept and the hardwood was treated. A small rug welcomed his feet, and a coat rack stood in the corner. If it wasn't for the large, jagged hole which spanned from the back wall to the ceiling, however intriguingly it showcased the coal-black sky and pale full moon, the place could have appeared restored and prepared for sale.

He knew not to ask about the hole. It was there for a reason, he planned to fix it, and beyond that it didn't matter.

The stairs to the second floor were completely caved in. He could tell parts were removed; all that remained were the few steps at the top and the bottom which were still firmly attached.

A door opened in a room somewhere above him. "Theo?" It was her. And, he remembered, this was his name.

His responding grin came paired with a confused squint. "Darling! How did you get up there?" It looked like the only feasible way up was to climb one of the support beams, and even this would prove hugely inconvenient.

She stepped past the wall and into his line of vision. He could tell she was waiting for him; she had time to get ready. Her brilliant red hair was shortened with tight ringlets. Her lips were tinted pink, and her eyes had that dark, smokey look. A white lace nightie hugged her waist and gave her the sort of cleavage any man would happily rub his face in. The sheer material billowed behind her as she walked, giving her the appearance of a gliding apparition. If she was wearing anything underneath, he couldn't tell.

Was this their honeymoon?

She leaned against the banister and smiled, waiting with a raised eyebrow. "Well?"

He laughed. "You're a dreamboat."

Her smile widened.

He was hoping by now something would've come back to him. He glanced about for anything that could trigger even the slightest of memories, but there was nothing. Finally he admitted, "I'm confused."

Her smile faded. "Is it happening again?"

"Is what happening again?" Something about it was familiar. He couldn't explain, and he didn't want to dwell on it long enough to try.

Concerned, she strode back into the room.

"Where are you going?" he called.

A few seconds later, the front door opened and he jumped aside. There she was. So however she made it upstairs, she had to go around.

She closed the door behind her. "Don't worry," she assured him, "This sort of thing has happened before, and it takes a while for you to readjust, but you always do."

Now he was worried. "What do you mean?" The sense of familiarity grew. Certain thoughts in his head couldn't be construed as words or even emotions. Whatever was happening, it was its own unique thing, and this was the sound it made.

"Do you remember how we met?"

He didn't, but he had to keep smiling. He didn't think he could smile if he admitted he didn't know. "How could I not?"

The sound it made, it was the sound of unravelling, of spiraling out, but it wasn't a sound effect. It was his own voice, in a made-up language, one he might've known when he was a child.

"What's your name?"

"Theodore Jackson Van Sloan." That seemed to roll off the tongue easily enough.

She stared into his eyes. Unsure of what else to do, he stared back. "So what are you confused about?" she asked.

He was breaking. This was the sound of shattering perception. Heart beating fast, despite the cold he began to sweat. He was losing it, whatever false language was in his head, it was beginning to tag onto real words and forcibly fizzle them into nothing. He had to bring them back, but he had to keep smiling.

He concentrated on her question. What was he confused about? What did *confused* mean? He glanced down at his attire, then back at the door. "Where was I?"

"You were taking a walk to clear your head."

Was this supposed to be funny? "Huh. I succeeded."

She smiled and kissed his cheek. Everything in him went numb. He couldn't understand why, so to the best of his ability, he kept smiling.

Was he losing his mind? Was this what it was like? *Well,* he figured, *I'm not dying.* Everyone lost their mind at some point; if it was bound to happen to him, why was it surprising that it happened now?

But no, not everyone lost their minds. He had it sideways, or backwards, or just wrong. Everyone died. Losing his mind—that wasn't normal.

"Don't worry," she said again, "It'll only get better with time."

What day was it? He remembered Mr. G-opolous assigned an essay; he only had the weekend to write it. But then, if he had a job and a house, he wouldn't have still been in high school. What did he do with his life since then? "How old am I?"

"Twenty," she readily answered.

His eyebrows rose. He knew he was an adult, but he didn't think he'd made it so much past eighteen. In any case, he was too old for school, but he remembered it like it was yesterday.

Another pang of panic. His fingers and toes were numb. Something was definitely off. When he tried hard enough, he saw something else. Everything appeared darker, more gray, and somehow this felt more realistic. He was breaking through.

Memories. He couldn't recall anything in its fullness, or place faces to people or settings to vague colors. All that seemed certain was a familiar sense of foreboding.

An old, familiar white noise in his head returned at full volume. The feeling he tried to shut out before, this was where it stemmed from. Whatever it was he couldn't remember, it was a nightmare.

"Theo?"

Just like that, he was back. The colors were vibrant again; the noise was gone. "Sorry," he muttered.

Although concerned, she put it aside with a smile, draping her arms over his shoulders.

He let his forehead rest against hers. "Are you about to lead me to the bedroom?"

"Not yet," she teased. "I wanna show you something first." She crossed to the coat rack, grabbing both her jacket and his.

He grimaced. "Come on now, darling, it's cold as fudge out there."

"Not any colder than it is in here."

He realized this was true. With the gap in the wall as big as it was, it would've been impossible for the room to retain any heat. This would explain why his extremities were numb. In any case, he wasn't about to be warm anytime soon.

After a defeated sigh, he grabbed his coat as she offered it and pulled it on. She let herself out, and he followed. They ventured around the side, past the waterless pool with its miniature forest inside. Two lawn chairs were left knocked over, broken beyond use. The yard was so overcome with tall grass and underbrush, it seemed to reclaim everything with an air of, *This is mine; you must leave.*

He must not have been walking fast enough; Winifred took his hand and led him faster. Eventually they were far enough to see what was left of the fence which spanned the yard's perimeter. It was difficult to distinguish what was a vine and what was a picket.

They kept walking. The underbrush grew thicker with no discernible path through it.

"There's probably an easier path somewhere else," he offered.

"We're already so far this way; no turning back now."

They weren't far enough for this to be a reasonable argument. He wouldn't have minded if he didn't have the idea of a heated bedroom, or at least a blanket and combined body heat, begging for him to ditch the cold and go home.

The bottom half of his robe and the hem of his coat kept catching in the small branches and thorns. It was time to start carrying the fabric by hand.

He shivered as they made it through the worst of it and all the animal-made paths became more apparent.

"We'll only be out here for about fifteen more minutes," she promised.

A soft breeze gradually picked up, whistling through the treetops overhead. He shuddered, then it was dark. Pitch black. He stopped walking. "Darling, I'm blind as a bat out here."

He noted the dark clouds which obscured the moon. It would rain, most likely. If it rained, they would freeze.

Winifred took his hand and carried on regardless. "We're almost there." How could she see anything?

Looking up, he saw the trees would thin out, wherever they were headed. It was a clearing. He held out a hand, as if for a tree in the instance he tripped, but there was nothing. Were they already there?

She led him a few more paces before slowing to a stop, letting go of his hand. She didn't speak, and he couldn't see what she was doing. There was only complete darkness.

"What did you want to show me?" he asked.

No answer.

"Darling?"

"You would like to see Alice again, wouldn't you?"

Somehow everything brightened at the sound of her name. He still couldn't see anything, but the darkness wasn't as dark. Yet, he wasn't sure what to think. He remembered Alice's face, but couldn't recall anything more. "She's our friend," he affirmed. This was of all he was certain.

"Call her."

"With what?"

"Your voice. She's looking for us; I think she might be lost."

"Why are we meeting in the woods?"

"It's a pretty spot. You'll see, once the clouds pass."

He might've been nuts, but normal people didn't meet in the woods.

He could hear her coy little grin as she reminded him, "The sooner she finds us, the sooner we can go inside."

"Alice!" he called.

Nothing.

He turned to where he assumed his wife was. "You're not gonna call her, too?"

No response. Dread spiraled from the outside in—

He pushed it out of his mind and did the only thing he could. "Alice!" he called again.

A distant rustle of leaves, suddenly louder and closer. He spun about, then it was silent. Still, he saw nothing.

The whisper floated to him on a breeze, and somehow he heard the strain on her voice, "What did she do to you?" She wasn't anywhere near him; she couldn't have made it past the line of trees.

She wasn't his wife.

"Alice?" His eyes adjusted just enough to tell where the woods started. Anything tall, narrow and dark could've been a person, but then it was most likely a tree.

Leaves crunched under a cautious first step. His eyes narrowed in, and finally he found her silhouette, slender and dark. When the clouds rolled ahead, he saw the extent of how nature worked against him. If it wasn't the darkness obscuring his vision, it would've been the fog. He squinted through it.

Moonlight caught her cheekbones, then her eyes. If she hadn't been wearing makeup, the shape might not have been so exaggerated, but now there could've been no mistake. This was Alice. The arch in her eyebrows meant pain, and the wideness in her eyes was fear.

She wasn't there because they agreed to meet. Nothing about this was meant to be pleasant. Terror sped his heart, and now there was nothing to comfort it.

32. The Clearing Revisited

Alice

Thmp... th, thmp... th — thmp...

Her heart accelerated the further she ran through the woods. "Jack!" she called.

No response.

"*Jack!*" she screamed again. He and Winnifred were close, but not enough to see or smell.

"*Alice!*"

She stopped short. "Jack!"

Silence. When she replayed his distant call in her head, and noted the rate of her pulse, she learned he was too far away to have heard her call for him. He'd escaped trance on his own and was looking for her.

"*Alice!*" he called again, louder this time, on the verge of panic.

Again she ran, and immediately her heart lurched fast enough for him to be in sight. She stopped where the trees began to thin. She could hear him breathing.

But she didn't hear Winifred.

She didn't trust this.

Alice turned her head and knew she would find him mere paces away. With the moon behind cover, it was through a darker purple filter everything appeared, as if under water. The clearing provided a pool of fourth-color light, and there Jack stood at the center, pale and practically glowing. His breaths came out in clouds of smoke. His chest was to her, but he didn't seem to see where she was.

Her throat closed. He wasn't dressed as the grim reaper anymore.

His shaggy hair was cut short, buzzed on the sides and combed back with a clean side part. Coat, pajama pants, robe, and slippers. This was what Theo wore whenever he wasn't ready for the day, but had to run a quick errand. The exact outfit, still torn from the last time he wore it, still stained with the opaque brown of old blood.

This was what he died in.

"What did she do to you?" she whispered to herself.

Somehow he heard, and he squinted. "Alice?"

After an attempt at a calming breath, she stepped forward. As the clouds passed overhead, the world flooded from deep violet to lavender, silvery white, and he looked like a ghost. As he observed her face, his expression shifted from an uncertain worry to a more definitive fear. He was feeding off her energy; she was scaring him. She didn't mean to—she didn't want to. "Jack," she replied.

He hesitated. "W-who's Jack?"

A flash of panic. "No. Don't do this to me, you're not…" She again considered none of this was real. Everything that happened since she left the crypt, when looking at it from an objective point of view, it wasn't realistic.

This reality was finally shattering.

"What is it?" Less afraid, Theo-Jack ventured some steps toward her. "Alice?"

"What—What's your name?"

Although he laughed, it was a poor mask for his discomfort. "No no, you can't tell me you don't know me."

"I do know you, but you need to tell me your name."

"Why?"

"Say it!"

He raised his palms as if to pacify a lunatic. "Okay, okay… Theodore Jackson Van Sloan."

"What do your friends call you?"

It was a distinction she didn't intend to make, but he caught it, the way she separated the idea of herself from his friends. It took him off guard, and there was a brief hiatus before he replied, "You call me Theo."

She shook her head, not at him but at the thought. Closing her eyes, she reminded herself, she had to remember what made sense. Even in the instance this was all in her head, her imagination thus far was consistent. Theo was dead. This was Jack, not a nightmare she could turn away from. She opened her eyes for confirmation. No runic bracelet, but he still had so many scars on his neck, and his nose was slightly crooked.

She had to think. Winifred wouldn't leave Jack alone in the woods for her. This...this was a trap. The girl was somewhere.

After stealing a glance from side to side, Alice decided it was safe to move toward him. Whenever his kidnapper did decide to show herself, Alice was most comfortable with Jack closest to her.

Slowly at first, she gradually came to run, keeping her pace slightly faster than human. He ran as well, meeting her halfway. Neither missed a beat in throwing their arms around the other, and she gasped when her heart sped the fastest it could. It was still such a rare thing; it still surprised her. All things considered, it brought new tears to her eyes, but she had to stay strong.

He was so cold. She wished she had body heat, or at least a scarf for him, but there was nothing.

"Have you seen Winifred?" he asked, face against her hair.

She knew he knew the answer before he asked, though still she replied, "I haven't."

"What's going on?"

"The sooner we leave, the better."

A faint *snap* from the treetops, and both shot their gazes skyward. There was nothing.

Slowly lowering her arms, Alice turned, keeping Jack at her back. Knowing who to expect, she gently spoke, "You can still come back from this."

No response.

Alice glanced back at Jack, hoping to glean how he was holding up so far. Although his eyes were wide with fear, there was also a curiosity to the furrow of his brow. He didn't remember how scared he should've been.

Quickly, she untied the bracelet Ruth had given her—her own runic beads for protection—and tied the accessory to his wrist instead.

He squinted at it, not like it was unfamiliar, but as if it confused him. "What…?"

"Trust me."

The words were hardly out before Winifred all but materialized at his back. In the time it took Alice to gather the air to yell, Winifred pulled him several feet away, grabbing him by the hair and forcing his head aside.

"Don't you dare!" Alice screamed.

Frantically he clawed at Winifred's hand, and immediately she pinned both his wrists back beneath his shoulder blades. If the bracelet didn't work now, it never would.

His breath quickened but he stopped fighting, either because he realized it was her or because it was useless.

His captor glared at Alice with eyes fierce as stone. If Alice tried to pry him away now, they'd end up breaking him. She had to wait for the opportune moment. "Don't worry," she told him, "she won't hurt you." She wanted to promise more. This hardly made him feel better.

"What's happening?" he rasped, arms and neck too awkwardly bent to manage anything louder.

Alice might have answered if it wasn't for the look in Winifred's eye. She was about to do something drastic, and Alice needed to be ready for it.

Silence. No one moved, or breathed. Slowly, Winifred turned her gaze to Jack's exposed throat.

"Don't you dare," Alice breathed.

Winifred parted her lips, and he flinched when she let her fangs glide along the length of his neck. But she wouldn't dare. Not right in front of her.

"Winifred," she warned.

When she shot Alice one last look—one of pain which gradually shifted to one of rage—Alice realized she was wrong. She *would* hurt him.

"*NO!*" Alice's voice raised to a bat-like pitch.

Winifred's teeth punctured.

Jack screamed, and Alice ran. His neck was glowing where blood spilled—

Theo's blood, metallic and sweet—

—and every atom in her wanted to take it for herself. She didn't know how she was about to get Winifred off of him—

Winifred released of her own accord, and he nearly fell before Alice held his shoulders, then put pressure over his neck, then held his face in her free hand. "Jack! Jack, listen to me, you'll make it through this!" Her hand was wet and glowing. She wanted to put it in her mouth.

He wasn't listening. "Behind you!"

She already knew; with reflexes she forgot she had, she spun around and found Winifred already within inches of her face, and without a thought Alice shoved and sent her flying into the tree at the far side of the clearing. Just as Winifred's back made contact with the trunk, it didn't get to splinter before Alice was upon her, pinning her arms above her head.

She heard Jack's footsteps running up to them.

"Stay back!" she yelled, but he didn't slow in the slightest.

Winifred emitted a small, defeated laugh. "I'm sorry."

Alice could've finished her then. It would've been easy. She could've done it. But, "You can still come back," she pleaded as Jack neared closer.

Winifred didn't respond, but stared at Alice for what felt like the longest time. The corners of her mouth quivered before she tucked them back and whispered, voice shaking, "I worked too hard for this to all fall apart. I need him. You understand."

Alice's heart raced, faster and faster, Jack practically upon her. Then —

A plunge through her back, breaking her ribs and piercing her heart. She couldn't gasp.

It throbbed.

It seared.

Everything slowed.

Winifred's little sniffles, Jack's panicked heartbeat, the whistling wind—everything echoed in her head before the ringing in her ears took over. This didn't make sense. But...

The end of a thin, sharpened, bloody branch protruded from her chest. The last thing she was physically capable to do was widen her eyes before she fell to her knees, paralyzed.

"Poetic, wouldn't you say? Alice? How he's killed you just as you killed him?"

She couldn't answer. This was it, then. This was how she died.

Winifred ducked to her level, and into her ear whispered, "When he grows old and frail, I will find you again." She kissed her cheek.

Alice completed her fall, landing on her back, and the stake delved deeper. The frozen earth shocked her bare skin, but then she felt nothing.

She couldn't see either of them anymore. There was only the cloudy sky, the black silhouette of spidering branches, and the dull glow of the hidden full moon. She hated how she couldn't see them anymore. She hated how she couldn't hear them.

Her head lulled back as she was lifted, then fell forward as her back raised further. It was Jack, holding her, stunned. He spoke, and although she couldn't hear him, she imagined he was praying. His Adams apple rose and fell, and she knew his throat was tight.

If this was how she died, she didn't think it would take so long. Maybe this was how she became a ghost; maybe she could still save him from beyond the grave.

He kept speaking, then he was pulled back, gone, and she was left again, on the ground with nothing to see but the sky. She needed to do something. At the very least, she needed to see, but when she tried to move, nothing happened. She recalled Ruth's basic rules of astral projection, though no matter how she focused, still, nothing happened.

If she wasn't a ghost, and if this was what killed her, why was she still here?

Time carried on. Nothing changed.

It was clear now. She wouldn't die. She was back to her immobile self, as she was beneath the crypt. But if she couldn't save him, what difference did it make if she was alive or dead?

Maybe someone would find her. Or, maybe she would have to wait for Winifred's return—another eighty years, no doubt.

She couldn't mark the passage of time. It was always dark beneath the crypt. No days, no nights.

Preparing for the long-haul, she focused on the overlapping tree branches above her, reimagining their shapes until...

The voice was gentle. *Again with this, Dollface?*

579

She could have smiled. She remembered his voice so well —not just its natural sound, but the way he used it. It was so full compared to Jack's. Proper. This man knew how to use his diaphragm.

Theo's shape sat beside her and all she saw was his face, too happy and unmarred to have been his doppelgänger's. He sighed, playfully shaking his head.

She wanted to cry. *I'm sorry,* she could have whispered.

What for? he asked.

You know.

He raised an eyebrow, waiting.

The parallels between the present and eighty years prior were overwhelming. There was a killer, and while Alice was the patsy then, now it was Jack. It seemed as if he was right when he spoke of karma, only she didn't believe he had done anything to deserve it. The energies of the universe, as horribly as they had affected him, seemed to have conspired more specifically against her. Jack was a mere casualty—a tool used to demonstrate to her what it would've felt like if the tables were turned—if Theo had killed her that night instead.

Theo kept watching her, growing exponentially more concerned as he read her thoughts. *Why would you think that?*

She knew tears would've begun their flow by now, if her body hadn't entirely shut down save for her sight and thought. However, because her body couldn't react, it appeared as if her surroundings reacted for her. While the world seemed to turn a more monochromatic blue, the upper corner of the sky alighted with a blinding, heavenly luminosity which faded into a deep navy gradient. There was something she needed to admit to herself, and something she needed to tell him. However saddened, she was grateful for the opportunity to do it now, even if he was just in her head.

I'm so sorry, she would have repeated. *There's no excuse. There wasn't a justifiable reason. I killed you because… because I was scared.*

He subtly squinted. Scared?

You wanted your ring back. You didn't want to wait for me, and I thought it meant that you —

That I didn't love you anymore?

When he put it that way, it didn't sound right. But she didn't want to assume anything else. She didn't want personal bias to warp her perception of reality.

Guilt is still a personal bias, he reminded her, *and I thought you knew me better than that. What did you think my last words would have been if you hadn't stopped me halfway?*

I know what I wanted them to be.

What else could they have been? 'No matter what happens, I will always'—what—'abhor cheesecake?' 'No matter what happens, I will always wear ugly sweaters for Christmas.' Or, no, 'No matter what happens, I will always surpass you in glass blowing ability.'

She could have laughed. The blue of the sky seemed to turn deeper, and the light radiating from the corner seemed to consume more of the sky. Two successive shooting stars trailed across her view. *You did seem to pick it up quickly,* she said.

He followed her gaze upward, appreciating the view. *You know I had practice beforehand.*

I know as much as I can assume.

There's no way I could have done so well my first try.

I know.

He smiled, glancing at her before peering toward the heavens once more. His face glowed in the moonlight, and he was so beautiful. She had the perfect view of his jaw, so clear and sharp, and his eyes were iridescent gemstones. *But come on, Dollface,* he murmured. *You know me better than that. I've loved you since the day we met. Why would I want the ring back?*

I don't know.

Think about it, he insisted. Think about me. Those last few weeks, you remember I was worried you would run away because of the neighbors. Then I proposed. Then you told me you had to go. Why would I want the ring back? You weren't actively listening, but I said it.

White light crept in from all corners of the sky and horizon, and it seemed she could see every star in the galaxy. It was breathtaking. Either the world was ending in the best of ways, or she was on the verge of an epiphany.

You're a man of tradition, she recalled.

He nodded, *Go on.*

You proposed because you were afraid I would leave; you thought if we were engaged, I would've stayed. When that didn't work, you realized... She was on a roll, but now it was halted.

She wasn't sure when Theo would have lain down, though now she imagined him beside her, face within kissing distance, also watching the sky.

What did I realize? he pressed.

You realized... You would have wanted a happy engagement.

He smiled, and she knew she was right. *I always planned to do it on your birthday,* he elaborated, gaze stuck skyward. *Halloween. I would have treated us to lunch before it was time to prepare for the festivities. Then, after Dr. Winston brought out your cake and we all sang Happy Birthday, I would have knelt on one knee as you closed your eyes and made a wish, so that when you blew out the candles and opened your eyes, you would see me there, and you would know your wish was granted.*

It was a huge relief when she found all of this rang true. It didn't feel like a biased answer; it felt right.

The different colors of the stars and satellites in the galaxies became more apparent, and each seemed to glow even brighter.

Both were silent before Theo shrugged and added, *Or, well, it all would have been something similar.* This was the moment he would have put an arm over her shoulder, pulling her into a comforting cuddle. *Very spectacular, darling; you would have loved it.*

As much as this all meant to her, it still didn't explain what might've been the most important question. *But why did I kill you?* she wondered.

He frowned, and it seemed as if he didn't know. *You hadn't eaten anything before then. How long had you gone without eating, since you turned?*

Weeks. Or, a month.

He nodded as if this was the obvious answer. New dom-suco, hadn't eaten for weeks, instincts pining to seal the transition with blood—sounds like a recipe for disaster.

But there's no excuse.

He grimaced, looking away. *Maybe not,* he finally conceded. *Maybe it was a horrible deed and you are completely to blame. And maybe it doesn't matter.*

I'm so sorry.

And see, that right there, that's what matters. He sat up for a better view of her face, and with a playful sternness he wagged a finger and added, *Just don't do it again.*

Although she was the one to imagine him as playful as he was, she didn't have it in her to be amused. With such a clear view of his features, she noted something which disturbed her. While his default expression was a grin, a scar interrupted his left eyebrow. Theo never had scars on his face.

Jack did.

The stars' sharpness in the galaxy faded, and now everything more-so resembled a fuzzy watercolor.

She didn't know what to think. *Who… Who are you?*

His head tilted as he gave it some thought. *Whoever you want me to be, I guess.* Jack's voice.

The watercolor faded, all the stars turned dim yellow, and the blackness of the sky conspired to snuff them out.

But... But why aren't you Theo? she pleaded.

It's okay, it's okay, he promised, taking her hands in his. *No one expects you to love a dead man forever.*

But I'll always love Theo.

Granted, but you know what I mean. If you come to love Jack just as much, it won't invalidate anything. You're allowed to love again.

Her chest felt both full and constricted. The stake didn't help. She didn't know how to respond. She wanted to reject it, but if at her core she truly didn't believe it, Theo-Jack wouldn't have said it.

What if I won't love him for the right reasons? she whispered.

Does it matter so long as is it isn't for the wrong reasons?

Deciding she needed time to herself, she stared past him, back at the sky, until she forgot altogether that he was supposed to be there. The stars returned to their white, twinkling pinpoints in the purple-blue heavens.

She might have loved Jack, or she might have loved him for the reminder of Theo that he was. In any case, for so long as this stake was stuck in her back, it didn't matter. For all the great any epiphany could've done, it came on too late.

33. The Deciding Moment
Theodore Jackson Van Sloan

He meant to help her, but his brain had pissed itself. Anything that followed was a malfunction of damaged receptors and confused reactions. When he was finally at her back, her breath caught and she stiffened, and his hand was wet. When he looked down…

He didn't understand. His hands were numb, and already balled for warmth. He didn't realize he held anything. Now there was blood on his hands. The side of his fist was flat with her back, and wrapped in his fingers was a wooden shank. He stabbed her, and now…

"No," he murmured, wide-eyed. He wanted to think it wasn't him; he didn't mean to. Yet he did. Clearly—it just happened, and he still held the weapon. He had to think, he wouldn't have done it if there wasn't some part of him that wanted to.

He remembered what they called him. Jack the Ripper. He was the killer. He was the psycho.

Alice didn't fall. He wasn't sure if she would, until her knees gave out. His gaze fell back to his hands before she completed her fall. He couldn't get over it. He literally had her blood on his hands.

His voice felt separate from his body. He might've laughed. He might've shouted when he said, "Darling? What… What just—"

"Shh, Theo, it's okay." It was as if she spoke to him through a thick glass casing.

He couldn't look away from his hands.

His legs buckled and he dropped to Alice's side. When his gaze caught her face, he stared. He had never seen her eyes so wide. The way she landed, it was too unnatural. The stake raised her chest, forcing her back and neck into the most unsettling of angles—

Sarah, throat open, chest raised, rock in her back—

—and all he wanted was for her to move, even the slightest bit. He wanted her face to relax. Maybe if she coughed, it meant he missed and she could be saved.

Careful not to touch the stake, he lifted her top half from the ground. Her head lulled back too easily; this didn't make him feel better. "Alice." He lifted her closer until gravity returned her chin to her neck. "Please. Alice."

He put the phone on the wet grass and held her. He had to reassure her. He couldn't sound scared. "You'll be alright, okay? You'll be alright."

Cold, frail fingers gently gripped his shoulders. "Theo—"

He slunk out of it. "You attacked me."

His wife knelt beside him, lightly resting her hands along the sides of his neck. "I had to," she pleaded. "It was the only way to catch her off guard."

"She—"

"Stood in the way," she finished for him. "She wanted to destroy everything we've built for ourselves. She's relentless—this was the only way."

However wary, he couldn't argue. He still couldn't look at her; he couldn't pry his eyes from Alice. She was frigid. Pale. But then, she always was. He wanted to think this meant she was okay, but she wasn't moving. She wasn't breathing.

"I killed her." He still couldn't hear himself, but he knew he was, at the very least, thinking it loudly. "I'm the Ripper."

"Theo, no." Carefully, yet with a strength he couldn't fight if he tried, Winifred pried his hands from the body and led him to his feet. Alice slumped back, coming to rest again with her chest raised, neck bent and face parallel to the sky.

Winifred turned his chin until he saw her. "You're not the Ripper," she promised, "There is no Ripper. Just Alice, and she's gone now. We're safe. You saved me."

He wasn't sure when he started shaking his head, but it was still shaking. He didn't feel like a hero. He felt like a psycho. But he didn't want to feel like a psycho.

He forced his focus on the face of his wife. She loved him. She had no reason to lie. He could trust her—he had to trust her. If he couldn't trust her, who could he trust? He didn't know anyone else, and of the two of them, she was the only one who knew what to do. She had a clear head.

His gaze wandered to her eyes—

Then it stuck. He couldn't look away.

Her hand traveled to the back of his head, caressing his hair. With perfect articulation, and never breaking eye contact, she stated, "You don't know anyone named Alice."

He waited for her to continue. The way it stood now, it didn't make sense. He glanced at the woman's body; she was definitely there. And her name was definitely Alice. But his wife had nothing to add.

"I don't understand," he admitted.

Her eyebrows narrowed, as if her explanation should've been enough. Then there was something else. Desperate, she held his face between both hands, still staring into his eyes. "Listen to me, Theo."

This wasn't right either. None of this was right. He remembered, "No one calls me that."

"Everyone calls you that."

He shook his head again. "This is insane. This is insane."

Now her arms were trembling. "No."

He couldn't stop glancing back at Alice. Lowering Winifred's fingers from his face, he took a step toward the body—

Winifred wouldn't let go of his hands.

His chest shuddered. "Please, I can't leave her like this." He pulled, but her grip only tightened. "Wyn?"

Still not letting go, she began the walk back past the line of trees. He kept pulling and wriggling his fingers, but her hold was impossibly strong. He knew—he could feel it—if he pulled too hard, he would break his hand. He pulled anyway—

This time when her grip tightened, something snapped. His chest expanded with a full, grating gasp, and his throat caught and he cried, "*Wyn, what the shit!*"

She kept walking, and even though he followed of his own accord now, she didn't loosen her hold. The hollow ache in his chest came paired with an aggressive nausea.

"We'll get you someplace warm; someplace you won't be distracted," she promised. "You'll feel better once you forget about her."

"What are you talking about?!" His fingers and palm were throbbing, burning, mind-numbing.

She spun on him. "There's nothing left to come between us! Anything you want—anything you can possibly ask for —I can give that to you! *Why can't you be happy with that?*"

"*Because you're fucking nuts —!*"

His head whipped to the side, the rest of his body staggering to catch up. He held his cheek, which stung, then ached. Looking down at his fingers, he found fresh blood.

The bridge of his nose tickled, though he didn't know what emotion to attribute to it, or if it was a purely physical reaction.

Winifred's eyes were wide again, like she was innocent and scared again. It was as if she wanted to apologize, but didn't know how. Instead, she whispered an explanation, or a plea. "You can't leave me. Not after everything I've done to keep you." Her chin quivered as she grasped his wrists, his bracelet awkwardly caught in between. "You'll learn to love me again. It doesn't have to happen right now; I can wait. But please, for now you have to listen. Whatever you think you're remembering, if she had anything to do with it, you can't trust it."

Of all the things he was certain, the only inconsistency was her.

He remembered what Alice called him. "My name is Jack." This felt right. The innate fear which weakened him before, it faded now. Finally, things were making sense again. "My name is Jack, and... We're not married."

"But we are; I can show you the papers—we've been married since you turned eighteen. Please, I know it's happening again, just let me help you."

More things came flooding back. He had a family—Grandma Ruth, Mom, Gabby, and his missing dad. He was still in school, and there was Crystal, and Adam seemed like the sort of guy he could get along with. The fresher scars on George's neck made him wonder if his old friend really had a choice in not seeing him anymore.

And Wyn…

Imaginary darkness spiraled out from the shadows and silhouettes of the trees and underbrush. There was a block placed before this memory, though he couldn't say if it was his own doing or hers. The spirals retreated when he considered letting it be, but consciously he knew he had to power through. Setting his jaw, though the darkness returned—

The bedroom ceiling—

His aching neck—

Wyn, on top of him—

He couldn't breathe—

The loss of his senses—

So much blood, he lost so much blood—

Sarah…

His breaths hastened.

There was screaming. But it wasn't him.

Wyn screamed, face stretched, clutching her fingers. This was convenient, but he didn't know why it was happening.

He peered down at his hands. The bracelet on his wrist glowed red, like it was hot. Yet he felt nothing.

As Wyn began to catch her breath, he thrust his wrist to her face. Screams renewed, sickeningly primal with agony, she shoved him away and he landed right on his ass. Holding her face, shoulders hunched as she writhed and howled, she staggered backward until she also fell, curling further into herself.

He didn't waste any time. Scrambling to his feet, he ran. If a stake was all that was needed to kill Alice, that same stake would work on Wyn. He couldn't take any chances.

He was upon Alice's body soon enough. "I'm so sorry, I'm so sorry." Kneeling, he lifted her by the back again, as if into a hug, so that he may grasp the stake. It was in deep, stuck, as if anchored. Holding her closer, hand flat with her spine, he focused his strength and pulled harder. For a second it didn't move. Then, when the resistance released—

The sound wasn't what he registered at first, but his hand rose with her back, her chest expanding. All the while, she inhaled sharply, deeply, voice catching and rasping. Her arms wrapped around him, hard, and he screamed.

"Thank you," she gasped, "Thank you."

~Alice~

Splinters caught in her flesh, burning, as Jack pulled the stake. The pressure in her chest lifted. The ribs in her back cracked into place as her muscle tissue and skin threaded back together. The sound she emitted, she wasn't sure if it was a surprised gasp or the wheeze of oxygen moving from the air pocket under her skin, back into her lungs. The puncture in the organ sealed. She was reassembled.

When she noted Jack struggling in her embrace, she released and he pulled back, just enough to see her face. His eyes were wide, his mouth open, and he never let go of the stake. "What—?!"

Now she heard screaming and scrambled to her feet, pulling him up with her, gently but quickly. Turning around, she found Winifred in the distance, clawing at her face as she wailed.

"You used the runes," Alice realized.

"I… Yeah?"

"This way, before she recovers," she prodded.

He nodded. She ran a human speed, and he kept pace beside her, knuckles white with his grip on the stake. Exercise would keep him warm, she hoped.

He kept his other hand close to his chest, wrist bent slightly back, fingers stiff, wounded.

"Is your hand broken?" she asked.

He glanced down and panted, "Don't know."

She knew Winifred would catch up easily, if she wanted to. The girl didn't have the element of surprise anymore, and now she was outnumbered. If she was smart, she would have stayed back.

But the leaves rustled exponentially louder with her return.

"You're being foolish!" Alice shouted into the woods. The leaves rustled past them, so she considered perhaps the girl was on her way elsewhere.

They followed the path around a bend, and —

Jack yelled and jumped back. There stood Winifred, shaking, curls loosened and dangling over her widened eyes. As Alice put herself in Jack's way, she noted the girl's hands half-raised in surrender, elbows to her sides. Her eyes glistened, tears flowing freely over her newly singed face. Her cheek was completely blackened where the runes had met her skin.

For a second all anyone could hear was their own staggered breathing.

"I don't come back from this," Winifred finally rasped. "I know. I know." A slow, shuddering inhale, and her tone remained low and hoarse. "But I miss him so much. And I had to. It isn't love if you don't try everything. Right? Absolutely everything, to bring him back?" After another deep breath, her voice broke nasal pitch. "I just wanted to bring him back. I had to try. I had to try." She rose her hand to her face as if to catch her tears before they fell. For every tear that passed through, she gasped and winced as they rolled over her fresh burns.

Unsure of how to react, Alice peered over her shoulder at Jack, as if he might've had a better handle on the situation. He didn't. Wide-eyed, he only glanced at her before turning his attention back to Winifred.

"You've injured him," Alice muttered before looking back.

The girl sobbed, voice strained when she mewled, "I know. I didn't—I mean—" Another sob. "I never intended… I snapped." Now her voice calmed ever so slightly. "Alice, I told you I would, and I couldn't… I couldn't bear the thought of losing him again, after everything I've... I've worked so hard for this. Only this." Her gaze lowered to her feet, hand still over her mouth. "I don't have anything else."

When Alice exchanged another look with Jack, she saw he was frozen stiff. "Follow the path, veer left," she told him. "It will lead you to Bishop's place. Hurry."

After glancing between her and his captor, he nodded and wandered ahead, extra cautious as he came to pass the latter woman. As he became more certain in his actions, he picked up speed and eventually ran. Winifred watched him briefly before she sobbed again and returned her gaze downward, shaking her head.

"I don't come back from this," she croaked again once he was out of earshot. "He'll never forgive me. You'll never forgive me."

Alice wanted to agree; or berate her, at the very least. She *gave* Winifred a chance. She gave her — so — many — chances, and came out the greatest fool for it.

She would have been an even greater fool, though, if she expected Winifred to change overnight. If this was her one hiccup... If she was finally, honestly, willing to give a new slate a chance...

Alice faced away and closed her eyes in concentration. "You tried to have him kill me."

"Not kill you," Winifred spouted, "I knew it wouldn't kill you; when Theo's father—"

"Did you intend for anyone to find me within the year—or even the decade?"

Now Winifred's mouth closed, and her chin quivered.

Alice continued, "You've murdered beyond dietary necessity. You instilled terror across this whole town, intentionally—"

"The domsuco in New York—"

"They're sick, too!" Alice snapped, not caring to hear an excuse. "But I haven't even *touched* on what you've done to Jack!" She flung a hand toward the path he took to leave.

Winifred kept her gaze lowered, clearly lacking a sound response. This time when she sobbed, her knees sank and she crumpled to the forest floor, covering her face. She spoke, though her throat was too strained for much to come out besides the occasional consonant. Finally Alice realized the girl repeated, over and over again, "Just kill me..."

Although this rang something in her core, Alice couldn't muster sympathy, and she wasn't sure if she was meant to. Winifred's actions had stretched beyond what was monstrous—her human empathy so genuinely forgotten, she couldn't consider why her actions were wrong.

Perhaps evil was never a conscious intention. Perhaps it was a primal instinct, which had in some cases convinced the mind, "This is permitted."

Alice had this thought before. This decision, which was too easy to make—too quick to register as unexpected. Her soul had sat aside and she had let something else take over, but she still had no one to blame but herself. This was how she killed Theo.

At the same time, Alice felt remorse the very moment she returned to her senses, and resolved to never allow herself to fall so far again. This was the clear difference between their two situations. Alice knew to stop. Winifred didn't.

Alice had to think. She had already promised herself to do what was morally right, no matter what. While she consciously thought any regular hero would kill this villain, this was a situation in which she didn't have to. Winifred surrendered. This wasn't the time to make an emotional decision.

She would take Winifred as a prisoner and ask for Bishop's perspective. Alice was prepared to keep a constant watch on her for the rest of time, if she had to, but if Winifred couldn't be trusted to change...

Tears threatened to wet her eyes. She hated being in this position. If Winifred proved to be too far gone, Alice would have to be the one to handle it. If there was a such thing as killing someone out of love...

She felt the corners of her own mouth stretch back, and she had to take a breath to keep herself together. She shouldn't have buried herself. Winifred didn't need to end up this way.

Alice had to be smart about how she took her in.

Feeling like a ghost, she took some steps closer and sank to the forest floor before her. "I'll leave here with you," she promised, the lie too believable, which upset her further. She took a shuttering breath and continued, "We'll reintroduce ourselves to society—both of us, and it could be like we're human again. Without any of the mortal setbacks."

Winifred looked up at her, small and surprised, like an abused child. "But no more hypnotism?"

"That's right," Alice whispered with a reassuring grin, "no more hypnotism."

"How will we eat?"

"Bishop has connections in this hospital; I'm sure we can arrange something similar."

"We can go to France?"

Alice nodded, throat sore as she kept her sobs at bay.

While this seemed to be a relief, it only made Winifred cry harder. When she peered up at Alice and held out her arms, Alice reciprocated; she hugged her back, fresh tears down her face. If she had to kill her later...this was goodbye.

Both heard the gradual change in Alice's heartbeat. Jack hadn't traveled so far ahead in the first place, and now he was headed back.

With her chin resting over Winifred's shoulder, Alice watched the path, waiting. The girl in her arms only continued to weep.

Slowly he emerged, shuffling his slippers on shaky legs. Because he didn't have the hands to button his jacket closed, he wrapped himself as best he could with the arm to his injured hand. His other hand still gripped the stake, tightly. Alice could only assume he had heard everything. He stared at Winifred, then at Alice. While his eyes weren't wide anymore, he was still clearly dazed.

She didn't know what else to do besides keep her hold around Winifred. "It's over, Jack," she finally managed. "Follow the path to Bishop's place. He'll have a fire going, and he'll arrange a ride home for you."

He paused when she spoke, allowing himself some time to absorb her words before he continued his walk closer. It was only when Winifred was directly before him that he stopped. After peering from Alice, to the girl, then back again, he swallowed the apparent lump in his throat. Then darkly laughed. "So she gets to say sorry, and that's it? That's enough?"

Winifred already shook, yet Alice felt the difference when her back tensed.

Alice held her closer, then peered back up at Jack. She didn't know how to answer. She wanted to reassure him, but she couldn't tip Winifred off to her true intentions.

He spoke slowly; forcedly calm and clear. "Whatever she told you is a lie. It's what she does. She lies, and then she starts crying. She's playing you."

Winifred hadn't lied about what Marius had done to her. But this wasn't worth arguing. "Then so be it," Alice said instead. "She can play me in France, and you can enjoy the company of girls who won't die for knowing you."

605

Nothing in his expression indicated he found this acceptable. After staring at Winifred's back for a long, painstaking moment, he dropped his gaze and clenched his teeth. "Wyn," he finally said.

She sniffled, allowing a moment to compose herself enough to answer. "What?"

"Stand up."

Still Alice watched Jack's face, wishing for some indication as to where he would go with this.

After a slow inhale and shuddering exhale, Winifred peered up at Alice, as if awaiting her opinion. Alice wasn't sure if her own face helped at all in the girl's decision, but eventually she rose to her feet, stiff as she turned around and faced him. However uncertain, Alice stood as well.

"Look at me," he growled.

A beat, and Alice assumed Winifred was looking.

Jack stared back, waiting. "Well?"

"There's nothing I can say that will be enough," Winifred mumbled. "I don't know what you want from me."

"Ask me."

Silence. "What do you want from me?"

Jack watched her eyes, a war waging within his own, and Alice figured not even he was sure what he wanted. Eventually a small, manic chuckle erupted from the back of his throat. "Wanna know what's fucked up?"

No response. Both knew he would divulge regardless.

"If I had to choose between having not one worry for the rest of my days, or fucking just running you through right now…" His voice cracked, so he stopped, clamping his lips between his teeth again.

"I can change," she pleaded.

"*I don't care if you change!*" he screamed, and both women jumped.

"Jack," Alice warned, stepping around to Winifred's side, preparing to come between them. She couldn't allow him to prove Marius right. Jack couldn't be the one to kill Winifred.

Again, he only glanced at Alice before returning his glare to Winifred. Gaze shifting between her eyes, he pressed his lips more firmly together, nostrils flared. "I don't fucking care."

Silence. All either did was stare at the other. His breaths slowed, and it seemed as though he would calm. When Alice peered back at Winifred, she realized why. The girl was putting him back under trance.

"That isn't necessary," Alice murmured, "Let him go."

The girl wouldn't look away.

"*Winifred.*"

Finally she broke her gaze and found Alice, and Jack gasped. "I wasn't going to make him do anything!" the girl pleaded.

"Forcing him under trance *is* making him do something!"

Jack pushed Alice aside with a full-body shove, and she was too caught off guard to prepare for what happened next. She miscalculated. Winifred was supposed to stop him. She had the reflexes, but she only stood there, wide-eyed. Perhaps she had frozen.

Or perhaps she didn't want to live in a world in which he hated her.

"*No!*" Alice screamed as his stake met its mark. She gripped his hand around the weapon, but...

An elongated, tortured scream ripped from Winifred's throat as she threw her head back, eyes wide and hands curling inward. It was as if she was being burned alive. She crumbled away into ashes, the ashes further disintegrated into a dark gray fog, and the stake continued forward before Alice held his hand still.

He didn't look at her, but kept his wide-eyed focus on the spot where Winifred last stood. His arms shook, and she was sure hers did, too. "That didn't happen to you," he whispered.

When his gaze caught hers, she realized she had been staring at him. Immediately he seemed disarmed, eyebrows angling up in the middle. "That didn't happen to you," he said again, defensive yet pleading.

Too much was still processing. There was supposed to be the chance Bishop would know what to do with her, but now…

Jack winced and gasped, dropping his gaze, startled. His face glowed with the reflection of whatever fresh blood was on the ground. "What…?"

Her throat felt caught between sobbing and gagging. The rest of her didn't know how to react, so it seemed her bodily response was suspended until then. "You—" The tightness in her throat cut her off, though she wasn't sure what she was saying. She found a new register in her voice—higher, and less strained. "Winifred?"

"My foot's bleeding." He might've been surprised.

Finally she remembered to release his grip around the stake. He backed away in an unbalanced haze, reaching out for a tree well before he neared one. His fingertips met bark and he winced. This was his bad hand. Leaning with his back to the trunk, her removed his blood-drenched slipper.

She dropped to her knees before Winifred's pile of clothes. There wasn't a body to hold. The lack of a body seemed to enforce the idea of the monster she had become, but even monsters had human hearts. Winifred was human at her core.

A whispered "What the fuck?" floated to her on a breeze. She couldn't look up yet. She traced her fingers over the soft fabric of the girl's coat. Alice had borrowed this garment on several occasions. Winifred had tried to give it to her, but Alice saw how much she liked it; this was a gift she couldn't ever accept.

Her thoughts quieted enough to hear Jack again. She heard in his breath how he shivered, and through the shivers he either sobbed or dry heaved.

"The fuck's my toe?" he rasped, "Where the fuck... How..."

Her hands shook. Her chest expanded. She took in too much air—too much energy. She didn't know what to do with it.

She needed to...

She needed

Blue and purple woods, bright and silvered, flashed past her as she sped. Her ears rang, and her throat rattled and scratched, hurting—

This was screaming—she was screaming.

The overwhelming energy felt suspended and trapped in her gut. Screaming wasn't enough; she needed—

Rough, cold bark smarted against her forearms, her fists, her hands—everything at once.

Wood splintered, cracked, and boomed as trees fell.

Jack's face, suddenly closer.

He yelped, wide-eyed, staggering backward as Alice shrieked, "*Why didn't you go!* I told you to run! I told you to veer left to Bishop's! *What part of that didn't you understand!*"

His surprise fell away when he screamed back, a fire from his core matching hers, "*She was playing you!* The second you let your guard down, you'd find another stake in your heart!"

"I had a plan!"

"*How many more girls would've died!*"

"I would have watched her! She could have changed, or I could have stopped her!" She spun, pacing away. She couldn't be angry at Jack; she couldn't blame him—she couldn't prove Marius right, even as Jack did. She couldn't be angry at Jack, she couldn't be angry at Jack, it wasn't his fault—

No, she wasn't angry at Jack. If *Winifred* hadn't completely lost her damn mind—

If Alice hadn't let the town bury her—

"I should have come back sooner," she warbled, "I shouldn't have ever... She didn't have anyone to..."

Now wasn't the time for her to lose it; she had to pull herself together, just long enough. Just long enough.

Closing her eyes, she gathered her thoughts on a deep breath, even as her arms trembled.

Eyes warm, she slowly turned back to Jack. He still looked like the man whose identity was forced upon him, wearing a trend which didn't reflect himself in the slightest, hair short and combed back. His chest heaved with his every breath, and he stood tensed, watching her with caution. Traces of blood faintly glowed on his face and neck, and he still had his injured hand held safely toward his middle. She noted his bare foot—still removed from the slipper—bright and wet with fresh blood.

His pinky toe was gone.

"What happened?" she whispered, gaze stuck on his foot so he'd know to what she referenced.

He didn't answer. Just stared back.

"I'm sorry," she said. "I'm sorry. We… We need to stop the bleeding and get inside."

It was as if he didn't hear her.

"Jack?"

He staggered back, past the tree, croaking something that sounded like, "No."

She watched him, silent. Then began her approach.

He held up the stake, sharp end her way, and again she paused. Both knew she could still best him in this situation, though it put her off balance. She didn't realize he would view her as a threat now, too.

His gaze flickered back and forth between her eyes. "How do I know…" His Adams apple rose and fell. "How do I know I can trust you? Or that you haven't also been putting thoughts in my head?"

There wasn't any sure way of proving this.

He continued, "What happened between you and the cheerleaders? Before you took them to the hospital?"

She wasn't sure how he knew, but he knew Winifred had nothing to do with it. Lying wouldn't help the situation, so she answered, "An accident which won't happen again."

"And I should just trust you on that?"

There wasn't an answer for this. Trust was earned; who was she to tell him to trust her?

Now when she stepped forward, he held his ground. She continued a steady approach, and he remained with his weapon drawn. It was to this wrist the runic bracelet was attached.

She was as close as he would allow, now—stopping once the tip of the stake touched the bloody hole in her dress from the first time he used it. When he didn't move, she raised her hand to his wrist with painstaking slowness, bracing herself for the worst. Shutting her eyes, she closed the distance. As she traced her fingers over the interwoven rope and wooden beads, she realized…

"You trust me," she sighed on a relieved breath as nothing happened. Her gaze returned to his. Where he was guarded before, the wall lowered and now there was unfiltered horror. Pain. Her heart slowed as he lowered his hand, dropping the stake.

His gaze locked on her old wound. "I got your heart, didn't I?"

He did.

"It wasn't you," she assured him.

He shook his head. "It was me. I was there."

"You didn't know what you were doing."

"And I... killed her."

He did. "You... You put an end to all of this," she decided. "Permanently." She didn't know if this was his intention, or if it was too immediate of a reaction for him to have truly intended one thing over another. Alice was the only context he'd had for a staked domsuco, so if he had approached this rationally, he had only intended to paralyze Winifred. Not kill her.

Silent and still he stared, and it seemed to finally hit him. His voice carried the vulnerability of a hurt child when he asked, "It... It's over?"

"It's over."

His lips pressed together in a hard line. His chin quivered. He sobbed.

As if to ask permission, she placed a careful hand over his shoulder. When he didn't recoil, but instead seemed to melt, permission was granted and she pulled him into her embrace. He leaned into it, shaking, sobbing into her shoulder.

"It's okay," she whispered, throat tight, "It's okay."

The following sobs seemed to rip from the back of his throat. It was as if he'd been stabbed himself, as if it physically pained him. "You're alive."

"I am, I'm fine," she assured him, and now her nose sounded stuffed as the bridge tingled. "I'm not sure if I *can* die."

Now she wasn't sure if it was laughing or sobbing. "That's perfect," he said. "God, that's perfect."

They were silhouettes in the fog, and the moonbeams glowed through the trees behind them. The first snowflake fell.

The Aftermath,
2011

34. Explaining To Grandma
Jack

He wasn't as cold as Alice had feared. After she tore off the hem of her skirt and wrapped his bleeding foot, she tried to steer them toward Bishop's house, but he refused. He needed to get home. His family needed to know he was okay, and he needed to change. He needed the familiar reminder of his identity. He needed his clothes.

Wyn, face contorted, pain unfiltered, screaming and snapping her head all the way back like she was possessed —

He didn't want to think about it, but it was all he kept seeing. Her face before she *disintegrated.*

But he had decent justification for killing her. While it was an accident, he regretted nothing. How many more girls would've died if he hadn't?

They made it out of the woods and to the side of the scenic road. The snow fell more consistently now, wetting the pavement, but it hadn't yet begun to stick. There wasn't much further to go. He only wished slippers were easier to walk in, and that he didn't need to shuffle everywhere to ensure they stayed on. He couldn't feel his feet, so he couldn't easily tell whenever they slid out to the sides, or rode too far off.

"I can carry you," Alice offered as he fixed his shoe back into place. "We could be there within seconds."

He didn't look at her, but shook his head. He knew she had already figured his answer, otherwise she would've suggested this sooner.

The snow thickened, soothing and peaceful. Snowflakes occasionally caught on his eyelashes, and he felt like a part of nature. It was nice to not be himself in that moment.

Finally he stole a look askance, learning Alice had been watching him all along. Snowflakes caught in her eyelashes as well, and in her straight black hair, which had by now completely fallen out of its braid.

"We're almost there," he murmured, as if it mattered how soon she got warm.

She nodded all the same, going with it. It was almost funny, knowing how capable she was, then remembering all the times he thought he needed to keep her safe. It was a weird sort of joke.

Within the minute, they strolled up his steep driveway.

"How is your neck feeling?" she asked

He forgot that was another thing injured that night. "Sore. But it's not like she hit an artery, so. It's fine."

Again she nodded to herself.

"Still don't know how my toe came off," he said. It wasn't even in his slipper when he took it off; it was just *gone*.

Alice twisted her mouth, thinking. "The price for freedom, I suppose. I don't want to guess wildly and put nonsense thoughts in your head; I'd rather confer with Bishop before I tell you more."

He nodded. "And Bishop's...like you?"

Her mouth remained twisted. "Like me," she conceded, though something about the way she said it made him think their similarities only went so far.

Having made it up the hill, he noted the lack of cars in the driveway. He couldn't guess where Gabby or his mom would've been, or if Grandma Ruth would have gone with them.

Side-by-side, he and Alice took to the porch steps. After checking his pockets, he wrapped his knuckles against the front door. He hoped *someone* was home. He didn't have his keys.

He watched the window to the side. For a second nothing happened.

The blinds lifted and her eyes peered through. Only visible for a second, they widened before the blinds fell back into place, and the doorknob desperately rattled with the jangle of keys.

"She shouldn't see you like this," Alice murmured.

He hadn't considered that, but, "Too late."

The door flew open, and there stood his grandmother, short and frail. Hand hovering over her mouth, her gaze snapped back and forth between them. Through her fingers, it seemed her lips parted and closed, as if she was unsure of which question to ask first. Finally she pulled them in, closing the door behind them.

It almost burned, the warmth of central heating. The muscles in his face loosened, and he had almost forgotten what it was like to feel his fingers and toes. He kicked off the slippers, which were now frigid and wet. The hardwood felt amazing beneath his bare feet.

"I'll make you tea," Grandma Ruth decided. "If you drink the tea, you're really here."

He didn't hear at first, as if he still needed his senses to defrost. When her words registered, his brow furrowed. "What else would I be?"

She held up a hand as if to say, "Don't ask," then hobbled into the kitchen.

Jack followed, and Alice trailed behind him. "You look like her brother," she explained. He didn't doubt it, but it still didn't explain anything, or how Alice would know that.

He heard the sink turn on and found Grandma standing there with a tea kettle. She mumbled, "If this was in my head, you'd both be older. The last time I saw them, they were…" After cutting the water and placing the kettle on the stove, she turned to Alice. "And your face wouldn't be green."

He was surprised she noticed. The make-up was so pale, and faded now, that he forgot to acknowledge it himself.

It seemed like Alice had forgotten as well. Absently, she touched her face then checked her fingers. If she remembered why her face was green, it didn't show.

"What brings you both here today?" The old woman asked.

He didn't think she had dementia yet. Disconcerted, he answered, "Well, I live here." Looking at Alice, he added, "And uh. She's the reason I'm still here."

Grandma Ruth removed three mugs from the overhead cabinet, placing them on the counter beside the stove. "Funny, in a dark sense. Interesting." From another cabinet she withdrew a box of teas. "She told us she was the reason you died."

"Grandma, I'm not dead." When he glanced at Alice, he expected some form of confirmation. Instead he found her eyes distant, staring. For a second he thought maybe he was wrong.

Grandma paused. When she recommenced her motion, she slowly placed the tea box on the counter beside the mugs. "Jack," she muttered, as if she should've known. When she peered back at him, however, she was confused again, almost hurt. "But why do you have your hair like that? How did… Why do you wear what he died in?"

He wore… What?

He peered over his attire again. More pieces to the puzzle came together. He knew the answer, but for verification he asked, "This was your brother's?"

She nodded.

"And… his name was Theo."

"You look just like him."

For a second he might not have been breathing. Wyn was his grandmother's age. There was a reason she chose to torment him, and no one else. Every detail she forced on him, it was all too specific for there to be any other reason. She wanted him to be… And now he was wearing the clothes he…

"I'm gonna shower," he decided. He didn't wait for either of them to respond, but strode down the hall without another word. He had the jacket off before he reached the bathroom door, and he shed the robe as he entered.

"*Fuck!*" he hissed when he tried to use his injured hand. He felt the pain in his chest, again like he would throw up, and all the while he stared at his fingers. They were red and swollen. They might've been broken, but not obviously so. He'd had broken fingers before, so he knew all he had to do was keep them straight for a while and not move them. He would make himself a splint after he showered.

He carefully finished stripping, trashed the blood-soaked makeshift bandages from his foot, and stepped into the shower. Usually he'd have the water steaming hot, but he knew not to do that to himself now. Even with the water lukewarm, if felt scorching.

His mind replayed the events of that night, and although it still disturbed him, he was too exhausted to react accordingly. Mostly he tried to sort out the details between what was a real memory and what was a piece of the life Wyn had implanted in his mind. He recalled being a child and swimming in the pool in his backyard, but there never was a pool in his backyard, so this never happened. He knew his sister was Gabby, though still at the thought of "sister," he'd also think of Ruth, who, although she was his grandmother, he didn't associate with "Grandma." He couldn't say if Crystal's death was a real memory, though he didn't want to think it was.

His movements slowed until he wasn't moving at all. Something clicked —

Alice, wide-eyed and hair matted, pinning him to the wall outside the diner bathrooms, a crushed stake raised above her head. "Theo?" she whispered, seconds before her gaze went distant and she went limp. Quickly he caught her by the shoulders —

Dr. Winston, staring into his eyes until he went under trance —

Jack blinked back to the present. He didn't need this memory to reach his conclusion, though it contributed more concrete grounds. Grandma Ruth said Alice was rumored to have killed Theo. She was the Japanese girl from her stories, who the neighbors buried in Erie, where the cheerleaders were attacked. They had to have been what woke her up; when Alice found him at the diner, it looked like she wore what she died in—dried blood down her shirt. This was that same day the girls were attacked. But how did she find him so quickly? And why was she trying to stab him?

When the water suddenly went cold, Jack finished his shower, dried off, re-bandaged his foot, made a splint for his fingers from the first aid kit he'd known he'd need since last year, wrapped a towel about his waist and stepped into the hallway. He saw Theo's jacket and robe still on the floor, and he intended to eventually deal with it, but not now.

Entering the kitchen, he found his grandmother at the table, a mug of tea in her grasp and two others left untouched before the seats to either side.

"Where's Alice?" he asked.

"Showering upstairs. If I had known she couldn't drink tea, I wouldn't have made so much."

"Does she drink anything, did she say? Or eat?"

"Blood. Just blood."

"That's…" He was about to say 'freaky,' but remembered she would probably hear him. "Okay," he finished.

Grandma Ruth shrugged, bringing the mug to her lips with an air of, *It's all beyond me.*

He glanced back at the clothes in the hallway, anticipating all she'd have to say about him being a slob, and that she wasn't his maid. "I'll get that after I change."

"I assume you don't want to keep any of it?"

"I don't."

"Then I'll release its energies back into the universe, banishing the darkness now attached and reuniting the rest with Theo's memory, so he may finally rest in peace." When she met Jack's blank stare, she put it in layman's terms. "I'll burn it all in ceremonious fire. You're welcome to watch, if you like."

"I, uh. I don't know. Don't wait up for me."

She acknowledged this with a nod, and he took a few steps toward the basement before she asked, "Where's the body?"

He paused and didn't think to look back. He was hoping no one would bring it up. He'd actually killed someone that night.

"Alice told me what happened," Grandma elaborated, as if he was wondering how she knew. "How she handled it… I'd say it was a long time coming."

So Alice took the blame for Wyn's death, and Grandma Ruth approved of murder. This hardly made him feel better. "There, uh. There is no body."

She didn't respond.

Feeling the conversation was done, he finished his cross to the basement door, then proceeded down the stairs and to his room.

Wyn, surprising him with a cake for his birthday.

Wyn, smiling from the second floor, leaning against the railing.

His wife —

He didn't have a wife.

Winifred, taking his hands in hers, promising she would help him through this, he was confused—

It all felt so real.

She told him, "It's okay, Theo, this has happened before."

He wasn't sure what he saw anymore. He could've been in his room, or he could've been back at the house with his wife.

"You're here," she promised. "And I'm here, I'm fine."

But he was pretty sure he was still in his room, so he didn't respond. No one was about to catch him talking to himself.

She sat on the bed. If she was alive, it meant he didn't kill her. If none of that was real, it meant none of the other stuff was, either. She never hurt him. He was worried about nothing. He remembered he had a history of recalling false memories. But then, he wouldn't have known this if she hadn't told him, and if she couldn't be trusted…

35. Rising Tensions

Alice

Barefoot and hair wet, Alice stepped down the cold basement steps, holding her shoes, stockings and dress in one arm. Ruth and Gabby were much smaller than herself, so Ruth had her borrow Jack's clothes from the laundry room instead. His clothes were roughly a size too big. The dark gray shirt hung loosely over her slender frame, the sleeves reaching past her wrists. The hems to the desaturated red and black flannel pants were faded where Jack would have consistently stepped on them, and they fell at about the same length for Alice.

She knocked on the door at the end of the stairwell.

"I'm changing," answered his gravelly voice, muffled through the wall.

"Take your time," she replied.

While she didn't hear movement before, she now heard his steps on the floor and the ruffling of fabric. The door opened a few seconds later, and immediately she registered the paleness of bare skin.

He wasn't wearing a shirt. She hadn't seen him without a shirt before. Yes, he'd been shirtless beneath the robe, but he was covered then; and, well, now he wasn't.

She was staring. She had to stop. The cut of his stomach muscles was like an arrow pointing downward.

"Hey," he softly greeted.

Clearing her throat, she intended to reel herself back in, but still she stared. She had never seen muscles shaped this way. Never in person.

Finally she pried her eyes from his waist and found his gaze, praying she hadn't made him uncomfortable. Nothing in his expression indicated such, and finally she replied, "Hey."

He watched her eyes, reading her, before dropping his gaze to his hand atop the doorknob. "Weird question, but… You're real, right?"

A flash of panic. From the perspective of a hallucination, would *she* be perceived as the imaginary one? Was she still under the Crypt, or in an asylum somewhere?

His brow subtly furrowed, wary and concerned. "That wasn't supposed to be a trick question." Someone had told her this before.

She replied with all that was certain. "*I'm* real, yes."

His expression remained. "Meaning?"

I have eaten, therefore I am sated, therefore this is real. "Forgive me," she replied, "I... Before I met you, when I was still a—hermit, I..." Words were difficult; exhaustion blocked her means of translating thoughts to phrases. Where could she start?

She closed her eyes and focused. "There was no sound. No light, no people, no movement. Just eighty years' worth of vivid hallucinations. It's difficult to confirm anything." Finished, she opened her eyes.

Something in his demeanor shifted. While he was still concerned, it was in a more empathetic sense. "That's right, I figured—" A pause as his gaze went distant, and it seemed another thought interrupted. "So you don't know what's real, either, then. Right?"

Now certain she was there, it was her turn to be concerned for him. "God no," she breathed, watching his face, "Not you, too?"

He humorlessly laughed, returning his gaze to his hand on the doorknob. "Now that I know hypnotism's a thing, it's hard to say what's my own thought, what's a real memory, what's really happening…"

She nodded her understanding, but didn't know how to reassure him. "To my knowledge, we are both here."

"Alright."

Silence.

He opened the door wider and stepped aside. It hadn't occurred to her that they had been standing at the threshold all this time. Accepting the invitation, she entered.

"Ruth called the school and the. Rainy Day. Where your mother works," she said. "She and Gabby are on their way home."

Absently he nodded.

"How are you faring otherwise?" she asked.

"I, uh." He shrugged. It was silent for a long moment before she figured this was the extent of his answer.

He closed the door behind her and crossed to his nightstand, pulling open a drawer and removing a flask. His movements slowed before he shook the container. Not a sound emitted, and while she was sure he knew this, he twisted the cap open and put it to his lips anyway. Tilted it back. Still, there was nothing.

"God fucking damn it," he huffed as he tossed it aside, letting his knees sink until he sat at the edge of his bed. He gripped his hair before sliding his fingers aside his head, pausing when he ran out of hair sooner than expected. "God fucking damn it."

She wanted to say something, but didn't know what. "I'm sorry," she finally decided.

"For?"

There were too many answers to choose from. "I should've caught on quicker. I knew her, and all this... I should've seen it sooner." *I should've listened to Crystal.* She crossed her arms over her midsection. *Crystal...*

His mouth opened. It seemed as though he had to remove his mind from his body before he managed, "Do you hate me now?"

"Anybody would've done the same," she answered, "and I cannot blame you."

"Phrasing," he grumbled. "Just because you understand, doesn't mean you don't hate me."

"I could never hate you," she promised, confident this would hold true tomorrow and the next day. She wouldn't prove Marius right, and she couldn't let Jack think otherwise. "You didn't know you would kill her," she said.

He nodded, though still he seemed distracted. Nervous.

She pressed her lips together. "It should've been me," she said.

"What should've been you?"

"I should've… It shouldn't have been you."

He subtly scrunched his mouth, and she was relieved to see she didn't need to outright say what she meant. "You wouldn't want me to avenge myself?" he asked.

She shook her head. Revenge tarnished the soul; forgiveness allowed for the same practical results. But he wasn't ready to hear this.

She couldn't read how he felt about this answer; his face was too lax to convey anything beyond deep exhaustion.

"So… you *didn't* plan to run away with her," he said.

She shook her head. "I didn't know what to do with her. I don't know if there's such a thing as domsuco prison, but I had to get her to come with me, one way or another."

"And I fucked it up." He shook his head at himself. Finally he grabbed open the drawer in his nightstand again. After little rummaging, he withdrew a small glass pipe and a metal, circular box. Upon opening the box and seeing what was inside, he grumbled, "Thank God." There was cannabis, already shredded. He placed the box down on the nightstand and commenced packing the weed into the end of the pipe. When he peered up at her and seemed to realize she didn't know what to do with herself, he patted the bed space beside him, inviting her to sit.

Like last time, she hesitated. He was still shirtless, and the closeness might've been too much for her to handle. At the end of the day, however, she was too exhausted, and selfish, to turn it down. She took her seat—one she thought was an appropriate distance away.

The mattress sank, forcing them to lean into the other, and her heart raced. She had misgauged again.

"Sorry," she muttered, attempting to scoot aside. The fabric of her pajama pants caught beneath her legs, and temporarily she was trapped.

"You don't have to," he offered. "Or, uh. Whatever makes you comfortable, but I don't mind—" He cut himself off, clamping his lips between his teeth, gaze lost as he struggled for words. "Get comfortable," he decided, promptly returning his attention to the pipe. Without the full view of his face, she wasn't sure how to interpret this. But, again, she was too exhausted and, ultimately, too selfish to decline.

She set her folded clothes down on her other side, and her shoes on the floor. Once she had braced herself for the pace of her heart which would follow, she allowed gravity to run its course, coming to rest with her cheek flat with his cool, bare shoulder.

Thmpthmpthmp —

Again he paused, and although he recommenced his action shortly after, his movements were slowed, distracted. With her ear so close to his back, she clearly heard his heart match hers in intensity. His breath had shallowed.

It felt right. Each sensation was too pleasant and familiar to have been wrong. But the grating claws of guilt began to slowly peel her, combatting this notion all too vehemently.

She reasoned with herself: it was the stress of the night which especially drove her to seek such comforts—that was all. Anything she felt as a result was purely surface. Nothing more. So she remained with her face to his shoulder, eyes closing so she may properly appreciate this while it lasted. She doubted she would let herself get so close again.

Now when his movement ceased, she knew it was because he had finished. Carefully, as if not to disturb her, he began to turn. To allow him greater freedom, she pulled back. He said nothing, but grimaced in protest. Still, he faced her fully in such a way that made leaning against him less of an option.

Pipe in one grasp and pack of matches in the other, he offered her both. "Want green hit?"

Remembering how she had hated it the last time, she almost refused, but... Well, for the moment she liked the idea of not having her wits. The Ripper was gone, and Marius was drugged and restrained in a bathtub.

She nodded, and if it surprised him it didn't show.

He handed her the matches first. "Sorry my regular shit's with my clothes back at... the abandoned house."

Again she nodded, accepting the matches. As she pulled one from the pack and began to strike, he placed the pipe on the nightstand and stood, picking his towel up from the floor and pressing it against the crack beneath his bedroom door. "To keep the smoke in," he explained, "and the smell."

She wondered if this worked for the extent of a human's senses, for she always smelled the weed on him regardless.

Having lit the match, she grasped the pipe. Remembering her lessons from last time, she looked for the small hole which her thumb was supposed to cover on the side.

"No carb," he said as he reclaimed his seat beside her, the mattress sinking so his arm pressed against hers. "You just

hit it. Might have to pull kinda hard, though; I don't remember the last time I cleaned it."

This made things simpler. Taking his advice, she lit the
end and inhaled with her full force. Immediately she turned
away with a high-pitched cough, waving out the match and
pushing the piece back into his grasp. She couldn't stop.
"My God," she wheezed between coughs.

He squeezed his eyes shut, gripping his forehead. "Sorry,
I was wrong—did *not* mean for that to happen."

She might've snapped back with something witty if she
could've stopped coughing. Her ears felt hot.

Now it was his turn, and he took it without incident.
When he offered her the next hit, she shook her head; her
lungs needed a chance to recover. He nodded his understanding and continued to smoke.

By the time her coughs calmed, the overall atmosphere
seemed to mellow out as well. Her eyes were dry and her
head felt full of cotton. She was feeling it.

She wished to rest her face on him again. But she didn't
know how to go about it. While this was at the back of her
mind before, it felt more present now. She supposed the
high had something to do with this, but that didn't make this
less of a dilemma.

His voice nearly cracked when he finally spoke, "I'm so sorry." He cleared his throat, pausing as if to ensure he was recovered before he continued. "I didn't mean to, but... If I wanted to take it all back, it would only be because I hate that it hurts you."

Silence. She rested an uncertain—albeit comforting—hand over his back. It was cool where the moisture from his shower met the chill of the basement air, but through this surface touch she felt the warmth which meant he was alive. She didn't think anything of it until she realized his breath had gone shallow again, which invited hers to follow suit. If she thought she didn't care before, she especially didn't care now. She liked the effect she had on him, and the effect he had on her. She wanted more.

He sighed. "You don't have to." The words were soft, defeated. If this was his way of telling her to let go, she wasn't convinced.

Still, it was important that she asked, "Would you rather I didn't?"

"I'd think *you'd* rather you didn't." He paused, squinting into the distance as if to replay his words.

"I..." She realized she needed to replay his words as well, but as she gave them more thought, she learned she didn't have the focus to draw any sound conclusion. "I hate being high; why did I do this?"

He lightly laughed. "Sorry, I remembered that as soon as you said yes. I wasn't about to deny you, though."

"So then I'm undeniable?"

"Yeah…" He trailed off as he seemed to realize what he said. "Fuck," he grumbled as he suddenly stood, crossing to his dresser. "I should put a shirt on."

"You don't—" She cut herself off, lips together and eyes searching for something else to say by the time he peered back. She had crossed the line. She should've controlled herself. "I didn't mean…" She dropped her gaze to her hands in her lap. She wouldn't be any better for him than Winifred, if she continued on this path. "I should go," she decided.

"Go?"

Nodding with increasing certainty, she again said, "I should go."

"Why are you going?"

She stood and shook out her pants so the fabric ended up on its intended side. "The Ripper is dead, you have your family for support, you can have a life again, and I'll only get in the way."

His speech accelerated with the beginnings of panic. "What— How will you get in the way; what do you mean? Where is this coming from?"

Too many questions. She didn't have the mind to form answers. Of all she was certain was that it was for the best. Or, was she overreacting? Why was she high? "I can't," she whispered, shaking her head as she crossed to the door.

"You're not taking it personally that I'm putting a shirt on?"

"I'm not." She twisted the doorknob.

"Well hold on," he blurted as he reached for her hand. When they made contact—

Thmpthmpthmp—

She sharply gasped, hand flying to her heart.

"Sorry!" He retreated. "Sorry, I forgot, you don't like that, just—*fuck*—Please. Please explain."

Still catching her breath, she eventually brought her focus to his eyes. They were wide.

He still didn't know about her heart.

"Oh," she sighed, turning her back to the door so she may face him fully. Her eyes watered, but she blinked the tears away before they could fully form. Why was she crying? *Why was she high?* Now her eyelashes glistened. "It's, um."

She bit her lip. It had been a while since she last had to explain this to anyone.

Deciding that it was best to show him, she rolled up her sleeve and held out her wrist. "My pulse."

"You don't have one," he guessed.

She liked that he was finally open to the impossible, but still, refraining from an explanation, she only pushed her wrist closer to him.

Although anxiety remained clear in his countenance, there now was a seemingly nagging curiosity to accompany it. Eyebrows semi-scrunched, he painstakingly lifted his hand to her wrist, as if to ensure he wouldn't startle her again. She was impatient, but she didn't have the mind to tell him to hurry.

When his fingers finally met their mark, she asked, "Do you feel it?"

Silence. He pressed his fingers more firmly, and gradually his face relaxed. His mouth fell open, and it was a moment before he seemed capable to articulate, "Yeah, that's fast."

"Do you want to feel it at its fastest?"

"Fastest?"

She knew she wouldn't need to elaborate, so she waited.

"I'm curious," he ventured.

"Put your hand over my heart."

His gaze lowered to her chest and he hesitated. Perhaps she had asked too much. Just as she gathered the air to alter her suggestion, he let his palm rest over her upper chest.

THMPTHMPTHMPTHMP—

She winced with the sharp intake of breath. He stared where his hand rose and fell with her every breath, and she realized she all but panted.

His voice came from the very back of his throat. "So… what are you saying?"

"You—literally—make my heart race. It is what it is." Goodness, she practically sounded in the throes of passion. His hand over her heart felt amazing.

Although he nodded, he seemed dazed. "Is it… like that for everyone?"

She had to focus on her breathing. "Not everyone," she finally managed. "Theo. Marius. Now, you."

Silence. He still didn't know who Marius was. "What does it mean?" he asked. Marius would be a question for another time, she figured.

With a small shrug, she shook her head. Gradually she grew accustomed to this new rate, and while it still felt dynamite, she could speak easier. "I've asked myself for so long, and gave it so much thought. There isn't enough information. The only thing all of you have in common is you're all men who have changed my life drastically."

"I… Drastically?"

"And you smell similarly."

His lips parted and he raised his gaze to hers. She couldn't look away; she was submersed in a pool of russet brown with glistening tawny highlights, and the longer she stared, the wider his pupils seemed. "I don't want you to go," he muttered, voice forcedly even.

His sincerity overwhelmed her, and she hadn't recovered when she whispered a delayed, "I don't want to go."

"Then I don't get it." He watched her eyes as if searching for an answer, and so she watched his in turn. While she knew their shape well in having known Theo, there was an intensity to Jack's—a history—which was uniquely his.

Her gaze fell to the sharpness of his cheekbones, where his bandage interrupted the smooth surface of his fair skin. She didn't realize she was trembling until she lifted her hand, hesitating before she could reach his face. He stood utterly still, as if waiting. Still, she had to be sure she wasn't crossing lines again.

"May I?" she whispered.

The words were hardly out before he nodded.

It was difficult to focus with her heart beating the way it was. There was a moment before she remembered what she was doing, and another before she touched her fingers to the space just beneath his bruise. His eyelids fluttered and seemed to involuntarily close as she gently traced a line from his cheekbone to his hairline, pushing his hair back —

Theo, nuzzling her palm when it opened —

Jack nuzzled her hand the same way, beckoning a pang to her chest. Her breath staggered from the back of her throat.

He moved his injured hand to her side, and with the one which had rested over her heart he felt his way to the back of her neck, his thumb massaging the base of her head. Now it was her turn for her eyes to close, but she didn't want to stop looking at him, so she recovered as quickly as she could.

Her gaze first found his lips. They were too inviting.

He rested his forehead against hers.

She gave in — she pressed her free hand to his abdomen, feeling the contour of each muscle as she made her way up his chest. It seemed like a knee-jerk reaction when he growled and leaned in, pinning her to the door. Though startled, she loved it. As his head tilted one direction, hers tilted the other. She released a shaky, shallow breath before she rose her lips to his, and he to hers.

The kiss was gentle. In a way, cushioned. Neither moved in the few seconds that followed, and she had to wonder if this was really happening.

With significantly less hesitation, he went in for another. She readily accepted, pressing her lips to his once, then again.

It was with whatever was left of his voice that he whispered, "Please don't go."

She didn't know he would speak until she was already kissing him again, and he reciprocated with just as much fervor.

"Stay," he rasped when his lips were free again. "Stay."

Theo, hair wet, squinting through the downpour, holding her, voice fighting to hold strong, "You're scaring me, Dollface. You have to come back."

Her mind left her body in that split instant, and she realized Jack had kissed her again. She did nothing back. Her eyes felt hot and her head hurt.

He paused, then pulled back. When she registered the look on his face, it was as if he was worried he'd broken something. The wideness in his eyes—

Theo, wide-eyed and gasping, grasping his bleeding neck. His heart seemed to call to her with its every frantic beat—

She couldn't recover after this one. Her mouth stretched back, and she knew she was done. A full, throaty sob escaped before her knees sank.

He lowered himself with her; she sat while he crouched. "I'm sorry, I'm. *Fuck,*" he hissed.

She couldn't handle this. He thought he'd done something wrong, and this brought another pang to her chest which made it even more difficult to say anything—to tell him it wasn't his fault she was like this. She shook her head and hoped he would grasp the message.

She needed to stop.

She couldn't. Something wasn't right.

She couldn't—

A flash of confusion. She couldn't feel her fingers.

She couldn't—

Her head felt light. She couldn't think straight. She didn't realize how little she saw until she tried to find his face. Her peripherals were hazy. Her chest was tight; she couldn't get a full breath.

A flash of panic.

She had to pull herself together. Jack was dealing with enough—she had to stop this, whatever it was. She had to stop.

Her arms were shaking. It was familiar. It wasn't crying—it was so much more. She was making a fool of herself. Her stomach rose, and seemed to remain in a state of suspension. Her throat felt tight, and if she was screaming she couldn't hear it. She held her hand over her mouth just in case.

"Alice, listen to me." It sounded like a distant call, even while he was just in front of her. His voice was comforting in its sternness, however muffled through the confusion in her head. "Breathe."

But if she wasn't breathing, she wasn't screaming, and she preferred it this way.

"Alice," he said again, ducking his face until his eyes were in her line of view. Now she had no choice but to look, and this was a good thing. She remembered the rules she had given him for their mesmerism session—she needed a tether to reality. These were her tether, and so she stared.

"Breathe," he said.

For argument's sake, she tried, and succeeded in a full, sharp gasp. This seemed to open the floodgates and tears streamed down her face. "No," she groaned.

"No, it's okay," he promised. "It's okay."

Another sharp gasp. "I'm sorry."

"It's okay," he said again.

Although it still hurt to speak, he deserved an explanation. "You look—just like him." Before another sob could escape, she deliberately slowed her breath. Perhaps if she could slow her breathing, she could find her calm.

He sighed, dropping his gaze as his thoughts enveloped him. "I know." Without his eyes, she needed his hand. Without full feeling in her fingers, her hand dragged along the cement floor until she found the interruption. Immediately he held it.

Then, after giving her shoulder a gentle squeeze, he stood, stepping away. But she didn't want him to go.

Her heart subtly slowed.

Her mind somewhat quieted.

Breathing was easier. Now when she inhaled, she felt she could expand her lungs fully. While the calm gradually returned, the steady stream of tears continued.

Her heart remained at roughly the same speed when he returned a moment later, kneeling some feet away from her. He wore a shirt now—a cut which, in her time, had been reserved for men's undergarments, but now seemed to be in casual style. The sleeves stopped past the shoulder. The material was dyed black, a simplified image printed over the front. Additionally he wore a knit hat, burgundy with a black stripe which ran all the way around.

She wondered if he did this intentionally—if he knew this would differentiate his look from Theo's just enough. "I'm sorry," she croaked. "I don't know what happened."

"Panic attack."

"What?"

"It's what it looked like, anyway. Felt like you were dying?"

She quieted. Nodded.

"Yeah. Weed might not be your thing, then. Or, I don't know. Different strains, different affects. All get you high."

Now she wondered if she was dying those past times it happened, before her transition. If, before her transition the one time Theo left town, she wasn't in mortal danger of heart failure, but merely scared herself and fainted.

"I didn't mean for you to—distance yourself," she managed. "You didn't have to—"

"This didn't help at all?"

While it did, she didn't want to say so. She wanted him closer, and... Well, she liked him without a shirt on. And she liked his hair—regardless of how it was styled or cut. She liked seeing it.

She let her hand drop from her face. Breathing became easier.

"Where do you want me?" he asked.

She dropped her gaze to the floor beside her. She knew what she wanted to say, but she didn't want to have to say it. It was easier not to speak.

Thankfully he understood, remaining low to the ground as he crossed to her side. When he leaned back, she remembered how close they had been to the door. Peering behind herself, she found he had made it a comfortable backrest.

"Hey," he said again.

She followed his lead and leaned back as well, into him. He adjusted his arm so it wrapped over her shoulder, and so gravity had her settle closer to him, back hunched with her elbows between her knees, face to his chest.

"It's okay," he muttered. "Don't gotta be strong all the time."

While her panic had subsided, her tears renewed. "I've tried so hard—not to be that woman."

"What woman?"

"The typical woman. Emotional, hysterical—when it doesn't solve anything."

She wasn't looking at his face, though in his silence she sensed something in his expression change. He emitted a quick breath from his nose. "Now that I know where you've been the last eight decades, moments like these make sense."

She looked up at him.

He looked down at her. "Was I a woman when I lost my shit earlier?"

She wasn't sure to which instance he referred, but she didn't think so. However, she never had the popular opinion on matters like these. Bishop might have told him to man up.

"Right," Jack murmured, turning his gaze to the back wall. "Don't answer that."

"You were human."

He scrunched his mouth, as if unsure of her sincerity. Finally he squeezed her shoulder and said, "So are you. Where it matters."

Neither moved or said anything. She felt so small under his arm. Secure. His hand covered all of her shoulder.

"There's always Grandma," he muttered under his breath.

"Hm?"

A pause. She wasn't supposed to have heard.

"I, um." He cleared his throat. "Well… Everyone's busy, or they leave, or they die, but my grandma? She might have another twenty years, right?"

He still thought she was leaving.

"I won't go," she said. Now that she knew the extent of how he wanted her to stay, she couldn't.

His air exhaled in a quick burst of relief, and he rested his head against hers. "Thank you."

"I didn't mean to—scare you."

A laugh. "I know. You were being a hero."

"Hero." She sniffled through her smile. "Is this what heroes do?"

"Guilt themselves into pushing their friends away, for fear of hurting them otherwise? Yeah, it's a cliché. And dumb."

"What if I'm no better than Winifred?"

"I can tell you right now, you don't gotta worry about that. You never put me under trance without me knowing."

He still didn't know. She wasn't sure how to tell him. Her breaths calmed further as she tried to find the words to begin, and now it was quiet.

He spoke first. "But, uh…" A low laugh. "Talk about clichés, uh… Where do we stand?"

This was a good question. "I don't think I hate you."

Softly, he scoffed, "That's a good start."

"…Friends," she offered.

"Sweet." Silence. "Friends cuddle?"

She shrugged, but didn't have the energy or the will *not* to cuddle.

He shrugged back. "I dig it."

Silence. Sweet, comforting silence. She wondered if she had the ability to fall asleep.

Muffled through the ceiling was the sound of the front door opening. Two sets of hurried footsteps trampled over the floorboards, and the voice of his mother called at breaking pitch, "Jack!"

36. A Closing Spell

Alice

Alice offered to get the bonfire started in the backyard while Jack and his family reunited. Although he had only been missing for a couple of hours at most, she knew it was enough to utterly frighten anyone who cared for him. She didn't want to intrude on a moment.

The Van Sloans had a decent fire pit. It didn't look like anything bought, or constructed by professionals, but there was a quaint simplicity to it which Alice appreciated. A hole was dug out, maybe a half-foot deep and three feet wide, and loosely stacked bricks encircled it. Collapsable canvas chairs sat around the perimeter, and a large poking-stick leaned against a nearby tree. Some distance behind it was a pile of found firewood—kindling and storm-torn branches alike—with a tarp tied above for protection from the elements.

Alice built the fire so the flames stretched nearly a foot above her head from where she sat. It was easy to let her mind wander in the layers of passages the burning logs had created. As her gaze fixed between two smoldering splinters, her thoughts overtook her.

She couldn't believe herself. Winifred was hardly an hour dead, and... Alice kissed Jack. She should've controlled herself. She should've waited. Rather, she shouldn't have had these impulses to begin with. She still wasn't sure if he was drawn to her of his own free will or if this was something carried over from the first time she had charmed him. She still wasn't sure if she was attracted to him or to his semblance to Theo.

She hugged her knees to her chest, letting her chin rest in the nook in between. She couldn't believe she let herself break down in front of him. As if he wasn't already dealing with enough on his own.

She had heard him and his family chatting all along, though only looked up when the back door slid open. Gabby stepped out first, eyes distant as she descended the porch steps. Behind her was Jack and his mother, whose face was wet with tears. He kept an arm over her shoulder as he closed the door behind them. They moved slowly, Jack being careful with his injured foot. When the woman caught Alice's gaze, she took a few calming breaths and walked faster, out of Jack's hold. As she came to pass Gabby, the latter peered back at her sibling and waited for him to catch up. As he neared, she wrapped her arms around his middle and he held her back. In this manner they continued Jack's slow walk.

Ms. Van Sloan wiped her cheeks and chin as she neared close enough for the glow of the fire to reach her, and Alice stood.

"So you're the one from my mother's stories?" the woman asked.

There wasn't a point in lying, although Alice considered it. She nodded.

Jack's mother mimicked the motion. It was bizarre, seeing the same faces he made reflected in hers. The same default caution, regardless of if it was appropriate or not.

The woman put out a hand, and finally Alice learned her first name. "I'm Lydia."

"Pleasure to meet you, Lydia. I'm Alice." She accepted the hand, and they shook.

"You saved my son."

"I helped."

Jack exhaled a quick laugh through his nose. Gabby subtly grinned as if she understood. By now they had reached the fire, coming to stand on their mother's other side.

When Alice heard the sliding door open again, she glanced up in time to see Ruth leave the house, Theo's old clothes bundled under one arm and a canvas bag in the grasp of the other.

Lydia never looked away from her son's fearless heroine. She smiled, expression pinched as the corners of her mouth quivered. "I can't believe it. It worked. My mother's crazy spells actually—" She sniffled, then laughed. "She said we would summon something so powerful, we would immediately see the results. I never would have guessed…"

Alice remembered the last thing imaginary-Theo had told her in the Crypt. *You're being summoned. Good luck.* It wasn't a coincidence, then, when she returned the way she did—she felt it in her subconscious.

"Did you know?" Gabby asked.

Alice didn't expect her to say anything, so it was a moment before her gaze found hers.

Gabby must've noticed her confusion, for she reiterated, "Like, did you know you were being summoned, or were you just kinda doing your thing and it happened to work out that way?"

"I… Well, my heart started beating again, so I had to investigate."

If Jack was already looking at Alice before, his gaze was more focused now. "When did this happen?"

Ruth had walked close enough to hear, so she muttered, "We cast the spell, Lestat runs away, you and Gabby post fliers in Erie—"

"Almost," Gabby mumbled. "Couldn't cross county lines."

"But you get close enough," the old woman amended, "for Alice to feel it."

When none of the others appeared confused, Alice knew Jack had told them about her heart. Or, Ruth. Ruth might've known.

After placing the clothes and bag on one of the nearby canvas chairs, Ruth let out a breath. "Anyone who doesn't plan to stay for the duration of the spell, please step back from the circle."

All the others exchanged glances. None moved.

Ruth nodded to herself. "Alright. Now let's make a circle."

Alice turned back to the fire, though didn't have to otherwise move. Lydia did the same beside her, as did Gabby on the woman's other side. Jack noted the wide gap between Alice and Ruth, so took it upon himself to fill it.

Once everyone was situated, Ruth rummaged through her bag and withdrew a box of salt. After sliding the lid back, she crossed behind Gabby and let a thin, steady stream pour to the ground. Slowly she led it behind Lydia, then Alice, then Jack, until it was time for her to stand in her spot and close herself in. She shut the container and placed it back in the bag.

Gabby glanced from face to face, as if in the hopes of gleaning everyone else's response to the situation — if they knew what they were doing, or if they were as lost as she was. "Is there something we should all be doing? Holding hands, or…?"

Ruth nodded. "You can hold hands. The more energy put into this, the better."

So they did. Alice took Lydia's hand, and when it was Jack's turn, their eyes locked. He was asking permission.

All was well for so long as she saw it coming, so she held her hand out to him.

Thmp thmp thmp —

And when his grasp found hers —

Thmp Thmp Thmp Thmp —

It felt electric; tingly. Right. She offered an embarrassed smile. He weakly smiled back.

Ruth cleared her throat. "I'll begin now." And she did. She addressed the proper deities and spoke in rhyme. When it came time to burn Theo's old clothes, however, she paused, then peered at Jack and Alice.

"It may be in our best interest if the three of us tossed a garment in the fire," she said, cutting herself off before she completely finished. "All of us, even. We've all bared the consequences of Winifred Dodds having never let go of Theo's memory. Like her, some of us may need assistance in letting go ourselves." She peered at Alice when she said this, and so the others did as well. Alice didn't know what to do with the attention.

When everyone figured Ruth wouldn't say more, they acknowledged this in staggered nods. Ruth nodded back, handing Gabby the robe as she said, "Pass this down."

She did, and as this process continued, it ended with Lydia holding the robe, Gabby the jacket, Ruth the pants, Jack the bloody slipper, and Alice the other. At Ruth's instruction, each closed their eyes and held their garment for a moment longer. They were meant to imagine the item encompassing every negative energy the past year had presented, and once they felt they were ready, one by one, they tossed their respective items into the bonfire.

Ruth motioned for Jack and Gabby's hands. Each took hold, and the rest were prompted to resume position as well.

The old woman addressed the deities once again, "And with the burning of the garments in which he perished, we banish whatever may bar us from moving on. We allow my brother, Theodore Jackson Van Sloan, to guide us in spirit as he sees fit, to live on only in our memories, and, ultimately, to rest in peace. So mote it be, with harm to none."

37. The Funeral

Alice

In addition to the Robinson family, it appeared as if the entire community was in attendance—all of the high school students, their parents and siblings, the Crawford County police force, as well as the media—photographers, and journalists with notepads and pens.

Alice watched from the shade of such a distant tree that, if anyone noticed, they'd see she was an outsider looking in. She had to be present; she was responsible for Crystal's death, after all. If it wasn't for her, Crystal would never have gotten involved. But at the same time, she didn't belong with the rest of the funeral crowd. They knew Crystal for more than just a few days, even if some of them didn't know her as well. They belonged to the same community. Alice mourned for her killer. She couldn't join them in hating Winifred, and she couldn't compare her own grief to theirs.

Crystal's mother, an officer, spoke at the podium now. Her face contorted to keep its strong front, but still her eyes were red and her nose was running. Prepared, she dabbed with a tissue and commenced, "Well, it's finally happened to *me,* hasn't it." She bitterly laughed. "As careful and as strict as we've been, and just as we're closing in on the bitch, she had to take that *one more…*" She cut herself off, looking to the sky as she blinked the tears out of her eyes. "I'm sorry. I know I'm not the only mother to lose a child to the Ripper. But this was *my* baby." Again she stopped, dabbing her nose.

Someone sobbed once, loudly, in the silence.

Crystal's mother cleared her throat, straightening herself. Something about her stance reminded Alice of a politician — one who might proceed with the tact to avoid insulting any-one — but as the woman scanned the crowd, her teeth clenched, and her words fell like sweet venom. "Imagine how much sooner we could have stopped this if we were looking the right direction." She let her gaze fall on the journalists. "If we didn't run amuck with speculation for the sake of a good story — for a quick buck."

One of the writers visibly shrank, eyes intent on her notes.

"If we didn't take our anger out on a teenage boy, because it was easy and convenient."

The crowd was silent, uneasy. Some turned their heads, and when enough kept their gaze on a single focus, from afar Alice found their object of attention. Jack.

He shifted his weight, his good hand balled in his pocket while his other remained in the cold, in its brace. His neck healed well, as did his face which now only held the faint purple of a bruise. He kept his head under a new black knit hat—bought to replace the one he wouldn't dare to seek out at the old mayor's house, and to cover the forced haircut which affronted his very identity.

He stared straight at the podium to avoid anyone's eye. He stood with Gabby, Lydia, and Ruth, all in black, all dead center of the crowd. Adam and George were nearby.

Officer Robinson turned to her colleagues—the other officers. With her mouth away from the microphone, Alice wasn't sure how many of the others heard, "I *told* you the evidence didn't add up."

Silence. The officer with blonde hair, blue eyes and a rough demeanor seemed to resonate with this the most, shaking his head at himself.

Officer Robinson turned back to the crowd. "I urge all of us, as a community, to formally apologize to Jack, and to thank him and his new friend for finally putting an end to that *bitch*—" She caught herself when her voice went especially hoarse. "Thank you, Jack and Alice. Thank you."

The crowd muttered in solemn agreement.

Alice's gut twisted. She didn't deserve this thanks. Heads turned, and continued turning, as Alice assumed they were hoping to see her. She stepped behind her tree before they could. She didn't need this attention.

The voices from the funeral took a backseat as her mind went on a tangent. She couldn't exist outside of society the same way Winifred had. This was the sort of lonely, isolated existence which had started the girl down her wicked path in the first place—she had lost touch with people because she didn't *know* any of them. While Alice didn't know where to start, was there a better time than now? She was new, and a hero in their eyes. They were curious about her, and if she alienated them now, they wouldn't be as interested in getting to know her later.

The thought of meeting them made her nervous, and she softly laughed to herself. Here she was, an all powerful domsuco—the Domglory, at that—and she was afraid of *people*.

Decided, she didn't head directly toward the crowd from her tree, but walked around. She didn't need anyone to realize she was being a stranger and watching from afar all along. From the back of the crowd, she weaved her way through, heart accelerating, until she found familiar faces.

She stood when her shoulder was behind Jack's, subtly leaning toward him to mutter, *"Here* you are."

She thought he would jump, but he smirked. He kept his attention forward when he muttered back, "You mean you were down here looking for me all this time, not hiding behind a tree?"

Her face felt warm.

"Glad you found me," he said. She could hear the snicker in his voice, and she was no less embarrassed for it.

Officer Robinson stepped down from the podium, and the funeral conductor—an old man with kind eyes and tufts of gray hair above his ears—took her place. "If anyone else has any words, you may speak now."

A brief silence. No one made a motion to step forth, though most seemed on the lookout for anyone who might.

"Any friends?" the officiant prompted, "Family? One of our vampire hunters, perhaps?"

A soft echo of chuckles, even while some hearts sped at the reminder. Winifred had exposed her ability to a full gym of students and staff, putting them all under trance without giving them any orders, so they all remembered everything they saw and felt. Alice wasn't sure how many people saw herself speed away in the blink of an eye, but enough had. There were too many heads to put under trance—Bishop tried. While some forgot, the reminder from whoever was left quickly allowed them to remember again.

She and Bishop talked about what to do about this. They were still talking about it. If they enlisted the help of more domsuco, they would have an easier time of keeping everything contained.

Heads were turning again. People found Jack again, and she felt their eyes on herself as well.

She and Jack exchanged a look, as if they simultaneously asked the other, *You wanna?* He nodded toward the podium, then led the way as she followed.

Finally past the crowd, they could see the fresh dirt of Crystal's grave. Her closed oak casket. Her new marble tombstone. Her family and closest friends all were seated, Luke bleary-eyed in the second row with Troy and a few of the cheerleaders.

"You wanna go first?" Jack breathed as they neared the front. The words were hardly out before she shook her head. She never was one for public speaking—that was Theo's job.

He bit his lip, and both slowed to a stop to stand alongside the front row of seats. "Same," he admitted. "But... I kinda have to, don't I."

She knew what he meant. This would be the first time he said anything while his peers were willing to listen to him. His first words as an innocent man. He needed to leave an impression; he needed to squash any lingering accusations.

After a quick breath in preparation, he jogged to the podium. Sprinkled gasps took the crowd as some noticed his magnitude of scars which they wouldn't have been able to see before.

As if feeling their stare, Jack pressed his good hand alongside his neck. "Uh. Yeah," he started, scanning the crowd before letting his gaze drop to the podium. "I uh. I didn't know her that well. I mean, this last year, I didn't know *anyone* anymore, but—besides the point, right." He scrunched his mouth, still finding his words. "In those last couple of days—that was all it took, two days—I think I learned about her, the most important things you can learn about a person." He turned his attention back to the crowd, presenting his thoughts as if allowing anyone to claim he was wrong. "How a person responds to crisis. If they face it head-on, or hide under the bed until it goes away." He paused. No one challenged him. "Crystal faced it head-on. She knew the risk—she straight expected she would die for her part in stopping W... the Ripper." He cleared his throat, and while he was on a roll before, it seemed he had distract-ed himself.

"Crystal might be the bravest person I know. Knew— fuck," he mumbled, then continued as if hoping no one would notice the blunder, "The Ripper couldn't influence her. She remembered everything, she came to me with what she knew, and she did it knowing it'd bring us a step closer to stopping the deaths, even if she wouldn't live to see it. If it wasn't for her, we'd all still be..." He silenced, and Alice all but watched his different, inappropriate options filter through his head. "Where we were," he decided.

Some murmurs of agreement from the crowd.

Jack turned to Crystal's grave. "Thanks." Silence as the word hung in the air, then he turned back to the crowd, hardly lifting his gaze before he absently nodded in departure and stepped away from the podium. "You're up," he told Alice as he neared.

Her head was reeling. There was something about what he said... Crystal's part in everything... If she had known what she knew sooner—if Jack could have spoken to anyone sooner—if there were more people who couldn't be affected by a domsuco's influence... Bishop seemed to think a penchant for truth was what allowed a person to withstand charm. Jack had begun to build a tolerance to it.

Absently she crossed to the podium, still thinking. It partially surprised her when she already stood before it, holding it lightly by either side. "What he said," she uttered, still distracted, and those who heard her chuckled.

She looked up, peering from face to face, reading them. They would eat up anything she said. She was a person who knew more about the situation than they did; they were vulnerable and wanted to be pointed in the right direction. She was their hero; their vampire hunter. They believed she killed Winifred.

They didn't want to stay in the dark, or go back to blissful ignorance. They wanted to know.

They deserved to know.

Decided, Alice's voice gained more strength. "In the days following..." She didn't want to say *Crystal's death*, so instead went with, "the dance... I've given this endless thought. I wasn't planning to do this here and now, but, well, it seems all of Sabertown is present, so why not."

Everything went eerily silent. None fidgeted, none sobbed or sniffled, and all side conversations stopped. Most who were seated had leaned forward.

Uncomfortable with the attention, Alice powered ahead as best she could. "I used to live here, a long time ago. The deaths then were equally common and brutal, and eventually people caught on and realized their Ripper wasn't like any typical serial killer. They knew just enough to be afraid, but not enough to know how to handle it. It started a witch hunt. If they had the truth, they would have known what to look for. They wouldn't have blamed the easiest scapegoat. They could have stopped the deaths sooner."

Jack's expression could have been comical if the situation was different. His eyes were wide with concern while his eyebrows were narrowed in confusion. "What are you doing?" he intoned, and besides the people directly beside him, she knew she was the only other person who heard.

She continued, "It may be a shaky first step. You may indefinitely have trouble sleeping at night. But knowledge is power. It will leave you more prepared, but not necessarily safer. I will leave you with the choice. Check your necks for old wounds. If you're marked, there's likely something you don't remember."

Now the hushed chatter began, even as she spoke, and some astonished gasps echoed as the congregation checked their necks and found wounds they wouldn't have noticed just a moment ago.

"See me if you'd like to remember, or see me if you'd rather forget," Alice announced over the noise, "But dash it all if we allow history to repeat itself." She peered back at Crystal's grave, imagining this was what the girl would have wanted. Progress. Free will. Alice offered a quick nod in farewell, but before she could step away from the podium, she noticed an off-palpitation in her heart.

Jack hadn't moved. She hadn't moved. Not enough for this to happen. Which meant—

She clutched her chest at a sudden ache.

Marius.

What Did You Think of <u>Forgive The Monster: The Isolated</u>?

First of all, thank you for purchasing this book. I know you could have picked any number of other books to read, but you picked this one and for that I am truly grateful. I hope it engaged you and transported you entirely.

If so, I would hugely appreciate if you could share <u>Forgive the Monster</u> with your friends and family by posting to Facebook and Twitter. I'd also like to hear from you, if you could take some time to post a review on Amazon. Your feedback and support will help me improve my writing craft for future projects and make this book even better.

Thank you, and happy reading for books to come!

About the Author

Diana Regolizio completed her first urban fantasy novel in 2004. At four-hundred pages long, it was a noteworthy accomplishment for an eleven-year-old—one which will hopefully never become available to the public eye.

Having since left her home in Newton, New Jersey to pursue her passion for storytelling, she earned her Bachelors Degree in Dramatic Writing from the Savannah College of Art and Design, where her focus temporarily shifted from novels to screenplays. Her Cinderella-verse feature length script, *If the Shoe Fits*, made her a finalist in the ScreenCraft True Story & Public Domain Competition. As for *Forgive the Monster*, the pilot adaptation earned a quarter-finalist placement in a much broader ScreenCraft category; the TV Pilot Script Competition.

With so many stories to write and worlds to explore, Diana will continue to pursue her different passions in waves. When she isn't in her own world, she's dancing with her hippie friends or taking color pencil commissions for people who want to be drawn as their favorite anime character.

Made in the USA
Monee, IL
23 February 2021